Bad Romance

Part II

This is a work of fiction. Names, characters, places, and incidents either are the product of the author's imagination or used fictitiously, and any resemblance to any persons, living or dead, business establishments, events, or locales is entirely coincidental.

Bad Romance: Part II

Published by Ellington Baddox
Copyright © 2020 by Ellington Baddox
Cover art by Ellington Baddox
Editors BeJai Crume

ISBN-13: 978-163795-6564

Printed in the United States of America

First Edition: December 2020

To my Granddad who always believed in me. Hope I make you proud.

Table of Contents

Bad Romance Part II   Ellington Baddox

Numb

(November 25th, 2011)

Numb, that's the best way I can describe how I am. After I ran as far as my legs could take me, I gave up and just sat on the beach. Not to my surprise, Dmitri caught up with me. I didn't fight him. The moment he came running up to me I looked back. He was saying something, I couldn't tell you a single word that was said. Everything was silent. It was as if I went temporarily deaf. He looked angry. Perhaps he was reprimanding me. I don't know.

But his anger soon turned into sympathy. He put his hand on my shoulder and looked at me the way you look at a kid who just seen something so horrible that they couldn't possibly understand. I've been given that look a few times in my life. It never becomes any more comforting.

He asked me something. From what I can paint I guessed that I had purposefully blocked out all sounds; because I was able to hear him clearly the second time he asked if I could come back with him to his house. I didn't respond. I just got up and followed him. He continued to talk to me about something. Once again, I blocked out all sounds. The only reason why I'm even going back was because it's Dmitri. He would do anything for us. He always has our backs and is pretty much everyone's shoulder to cry on. He may be hard, cold, and downright cruel, but when it comes to the people he cares about, he's nothing but a teddy bear with sharp teeth.

I sit in the den staring at the crackling fireplace. Dmitri is in the hallway, out of sight, but well within ear range, going off on Craig.

"Does it look like I give a shit? No, seriously look me in the eyes and tell me if you can find this shit I should be giving."

Cassidy and Nick left to go see if I went home while Dmitri searched around his house. I don't know why Craig bothered to stay.

"There is nothing I can say that'll make you any less angry. So, tell me, what do you want to hear Dmitri?"

"I want you to leave my house. Do you realize what you did to her?"

"Dmitri-"

"Clearly you don't! She isn't the basket case Travis makes her out to be, but she isn't at the state where you can get into her head like that... Even if she was that it still wouldn't be okay!"

He is in there fighting my battle. I can't even say that I could fight it myself even if I wanted to. The moment I look at Craig I know I would be mute. My tongue would be as if it was ripped out of my mouth. My throat swollen shut. My lungs collapsed and my heart sunken deep within me. I trusted him so much. I was willing to give him so much. I feel as if a piece of me has been erased, that the memory of the good times and positive emotions are all gone. Everything feels so cloudy, so lost.

"That wasn't my intention, I didn't try, I barely got into her head-"

"The fact that you were in her head at all shows how much of a piece of shit you really are!"

"I didn't do a thing to her! If anything, I was the one who was helping her out!"

"Helping her out?! By directly putting her in harm's way and using her as bait?! Yeah, a fucking class act, Edwards."

Bait, he used me as bait. Hearing Dmitri say it really puts it in perspective. I should have stayed out on the beach. I don't want to hear any of this. I don't even have the capacity to block out sound anymore. I can't help but listen and hear all of the things that made me run in the first place. Hearing Craig's voice makes the small bit that is left of my heartbreak just a little bit more.

They are speaking to each other too low for me to understand them at this point. The sliding door in the den was left open, bringing a brisk chill into the room, it counters the warmth of the fire. The fire seems to be growing even though there has not been any added kindling. Or that could just be my mind formulating this ever-growing fire illusion. As I stare into this fire, I can't help but think about if there were any signs of deceit that I couldn't, didn't catch before. Everything Craig did, said, looked, felt so real, and genuine. That's why I fell for him, why I cheated on Travis... Why I even left Travis. That last thought makes my stomach drop. I risked and harmed my stable relationship for this, this sham.

"Don't talk to her, don't look at her, don't even breathe in her direction. If I catch you anywhere near her outside of sharing a class-" Dmitri goes silent or says something so low that I can't hear him.

"I didn't mean her any harm. I never did," Craig whispers.

The conversation goes silent, and so does the whole room. The waves outside go still, the fire stops cackling, everything is hush. Then I look to the opening doorway and I see him. Craig sulks past the walkway. His head low and his posture follows. It's a stark difference from his tall confident stature that he normally carries himself in. He looks over at me. Our eyes meet with an unfamiliar look, he looks worn, shameful, there's regret. He looks as if he is calling out a thousand apologies within the two seconds our eyes meet. The two seconds lasted much longer.

It wasn't until he left my vision and the door closed did I notice that I wasn't breathing that whole time. I take a moment to catch my breath in the quietest way possible. I don't want to cause any more worry to Dmitri.

As I stare at the ground trying to steady my breathing, sort of succeeding, I see Dmitri enter the room out of my peripherals. His wardrobe is nearly exclusively black, but he took off his sweater, and now his white t-shirt, that perfectly sculpted around his lean muscles, is shown. I didn't notice this before. Perhaps because I was having a bit of an out of body experience. Still am but to a lesser extent.

He looks exhausted, stressed. I caused this. I open my mouth to say something but still, I can't speak. His eyes dart over to me. His face quickly changes to warmth and comfort. He rushes to my side and sits beside me. He places his hand on my shoulder and massages the area between my shoulder and neck. I could melt into his arms. He is the only place I want to be right now.

"Are you okay, Belle," his voice low. Before I even get the chance to respond he takes his hand off my shoulder and slaps it on his lap. "Of course you're not, look at you! I'm sorry Belle. I didn't even know you guys were hanging out like that. I would have been more proactive. Craig can't be trusted, for obvious reasons, that you, unfortunately, know now. Shit, Belle." He buries his face in his hands. I can tell he feels super guilty. He rakes his fingers through his hair.

I want to be able to tell him that it isn't his fault. If I would have listened to him in the first place, I wouldn't have been in this mess at all. But all I can do is look at him, blank and expressionless. I try to move closer to him to hug him, my body is frozen though. "Dmitri," I manage to say. My voice is small, shaky. My throat starts to close up a little, my eyes start to become foggy from the incoming tears.

Instinctively Dmitri pulls me into his arms. Despite how cold Dmitri can be, it throws me off how warm he is. Instantly I feel myself loosen up. I wrap my arms around him and squeeze as hard as I can. I don't ever want to leave this embrace. I shut my eyes and let the pain melt away.

I'll never let go, no matter what happens I will be there

I hear Dmitri say in my head with a thick Romanian accent. He normally hides his accent unless he's drunk and can't control it. I pull away and look at him, puzzled.

"What?" He whispers.

"Did you say something?"

He looks confused, "no..." Great, now he thinks I am hearing voices. Which apparently, I am. I completely pull away and shake my head. I am completely losing it. I can't go home now, there is no way I can hide how disconnected I am. They will see right through me and treat me like a mental patient. I just need some air.

All of a sudden, the room feels very small. The air has been vacuumed sucked out the door. I can't get a single breath of clean air. Everything feels tainted and unclean. Every time I try to take a breath, no matter how deeply I breathe I feel as if I am being strangled.

"Belle?"

I try to take another breath, even deeper. My windpipe feels like it's being pinched shut. I need to get out of this room. I shoot up and b-line towards the sliding door. Before I get the chance to make it out Dmitri cuts me off, holding me by my shoulders.

"We need to get you home, I can roll the windows down and you can take some fresh air, but I am not letting you walk out to the beach again."

I nod without saying a word and sit back down on the couch. He backs away from me as if I am a lost feral animal. As he retreats out of the room to get, what I am guessing is his jacket and keys I am left to sit in the den to listen to my heartbeat, my lungs fill with air and release. A light cackle from the fireplace. My stomach rumbles, growls, twist, causing a pulsating sharp pain. I just want peace.

"I got my stuff. We are taking the Rolls. Are you ready?"

Without answering I robotically make my way over to him. With the faintest smile, I give a soft nod over to the door. Dmitri looks concerned but doesn't say anything, just hands me my bag.

I have never been inside his car; we've seen it from afar, but he is normally taking his motorcycle and Nick drives him to school. It really is a super nice car. It has this classic, expensive look to it. Matches him completely. I understand that all our families are well off, considering we all live in Malibu in nice homes, but it is one thing to get your 16-year-old a Range Rover or something of that matter, but a Rolls Royce? That's a bit insane to me. But then again, I do remember Dmitri revealing to us in the 6th grade that his family has a private jet, so perhaps it isn't that far off for the Vaduva family. I have never been in a car this nice before, other than Craig's Maserati.

The blood, all the blood on the back seat. I scrubbed and scrubbed to get it off. The red-stained my hands and Wendy. No matter how hard I scrubbed, I scrubbed my hands raw, it felt like the blood never left. Like the smell of the seawater was permanently in me. The sound of the gunshot still rang in my ear.

As soon as I situate myself in the car, trying to block out the pain, I take my phone out. 6 missed calls from my Dad, 10 from my Mom, 13 texts from Cassidy, and 14 from Nick. Nothing from Travis. Not even, I'm sorry text... How did this all happen over a course of a month? Why am I warm all of a sudden?

We're driving, I don't know how I didn't notice. And the heat is on, the fan is low, and the heat is set on high. It is a chilly night; the wind has been unforgiving. It seems like the moonlight found a way to brighten Dmitri's face. His calm composed look makes me feel safe, and almost like he is home. His eyes quickly pan over to me catching me in my gaze.

"You gotta stop staring at me so much without saying any words, Belle. It creeps me out," he teases, an attempt to make me smile. I want to, I can feel it in me, yet it doesn't show. He plays some classical music via Bluetooth. He says that not all the music is classical that some are baroque and romantic, and all that jazz. In my mind, it is all classical to me. I wouldn't dare to say it out loud, the last time we got a whole music history lesson. I feel so at ease here, driving with Dmitri. It feels so familiar.

Come, my love, I will take you away from all the pain. We don't have to be creatures in this state. A voice, that sounds almost like Dmitri's lulls to me in my ear. *Worry not, it'll all be over soon.* I slowly start to drift to sleep, the soothing voice like a lullaby in my head, calling me to dream, to get away from the mess I made.

"Belle!" I snap my head up, my eyes wide. We are in front of my house. Did I lose time? Dmitri is looking at me with a smile on his face. "You fell asleep, I didn't really want to wake you, but I figured me walking up to your doorstep with your body hanging almost lifeless in my arms after you disappeared on them would be highly suspicious." And he is right, it would be.

I don't want to go back; I don't want to go into that house and face everyone. Mom, dad, Lindsey, Josh, Cassidy, Nick. They will all be sitting in the living room no doubt just waiting for me to walk in. They would want explanations as to what happened tonight. I can't tell them the truth and I don't have the brain capacity to lie to them either. I groan and slam my head down on the surface in front of me, I let my tears freely fall, one after the other.

His hand slowly rubs my back in calming circles.

"Belle, it's going to be okay."

"How the hell is it going to be okay? Huh? Please explain how I am supposed to walk into that house acting like everything is okay when it is nowhere near okay? I can't even explain to them what happened! I, I can't give them a decimal amount of explanation as to what I did, why I did it, why I ran out. This whole situation is a one-way ticket to the mental hospital. It is insane, it defies all rational thinking!" I stammer off, hyperventilating. It feels like someone is clenching my lungs.

Out of the corner of my eye, I see Dmitri reach for me. Something within me snapped in panic. "Don't touch me!" I snap as I push him away.

He puts his hands up as if he surrenders. The car goes silent. I know everything is still, but I feel everything whirling around me. Breathing, focusing on breathing is good. In and out. In and out. In and out.

"Belle, Belle if you aren't ready to go inside, we can wait a while-"

"I can't just sit in your car and wait, and wait, and wait until I magically feel alright! There is not a single point in this night where I will be okay. Where I can face my family and friends and try to find a way to piece a logical explanation together that will make them not want to admit me into a mental hospital," I spurt out erratically.

He settles back into his seat and stares straight ahead. His eyes searching for a way to smooth things over. There was hardly ever a time where Dmitri is lost for words. He unlocks the doors, keeping his eyes straight. "Let's go in then. We can walk in; you say hi to everyone and go straight up to your room. I can talk to them, make up some stuff that is believable enough where they won't try to interrogate you."

I nod and open the door without a break in rhythm. It feels as if I am making the walk on death row. The streetlights are buzzing like a bee that just won't leave you alone. Despite the normally decently star-filled sky, it's vacant covered by the heavy drown of clouds. In and out. In and out. *Knock knock knock.*

We're at the front door, Dmitri just knocked. In any minute the door will open. Mom, Dad, Josh, Lindsey,

Cassidy, Nick, one of their faces will be on the other side looking at me as if they just had the weight of 10,000 bricks released from their back. There will be relief but tears from all the pain.

Without even a sound of the door unlocking or the knob turning, the door bursts open. "Jezebel, thank god! Sweetheart are you okay, what happened?" My Mom blubbers through tears never letting go of me.

I bite my lip to try to hold back the tears. I hate that I put everyone through that. I don't want to see the rest of their faces. I don't want to hear their concerned words. I feel a small push on my back. Dmitri is guiding me deeper into the house. I didn't even notice that my Mom let go.

Dmitri shut the door behind us. Cassidy shoots up out of her seat and lets out an audible gasp. They are all sitting in the living room. Giving me the look that I dreaded to see. I scan each of their eyes, with each second I can feel everything getting worse and worse. I gotta go. All I can muster is this weird peep sound, within a second Dmitri is at my side with his hand on my back.

"She still isn't doing the greatest. A lot happened; she just needs some rest, ya know. I can explain the whole thing." They murmur in agreement with Dmitri.

"Yeah, Jez, just head upstairs and get some rest," my Dad says exhausted.

I give a soft nod and walk off towards the stairs. Dmitri starts the lies as soon as my foot hits the stairs. I make it to the top of the stairs to look back one last time. Everyone is standing, hanging on his every word. Peace. All I want is peace.

Visitor

I have barely left my room since Friday. I only leave to eat, go to school, and go to practice. My parents try to make me feel better, checking in on me every hour. I know it breaks their heart seeing me like this but I don't know what to do. I can't tell them the truth so they would never understand, never be able to help me like they want. Almost everyday Dmitri has been coming over. Sometimes we will talk and other days, like today, there is silence. His only purpose for being here is to make sure that I am okay. I ask him questions about what Craig is and he never answers. He claims it is best that I don't know. Yet, I feel like that isn't true. Living in ignorance seem like it would be worse. He is the only person I feel relaxed around these days. I haven't been myself and the only time I feel happy or sane is when I am with Dmitri.

"Can you give me just a little bit of a hint. Give me the smallest bit of information," I beg. It is chilly outside but I needed some fresh air so we are sitting out by my pool, laying down on our stomachs. Dmitri is ignoring me as he glides his fingers through the water.

"If you spent a little less time dwelling on this, the easier it will be to heal."

I lightly splash water in his direction. "Alright Confucius."

He chuckles at me and splashes me back. "I'm serious Belle. I want you to be able to be normal again. You are freaking everyone out. You won't talk to Cas or Nick really. Your parents ask about you, you don't see the issue?"

"If I knew what he was I would feel more at ease and be less zombie like."

He gives me a skeptical "mhm" and stands up. I stay laying down but my stare follows him. He comes up behind sitting on top of me. I start to cough acting as if he knocked the wind out of me.

"Get your 200-pound ass off of me!" I giggle.

He shushes me and pushes my head down. He switches his position to kneeling with his legs on both sides of me. He starts rubbing my shoulders and upper back. It feels amazing. I go limp as I let him give me this massage.

"You need to relax, Belle. The less you know the better. Have you had any weird feelings, anyone been stalking you? Any weird dreams?"

I hum, he has magic hands... Wait, what did he just say? Did he just say something about dreams? I turn myself around, well as much as I can to face him. "Dreams? Did you just say dreams? Can they get in my dreams?!"

Dmitri looks at me like a deer in head lights. He shakes his head around trying to find a way to talk himself out of this. "Well, they can, um... All I can say is that they can have some kind of influence on your dreams."

Those dreams I was having before, was that them? Could that have been Craig himself? I wiggle and try to push Dmitri off of me. He moves himself and lets me free. I get up and stomp over to my door, arms crossed. Nothing is safe. How knows all they can do?! I should read that book I stole from Craig. I bet there will be answers there. But would it make me feel any better? What if it makes everything worse? I wanna go back to the time I didn't know about any of this. But was there ever a time I was free from this? Slowly they have been coming after me since I was six. Each time they get closer and closer. Bolder and bolder. My body goes cold and my mind blank. Darkness and emptiness is all that is left.

"Belle, please don't think about it. I know it is easier said than done-"

I scoff at him and brush him off. I stomp up to my room. I hear his footsteps behind me. This is the first time I wish he would go away. He doesn't, he never does. His support is almost suffocating right now.

I try to close the door in his face but he catches it. That makes me even more frustrated. I grab a pillow and groan loudly into it. When will this end? When will I know peace? I start to tremble and then collapse. I feel Dmitri's body wrapped around mine, his hair sweeping over my shoulder. He hushes me, rocking me until I stop shaking. "I wish I could make you feel better, give you a clear mind," he simpers in my ear. I hold him tighter. I just don't want him to ever let me go. In his arms is the only time I feel one hundred percent safe.

"*You messed up big time, Jezebel. You shouldn't have done that. Killing one of mine. Tsk tsk tsk. Didn't your daddy teach you to not be trigger happy? What am I gonna do with you? I can do anything I want, you're all alone. No one can help you. No one can protect you from me.*" Who are you? "*I'm a friend.*"

I jerk out of my sleep panting trying to catch my breath. I search around my dark room. My eyes adjusting to the darkness, I can just barely make out the furniture.

You're all mine. You're trapped. "Who's there?" I jerk my head around. Anything, give me anything. A pair or glowing eyes shine in the corner of my room filled with sinister energy. I screech at the top of my lungs. I gather up my covers and throw them off of me. I try to get out of my bed to run but I am frozen. Please god, no!

"Jez, baby what's wrong?!" My Dad bursts through the door with a bat in his hand. My Mom comes racing up behind him with his gun. I look back to where the eyes are and their gone. What the *hell* was that?

My mom turns on the lights and they both rush over to me. I can move but I don't want to. Frozen in fear I clutch my covers and stare at the corner where the eyes were. "Baby talk to me," My dad drops the bat and rushes to my side.

"I-I had a bad dream. I think I had sleep paralysis. I saw something."

"Is someone in your room?" Mom asks in an urgent whisper looking around to see if anyone is hidden.

I shake my head and then shrug. "I-I don't know," I barely get out. I want to call Dmitri.

My parents search my room for me. Trying to find any semblance of the threat. A part of me wishes they will find something. I want to feel a little less crazy. But there is nothing. Of course there is nothing. Why would I be granted any form of sanity.

My parents offer for me to come and sleep with them but I decline. Reluctantly they go back to their room and shut off my lights. I turn on the light by my bedside. I don't want to go back to sleep. I don't want to shut my eyes. What if that thing comes back? Who was that? Whose voice was that? It wasn't Craig, it wasn't Aiden. But he knew Aiden, the voice said I killed one of their own. What does this mean? What does this all mean? If I tell Dmitri about this, I wonder if he will break his tight lock he has on his information. Something or someone is after me, at least, I think. He could at least give me a small bit of knowledge. I text him, against the voice in the back of my head, I text him. In seconds I get back *I am on my way over.*

Minutes, Dmitri is over. It is 3am and I suspect no one is on the roads so we can easily speed. He taps on my window and I let him in. Like my parents, he does a quick scan of the room. Once again, nothing. I guess that is a good thing, it's gone. But that makes me feel more uneasy. It came into my dreams; it was here out of my dreams. It spoke to me, threatened me. And yet so quickly he was gone.

"I'm gonna stay here all night. As long as you need me Belle." Dmitri continues to investigate.

"Can you tell me what is going on now?"

"I don't know what is going on. All I know is that it appears someone is trying get into your head. I can't prevent it, but I will do all I can to make you feel as safe as possible."

I don't think he is lying to me. He doesn't know what is going on. And I can tell that this, what ever this is, is bothering him almost as much as me. I feel like this is the start of a very long journey. Before It was isolated incidents. I have never been attacked, sought after for a prolong period. What is this creature?

Dimmer

Cassidy told me to refrain from listening to any depressing music yet I couldn't stop myself. I want nothing more than to talk to Travis. Every time I try to get his attention, he acts like I'm not there. Could I blame him? After everything that happened. And he doesn't even know the worst part of it.

So now I sit in my room listening to Vince Vance and the Valiants "All I Want for Christmas Is You" on the verge of tears. I go through my pictures of us together on my phone. Where did it all go wrong? Why would I even think about cheating on him? The obvious answer would be Craig, but could he really be to blame? Even if he did get into my head, I still chose not to tell Travis. There were moments when I thought to break it off with Travis and be with Craig. Or I would forget Travis even existed when I was around Craig.

I need to talk to Travis, I will never have peace of mind until we get a chance to talk. This ended so coldly between us. I go over to my texts and try to find the perfect way of asking him to talk. He isn't working this weekend, I still have his schedule in my phone from when he gave it to me.

Can we please meet to talk? It can be public, but I really need to talk to you.

He immediately opens my text. I can see that he read it. I stare at my phone, chewing on my lip, waiting for his response. The three dots come and go until-

Meet me at my job in 15.

A wide grin spreads across my face. This doesn't mean anything good will come out of this but at least we get the chance to talk. I spring out of bed and tumble as I change out of my sweats into jeans and slip on a sweater. My hair looks like a rats nest so I smooth it to the best of my abilities into a bun.

As I race down stairs I tell my parents that I will be back soon, that I was going to starbucks. I am feeling surprisingly optimistic. The music quickly makes me change moods. "Last Christmas" starts playing. Of course. It couldn't be "Sleigh Ride" or "Silver Bells"?

I pull into Starbucks and I see him sitting there. He has two drinks in front of him. Let's do this. I walk over with a shy smile on my face, but it switches to a frown rather quickly. He looks annoyed and severely unhappy to see me. I sit down across from him and give a small smile and hi.

"I got you the peppermint mocha with cinnamon," he says in a small dry voice, gesturing at the second cup.

I thank him but it puts a pit in my stomach. I have no clue how this will go down. He got my favorite drink, but doesn't smile nor does he look remotely happy to see me.

He doesn't look at me, he keeps his eyes locked down at the table or when he takes a sip of his coffee, he looks to the sky. I appreciate him agreeing to meet with me but this is somehow worse than him ignoring me. It is clear that I will have to start. But how do I start this?

"Did you cheat on me?" Travis breaks the silence. I nearly choke on my mocha. I get my throat cleared then look at him. His eyes are filled with grief and moistened with the beginning formation of tears. How did he know?

"You had been really distant with me. Even when we were together it didn't seem like you were all there. And then at Dmitri's house, the way Dmitri and Craig were, it was... and then you broke up with me-"

"I asked to take a break."

He looks at me, tired and annoyed. "Taking a break is basically breaking up. If you feel like we need a break without each other, then that means you are done."

I take in a sharp breath. I suppose he is right. Maybe a break isn't what I needed. Maybe some time alone with just my thoughts to figure things out?

"Well, did you?" Travis continues.

I hate to have to admit this. I wanted to have more of a conversation before we got to this. "Yes," I say in a small voice filled with shame.

He picks up his cup and tries to take a sip but he can't. He flutters his eyes trying to hold back the tears. It breaks my heart. I want to get up right now and leave but what will that solve? What will that do? He deserves an explanation and an apology.

I reach for his hand but he pulls away. "Travis... I kissed Craig twice. Well, he kissed me first and I pulled away and scolded him for it. But then I kissed him a second time. I felt so bad and instantly regretted it and I wanted to tell you, but-"

"But? But what Jez? Why didn't you tell me? I'm sure you had plenty of times to do it!"

"I was scared, I wasn't sure how you would react, if you would want me anymore! I have been losing my mind since that extra credit project and even before that!"

"Is that why you cheated?"

"Yes!" I say a little too loud. Both of us in almost tears now. This is the first time I really thought about it. About why I cheated on him. I do feel like it is Craig's fault but there could have been something else there. "You made me feel so alone when it came to stuff like that, like the Malibu Beast. I told you about the weird things that would happen in my life and you basically wrote me off as being borderline schizophrenic. You kept trying to fix me, and I get it and appreciate that you tried to help. But even after seeing the Malibu Beast with your own eyes you wanted to dismiss the whole thing. You never came to me to ask me if I was seeing things or hearing things. If I was doing alright."

"You didn't come to me with it. How was I supposed to know?"

"I stopped because I got tired of feeling crazy whenever I told you something. You kept me safe and hidden from a lot of things. I felt normal most of the time. But when I needed support the most, when stuff like the extra credit project happened, I couldn't rely on you. Much like at Dmitri's house I figured you would reprimand me and treat me like a kid."

He rolls his eyes at me, it makes my blood boil a bit. He is doing it again. He always ends up doing it.

"Jez, what you do with Nick sometimes *is* super irresponsible. Sorry for not aiding and encouraging behavior like that. And I'm sorry I made you feel alone but the stuff you talked about did sound pretty crazy."

"Craig listened to me. He didn't make me feel crazy. For the first time I didn't feel alone in all this stuff. I felt like I could tell Craig anything."

"Yeah, it's called manipulation. He and his friends are really good at it. He doesn't care about you, he just wanted to get with you. He had years to get to know you and all of sudden he chooses now? He did what he needed to do to get you to trust him. Because you aren't like those other girls who he has been with. It takes work to get you to want to do anything." His voice is actually sweeter. A little more endearing. He's right. Craig did use me. He used me for not what Travis thinks but to get his answers.

I bury my face into my hands as the tears freefall.

"Travis, I am so sorry! I am an idiot, I didn't mean to hurt you, I should have thought. Everything happened so fast and I couldn't talk to you about the situation, and Nick is kind of a robot with things like this. Craig was there, well I thought he was there for me. And-" My voice breaks and I start to fully cry. I realized I messed up. I have apologized more than 50 times via text. But doing it in person. It makes me realize how much I aided in ruining my life and relationship.

I feel Travis get close to me. I open my eyes and embrace him, he holds me tight, he holds me like he used to with such care and love, like he will never let go. He pets the back of my head and says, "I know, I know things were really hard for you. And I'm sorry for not being there like you needed me to be. And I'm sorry I did what I did at Dmitri's." He parts from the hug and starts to distance himself from me. "But I need time Jez, I can't just jump back into this like nothing happened. You lied to me and cheated on me."

"We can work this out though, I'm not talking to Craig anymore. He is out of my life. I don't want him in my life. Travis," I reach out and take his hand. "I want you. I want to feel safe again."

He gives me a pity smile and slips his hand out of mine. "You know I care about you, and you mean a lot to me. But I'm not ready. And I don't think you are either. I can tell you are still mad at me for what I said at Dmitri's and how I made you feel 'schizophrenic'. As long as you're still bitter about that, we will never heal."

I nod to say I understand, because I do. While it would have been nice to get back together right now, right in this moment it wouldn't be healthy. He is right, I am still a little mad and hurt by his behavior. And being able to instant forgive me after I admitted to cheating on him, well that isn't realistic.

He stands up and leans down to give me a soft kiss on the forehead, He whispers bye and goes back to his car. Leaving me sitting alone at the table. Why does it feel like he is saying goodbye forever? A flame being blown out still leaves smoke, still has a lasting smell that lingers. There is something that indicates that the flame was ever there. This is like a dimmer, fading out into nothing until I am left in darkness. Nothing to show that there was ever light to be seen. I can't even get that bit of serenity.

Happy Holidays

Christmas, my favorite time of the year. I have been trying to get myself in the mood all month but hardly anything has worked. But tonight is our family's annual holiday party. It is Friday, December 16th. I have it circled on my calendar with red and green sharpie. It is sort of an all-day affair for the Bedeau's.

My parents took us out of school so we can all go out for breakfast. That was the highlight of the day so far. We went to this little bistro and just hung out together. It was the first time they didn't ask me if I was okay or gave me a concerned look. We just ate, talked, and laughed. Josh and Lindsey didn't even bicker. A Bedeau holiday party miracle.

After breakfast, we went into party mode. It takes a lot out of us but we blast Christmas music throughout the house and it always boosts our morale. Lindsey stepped up her game this year and got a checklist complete with a clipboard, to make sure that we stayed on our tasks. Josh rolled his eyes at her whenever she barked orders like a drill sergeant. The rest of us played into it. My Mom and dad were stuck in the kitchen for the bulk of the day cooking and baking. It is our most impressive spread we have all year. Not even thanksgiving can hold a light.

We do have a large crowd of people coming. Cassidy, Dmitri, and Nick are expected. Along with their parents. For the first time, the Vaduvas have been invited and I do believe they will be coming. Dmitri says he worked them over. Maci wanted to come but she is out of town with her family for the holidays. Lindsey and Josh have their friends come and a few of their parents. My parents have their buddies over as well as a few family members who are also in the LA area. The house is practically filled to capacity yet it always just feels cozy and nice.

I haven't lived in Illinois since I was 7, but every year, without fail, I yearn for the white Christmases I used to have. The time was brief, but it added an extra sense of magic. My Dad did go the full 9 yards this year and got a fake snow machine and littered our lawn with it. It's not the same but I do appreciate the effort. Josh and Lindsey were too young to remember the snow but still think the fake snow is a cute touch.

Like a well-oiled machine, we cleared the house and decked it out in all the holiday party décor for the night. It is 4:45 pm and we are about to leave to go to the school for the holiday concert. Nick spilled to our parents how Dmitri is in the concert and how it would be an amazing pregame to the party.

I've straightened my hair and pushed it back with a black velvet headband to match my velvet maroon long-sleeved skater dress. I have some cute white fluffy socks that have little red snowflakes poking out the top of my boots. I straighten out my dress and brush my hair. I look very festive but I don't feel it too much. While we get to see Dmitri perform tonight, we will also see Craig.

We all meet up, the Bedeau's, Papakonstatinos, and the Babicz/Aronthal's, and grab a seat next to the Vaduva's who were already sitting in the auditorium when we got there. Before the concert started the dads wasted no time chatting Mr. Vaduva's ear off. This was their first time meeting him and of course the first thing they mentioned was the striking similarity between him and Dmitri.

None of us, besides the Vaduva's, have ever been to the holiday concert and had no clue that it included the band, the orchestra, the jazz band, and two different choirs. The choirs started off the evening, some of their pieces dragged just a bit. But the band came on and picked up the pace. My favorite was that they played Sleigh Ride. I somehow missed Craig. When they sat down, the saxophones weren't really visible from my seat. Then the orchestra was up. Nick was telling me and Cassidy they were going to play Winter by Vivaldi and that Dmitri is doing the solo because no one else could play it as well as him. So they had to transpose it for the cello.

The piece was incredibly long but I was astonished by Dmitri. His solo was so fast, so intense, and he handled it like it was nothing. We knew he was a prodigy but oh my god! Lindsey's eyes lit up like a Christmas tree as she watched him play. At the end they had him stand up and take a separate bow. The crowd went insane and gave him a standing ovation. I saw that Mr. and Mrs. Vaduva looking so incredibly proud. Mrs. Vaduva even had tears in her eyes.

Riding off the high of watching Dmitri perform for the first time and blowing us all away, I nearly forgot about the fact that the jazz band was next. It is a smaller group than the band and he will no doubt be in front. They come out and just as I suspected, he was. Under the stage lights, he shined like a star. I tried to not look at him but it was hard. Right front and center. Turns out he had a few solos in their piece as well. They played the Nutcracker Suite, the one that was in Elf. Another long piece, but amazing nonetheless. Much like hearing Dmitri play for the first time, this was the first time I heard Craig play. And it nearly took my breath away. He was made to be on that stage playing. Unlike with Dmitri, while he was in the front there were still other musicians highlighted with him, yet all I could see and notice was him. Even when he wasn't playing.

After the concert was over Cassidy, Nick, and I rushed to the music room to find Dmitri to congratulate him. We found him relatively quickly. We practically jumped on him gushing about how amazing he did. Dmitri couldn't stop smiling and I think he blushed a little bit. Cassidy took out her phone and demanded that we take a commemorative selfie. The one ended up being five. After praising him and cracking a few jokes we let him free so he could change and meet up with our families.

As we walk down the hall, I catch a glimpse of Craig. He is talking to some bandmates as he puts on his jacket. I don't know why but something possessed me to stop and talk to him. I check to see if Nick and Cassidy are looking back for me. They aren't. I quickly scurry into the room and walk up to him. He doesn't see me; his back is to me. I haven't spoken to him since November 25th. Should I even be doing this? I bite my lip. No, no I shouldn't. I don't want to ruin the day.

I turn on my heels and go to exit the room, and then I hear, "Jezebel?" I stop, balling my hands into a fist. This is my fault. I pivot and face him. "Hi," I whisper weakly. He looks around before approaching me. He doesn't look happy. He doesn't want to see me as much as I him.

"Why are you here?"

I expected at least a hi back. He really doesn't want to talk to me. "I'm here with my family and my friends and their families... for Dmitri," I add the quick clarification.

He nods and stares at me blankly. I can tell he just wants to leave and so do I. But I can't end the conversation. I need the closure. "Can you tell me something?"

He raises his eyebrow in slight intrigue. "You said that you manipulated me to get your way of me trusting you. How far did you go? How much did you alter my thoughts, cause me to like you, make me want to cheat?!" I start to get louder as I trail off with my rambling questions. "How much did you get in my head?"

Craig takes in a big breath and moves me off to the side. He looks as if he wants to just escape from all of this. "I don't know why you chose to have this conversation right now, but I didn't manipulate you the way you think I did."

"What does that mean?" I jab crossing my arms.

"What that means is when I asked to be in a group with you and Nick, I did persuade you to let me in with little to no opposition. And when we were talking for the first time I did use it a little within the first couple of sentences.

But when I looked into your mind-" he stops as if he is wondering if he should say anything. "I saw that I didn't need to. I didn't go in your head beyond checking to see if you hated me. I never created any false feelings, Jezebel. What you felt for me was 100% organic."

I step back shaking my head. No, he is wrong. He is lying. "I don't believe you."

He rolls his eyes adjusting his sax case. "Okay, believe what you want. But I'm telling you the truth. What I- my feelings were real and so were yours. I know you feel guilty for cheating on Travis but that did not happen from my 'manipulation'. You can believe it or not but it is the honest truth."

I can feel the tears starting to well up in my eyes. That can't be right and I won't believe it to be. I shake my head and jog off. He doesn't call after me and a part of me sort of wishes that he does. But at the same time, if I never hear from him again, I will be elated.

Getting back to my house, my friends and family instantly felt and saw the shift in my mood and did everything to make me happy. As soon as we got into the house the Christmas music was blasting once again. Josh and Lindsey got me to do our perfectly choreographed dance to Little Saint Nick. We have been doing this dance for years, and it was quite the crowd pleaser. Everyone cheered and clapped as we did our big finish.

Everyone became enthralled with the Vaduva's. They couldn't stop listening to their stories and Mrs. Vaduva turned out to be the life of the party on the parents end. Mr. Vaduva looked uncomfortable but still managed to dazzle everyone. Then my Mom started to play the piano and the adults gathered around and listened as she played "The Christmas Song". Mrs. Papakonstatinos joined in accompanying her with song. They were like lounge performers; they began taking requests.

I and my friends snuck into the kitchen to do a little champagne toast. "To a merry Christmas and a happy Hanukkah. Now let's get festive and so wasted that we forget the night," Dmitri toasts. We all cheer as we laugh and drink down our glass of champagne.

I only had two glasses but it did really help relax me. I and my friends ran around giggling as we did an impromptu karaoke night for everyone. Cassidy and I sang "A Christmas to Remember". Cassidy was Dolly and I was Kenny. Dmitri and Nick hilariously sang "Santa Baby" cracking everyone up.

Dmitri was pretty drunk after the karaoke and to our demise, he found the mistletoe. He started to chase us around with it. He nearly tackled Nick as he planted a big sloppy kiss on him. He then hovered it over me and Cassidy. She is wearing bright red lipstick so she kissed me on the cheek leaving a perfect mark. Many laughs and pictures later we got to the portion where we all joined in the living room for a big speech from my Dad. He decided to go for a small tearjerker but mainly a lighthearted theme. It made everyone feel warm and fuzzy. We toasted our hot chocolates, eggnogs, hot apple cider, mulled liquor, what have you. It is one of my favorite parts of the Bedeau holiday party. It brings everyone together and makes us feel the true spirit of the holidays.

As the night winds down, my Dad started to talk to a very drunk Dmitri, which he couldn't hide very well, about his performance. If my Dad wasn't already in love with Dmitri, his performance tonight really sold it. My Dad got Dmitri to play the piano for the remaining guest, to do an impromptu duet with my Mom.

The last of us gather around the piano and listen. To me, Cassidy, and Nick's surprise Dmitri was still amazing at playing while drunk. Nick, Cassidy, and I are all hugged up together as we smile and listen. I wasn't sure how tonight was going to be, I thought that I wouldn't be able to enjoy one of my favorite days.

Before they leave, my friends and I sneak away up to my room and exchange gifts with one another. And also, to just take a moment to lie down and collect ourselves. As we lie back on my wrapping paper, gift bag, and tissue paper filled floor, I can't help but think about how happy and grateful I am to have them in my life. "I love you guys. Things have been pretty sucky for me lately. Thank you for being there." Tears start to stream down my cheek. It is the first time I am crying from relief rather than pain. They awe and roll over to me making a pile as we all hug each other. I can hear my favorite Christmas song softly playing from downstairs. "White Christmas".

Nothing Still

I cannot sleep. I haven't been able to sleep properly since our holiday party. Since I last saw Craig. Not being able to sleep on Christmas Eve wasn't bad. I just stayed up with Lindsey and Josh baking cookies and watching movies. The other nights though, nightmare after nightmare. Somedays I was free from them, but I was too afraid to close my eyes. Dmitri came over almost everyday to check up on me. I appreciate all that he has done for me since Black Friday, checking up on me, bringing me my favorite snacks, staying up late with me at night. Tonight he is coming, I texted him letting him know that I am not feeling at all at ease.

Knock, knock, knock! I spring out of my bed and race to my window. Dmitri has been coming through my window when he visits me at night. I open it and he comes climbing in. His hair is in a bun and he is wearing his pajamas; black tank and dark grey sweatpants. He pulls a pack of cigarettes out of his pocket.

"Want a smoke?"

I shake my head and decline his offer. He puts it back in his pocket and follows me over to my bed where I plop down face first in my pillow.

"There, there," he comforts as he rubs my back. "I can get you a really great sleeping drug my mom has. It will put you right out for the night."

"But if I sleep then I will have a nightmare, or sleep paralysis."

"But if you don't you will be sleep deprived and you will go crazy," he lies down facing me. He brushes my hair out of my face so our eyes meet. "You are starting to scare your family. They ask me questions about your sanity every time I am over."

"Good, they should be worried. My sanity isn't good right now."

Dmitri drops his hand from my hair and chuckles. I prop myself up on my forearms as he gets up out of my bed. He heads over to my bookcase running his fingers along my history encyclopedias. He picks up a crystal figurine that I got from Austria and examines it.

"I can't stay tonight, Belle." He peaks his eye over to me to see my reaction.

"Why not?" I ask in an unintentional whine.

"I am going to Romania and then Florida. We are leaving tonight. I will be back in four days. I actually just woke up." He notices the disappointed look on my face and returns to my side. "You know if I could stay I would."

I know he would. I cannot expect him to stop living his life just because I'm going through this, this insane thing. He has gone above and beyond what I expected. A tear drops on my hand. I started to cry without even noticing. I sit up and wipe away the tears trying to hide my face. I get so overwhelmed so easily these days. The littlest thing can set me off.

Dmitri pulls me into him. I hug him back deeply, so tight, if he wasn't so built it might have hurt him. He lightly rubs my back. "If you need anything text me. I can't get back to you, but at least you will have someone to talk to," he says in my ear, still not letting me go.

I nod and break from the hug. He makes sure one last time that I am good enough for him to leave. I reassure him and wave him off. Once he is out the window, I close my curtains and go back to my bed and lay face down in my pillow.

I can't sleep still. Every time I close my eyes all I could see were glowing eyes looking back at me, the shiver inducing whispers. I couldn't shake the possibility that someone was in my room. Everything within me wanted to call Travis, to hear his voice telling me that everything is okay but I know that that's not an option anymore. I don't even know if Craig made me have those feelings for him. He claims that he didn't, but how can I trust him? He could have influenced Travis to say what he said to me. He has never belittled me. Sure, he has been condescending towards me at times but he has never torn me down. I will never know the truth, nor will I ever find peace in this situation. All it did was open another dark door in my nightmare of a life.

I'm alone. No one can help me. Dmitri is doing all he can, but he cannot solve this issue. I can't tell my parents they would probably just pack us up and move us again. Or bring me to a psychiatric facility or to a psychiatrist, considering that I am sounding schizophrenic. Talking to Cassidy really helped last time and Nick would probably be overjoyed to get back into this supernatural investigation. But I don't want to involve them in anymore of these matters. I can't tell them what Craig is. What if he comes after them?

I sink my face into my hands, letting out a deep painfilled groan. Bitter silence, no crickets, no static, no cars going down the street, just silence. A silence so deep I feel like I am in an isolation chamber, stuck in solitary confinement. I will soon lose my sanity completely before I find any semblance of peace of mind.

Back and forth, left and right my life is being passed around like a ball. I haven't had full control of it in years.

I get a few hours of sanity when I am in practice. God, I can't wait to go back. Just a brief moment away from all of this crap.

How can I be normal without getting rid of this formidable fear I have. There is always going to be this growing fear that someone is coming after me. I could be paranoid but every part of me is telling me that I'm not. It could have been a hallucination. Black Friday was a very hysterical night for me. I'm not myself. I barely feel real. Nothing about what is happening to me feels real.

I hate to think about how much my simpler my life would be if I lived the type of life Travis wanted me to live. Be that perfect, obedient, careful girlfriend. Maybe I wouldn't have creatures trying to kill me. Every time I poke my head into something the people around me gets hurt, or I do.

It is a saying that you never remember pain. We all know that physical and emotional pain hurts, that sometimes it can even impact you so deep that it leaves a scar. Yet, we are incapable of remembering the exact feeling of the pain. The specific burn that it creates in your chest. The shock waves that flow through your nerves. It is why we can never fully stop ourselves from getting in situations that will inflict pain. How can you prepare for what you don't know? We think, it won't be that bad. That everyone goes through pain.

I am insanely guilty of doing the same. I know that digging farther will end up with me getting hurt either physically, mentality, emotionally, most likely the ladder.

Yet if I don't, what am I to do? Sit around going the rest of my life looking over my shoulder? Having restless nights, never feeling safe or relaxed?

The last time I felt truly away from all of this is when Travis and I went on our last date. Everything seemed so right then. The only worries were frivolous teenage things. The way he looked at me, held me, kissed me... but that is all over now I guess. Things could change...

Just like that night the Malibu Beast ruined our harmony. There isn't a single thought within me that is telling me to give up on us. Yet, I think back to when I talked to him at Starbucks. Things started off so coldly. I could see how much I hurt him but then things started to warm up. When he hugged me, I forgot all that was wrong in my life. When he touched me I wasn't reminded of everything that was taken from me. Travis was so genuine, no matter how Dmitri felt about him and his actions, I know that they were true.

Craig, I can't trust a single passing thought or feeling I had with him. He brought me deeper into all of this mess. I killed someone because of him. And now I sit with this book that might hold all my answers, these nightmares, because of him. I don't know what any of this means in this stupid book. Literally I cannot, it is all in Latin. I want to be rid of all the bad these little investigations of mine burdened me with. Yet, when I am not obsessing over the Beast my mind is on Travis. As of now I think I'd rather take the pain of fear rather than heart break.

I roll over in my bed and open the middle drawer of my nightstand. I remove the papers I placed on top to act as camouflage and pick up the book. I get up and move over to my desk. As I settle in, I mentally prepare for the possibility damning information that is inside. I forgot for a moment that it is completely written in Latin. Thank god it has drawings as to indicate the physical appearance of these creatures.

My best mode of action is to rely on an online Latin translator. It actually worked out really well. I was able to switch the language around when things didn't quite make sense. It was written in the 1200s so it was an interesting time typing everything out in a modern way of speaking so I could fully understand. My guess is that some of this information is outdated, but it is a start. I was able to locate he creature that is the Malibu Beast from the drawing. The fact that this book is the only one we were not allowed to touch, I should have known the creatures identity would be in here.

Ambobestia: A creature with immortality and incredible deception. Origin: Unknown. The lore is thought to come from a powerful curse. An ambobestia could never fully live amongst humans; despite their human appearance. Known to have three major weaknesses: nearly unfeedable hunger. Bright flashes of light (when in full beast form), and their head. The light disorientate their brain and its senses causing the creature to be vulnerable. While the only way to kill an ambobestia is to disconnect the head or to crush the head. One of the toughest creatures to kill. With their fatally sharp teeth, without much, one could easily eviscerate ones pray or attacker. The deception that these creatures perform are to doubt any validity of reality. An ambobestia could influence someone to harm or kill themselves, cause prolong torture by keeping the subject alive and conscious when in a state of near death. The creature is known to be able to enter people's dreams. When in the dreams they can cause harm to the target or extreme emotional distress. This has been known to carry on outside of the dream when the target is awake. The extremely cunning and dreadful creature is often marked by the insignia of a snake. This insignia can most often be seen on a door of a known trouble making ambobestia. The double headed snake is the basic symbol of the ambobestia. This is often proudly displayed in their homes.

I close my laptop. I cannot read anymore. I feel as if I shut a door that held an overwhelming amount of negative energy. Uncertainty and fear sets deep in my heart. I wanted to know the truth. I needed these answers. Yet, I feel as if I'd be better off not knowing what this ambobestia was. All I got out of it was that I am even more scared of what is to come.

So what, I know what it is, but I can't get rid of it. I'm right where I was before I read the book. Scared, alone, confused... I know what I need to do, who I need to talk to. I don't trust this, yet I have no choice.

I take an extra strong grip on the wheel. The pain begins to grow from the friction and my fingers tense up. I take two calming breaths and close my eyes. A gleaming orange light enters my darkened vision. As I slowly open my eyes the orange light turns yellow. The sun is shining past the cloud that previously hid it. The moment is brief, just long enough to give me the sensation of peace; it now hides behind another cloud.

Perhaps this meeting will be short. Maybe I will find satisfaction in the answer. Try and stay positive, I keep telling myself. A thing that is definitely easier said than done. I need to stop thinking, the more I debate about outcomes of the situation the worse it gets.

Craig's book gave me all the information I needed, yet here I am. I can't do this alone. Dmitri will never help me the way I want him to. He worries about the future of my wellbeing. While I am grateful for that, it is not what I need... Well at the very best what I want.

A car drives past me, startling me. The street is so quiet and it is somehow sunnier than the others. Pleasant morning birds chirp having pleasing conversations. Sitting here reminds me of the Malibu I knew. Peaceful.

A place away from the city where you can settle down and have a moment to yourself.

I look at the time on my radio, 11:22 A.M. It's Sunday, people will be coming from church soon, going out to brunch, maybe go for an afternoon golf. I told my parents that I would be back by 1. The sooner I can get this done the better. So I hope I keep to my word. I crack my neck and shake off the last bit of nerves. Here goes nothing.

I get out of my car and linger in the street. I don't want to do this, to put simply. Maybe I should go home. I shouldn't be involving anyone else in this mess. I turn back towards my car. Before I even get the chance to open the door I hear my name being called.

"Jez! Jez, I know you hear me!" Nick calls from his doorway. He is so loud that the people in the next subdivision can probably hear him. I drop my hand from the handle and face him.

"Hey Nick," I say solemnly, just loud enough to be audible from his distance.

"Well are you gonna come in?" He asks, still very loud.

After not replying for a whole half of a second, he enthusiastically beckons me in. I let out a small groan into my chest. This was a dumb decision. Then again, my only other options were to: talk to Dmitri, which would have ended with him scolding me. Ignore all my problems while still being haunted and hope I don't get killed. Or talk to Craig. The very last thing I want to do.

I lock my car and walk over to meet Nick.

"I didn't know you were coming. I was sitting in the living room and saw your car. What's up?" Nick says in nearly one breath leading me into his house.

"It was a spur of the moment decision. I need to talk to you about something-"

"Oh thank god! Is it about what happened on that Friday? I have been waiting, but Cas told me that you have to come and tell me. So I have been trying to be respectful."

With genuine excitement in his eyes, Nick grins at me with anticipation. I do not meet his enthusiasm.

"Can we go to your room? No one else can hear about this."

Nick finally reads how serious this is. He nods; without another word we walk up to his room. Nick's house has a very cozy aesthetic Both of his parents are very busy so he normally gets the house to himself, unless Adam is somewhere lurking around being a creep. I haven't heard any lewd comments, an obscene amount of cursing, or a loud conversation that lacks any form of substance, so I could say that this house is void of Adam and his neanderthal friends. One positive thing.

Nick opens his door and motions for me to come inside. I sit on his bed as he shuts his door. He eagerly walks up to me and plops down next to me, making me catch some air. He lies down and props his head up with his fists resting under his chin. Here we go.

I open my mouth to begin this dreaded conversation.

"So, what went down? Everything after you passed out from telling us off."

I think of a way to compose the explanation. I know that he was partially a part of the whole thing but it is still difficult to figure just the right thing to say. I know the moment I let everything out the more real it will become for me. That's how it always works. I can feel myself getting choked up already just thinking about it.

To my surprise, Nick jumps up and hugs me. I hold back the tears and hug him a little deeper. Nick isn't much of hugger in situations like this, him doing this makes me feel easy. As we part from the hug it was as if we had an unspoken understanding of saying sorry. Him being sorry about what happened to me and me being sorry about keeping him in the dark for so long.

I'm still searching for the right way to explain what I know. I don't want to tell him that Craig isn't human. I don't know what Craig would do if he ever found out that Nick knew. But it is such a large part as to why I am like this. How can I explain to him the deception without outing Craig for what he is?

"When I woke up from passing out, I heard Craig and Dmitri talking. Craig has been lying to us this whole time."

This sparks Nick's interests. "How so?"

I'm careful with my next words. "He knew what the Malibu Beast was. He knew the whole time and used us to get closer to who it was. Everything he has been telling us could have been a lie." Without disclosing what Craig is, everything sounds so minor. "He manipulated me and you too. He knew how dangerous Aiden was and put us in direct harms way just to figure out his name and face. I *killed* for him. I knock Aiden out, tied him up, shot him in the head and pushed his dead body in the ocean," I break off getting choked up again.

Nick pats my back. "How- how do you *know* he manipulated us? I only ask because with or without him we were going to do the investigation. Honestly, not even trying to pander to your feelings, killing Aiden was the right thing to do. He was a monster Jez, if you didn't pull that trigger you would have been the one on the news."

I know, I know that killing Aiden was out of self defense but it doesn't make me feel much better. I still think about his parents on the news, how heart broken they were.

"Jez?"

"I don't have direct proof that he manipulated us. And I know that we were planning on investigating anyway but he was never part of the plan. He was never supposed to be there. He gave us all the tools to make it seem like we were on to something. That we were really helping on finding out what Aiden was. We were pawns to him. He gave me so much security. I disclosed so much to him."

"And you think you did that because of him manipulating you?"

"I was happy with Travis. Breaking up never crossed my mind until we started the investigation with Craig."

"It could have been that you never really spent much time with him before and you genuinely liked him."

I never owned up to that possibility. It is much easier to deny and blame Craig for this. It makes so much more sense. I never thought of doing the things I did with him around. There is no way, *no way* that Craig had no influence in any of the things that I did. He said that he didn't though. That he influenced us to trust him easier but that's it... No. No it is not true.

"So what is it?"

"Huh?"

"The Malibu Beast, did you ever find out?"

"A creature called an ambobestia. It was in that book he forbade us from looking in. I stole it. During one of our study sessions."

Nick bugs his eyes out in shock. "You stole the book? Jesus Jez. An ambobestia huh? I have never heard of that creature. And I scoured through those books. Cover to cover. I do have to admit, him sending us on the goose chase trying to figure out what it was instead of focusing on who it was pretty crappy of him."

"What should I do?"

"With the information?"

"With the information, with Craig, with everything that has been happening to me."

"What has been happening to you?"

I forgot that I didn't tell him about what has been happening to me since the night. With these dreams that may not actually be dreams. "I have been having dreams that are almost like night terrors. I get sleep paralysis as well. I think it has to do with Aiden."

Nick doesn't respond. He looks away from me and gets up. Pacing around I can tell he is biting his tongue on a response.

"What is it Nick?"

He stops moving. He barely glances at me before he continues his pacing over to his window. "I don't want to upset you, Jez," he says with his back to me. "But I do really think that you should talk to Craig."

"No!" I snap back unintentionally. Nick flinches at my reaction. He slowly turns to face me, his eye filled with caution and regret.

"Jez, hear me out... I know him lying to us is bad, but all three of us did some stupid things during that investigation. He knew what the Malibu Beast was. He could probably give you answers on all of these weird dreams you have been having... don't be mad at me," he peeps cowering, waiting for my response.

I let down my wall and sigh. I know he is right. Craig is the only one I can go to for answers. Dmitri will never tell me. He would prefer if he could erase my memory, all of our memories of all events from our extra credit project onward. I'm not going to do it. I don't even want to hear his voice. Who knows all that his powers can do. He has already messed so much up.

"I know you can't trust him and you think he manipulated you, but have you entertained the idea that maybe, juuust maybe that you did what you did because you wanted to? Also, sure he sent us on a wild goose chase but he also led us to the truth, and that was Aiden. And once he found out who Aiden was he did say that we should stop the investigation."

"And then he called me up to come with him to the club with him to hunt down Aiden. He left you out, but he used me one last time for bait."

"That's pretty shitty, I gotta admit. But you did agree to go. Because you wanted to. Or he could have manipulated you, I don't know.

I haven't 'entertained the idea'. And I will never will. That could be that I am avoiding the truth, the truth of Nick being right. But if I admit that, that means that Travis and I can never be okay. That I wanted Craig over him. That I was so willing to share so much with Craig, much more than I did with Travis when we first met. That I truly liked Craig more than Travis that I was willing to mess up our near 2-year relationship. But that can't be right.

"Jez, you gotta talk to me a little more."

"He isn't what he seems. He is a snake!"

Nick looks at me quizzically. That is as close to the truth as I can get without endangering him. "I know you like him, Nick, but we cannot trust him. Dmitri was right to bar him from us."

He opens his mouth but quickly closes it. Nodding he joins me back on his bed. He probably still thinks that I am being crazy. If he only knew the truth.

Walking into Fire

I would have preferred if Thursday never arrived. January 5, 2012, we're all supposed to die from Armageddon in December so maybe no matter what I do, it won't matter. Who am I kidding, this is just going to be another Y2k. I managed to stay off social media this whole holiday season. I couldn't risk seeing Travis. I specifically stayed away on New Year's Eve and on New Year's. It would have been our 2-year anniversary. There is a tick in me that is itching to see if he posted something.

Going against my better judgment, I roll over and reached over to get my phone. Frantically I unlock it and get to Instagram. I don't really care about anyone else's posts too much right now, but I should try to naturally see if he posted instead of going to his page. The first post is Nick's post from New Year's, he was in Time Square with some of his cousins looking happier than ever. Next, some insignificant girl from school, followed by another, and then an insignificant boy from school. My heart beats a little faster with each post I passed. I don't know why I am searching to get my feelings hurt. Maci's post is a highlight of the year and I made it as a feature in the post. I feel very honored actually. Dmitri posted. That's weird, he never does. Even weirder, it is him and his dad; captioned, "bringing in the new year with my pops #clones". I can tell he is super drunk in this picture. I smile. These posts, at least Nick's, Maci's, and Dmitri's were actually a morale booster for me.

Then it hits me. Before I even see the post. I see Travis' name, Travofharts, Dmitri and Nick would make fun of that name often. I take a moment to breathe before I scroll down to fully look at it. I freeze, I have been looking for a post from him but I can't bring myself to look at whatever this might be. I should treat it like a band-aid and just look at it. With a swift motion I scroll down and there it is. On the beach, him and Candice. He has his arm wrapped around her waist and is kissing her cheek. She looks extremely pleased with herself with a satisfied grin. She is wrapped around him like, if she lets go she would blow away. My eyes pan down to the caption that reads, "I couldn't be happier to bring in the new year with this beautiful girl. She has been my rock, my release, and my happy place. Leaving the negativity in 2011"

Shit... I throw my phone at the other end of my bed. My heart, the last bit that was still somewhat held together has completely disintegrated. I know I am that 'negativity' that he is talking about. Any small piece of hope or optimism left the moment my eyes saw that post. I ruined everything and I have no one to blame but myself and I can't even clean up the mess. All I can do is sit in it.

I sat in my bed for thirty minutes crying, feeling sorry for myself. Hoping that maybe if I cry, I will feel something but all I feel is emptiness and anger from feeling so hollow. Everything I do today matters. How I walk into the school, how I carry myself around Travis and his new girlfriend, Candice, how I look at Craig, if I even have the balls to confront him. I still can't believe how quickly Travis moved on. And made it public on our anniversary no less. I can feel my face getting hot and my vision becoming blurry. I'm on my last pair of contacts and I'm not getting new ones until next month. I don't want to risk a crying fit messing up my lenses. I have to hold everything together.

Bzzz bzzz. My phone vibrates on my bed. Cassidy is calling. I hesitate to pick it up because she never calls before school so I know it will most likely end up being something about Travis. I know they all have had to see that post. Bzzz bzzz. I huff and slide to answer.

"Hey Cas," I say faking my composure the best I can.

"Jezzi... How are you doing, is everything okay?" She asks cautiously. I can hear the regret in her voice for even asking.

Shit. Tears start swelling then streaming down my face. The three words that break people faking their happiness, "are you okay?" If they have to ask it's always no and results in waterworks. Exhibit A.

"Jezzi, if you need you should take a personal day. You have been through a lot since black Friday. And it would be tota-"

"No, Cas I can't! I can't just take off of school because I took a break- well what I thought was a break but turned out to be a breakup because he is now dating the girl who I hated being around him because she was just a little too friendly!" I shout with tears coming out of my eyes staining my shirt.

Static silence fills the call. Cassidy is probably stunned with guilt by association. I didn't mean to outburst like that.

"Well, it wasn't just the breakup. You... killed someone. And something happened between you and

Craig, that I still don't know what that was. But nevertheless, you have been broken since. And I know you never said it out loud but I know that you loved Travis."

Those last words hit me like a semi-truck. I did love Travis. And he, well I thought he loved me. He was the best part of my two years. Up until that extra credit project we were great. Dimitri thought he was too controlling but he wasn't. He knew about my past and just wanted me to be safe. Our last date that we went on reminded me of the times that we used to have before our lives were in constant danger. I blew him off so much, I didn't spend the time I should have with him. I was too busy spending it with Craig... Craig, this is all his fault. I don't know what thoughts, what feelings were mine. I still don't. He could have been controlling me this whole time and I will never know. I tried talking to Travis multiple times after thanksgiving break. He didn't want to talk to me. Notably so.

"Jezzi, you there?"

"Yes, yes I'm here," I say shuffling into my bathroom to replace my contacts with my glasses. I hardly ever wear them, but they do compliment my face. They are navy blue browline glasses with a gold accent on the arms. While I'm here I put my hair in a ponytail and clear my face from the blubbering. "I'll be fine. I can't make the promise, but I will try my hardest to be as fine as I can be. I only have 2 classes with him anyway. Lunch too. But I'd imagine that he would be sitting with *her*." My eyes still look puffy but there isn't much I can do about that.

"I wish I had more than two classes with you."

"I'll be fine Cassi, I swear it. Cross my heart," I motion across by my heart as if she could see it.

"I'll take your word. See you soon."

I say a soft bye before hanging up. I look down at my shirt and I see the tear stains. I groan and rummage through my closet for a pullover hoodie. I find my black Adidas one and pull it over my head. People normally come back from winter break with brand new clothes, a new hairstyle, or a full new look. The purpose is to look your best. Going back to school after Thanksgiving was hard, having to see Craig and Travis. But they stayed out of my way. I thought that maybe Travis needed some time, that after the break, we would be okay. But he doesn't love me. He made that perfectly clear with the post he made. This is gonna be the longest day of my life. I may be acting a bit melodramatic, scratch that, I know I am acting melodramatic. Everyone will go through a breakup in their lifetime, yet no one prepares you for the sting that follows.

I look at myself in my full-length mirror. I look very basic and defeated. Not the look I wanted to stride into school with but c'est la vie. I smooth down my ponytail while letting out a huge puff of air. I need to pump myself up. It's the first day of school in the new year. I can do this. I start jumping in place, shaking out nerves. I'm a strong woman, I swerved the most popular guy in school, I have won state- and nation-wide medals and trophies in gymnastics, I killed a guy and dumped his body in the ocean. I am a badass.... And a murderer, who will most likely go to jail. I stop hopping around and get back into my thoughts. I could go to jail, I was the last person to touch him. My fingerprints are all over him, what if my hair got caught in his clothes. How long do fingerprints stay on a body if they have been underwater? It has been over a month, working on two, but I know they are still looking.

"Jez, you're going to be late! You are driving Josh and Lindsey as well!" my Mom calls from downstairs.

I take one last look in the mirror. You're a cheater, you have been dumped, and you're a murderer. But let everyone else see what they always do. That random redhead chick who is friends with Dmitri and Cassidy. I exit my room and head downstairs. Each step I mutter some words of encouragement to get myself ready to face school.

"Took you long enough," Josh grumbles. "Jez, you okay?" he questions looking at me with concern. Please don't start the wave.

"You have been acting really weird these past couple of days," Lindsey adds. I really don't need them to be nice and supportive little siblings at this moment. I swear to god if Lindsey touches my shoulder and gives me her trademark look, I'm gonna lose my mind. She radiates warmth and care and when she gives you that look it is a 99.9% guarantee that you will cry.

"Yeah, I'm good. Just tired and not really in the mood for school."

"Bullshit," Josh says hopping out of his seat, "who did something to you?" He may be my younger brother but guards me like a pit bull at times.

"Language Joshua," my Dad says in his coffee mug while taking a big sip. But he too looks at me with the same concern. I should have just slept over at Cassidy's to avoid this. I look around at my family looking at me almost the same way. Minus my Mom who is absent from the room. God bless. I spurt out a little fake laugh and a smile to match it.

"I'm fine really. Just really tired. Let's go." I race towards the door, grabbing my backpack and keys on the way. I motion for Josh and Lindsey to follow.

"Bye Mom, bye Dad!" I call already out the door. Walking at a suspiciously fast pace I get to my mini cooper and throw my backpack to the ground and quickly start the car. Josh in the passenger and Lindsey in the back, still highly confused by my behavior. Me smiling the way I am isn't helping the situation whatsoever, yet I cannot stop. I pull off flying down the street at record speed. They both take notice.

I want to get to school as soon as possible. The longer I linger around my family the more the suspicion grows. They don't even know about Craig. Having to face the reality of Travis was hard enough. I haven't seen Craig since December 16th, the day of the holiday concert. It made me fully realize that my feelings for him weren't completely gone. I keep telling myself that I never had feelings for him, that they were all created by him getting in my head. *"I never created any false feelings, Jezebel. What you felt for me was 100% organic."* His words that I refuse to believe ring in my head.

"This is garbage," I mutter out loud, unintentionally.

"I know, this traffic is torturous. We should have stopped at Starbucks. But you were in robot mode," Josh says exasperated. I've seemed to have gotten away with my outburst. I'll just go with it.

"I have had a lot on my mind. I just wanna get to school."

"Is it Travis?" Lindsey asks.

Hearing his name makes my heart sink. Josh reaches back and punches her. "You idiot, of course it's Travis, why even ask that?!"

"Because you never know!" She exclaims hitting him back.

I can feel my face getting warm again. The tears start to well up as Lindsey and Josh go back and forth with each other. An overwhelming pressure weighs down on me. Halted in traffic I look out the window to see rows of cars with people all looking like they want to end it all. Very few people actually enjoy making the commute. Nobody wants to go out into the world and face responsibility. It truly doesn't help the fact that I have to face two things that I really would not want to be privy to.

The sounds began to slowly drown out my thoughts; Lindsey and Josh fighting, the honking of cars because another one cuts them off to try to move just an inch closer to freedom from this hell. The smell of the overpowering peppermint air freshener. The sun is just barely reaching over the clouds mixed with a little bit of smog. The wind whirled between the cars and the gusts are high, matching the waves crashing down in high impact. I can't even tell if I'm moving if anything is moving relative to time.

"Jez!" My trance brakes by Josh.

I look over to him, not even sure if I'm showing any kind of expression.

"Do we have time to go to Starbucks?" He asks slowly. Or perhaps it was at a normal rate and I'm just losing it.

"Jezzi, watch the road!" Lindsey shouts, snapping my attention to normal once more. The road is clearer, we are actually running ahead of schedule.

"I too would like some Starbucks... If we can," Lindsey peeps, leaning forward at me.

"Um yeah, sure."

"You're paying right?" Josh inquires.

Lindsey hits Josh again, "You have your own money you leech!"

"She has Daddy's credit card so let's not have any of us spend our money!"

"Can the both of you shut up? Your yelling and fighting is making me go insane," I say in a mumble. But apparently, it was loud enough for them to hear. They both sit back and get quiet. I feel that for the first time in this commute I feel a sense of peace. The horns have stopped, the wind is barely a whistle. The waves crashing is more soothing rather than an attack on my ears.

"I don't think it is us who is making you go insane, we're not Travis," Lindsey mumbles coldly.

My jaw drops. I can't believe she said that to me. She is normally on my side.

"Damn Lin," Josh laughs.

I close my mouth and focus on the road. I shouldn't get these jerks anything.

I was able to make it to school in just enough time to go to my locker and rush off to class. Normally I would try to see my friends beforehand, but I needed to mentally prepare myself for first period, A.P. English, Craig is in that class. I decided not to get anything from Starbucks, I might not even eat my lunch. Here I go, into the fire.

In the Flames

irst Period. AP English. While I am free of Travis, I have to see Jude, Jeanette, Bridget, and Craig. How did I get so lucky to have them all in my class? At least Candice isn't in this class. She's too dumb. I feel a little smirk grow on my face as I think about it.

"Hey Red," Jude's voice boomed next to me. I haven't had to hear him since November. Gotta say, I don't miss it in the slightest. I wonder if Craig told him anything, they were both in the UK at the same time. They could have met up.

"Jude," I grumble acting as if I am searching for some notes. I don't even know why he is talking to me. Travis and I aren't together anymore. Craig and I don't talk. I know he has been away, but he has to know something. I continue to ignore him; I can see that he is still looking at me. I don't have time for his jokes or jabs.

"Jezebel." I turn my head. He called me by my real name, he has never done that. He doesn't have his stupid self-assured smirk. He has this foreign look in his eye, sympathy, concern, worry? "I just wanted to let you know that I think the whole situation, the breakup, with Travis is garbage. I know I tease you a lot and you're not that fond of me, but I think you're a really cool girl and he was an idiot to give up on you for Candice."

I sit stunned. I did not expect that from him. Candice is one of his best friends, or at least I thought she was. I can't find the words to express my shock. Or my gratitude even.

"Everyone thinks that he is such a king for getting 'top prize' Candice. But I have always hated how much she would come on to Travis. This whole situation is shit and you deserve better."

I bite my lip and try to hide my embarrassment. However, there isn't much I can do about my ever-growing red face. "Thank you," I squeak.

His cocky grin returns as he faces forward. Mrs. Galliher begins to talk about the importance of the so-called "American Dream" a good hint that we will be starting Gatsby soon. She did say that before Spring Break hits we will focus on Great Gatsby and Slaughterhouse Five. I tried to pregame a little bit but the only book I could focus on was Craig's.

Jude leans towards me, his eyes still facing front. "You might want to know that Craig still talks about you, a lot," he whispers between his teeth. I try not to show my satisfaction, he's a monster, he lied to me, he purposefully put my life in danger. Yet, hearing that makes me so happy, so giddy. I try to suppress the smile that is beaming inside of me. He talks about *me*; he actually likes me. He wasn't lying... I snap back into reality. I can't always be so naïve. Jude can be lying to me too. Everything about him and his friends is just so off.

"The 1920s are often commercialized as a fun and carefree time, full of parties, free will, new music, a world of new opportunities. It is shown as a time where people can make their dreams come true, the ultimate American Dream. But under all those flashy lights and the golden blanket of warmth was the harsh reality. The hyper idealized lifestyle of the 1920's era is often put into question through literature. Which is why, and you probably guessed it, we will start with The Great Gatsby."

As Mrs. Galliher hands out the books, miniature conversations murmured throughout the class. I take the time to peak over my shoulder to look at Craig, but he isn't here. I quickly look back before I catch the eye of Bridget or Jeanette. Why isn't he here? I shouldn't care, I'm not supposed to be communicating with him. I ignored him after Thanksgiving, this shouldn't be so hard. But all these dreams, that book... He'd understand and have some answers. But that's what got me into this whole mess.

History wasn't that bad. Travis walked in and went to the back of the class to an empty desk. Not even passing a glance in my direction. I felt a sting in my chest, but it didn't hurt as much as I imagined. I felt distracted by Jude's statement about Craig still talking about me. Why would he talk to Jude about me, I know the answer to that, but it doesn't seem right. His having real feelings for me is like me having a crush on a cow. I'm, humans, are his food source. Well according to that book they are carnivores and eat all meat. But still, their main source of food is human. And that's where they get most of their strength. That just doesn't seem right. Besides, I can't trust him. I have been saying that to myself on repeat since black Friday. I keep repeating the same thing to myself over and over again for almost two months now. With each repetition the less the words stick with me, the less I care.

"Jezebel," a voice lures me in my ear. I turn around. No one is paying attention to me, except for the occasional quick glance from the rest of my classmates walking in the halls. I continue my walk to the lunchroom. That was weird, I could have sworn I heard my name. It sounded like a male voice called. I can't pinpoint an exact person to that voice. It was almost hypnotic. "Jezebel," I stop in my tracks and look all around me. Once again no one is paying attention to me.

Everything goes quiet. My vision goes blurry, at least the vision of the people around me goes blurry. They move from all around me to the side and continue to walk forward. The hallway illuminates as a high pitch ring grows louder. I feel myself go into a daze. My sense of reality shifting. The hall begins to slowly spiral. The focal point does not waiver from the end of the hall. A dark figure appears from the light. A male? As I struggle to focus, I see glowing amber eyes.

"Jez!" Nick's voice snaps, clearing the hall like vacuum suction, the light, the ringing, the figure is gone. I blink and I'm no longer in the hallway but standing in front of our lunch table. What just happened to me? How did I get here?

"Hellooo, Jez, you're acting very weird and zombie-like. You have been just standing there staring off into nothing, kind of weirding me out," Nick looks at me disturbed and puzzled. I give him a similar look. I don't know what I just went through, what I just saw. I sit down. Nick unpacks his lunch and starts eating. I set my backpack on my knee as I bounce it up and down. I search for any clues or remnants of what I just saw. Everyone is being normal, acting normal as if nothing is wrong. No one looks suspicious.

"Can you stop shaking the table?" I dart my head back to Nick who is looking at me, taking a bite of his sandwich. "It's very annoying. I don't know why you are being so squirrelly. Did you talk to Craig yet? Ya know, about the book and nightmares?"

I freeze up, I nearly forgot about that book. About telling Nick about it. I should have kept everything very hush-hush like I wanted to do in the beginning. I should have, I should have, I should have. I keep saying that on repeat like a broken record. I can't reverse time no matter how much I dwell on everything that I did, nothing is gonna change it. "I need to stop being a little bitch," I mutter.

"Wow, well I wouldn't say that. You went through a lot Jez, and-"

"No, No Nick I can't keep living in this constant loop of me feeling bad for myself, I put myself in this situation. I cheated on Travis, he has every right to not want to be with me, I chose to do that project on the Malibu Beast, I wanted to invite Craig into this investigation. I'm the dumbass and I need to make it right." I stand up feeling determined. Nick looks at me with his mouth full of sandwich. He looks concerned and confused. Rightfully so, that was a complete 180 in mood.

"Um, Jez. Listen, not everything is your fault. The cheating, yeah that's your fault, not gonna lie. But truth be told Travis sucked, he dragged you down a lot. He was comfortable but comfort can be bad and harmful. I'm not 100% sure what happened between you and Craig, but from what you told me... It's not a very good reason to be mad at him if I am being completely honest. I get that you feel betrayed by his original motives, but you and I have done pretty stupid things and put our lives in danger many times. I really don't think he manipulated us the way you think. You were really happy when you were around him and you were yourself... Just saying."

He's right. He is 100% right. Or once again I am being stupid and forcing things to make sense. But I don't care. I have been avoiding the truth since November 25th. I thought that today was gonna be terrible and torturous. That the flames of the bridges that I burned were going to take me down. But I like it. I like the feeling of walking into this uncertainty, going right to the belly of the beast to confront everything head-on. 2012 is the start of me not being afraid to get a few burns from these flames.

I give Nick a brave little smirk and walk confidently over to the Elites' table. I feel eyes watching as I go over. No one took notice of me before, no one knew me past my hair but right now it is as if I am the Pope walking through. Maybe not that much awe, but this surge of power and might is electrifying. As I get closer to the table, I feel the heat growing. Their heads begin to turn and the sting from the glares nearly takes me down a few notches. I hold my head up high and cut a quick look at Travis. He places his arm around Candice as if it was instinct. I smile big and lock eyes with Jude, he sits at the center of the table where the light shines on him as if he is this divine oracle here to give me all my answers. I place my hands on the table and lean in.

"Jude, can I talk to you for one quick second, I have something very pressing to ask," I state precise and clear. I look over to Jeanette and Bridget who are giving me the coldest stare that could cut a diamond. Over to Travis and Candice, who are so snuggled up they could be conjoined twins. A bubbling force inside me is begging me to say something to them. "Travis, you're looking quite comfortable. Glad you have someone who has so little going on that she is more susceptible to your words of wisdom," I let slip out in the most sweet as pie tone I could possibly muster. I hear Jeanette audibly gasp. Travis' and Candice's face drops and looks as if they are ready to pounce me. "Didn't mean to offend, Jude, could we?" I rise up and motion towards a corner of the room. Jude looks amused and gets up to follow.

"What a bitch," I hear Bridget say to the rest of them. It makes me smile more. With each step I feel my confidence grow. I stop walking when we are at a good enough distance away from the tables. The area by the vending machines is pretty dead at this time.

"Red, what has gotten into you girl?" Jude asks looking very impressed and slightly turned on. Ew, I take a step back but keep my confident stance.

"I decided to stop feeling sorry for myself," at least for now but I wanna keep riding on this high. "I need to talk to Craig. I have something for him and have some questions to ask. Where is he today?" His look of slight arousal leaves but his smirk stays. God, he grosses me out so much.

"He isn't in the country yet. He went to England over winter break. He will be back late tonight but will mostly crash as soon as he gets home."

"Oh," I say disappointed. My confidence shrinks just a little. Perhaps this whole thing is a bit ambitious. The space between us tightens. I look at Jude as he gets closer to me. I attempt to protest and resist this ever-closing space.

"He is having his party tomorrow night, it's his 17th birthday. Only gold invitation holders are allowed. But I happen to know that he would love to see you. I'll slip the invitation in your locker." I look up at him, his eyes are scheming. Should I trust this? At least at the last party I had my friends there.

"Dmitri, is he invited?" I ask, if he sees me there, he will probably exile me from his life. He had a golden invitation to the last party. Jude nods and heads back to his table.

I'm not sure what I am doing. What my plan of action is exactly but I have an in, and if anything goes wrong at least Dmitri will be there, most likely at the bar.

Crash Your Party

J ude kept to his word, when I went back to my locker the gold invitation was there. Still baffles me that they feel so entitled to have this exclusive invitation. With a barcode! The only other thing they need to add is a doorman to double-check people. I never asked him, but I wonder if it was Craig's idea. Ninety percent of the parties are at his house. But he doesn't seem to be that snobbish.

I was debating back and forth on whether I should tell Dmitri. He could be my ride and my safety net in the event that something goes wrong. But, on the other hand, if he knew that I was coming he would do everything in his power to keep me away. I should take that as a hint to stay away seeing that Dmitri has done nothing but try to keep this world hidden from us. Yet, I can't find any bit of me that cares anymore at this point.

I finished off my day with the usual; trying to cram as much homework as I can for two hours, then onto nearly losing my mind in traffic trying to make it through that hour commute to gymnastics. I have two beautiful hours of silence from all the thoughts that have been swirling in my head while I am at practice. If I didn't clear my mind, I could injure myself and I do not want to be out again. I have been working on my floor routine. With every second of that minute and 30 I feel like all the thoughts, the worry goes away. All I can hear is my coach, teammates, and The Eurythmics. When I got home, I got my first night of full night's sleep without a weird nightmare or slight sleep paralysis since Black Friday.

Finally, it's Friday and in twenty minutes I'm going to be at this party. I have one goal, but to get to it I need to blend in so no one detects me, i.e. Bridget, Jeanette, Candice, I'm guessing Travis will be there, but most importantly Dmitri. I took the time to curl my hair, even though it is already naturally wavy, and to do my makeup. I keep to the guidelines that Cassidy gave me back in October at the last party we went to. However, this time I decided that I need to look nothing like myself. I went shopping to get an outfit for tonight. Chunky black heels, a pink fringe feather skirt, and a white sleeveless top. As I look at myself in the mirror, I barely even feel like myself. I smooth out the feathers in my skirt and sigh. Turning on the balls of my feet I continue to check myself out. I'm ready.

My parents looked at me questionably when I finally came downstairs. I told them that I wanted to try something new for this party. The best way for me to be able to get Craig to talk to me is to bring up the book. The last time he spoke to me was the day of the holiday concert and he was very reluctant to do so. I don't know what his reaction will be, but I know it will get his attention.

Just like at the party in October cars line the driveway. I gaze upon them through the bars of the golden gates. It looks as if things glimmer and glow, sparkling and beckoning me to come in. Hypnotic and exciting. I drive up to the scanner with the invitation. Within seconds the gates open.

Walking up to the door I can hear the music blasting through before the door is even opened. When I open the door, the music surrounds me luring me to go in deeper. I feel as if I am walking on air as I make my way through the crowd. Guys look me up and down, giving me sly smiles. I give little coy smiles, playing with my hair. Little conversations are loud enough for me to hear, I giggle at a few that I catch. The lighting makes me feel like I'm at a club. Dark to only be illuminated by the different colored lights. The Elites know how to throw a party, they give us that crazy high school party fantasy.

In the main walk-in area of the house, everyone is either drinking something or smoking something. I see a few people popping things, laughing way too loud, or eating some finger foods. Not far from view, the open dancing area where the main sound system is, the girls are dancing as if they are trying to win at drawing the most attention. The guys close behind them grinding or hyping up someone.

I make my way over to the den where it is a bit more relaxed. Every room in this house has a different mood. The people here are still in the drinking or smoking something branch, but they seem more relaxed. Mostly everyone is sitting, with a few standers still broadcasting the same vibes. While it is still chaotic, it is calm chaos. And that's when I see Dmitri. I quickly put myself behind a pillar but peek my head out to look at what he's doing. With no surprise, he has a drink in his hand. He is pouring up vodka shots for everyone. He is sitting extremely close to this girl with a short black dress and a blunt dark bob. It suits her well. She looks sexy and alluring. I have never seen her around the school. Everyone grabs a shot and raises it as Dmitri calls out "bottoms up!" At various rates, they take down the drink. Of course, Dmitri is the first to finish. Doesn't even wince. Just sticks out his tongue and slams the glass down. As people finish laughter begins and excited chanting. Dmitri looks at the girl next to him and says something inaudible that makes her smile. Not even a second later they are making out. Well at least he is having fun.

"Red!" I jump and sharply turn around ready to attack. Jude. Who else? I grab his arm and drag him out of view of the den to limit my chances of getting caught by Dmitri. He puts up very little resistance. He more so looks amused.

"Red if you wanted me alone all you had to do was tell me, didn't need to be so forceful." I want to vomit. My face shows it, which promptly makes Jude laugh.

He has a joint tucked behind his ear like a pencil. His hair is a bit disheveled but in a relaxed sexy way. Even though he makes me want to hurl and sometimes gives me the urge to punch him in his smug face, I cannot deny that he looks really attractive tonight.

I shake my head and get back to the point of me being here. I almost got so swept up in the party. I see why everyone wants to be at these. "Do you know where Craig is? I haven't spotted him yet," I strain to get my voice to carry over the music. I didn't realize that there was a speaker right above our heads.

"Well, he isn't in the jazz room," he takes the joint from behind his ear and lights it. Taking in a big huff, "I was just in there and he was not." He is considerate enough to turn his head, so he isn't blowing smoke directly in my face. I really don't understand how people handle the smell of weed.

"He could be anywhere to be honest, but my guess is that he is in one of two places. Both are in the basement where Bridget hasn't been. He has been hiding from her all night." He looks me up and down real quick. "But you look good though, great legs."

I make another disgusted face and audibly react in disgust. Once again it makes him laugh. He pats me on the back. "I love messing with you Red."

I knock him off and scowl. "What are the rooms?"

He goes on to explain exactly where the rooms are located, straight down the hall, right before you get to the back-patio door there is one that leads to the basement. Once downstairs there is a break in the hall, on the left side is a gaming room that leads into a home theater, and to the right, an indoor pool.

"He has an indoor pool?" I ask astonished. I knew his place was a labyrinth of wealth but an indoor pool? That Just seems a bit like overkill.

Jude nods, "It's pretty incredible, the ceiling is a screen that mirrors the night sky. But, if you can't find him there, I highly doubt that he would be here on the main floor. Your next best bet would be his room. He would be alone, not exactly enjoying the party himself but appreciating the fun that everyone else is having. Having a Gatsby moment." I look at him confused. We were assigned to read the first chapter however I have zero clue what he is talking about. He sees my confusion and explains how he read the book over break, so he didn't have to deal with it later. He says that I will get it soon enough.

"I would tell you where his room is but I'm sure you know exactly where that is," he winks at me.

My jaw drops. I can't deny it, I do know where his room is but not for the reason he thinks. I try to protest but he beats me to it. "Chill, I know you guys didn't do anything; well except kiss." He sees the shock on my face. I didn't know dudes talk about things like that with each other. I feel so embarrassed. "I went to his place in Surrey over Winter break and he told me everything. He was feeling super guilty." He looks more serious and gets closer to me. "He really is sorry Jezebel. I know you're nervous about things but he's gonna be really happy to see you."

He gives me a reassuring squeeze on my shoulder and began to walk off. "Wait, Jude!" I call. He stops and comes back, looking a bit puzzled.

"Could you do me a favor?" My nerves make my voice a bit shaky. "I am trying to stay under the radar as much as I can, so could you distract Bridget. I just don't want to risk anyone seeing me. Especially her."

I bite my lip in anticipation of his answer.

"Well, I am supposed to stay away from her tonight. But for you, anything," he sticks his tongue out laughing.

With that, he walks towards the kitchen. I follow along the walls and see him approach Bridget. She is in the middle of a group of girls. All of them pretty but she stands out like a goddess. Her golden locks perfectly curled as they frame her face in the most flattering silhouette. She stands tall and confident. Her outfit sort of mirrors mines, except she fits the look 10 times better than me. I have no clue why Craig would want me over that.

Jude leans in and whispers something in her ear. She smiles sneakily and says something back. He shares some banter with the girls around her. Everyone laughs. Watching them interact is like watching a scene from a Greek story. Beautiful aristocrats interacting in a room covered with marble and gold. Everything is so electrifying and unattainable. It can only be marveled at from afar.

I break away from the trance of their vision and head down the hall to the basement. The music fades away back here. I feel as if I could finally think. With all the noise I felt swept up in the magic of the party. I can hear the soft bass from the music that is playing in the basement. As soon as I open the door the music hits like a ton of bricks, somehow it sounds louder than the music on the main floor.

As Jude said, the hall breaks off into two different paths. I choose to go left first into the gaming room. I expected to see an Xbox, PlayStation, perhaps a Wii, but there are full-on arcade games, air hockey, a pool table, and ping pong table. Currently, the ping pong table is being used for beer pong. And the pool table currently has some dudes taking body shots off some girls. I scan the room trying not to get distracted by all that is happening.

Between the music, excited screams, and the arcade sounds I can't pull together any conversations or my thoughts really. Everything in this room is bright and colorful. The flashing lights of the games catch my eye as the center of attention.

I scan and scan but from what I can see there is no Craig. The room is large and there is a good amount of people in it. But Craig never blends in. He always has a way of standing out. I make my exit, the longer I stay in here the harder it will be to leave. I can't believe I didn't know about this room at the last party, I would have stayed in here all night.

Back in the hallway the sound of a splash and people cheering sounds. I can't believe they have an indoor pool, so excessive. Opening the door allows for the smell of chlorine to flood out. It's one of those comforting smells that aren't supposed to be, like gasoline in the summer. The water on the floor is making walking in these heels even harder than it already was.

I take a moment to take in the room. The ceiling is just like Jude said, it replicates the night sky. It's so mesmerizing and romantic. The walls and décor mirror a Grecco Roman bathhouse. At the end of the pool sits a waterfall fixture that would normally give a relaxing pitter-patter of water. Now it is being drowned out by the music.

Scanning the room, the first people I notice are no other than Candice and Travis. I swear she stays by the pool just so she can show off her boobs. They sit on a lounger that is clearly made for one person, but they are snuggled up on it together. Cheering along with the rest of the crowd watching people play chicken. Candice seductively captures Travis' face and begins to tease him. He takes her by her waist and pulls her in. Seeing my ex make out with his new, hot girlfriend is not something I want to be a part of. The guys begin to hoot like a bunch of drunk idiots when they take notice of them.

They seem to feed into the crowd and put on more of a show. With her on top of him, he grabs her butt and squeezes. Disgusting. So trashy. I disengage from that and continue along the room.

"We Found Love" starts, the opening notes gets people excited. Cassi loves this song; I wish she was here with me. Wait. Is that him? Across the other end of the pool, I see him. Craig Edwards, like I said he never blends in. There is nothing but artificial light but it's as if the ceiling opened to let in the moonlight to shine down on him like a natural spotlight. He is wearing dark blue jeans with a black short-sleeve button-down shirt that has a pale pink and white flower pattern. Both hug his body perfectly. His hair is perfectly quaffed as usual. It looks just a hair longer than when I saw him last. The room and the people become a blur, nothing but background around him. I need to get to him.

I rush over to him just as the music is revving up for the bass drop. I feel even more anxious to try to get to him that I start to run to beat the time. I stop just close enough that I could be in his view. I need someone to get him for me. As some dude who looks vaguely familiar from school passes by, I grab his arm to get his attention.

"Hey, could you get Craig for me?" I ask. He looks confused and unwilling. "Tell him that Bridget is good and distracted, and that his little birthday gift is waiting for him around the corner," I coo trying to sound as sexy as possible.

It must have been good because now he is looking at me as if he wants to take me for himself. "Yeah, I'll let him know." He takes one final look at me and walks over to Craig. I peak around a column to watch.

He pats Craig's shoulder and they do that bro handshake thing. I can't hear them but from reading his lips I get that he tells Craig exactly what I told him. Craig looks confused but intrigued. He looks around the room, but then the dude points towards me, to the corner where I should be now. Craig turns his head over in the direction and I bolt.

I get behind the corner and try to mentally prepare myself for him. I hope he didn't see me. My heart pounds in anticipation. What will he say, what will he do? Just then I see a shadow come into view.

"Are you my birthday gift?" His voice sounds a bit sleazy, very abnormal to how he has ever spoken to me.

He rounds the corner, his confident, sexy smile fades as he realizes it's me. Now it looks as if he saw a ghost. Eyes big, his body frozen and stiff.

"Happy birthday," I say shrugging. Having him this close to me feels amazing. Looking into his eyes again, being able to smell that fresh and clean scent that he always smells like. Just then, "Give Me Everything" plays. It's the same song that played when I first felt a real connection to him, the song we danced to at his party in October. It feels so full circle.

"H-Wh-How are you here?" Craig asks dumbfounded. "Did you come with Dmitri; I don't remember you coming in with him?"

"No! No, he doesn't know I'm here. Jude is actually the reason I am here. And don't worry about Bridget, I have Jude distracting her."

He looks unconvinced. He is trying to say something, but it seems like the words are caught in his throat. He looks around to see if anyone sees us.

"Jezebel... I am very happy to see you, don't get me wrong. All I could think about over winter break was how much I messed up. But I can't talk to you. I definitely cannot be seen with you. If Dmitri-"

"He doesn't know I'm here and Jude is the only person who has noticed that I exist tonight."

"You know Travis and Candice are down here."

"Yeah, they were the first I noticed," I bitterly say between my teeth.

We stand in silence. He looks everywhere but at me. Can't say I blame him for the paranoia. I have been the whole night, up until this moment. Now that I am with Craig, I feel invincible. I wouldn't even care if Dmitri were to catch us.

He looks back at me. His eyes a bit pleading with a hint of happiness. "I would be lying if I said that I didn't want to steal you away right now. But we can't talk anymore. I realized when I was in Surrey that you are much better off and safer without me in your life. The more you're with me the more you're exposed to things that can harm you. I can't have that on my conscience." He places his hand on my cheek. I could melt, it feels so warm. "I care too much about you to have you put into that kind of situation again."

As he takes away his hand it feels like I'm losing a part of myself. As he turns and walks away my heart begins to pound. I can't lose him. "I know that your kind is called an ambobestia, often called an ambo!" He stops walking and stands stiff. "You're immortal, and a carnivore. But you're stronger and healthier if you mainly eat humans. You have telepathic and telekinetic powers," I call out.

He rushes over to me hushing me. If he didn't look panicked before he looks crazed now. He looks around seeing if anyone heard. But of course they didn't, they are still preoccupied with their nefarious activities.

"How the hell do you know all that? Did Dmitri tell you? Jude?!"

I pull my mini backpack to the front and pull out the book. His jaw drops. Eyes wild and furious. "I stole your book a while ago," I try to say innocently flashing doe eyes. I don't think it works.

He snatches the book from me. "Follow me. Now." His voice stern. I have only heard that tone when he went off on Travis. But he has good reason to be this way. I did steal from him. Without protest, I follow behind him. I nearly have to break out in a slow jog to keep up. I regret this heel choice.

He storms through the room straight into the hall, up the stairs without looking back to see if I was there. Once on the main floor he took some more caution, looking for Bridget most likely. He quickens his pace making it up the stairs. I can't do stairs that fast, he's gonna have to wait for me. As I make it to the top of the stairs, I notice that he isn't there. I guess he doesn't have to wait.

I creep and peak through the doors to see if I can find him. But also fearful of the possibility of there being someone hooking up.

"Jezebel," an aggressive whisper sounds. It's Craig, he is poking his head out of his doorway. I scurry over to him. Once I am inside, he shuts the door. His arm is weighted down on the door. My back is pressed against it. I look him in the eyes, his gaze meets mine. I want to kiss him so badly. I want to passionately make out with him as we make our way to his perfectly made bed like in the movies.

"Why the hell did you think it was a good idea to take that book. What possessed you to think, hey stealing sounds fun and a great idea."

"Had I asked you, you wouldn't have let me have it. And I see why not now," my voice small.

His eyes are full of rage and fire, his pupils begin to change, they shift into a thin strip much like a lizard or a cat. What the hell? He grits his teeth, they are long and razor-sharp; they look like they can tear through flesh easily. No, no, oh god no. I sink into myself sliding down the door. My body trembling from fear. I shouldn't have come. I should have given the book to Dmitri. I don't know why I thought this would work. This is the end. I'm dead. I'm dead.

He moved from above me and grunts and groans as he buries his face in his hands. "Damn it," he mutters, his voice hoarse.

When he turns around, he looks normal. I hug my legs to my chest to become as small as possible. I can't move, all I can do is make myself as small as I can to feel like I'm not here.

"Jezebel," he rushes down to me. I scooch closer to the door, I have nowhere else to go. "Jezebel, I'm sorry I didn't mean- I can't control it all the time. I'm not going to hurt you, I swear."

I shake my head and try to find a place that I can scoot to get away but every place leads to a wall. I don't want to be here anymore. I don't want to be in his presence. I don't want to tell him about the dreams and weird experiences. I just want to leave.

"Jezebel," he tried to comfort me by putting his hand on my arm, it feels warm and soothing. "If you want to leave you can. I'll get you out without notice... I'm sorry." His voice soft. His accent has always been very soothing to me. "Do you need help getting up?"

I uncurl. I look him in his eyes. They are back to the familiar look that I know and love. Come on he says to me in a voice so soft that it barely comes out. He takes my hands and helps me up. He looks at me for a second. He reaches for my face. He cups my cheeks with both hands, using his thumbs he wipes away my tears that I didn't even know I had.

"Can't go downstairs with tears in your eyes. That won't help you go unnoticed. Not to mention if Dmitri sees you, he will make this into a mass homicide really quick," he jokes in an attempt to lighten the mood. A slight smile spreads across my face.

He opens the door and lets me out, he follows behind. Before we get to the stairs, he instructs me to wait until he gets all the people in the kitchen who's down there.

"The birthday boy is ready for the cake!" He calls as he excitedly jogs down the stairs. Everybody cheers and hollers. I peek over the edge and see them all flock to him as he strides into the kitchen. On command, Jude brings out this giant fantastic cake with sparkler like candles. As the chorus starts with Happy Birthday, I take my queue to exit. Before I go towards the door, I take one last look at the scene. The golden sparks radiate his face and his brilliant smile. Bridget has her arm around him keeping her eyes on him in a lovingly way. Jude and other guys around him shake his shoulders in an encouraging manner. When they get to the end Bridget tells him to make a wish. His eyes find mines, filled with want and yearning. It was as if he was saying "You're my wish". Looking back at the cake he blows out the candles. As everyone cheers, he smiles but I can tell he isn't truly happy.

Trying to not press my luck too much I make my exit. It feels like I am walking away from Craig for good. That this was our final chapter together. Pain spreads from my heart. He scares me but I don't want it to be over.

Run and Hide

Have you ever wanted someone so bad, but you knew that you couldn't have them? I lay on my bed staring up at the ceiling watching my fan spin around and around. There is a slight jingle from the little chains that hang by the lights. One to turn on the fan and the other for the light. The arms go around and around in a consistent fast motion. Putting me in a trance, free to do nothing but think and hear the white noise around me.

I want Craig, I realized that I truly wanted him when I saw him at the party. I don't want to get back together with Travis. I wasn't in love with him, at least when Craig became close to me. I had love for him but I never wanted him, to just be near him as much as I wanted with Craig.

I feel so safe yet on edge whenever I am around him. That I could do anything but also that in a moment's notice my life can be over. He started to transform right in front of my eyes.

His pupils begin to change. They shift into a thin strip much like a lizard or a cat. He grits his teeth. They are long and razor-sharp; they look like they can tear through flesh easily. The image of his eyes flicker in my head like a violent, harsh jump scare.

I shake my head with my eyes shut tight, getting the image out of my head. He's a monster, he can eat me, he probably wants to eat me, he can manipulate my mind. But he's so beautiful, he makes me laugh, he cares about me enough to stay away from me. He doesn't make me feel weak.

I fear him. I fear the fact that I can't 100% trust him. I fear that I won't be able to ever know if he is messing with my head. It will be a constant thought rolling around on whether or not he just says all the right things because he knows exactly what I'm thinking.

But I love his smile. The way his eyes light up when he sees me. He looks so engaged in everything I have to say. He always looks deep into my eyes. His accent and the way he says my name.

Clink, clink, clink. The arms of the fan spin around fifteen times. My family's footsteps travel about the hall. A gentle creak sounds every time someone steps on that one faulty floorboard. My parents have been trading off on who is gonna call to get it fixed. *Clink, clink, clink, clink.* twenty times this count. I can hear the dust settling in the room. It's the sound of heavy silence with a low, deep something that patters in your ears. I can't remember the last time I blinked.

I need to find a way to clear my mind. Should I shower? No. Perhaps go to the gun range? No, I would need my Dad to go with me, and if I ask he will be able to know that something is up. Should I contact Dmitri and see if I could get drunk with him and forget all of my thoughts? I should just go to the park. Some fresh air will do me some good.

As I sit on the swing, I look at the desolate park. It's half past 8 pm and there isn't a soul in sight. The freak out of the murder of Aiden, coupled with the lack of Beast sightings is still making people very uneasy. The non-presence of the Beast is making people feel panicked because it's like the quiet times of war. You just have this constant unshaken feeling that something bad is gonna happen, that an attack will come soon. They don't know with Aiden dead that no more attacks will happen. At least, I hope.

As the breeze moves past me. It cuts through my jacket, causing goosebumps to rise on my arms. Other than the sound of leaves shaking in the trees from the wind there's nothing. I would prefer it if the park stayed like this. Occasionally I think I can hear the alarms that went off the night of the last attack.

I feel like I am spiraling into insanity. I just keep repeating the same things to myself over and over again. I think something new will arise out of it. That I will come to a new conclusion, But the truth is, is that I know where this is going. I know he is an ambo; I know what he is capable of. I fear him. I close my eyes and see him transforming. I imagine him as Aiden was. The massive, demonic-looking creature that stood over me. Ready to kill me, dragging me through the sand, bloody, scared. At his party, when he began to transform, it felt as if the sun was eclipsing. That I was losing all that was warm and bright. Everything became as harrowing and cold as a snow-filled graveyard.

But I want that. I want his beauty, kindness, and charm. That horrid, grotesque, beast that he is. The intensity excites me. I want everything that Craig has to offer. I'm crazy for wanting this. I want to hold him, kiss him, hear him say my name.

"Jezebel."

Springing up from the swing I swiftly take my gun from my bag. As I turn to aim, I see Craig standing at the edge of the park, a few feet away from me. In perfect illumination as always. It's almost angelic. Him showing up, right when I was thinking of him, to want to hear him say my name is as if my prayers have been answered. Or he was following me and listening to my thoughts.

"Why are you here? How did you know I was here? Did you follow me?" I accuse.

Cautiously he begins walking towards me. I instinctively raise my gun up and aim at his chest. He stops cold and raising his hands.

"Woah, Jezebel I'm not here to attack you or anything. I just wanted to talk," he says taking small steps forward.

"Don't take another step towards me! If you move one inch, I will shoot a bullet right through your chest!" My voice shakes a bit, but I keep my strong stance, keeping my gun steady.

"How did you know I was here," I demand, taking my time with each word. My heart is beating fast yet steady.

He doesn't dare to move an inch, "I didn't follow you. I didn't read your mind or anything. I went to your house and asked your mum if I could talk to you and she told me that you were here."

I lower my gun a bit. At that moment it felt like the world stopped spinning. Everything feels so still, frozen. I've had this feeling before. I look around me. There is no wind, no sounds of the ocean. No seagulls. The trees, grass, everything is frozen. My eyes cut back to him. Aiming right off his right ear I take a shot.

With the crack of the bullet leaving the barrel Craig jumps back, the sounds of the wind, ocean, and gulls come back. That son of a bitch. I keep my gun aimed at him. No matter how much fear is boiling within me; I know what he is capable of. I've seen it in action thanks to Aiden, but he can't see that fear. I have to remain unyielding.

"That trick was used on me before."

"Are you mental? You almost shot me!"

"If I wanted to shoot you, you would have been. Why did you want to talk to me? You had the chance at your party."

I feel a bit cocky, knowing I have the upper hand in this. But also, it makes me wonder, looking at him he doesn't look as if he wants to attack. Nothing about him screams predator.

"Jezebel, I don't want to hurt you. I honestly just want to talk. I know I used my powers, but I just didn't want anyone disturbing us. Please, hear me out," he pleads sounding tired. A bit broken. I can feel my hardened demeanor weakening. I wanted this. I wanted him in my life. Here he is pleading to talk to me.

I shake the feeling and back away from him even more. I don't dare turn my back to him. I make my way over to the jungle gym. Not the best place to post up but it's the closest.

"I don't want to hear from you right now... I would prefer it if you left," I hesitate. Not even sure if that is a true statement.

"Fine, but I'm not leaving. I'll just sit here until you feel ready to talk, or until you leave," he huffs sitting down on the concrete ledge at the edge of the park. "I can't let you walk away again. I couldn't get my mind off of you since my party. Seeing you when I turned the corner. It felt like a shock wave."

Butterflies flutter in my stomach hearing him say that. Even though he is shaken, every word that comes out of his mouth is like silk. In the front of my mind all I can think is to drop Wendy and run to him. But in the back, I remember why I am posted up in this jungle gym with a pistol.

He goes silent, not even looking at me. His eyes wander about the park, the sky, and the ground. I relax and sink into the ropes. Trying to not let my mind wander into any holes or loops of thoughts. I want to escape in the silence.

I don't know how much time passes. It could have been minutes or hours, but it feels like an eternity. Neither of us spoke. Just radio silence between the both of us. It's driving me mad. With each squawk from a seagull, chirp of a cricket, splash from the ocean, rustle of leaves, made me grow more and more restless. The park was so quiet when I was here alone. These extra annoyances weren't present. All of the sounds around me have become hyper noticeable, it's overwhelming.

Craig is now lying down; his body effortlessly hangs as if he was posing. His hair looks even richer in the low light. I don't know how the perfect lighting always finds him. It casts a perfect shadow on his jaw, cutting just right. His crystal blue eyes glimmer as he turns his head to face the park. But just for a moment. His chest puffs as he takes a deep sigh and continues to stare at the sky.

I can't take this anymore. I can't sit up here anymore; for one my legs are starting to cramp, but also it is getting far too late. I ease my way off the jungle gym. I make my way over to my car, but as I walk closer and closer to the park's edge, I realize that I have to go past Craig, of course. He doesn't notice that I got up, he now has his head facing towards the parking lot area. Maybe I can sneak past him.

"You know, this is ridiculous. I'm sorry," Craig groans standing up. He turns and faces me and steps in my direction.

Without thinking I raise my gun and pull the trigger. Within seconds the blood spreads on his shirt, I struck him. Right in the heart. He crumbles to the ground. Oh shit. No, no, no, no!

I run over to him dropping to my knees. Maybe I didn't hit his heart. Maybe I just missed it. I put my ear next to his chest. Nothing. I franticly take hold of his wrist, nothing. I didn't want to kill him. I didn't mean to kill him. Oh no, oh no, oh no. I unbutton his shirt to see the wound, the blood spreads down and reaches my hand. I tremble and shake. I don't know what to do. Just constant words of panic fly through my mind. I don't know what to do, I don't know what to do. Should I call an ambulance? But I have the gun right here, they will know it's me. If I was worried about going to jail before I would definitely go now. I told him not to come towards me. Why did he come towards me? He wasn't a threat; he wasn't trying to attack me. Oh god…

I put my arm around his back to lift him up towards me. He is heavier than Aiden was. I rest his head in my lap. I stroke his hair as I gaze upon his lifeless face. Tears trickle down my cheek hitting his. Craig, oh no. I start to choke on my tears as the lump in my throat grows larger. I don't want to leave; I want to just hold him and hope that everything will be alright. But I know it won't. I should call Dmitri, but that means this time will be over. I don't want him to be put in a body bag, I don't want to have to put his family and his friends through that grief. Aiden was a monster; Craig was just a teenager. As I sit here, looking at him like this, I see he didn't want to hurt me, that everything he said was true. That book said that they are creatures of the senses, including the "sixth sense" of presence. If he was actually on guard to attack me, he would have deflected the bullet. Maybe not completely away from his body, but from away from anything vital. He could have killed me so quickly but instead he wanted to talk, he wanted to know me, he wanted me to feel safe. I'm the monster.

I feel some strange skin-crawling movement on my hand that is rested on his chest where the wound is. I pick it up to see if there is a bug. To my surprise, it's him, the wound looks as if it is repairing itself. The bullet levitates out first. Then the muscles reattach, slowly. It's freaking me out, but I can't look away. As healing makes its way to his skin the wound closes, no scab, bruise, or discoloration. It's as if it didn't happen. I press my hand on his chest, I feel the faintest heartbeat. *Thump thump, thump thump.* It grows stronger and faster with each passing second.

His eyes pop open as if he were reborn. I squeal covering my mouth. He's alive! The tears fall faster but in happiness and joy instead of sorrow.

"Bloody hell," he whispers, panting as he is able to breathe again. His eyes bewildered. "You shot me, you killed me!" He scrambles to get up backing away from me in fear. I'd never thought he would be the one who fears me.

"I said to not take another step," I weakly simper. I stay sitting on the ground, still in shock as to what just happened. "But I didn't kill you, you're alive and talking."

"You temporarily killed me, and if I wasn't as advanced in my powers as I am you could have permanently killed me. Jesus, I forgot all about that, it has been like an hour and a half. We have been sitting here in silence. Jezebel, if I wanted to hurt you, do you really think I would wait this long?!"

I shake my head looking down to wipe away my tears.

He groans and I can feel his body heat next to mines. I look up and he is sitting right in front of me. "I'm sorry I yelled. It's kind of hard and extremely painful to get shot and resurrect. Didn't think I would need to be on guard around you. Granted you did point a gun at me the moment you saw me... I shouldn't have come. I should have left when you asked." He takes a second to look at me a bit longer before getting up. Before he has the chance to walk away, I catch his hand to stop him. He looks back at me.

"Please don't go," I whimper through tears. In one swift motion, Craig helps me off the ground and wraps his arms around my waist in a deep warm embrace that melts my heart. I pull him in tighter with my arms around his neck, as I stand on my tippy toes to be as close as possible. Everything about this feels extremely right, feels like no matter how scared I am, no matter what I do, how terrible the world is around me, I'll be alright.

"I'm so sorry, I didn't mean to kill you," broken through tears I say into his neck.

He pulls back and wipes away my tears, smiling at me. "I shouldn't have taken that step. You did warn me."

I laugh and nestle my head into his chest. But then I feel wetness on my arm. The blood. I forgot his blood is still on my hands. I break apart and see the blood from his chest has gotten on me as well. Oh my god, it is probably on my face. Craig is holding back laughter as he looks at me. The blood is on my face. "I have a towel and some water bottles in my car, we can get that off you," Craig chuckles.

I follow his lead back to his car, which is right next to mine.

As I clean myself off, I can't help but think of how right that felt. How whenever I'm with him everything feels so natural, and light. Even when I am cleaning his blood off of me. I can't help but smile at him.

"What?" He questions

"I believe you; you don't have to explain yourself for the ten thousandth time. I got it from the first time you told me. It would be a lie if I said that I don't have any fears towards you; but I'm willing to take the risk to have all that you are."

He smiles but he looks weary. He drops the towel in his trunk and closes it. As he leans against his car for support, he pulls me in by my hands, slowly guiding me closer to him.

"I love hearing that Jezebel, I really do. But I would be a complete and total arse if I didn't give you the full story about who I and my family are. It is pretty late, and we have school tomorrow; I think we should both get home. I can drive you to school tomorrow if you'd like, and I can explain it all on the way there."

The fact that he needs to give me more information on his supernatural life worries me. But this is what I need to hear. And if it is too much I can always get a ride back from Nick or maybe Cassidy. I nod, "Yeah, we can do that." I bite my lip in anticipation. He smiles back at me. I want to kiss him. I wonder if he is reading my mind. I don't need to read his to tell he is thinking the same thing. Yet, he drops my hand and rises off his car. I back up to give him space. I'm a bit disappointed.

"Then, I will see you tomorrow, 7:15," he waves as he gets into his car.

I smile and give a small wave back. "7:15, see you then". I slip into my car, taking a moment to revel in excitement. 7:15.

Falling

After all this time, I have been moping around since November, I feel clear. The sun feels sweeter on my skin. I move around my room dancing to my 70's playlist. Everything is rosy and carefree. I braid a little daisy in my hair and add just a little extra blush to my cheeks.

With a big cheesy grin, I float about my room putting on a performance for my stuffed animals. I feel a bit ridiculous, but I haven't felt this happy in a long time. I don't even think I was this happy when I was with Travis since the first year we were together.

Knock knock knock. I turn down my music and trot over to the door. "Oui?" I chirp through the crack of the door.

"Are you naked or something, open the door," Josh bullies his way through. His hair is disheveled, eyes a bit reddened. I forgot that it is 6 AM. He looks around my room then back at me in disgust. "Now listen here, I'm happy that you are happy. You've been moping around this place for a long time. But you know what I can't deal with, Jezebel? This loud ass music at 6 AM, over here acting like you are in a music video. Mom, Dad, and Lindsey may be able to rest without your music getting to them since their rooms aren't right next door. But this one, this one right here is right next to you. And you know I'm a light sleeper. Shut it down... Glad you're happy." He takes one last look at me, scowls, and shuts the door.

Suddenly my room looks less rosy. The Music sounds more of background noise rather than a surround sound of bliss. I'm not in a dreamland music video. Craig said that he had to tell me something about his family and him before we date. That didn't occur to me before. No, no it doesn't matter. I turn my music back up, not at the full level as it was before, and continue to bop around my room singing the lyrics *It's too late, to turn back now, I believe, I believe, I believe I'm falling in love.*

I have never been ready this early for school. It's 6:45 and the whole house is up. It seems that between my music video and Josh's pissy attitude the whole house woke up and is ready for the day. Except for my Dad, he is a heavy sleeper. My Mom is baking some extra donuts for the bakery for this large order. Lindsey is trying to negotiate one from her, and Josh is watching YouTube while angrily drinking a frappe.

Bzz bzz. Not even a second passes before I look at my phone. It's Craig. A sweet little smile spreads across my face, my heart flutters.

"What are you blushing about? Are you and Travis back together?" My Mom asks in a teasing tone.

I thought nothing could erase the happiness I was feeling but I was wrong. My Mom takes notice of my now dropped expression and I see the immediate regret on her face.

"Oh Jez, baby I'm sorry I honestly thought," she begins to walk towards me. Not this again. I've had 2 months of them walking on eggs shells around me.

"No, no, no, it's fine," I rush, putting on a fake smile. "It's not Travis. It's our group chat, it's Cassidy," I chuckle.

"I'm glad to see you smiling again," she says. She turns to finish her baking.

My Dad comes floating into the kitchen, he's always in a good mood though. He hugs my Mom from behind and kisses her on the cheek, "Good morning my sweet Raven,"

"Christophe if you do not get off of me." She hates being touched or bothered while she is baking.

I giggle as he backs away. He nudges me and says good morning as he makes his way into the living room.

Bzz bzz. Craig! I almost forgot. I open the texts, *Hey, so I completely forgot that I take my siblings to school. So, they are coming with, which will ruin our talking time. But I still would like to take you to school.*

Actually, because I can and idc, I can pick you up at 7 instead and drop them off early they can just hang out in the quad and we can still get the chat in.

I forgot that I take Josh and Lindsey too. I have priorities today and I need these two to cooperate with me and not ruin my chance with Craig. I forgot to ask if they could even come along. I tell him about me taking my siblings too. Seconds later he just says, "bring em along".

Lindsey sits next to me and flashes her doe eyes, "Jezzi, mom hates me and won't feed me so could we leave early so we can go to Dunkin?" My Mom shoots her a sharp look, but Lindsey pretends she doesn't see. She is insanely sweet, but she knows how to put on the dramatics.

"Well since you're starving and clearly being neglected, I'll see what I can do. I have to ask first," I tease, picking up my phone to text Craig. She looks at me confused and a little annoyed.

"Since when do you need permission to get food before school?" Lindsey inquires, looking at me with an untrusting eye. As she gets older the sassier, she becomes, she's just like mom.

I finish my orange juice and scooch out of my seat. "Well, we are getting a ride today. So, I would have to check if it's okay."

I make my exit, going to the living room. 6:50, Only ten more minutes. I can try to power read the remaining pages of the Great Gatsby that I was assigned. I situate myself on the couch, but before I get the chance to read a word Josh is hovering over me and Lindsey is sitting next to me.

The interrogation starts with Josh, he guesses Dmitri. He's been around a lot since black Friday, apparently, it's been speculated between Josh and Lindsey that we started to secretly date.

"Dad loves him so if you guys are dating it wouldn't be terrible. Also, he has a motorcycle so that's cool," Josh says.

"He is kind of scary. He seems very intense. I think he smokes. We don't need that kind of bad influence around the house," Lindsey lectures.

Josh proceeds to tease her about being too goody goody, accusing her of being stuck up. They go back and forth about the pros and cons of us dating. "We're not dating, also, it's not him," I grumble over the book. I still try to get in the last pages. I open my mouth to say that it's Craig but then Lindsey cuts me off going to the next suspect, Nick.

Lindsey and Josh are both in agreement on the fact that Nick is a fine person, but he talks too much and is a bit weird. I don't give them an answer but continue to read. They take my silence as it being the wrong answer and move on to Cassidy.

"I love Cassi, she's the best. Also, she has better taste in music than you. No offense, it's just a better way to start the morning," Lindsey reassures.

"Cassidy is a babe. God, I adore that girl. Everything about her is sexy. I could talk to her for hours, running my hands through her luxurious hair," Josh dreams.

My face turns sour and disgusted. I hate how much he pervs on her. And I am offended by the music comment.

"First of all, I have great taste in music, you just lack variety. And second," I turn sharply to Josh, "You disgusting perv, you are 12 you shouldn't be talking like that, you haven't even kissed anyone yet and you have barely gone through puberty!"

"I'm gonna be 13 next month, it's only 4 years, age is nothing but a number."

I audibly gag, "I would much rather be waterboarded than have to hear you say those words again. I wish I was kidnapped and turned into a sleeper agent so that my memory could be erased. You're freaking disgusting... Anyway, it's not Cassi either... it's Craig, Craig Edwards."

Lindsey looks confused, she doesn't know who he is. She has never met him. Josh perks up. I believe he has met him through his little sister Erin. Josh goes into a gushing session about how much he admires him. His style, how he is multitalented. He loves his car and the fact that he smokes weed. If I didn't know any better, I would think that he was the one with the crush on him.

"Since when are you two friends? He is a legend!"

Bzz bzz. I look at the text, *I'm here.* 7:00, right on time. "He's here let's go," I say as I get up and put my jacket on. I don't know how awkward this car ride will be but at the very least I am free of this interrogation.

I was looking forward to this very moment all night. I was bouncing off the walls this morning daydreaming about how it would be. He would pull up in his Maserati, be standing by the passenger side so he could open the door for me. He would have some Dunkin or Starbucks waiting for me. When I got in the car Michael Bublé would be playing, for some nice easy listening. Everything would be perfect. But this, this reality is awkward.

When we came out, I see a Mercedes SUV. Erin came bursting out of the car squealing in excitement to see Josh, as if she didn't just see him three days ago. Unbeknownst to me or Craig, Craig's little brother Jimmy is obsessed with Lindsey. So, she felt extremely awkward and uncomfortable when getting into the back seat having to sit next to him. Josh and Erin went on and on about how they are going to have a joint birthday party next month, because their birthdays are a day apart. I could see Lindsey being the most uncomfortable she has ever been as Jimmy tries to carry on small talk.

Craig barely looks at me. Occasionally he will pass a glance in my direction but for the most part, his eyes are glued to the road, hands gripped to the wheel. His body language is so tense. I can see the muscles in his neck tighten as he clenches his jaw. The friction between his hands and the wheel causes the rubber to squeak. I tried to initiate a conversation 3 times, but it was like eating a full sleeve of saltines with no water.

The last time I saw him, things were tense, but it ended on a good note. I hadn't seen him in a month and when I finally did, it was in a club lit house and in a park at night. His beauty is accentuated during the day. His sun-kissed skin almost glows during the day, the contour of his jaw is striking yet soft. Some guys look of the precise perfection as a chiseled stone, Dmitri favors that. But Craig, he looks perfect but as if he was sculpted. Soft yet prominent. When the sun shines on the side of his face it bounces off his eyes like the sun on the ocean. They look deep in thought. I wonder what is eating at him.

His family. I wonder what it is about his family that is making him act so tense. They could be criminals, rouge running away from the law. Perhaps even enemies of the state. No, they can't be, they are too out in the open to be anything like that. What if they are in a cult or agents? I excite myself thinking of the possibilities of what could be this detail. It has to be something bad.

"You look pretty," Craig says softly.

I break from my train of thought. He is smiling at me, it's weak but his eyes are bright. "I like the daisy," his voice soft and gentle. He is speaking so low that only the two of us can hear. Despite the car having four other people in it, it feels like it is just us. His gaze is one that would instantly make someone blush. It gives the illusion that there is nothing else but you two. I feel like I could melt.

He focuses his attention back on the road. The moment doesn't fade, it's not an illusion only held by his eyes. He just makes me feel like that. I need to stop drooling, it may feel like it is just us, but there are four preteens in the back. And I am pretty sure two of them have the ability to read my mind. I also need to think of a response.

"Thanks... I tried this morning," I say low enough just for him to hear.

"Oh yeah? Me too," he responds without missing a beat. I clear my eyes over to him; his head is cocked with a wicked alluring grin on his face. He gently bites down on the straw of his iced coffee. The signature confidence that makes girls swoon is back. The silent awkwardness is gone without a trace. And I find myself unable to look away from him.

He takes a sip of the coffee and puts it down. "Believe it or not, Jezebel," His voice is so deep and beckoning that it makes me shudder a bit, "I was feeling quite nervous myself. What I have to tell you is pretty big. I just got you back and I would hate to lose you again."

I can feel myself going in full love lost puppy mode, hanging on his every word. *You won't ever lose me.* I almost let that thought out of my mouth. I shake my head slightly and snap out of it. This feels like when I first interacted with him at his party back in October. He was larger than life then, he felt unreal. Like it was all a fantasy.

I look back at him, he is focusing on the road, he looks just as tense before, annoyed. Everything feels dull and tiresome. He notices me staring. He flashes me a quick smile and goes back to the road. What the hell?

Finally arriving at the school, the siblings promptly exit the SUV. Lindsey gives me a glaring look of "why did you do this to me" before exiting. I give her a soft sorry and cringe. To be fair, neither of us had any clue. Craig and I go over to a bench and sit beside each other, luckily there aren't too many people here right now.

I attempt to start up a conversation, but he immediately cuts in with an apology. In his words, he finds Erin's "middle school banter" to be extremely annoying. He says that there is a difference between talking to her when she isn't around her friends. "She's still annoying, but little sister annoying," he finishes. I agree with him, telling him how Josh is the same way. He then goes on to apologize about Jimmy, saying that he does not have the Edwards' charm despite his looks. According to him he is terribly awkward and believes artwork is the ultimate way to an 11-year old's heart. I told him that it would have gotten me when I was 11. We laugh, and everything feels like normal again. It feels light and natural.

He takes a moment to look at me. Every time he looks at me like this it instantly makes me blush. "I'm sorry, I just haven't seen you in a while, I was a bit faded at my party. You just look so pretty," he says playing with my fingers, interlacing his in between mine, this makes me blush even more.

"But," he says as he abruptly stops playing with my fingers. I stop smiling, confused. "I need to be honest about something. Well, I have to be honest about a few things. But first, I used my powers in the car." He what? I scowl at him and scoot away. I knew something was weird. I should have known he was in my head.

"I did what is called an illusion of the mind. I wanted to talk to you, to let you know the things I said in the illusion. I wanted to be charming and sweet, but I was just way too tense in the car with our siblings and I was feeling nervous so I casted that into your mind. I wasn't manipulating you, I just needed to communicate with you one on one somehow."

I go silent and just look at him blankly. I feel violated in a way. I thought that I would be able to tell if he was in my head. It sickens me to know he can get in so easily without me even noticing a bit.

He reaches for my hand and calls my name. I snatch it away and give him a burning look. "Don't touch me. And stay out of my head. I can't be with you if I never know what is real and what is fake."

"Yes, it was an illusion but if our siblings weren't in the car it would have happened," he says exasperated.

"I don't need the world to be rosy, I don't need to feel all bubbly and perfect all the time when I am around you. We, well one of us is human... imperfection is bound to happen."

He nods. "You're right, I'm sorry."

We sit in silence for a moment. I like the moments when I forget that he isn't human. It makes everything less complicated, but that is a given.

"I really like you; I wish things didn't have to have this complication... I need to tell you everything about my family." Here we go. I settle in and turn into him, giving my full attention.

I was expecting to hear something along the lines of his family being fugitives, a danger to society, bloodthirsty murders. They seem so put together, shiny, and perfect; that would be the typical shocker that would follow. But no, that was far from what he told me.

My family and I are the most powerful ambos... In the world. It is a centuries-old bloodline of power. It's not just me and my family here, it spans to every Edwards that lived or will live. Because of that power that we hold we are important beings in the state of our world. There is another dimension beyond the one you know, and it's called the Immortal Realm. It was created in the 14th century by powerful wizards, witches, and ambos. My multi great grandmother being the main one. In the late 16th century, there was the formation of our government, so to say, called the Council. It is ran by the top four supernatural of the land; that being vampires, werewolves, witches and wizards, and ambos. And of those, four families hold the most power. The Edwards are the family of the ambos. Within the Council there are three high courts where the highest crimes against the land are conducted. And within them, as well as beneath them, all the laws and continuous running of our realm is held. Below that is much like governors, mayors, and police officers. Normally with age are the most powerful amongst the family. However, sometimes that doesn't happen. My Dad, born in 1970 is the 3rd most powerful ambo in the world and he is the 3rd high court representative. What that means is that being with me is the equivalent of dating the child of the president or someone from the royal family. And with that comes a lot of risk on its own. However, you, specifically, are an enemy of the realm. Not because you are human, but for the fact that you, Jezebel Bedeau, are on the most wanted list. You knowing about the reality of supernatural creatures and even worse the immortal realm, puts a massive target on your back.

I sat in complete utter shock. I try to digest everything that was just presented to me. With everything he told me multiple questions followed. Why is there a separate realm, and why isn't he in it? If vampires, witches, wizards, and werewolves exist what else does? And since his dad is in such high standing what happens when he finds out that we're dating? And most importantly what the hell did I do to become an enemy of a realm that I didn't even know existed until this very moment?

"You have questions, don't you?"

Yeah, no shit I have questions! No, no, I need to keep it cordial. He didn't need to disclose all this information.

I flip my hair and adjust myself. "Yes, I do have some questions."

"Shoot."

"Is this reason as to why I am an enemy of your realm a big secret that I can't know for my own benefit?" I put air quotes around "my own benefit".

He lets out a puff of air and pulls his fingers through his hair. "Yes, it is. You don't need the air quotes. I am putting myself in danger telling you all this stuff too. To be a hundred percent real with you, it is actually against the law. And while I am being real, if you were to know why you are an enemy the 1st high court would summon you and they would behead you on the spot with their 'Ax of Justice'. I want to tell you as much truth as I can while keeping you and me alive."

An Ax of Justice? He is risking his life just telling me things. Normal relationships aren't like this, they aren't filled with little bits of information that could lead to death. There are numerous red flags being waved in my face, but I have gone color blind. "Dating someone with power is pretty hot," I flirt scooting closer to him.

He looks at me as if I am crazy. He may be right in that aspect. I feel crazy for saying that. But it is true, the power thing is hot. But it would be a lie if I said that I wasn't afraid of all the things that could follow. But right now, my heart is telling me that the risk is worth it. I want to be with him, and god I want to kiss him.

I grab the collar of his jacket and pull myself closer to him so that our faces are so close that I could feel the heat of him. My lips brush up against his. He chuckles, "I knew I was right when I said that you were mad," he murmurs right before kissing me. Little butterflies flutter in my stomach, reaching my chest making me feel flushed.

I pull him in closer but as soon as I do it is as if he is ripped away from me. I open my eyes to see Dmitri standing in front of me, gripping Craig by the neck. In all of that, I forgot that we were in public.

"I'm going to snap your neck," Dmitri grits between his teeth. He tightens his grip just enough to make Craig strain.

Nick rushes up out of breath. "I'm sorry Jez, I tried to stop him, I'm 5'8 and he's a 6-foot 5 muscled beast. I never noticed the body type and height imbalance until I tried to overpower him," he says taking deep breaths in between phrases.

I shake my head and get up. "Put him down, I don't need saving from him. I'm fine Dmitri, I'm not scared. I feel safer being with him," I assert, putting in some white lies. I don't need Dmitri going guard dog on me.

He cuts his glare over to me and drops his grip. Craig coughs and rubs his neck. Dmitri steps up to me, looking down to look me in the eyes. I stand up straight, making myself as big as I could. My eyes, strong and stern.

"You really want to be with him? After everything that happened?"

"Yes"

He shakes his head, "I never pegged you as a dumb bitch. Guess I was wrong."

My jaw drops. He raises his eyebrows in a cold-hearted manner and walks off. Nick calls after him, jogging up behind him. I look back at Craig, who looks just as shocked as me. My face starts to get hot and I can feel some tears starting to form. I guess I am a weak bitch too.

As if it was instinct, Craig takes my hand and smiles at me in a comforting way. "He's right you know; we are dumb bitches." I look at him puzzled by his statement. "But," he continues, "I'm more than happy to be a dumb bitch if that means we get to be together."

I try to hold back laughter but end up giving in. That is a ridiculous statement, but it made me feel better.

Infamous Star

Walking into school no one seemed to notice much, they've seen me and Craig talking to each other in the halls before. We didn't make much of a scene, no handholding, parting kisses. He didn't move his seat in first period to be next to me. Everything seemed normal. It was how I liked it. Seeing how negatively Dmitri reacted, to be fair Dmitri does believe that Craig will kill me or that has some ulterior motive, It does make me wonder. He has never liked Travis but he has never acted too strongly about me being with him. How dangerous is Craig?

It has been distracting me all day, I haven't been participating in class and my friends have taken notice.

Nick told Cassidy about what happened and she wanted to comfort me about it but I wasn't really there. When lunch came around, I had a different kind of distraction. All of the stares and whispers. Craig met me outside of my class, leaning against the wall. When his eyes met mine, he lit up and grinned. Out of instinct he held his hand out for me to take it. Reluctantly I took hold of it. I knew that this would cause a connection to our student body and shoot the electric waves throughout.

Sure enough, everyone was looking. It always starts off with one. A girl notices us from admiring Craig. His eyes normally wonder a bit and dazzles the crowd but when his focus didn't shift, she looks down. Seeing hour hands interlocked she looks back up at him and then at me. The first lightbulb goes off. She whispers to her friends and they look and then more people notice the stares and join in. The halls become loud with whispers and some not so soft comments. I feel small and like an animal at the zoo, while Craig is on cloud nine as if nothing is happening. Every guy and girl we pass look at us as if we're taboo. At first, I knew that this was going to be a bit of a shock but then it hit me. Bridget. Craig and Bridget have been a power couple since the 8th grade. Girls feared Bridget and would never dare to talk to Craig openly. Guys pined after her just waiting for their opening. She is going to kill me.

The power that Bridget felt when being known as Craig's girl and becoming a threat is heavily present now. People don't look right through you, they look at you with envy, awe, and a little bit of hatred. But Bridget stood tall, a model, a goddess that decided to grace its presence in California. And I'm a 5'3 average girl who somehow managed to sneak her way onto Mount Olympus. The looks didn't quite match. No one yearned to be me, to look how I look, dress how I dress, be as gregarious. I am the least bit intimidating, hence why girls weren't so afraid to talk to Travis the way they were Craig.

I can see now, how I stand amongst my classmates. I was nothing to them but now it's like I am the biggest star. Fresh new blood to hit the scene. It is the first time anyone has really seen me. I was more so shadowed by Travis, Cassidy, and Dmitri but with Craig, I'm in the spotlight. Not sure if it is a good thing or if it is bad.

"Not sure if you noticed, but everyone keeps staring at us," Craig murmurs in my ear. The hair on my neck stands up. So, he has been aware of it all.

"How can you not... What are they saying?" Knowing fully of his powers I want to be able to hear what he hears; the curiosity has always tickled me about the thoughts of others.

Craig looks down at me and smiles amused. "Don't you think that is an invasion of people's privacy? I don't listen all the time. I try to tune people out at school. Too many voices."

I feel a bit shameful for asking. I wouldn't like it too much if someone was listening to my thoughts all day. But some of these looks, they are venomous and it is burning a hole in my mind. But then something possesses me, a wave of confidence. I hold my head higher, my gate is strong and confident. As the people pass by, I feel like I am going in slow motion. I don't avoid eye contact and give anyone who wants to stare a smirk.

As we enter the lunchroom the show really started. The sheep, who usually follow behind Craig the moment he walks in the room, quickly took notice. They make a bit of an uproar causing the others around them to look as well.

"We should sit at a separate table for today," Craig says as he leads me to an empty table. As soon as he lets go of my hand, I feel embarrassed, anxious. The whispers are louder and the stares and glares feel sharper.

"Did you do something?" I ask looking around me, the people try not to make it obvious with their staring but I still catch a few. I look back at Craig who has his hand over his food, it starts to glow like a toaster oven. "What are you doing?" I hiss getting close to him. Does he always use his powers like that out in the open?

He chuckles and continues, "It's nothing, I do it all the time. No one notices. I am just heating up my food." I start to pick at my food but I feel too anxious to eat. I wonder if my friends are here. I poke my head behind me to try to catch a glimpse of my usual table but instead I catch Travis walking in. He looks at both of us in complete disgust. He gives an all-knowing smirk and rolls his eyes. My blood starts to boil but at the same time my heart breaks. He has every right to be mad at me, but he moved on, quicker than me, so who is he to judge.

"That dick!" Bridget's voice carries as she stands glaring a few feet from us. Jeanette and Candice are with her. Their looks are searing as they call the both of us a few choice names.

"Did you-"

"Yes, I told Bridget, she knew how I felt about you since Christmas. After we left the park, I told her about what happened between the two of us. She just didn't expect that I would be public about us. She will get over it," Craig answers, cutting me off in a nonchalant tone.

I look back at them, who are now walking in our direction. They look like they are about to jump me. I quickly cut my gaze to my table again and see Cassidy and Nick sitting there. They see them approaching me too. Cassidy mouths 'we got your back' as Nick nods and gives a thumbs up. But when I look back to the girls, they are holding their heads in pain. Bridget scowls at Craig and stomps off to the Elites' table.

"What did you just do?" I didn't see a change in Craig but I just know that he did something.

"Don't worry about it Jezebel," he gently tucks a piece of my hair behind my ear. "You don't need to hear any of these thoughts, they are pointless and not worth your worry. It is just first-day shock, I promise."

He gives me a reassuring smile but I can't give one back, I'm going to be looked at as the girl who took Craig away from the queen bee. I am going to go from hardly even noticeable to infamous. This isn't just some high school thing. They are like socialites. Beyond the school walls their families were very well known.

"It's not all bad you know, their thoughts. A lot of people are impressed by you." I shake my head and focus on my lunch. I wonder how long this is going to last. A few days, a week? I need to stop pondering about this. It doesn't matter, like Craig said it wasn't worth my time. I shouldn't care about what they think. I am with Craig Edwards; he is unbothered by what everyone thinks of him and us and he can actually hear them. He just keeps looking at me, with a warm smile.

I shake the feeling of self-doubt and anxiety and just enjoy the moment. I don't want to sit here moping. I perk up and smile back at him and start talking about Gatsby.

"You know, at your party, Jude made a reference comparing you to Gatsby."

"Oh yeah? Does he think I'm delusional?"

"That's your take on Gatsby?"

"I finished the book already, romanticizing it is. A lovely written description of the idea of romanticizing wealth, the 20's, and the American dream. If you can argue that is even real. But the man was delusional. He never left out of that dream of his. Every character is flawed and for a reason. It is showing how even if you cover everything with gold and marvelous things, you still cannot fully hide the shit that is underneath it. There are always secrets under all that masking."

"Huh... I got to the first party scene and I got that Jude was saying how you throw these parties for everyone else and that you don't really enjoy them."

Craig bursts out laughing after a quick moment of silence. "I didn't mean to sound so pretentious, I'm sorry. You should have shut me up."

"No, no you were really passionate, I didn't want to stop you. What are your thoughts on Shakespeare while we are at it?"

I laugh with him. Maybe this won't be too bad. When I am not just sitting in silence waiting for someone to say something, being with Craig has been the easiest thing I have done within these past few months. What they are saying or thinking can't be *that* bad.

Heated

I didn't think that school was going to be the hardest part to get through this week. Between the stares and whispers of classmates and the iced-out behavior of Dmitri, going home was the best part of my day. The Elites had no problem icing me out and giving Craig the 3rd degree. But they didn't kick him out, he holds the most power over them, but the girls made it perfectly clear that they were pissed at him. Travis still had the audacity to sit at the table, but Craig took every chance he could get to make little digs at him.

I didn't want to be a part of that drama, so I chose to stay at my table. That inadvertently caused more eyes on us because we weren't sitting together. It started going around that it was because I fear Bridget and the other girls, so I'm "staying in my place". I resented that most of all. I'm not seen as an equal amongst their crowd. The guys feel as if he downgraded and the girls are jealous and confused why he would pick me out of all the other "better options". Monday through Thursday it was nonstop, behind my back whispers and rumors about me. It got to the point that I had a full breakdown Thursday night at gymnastics.

Maci came back to my house with me that night to keep me company and in good spirits. I didn't want to tell anyone else about it. She is so removed from the situation; she has only heard of Craig through the grapevine. When I showed her a picture of him, she told me that we looked cute together. I know she is biased, but it made me feel a little better. A part of me would like to pack up and spend the weekend with her in Beverly Hills. Malibu has been giving me nothing but headaches and nightmares. I have a constant feeling that someone is watching me. Occasionally in dreams I see a shadow figure just standing and observing me. Sometimes I think I see it in real life. But when I was with Maci, I felt at ease for the first time, it was refreshing, to say the least.

My communication with Craig has been very limited. I have told him I have been feeling overwhelmed, but I haven't gone to great extent with the explanation. He doesn't try to pry but he really wants to see me. I keep coming up with excuses for him not to, but in reality, I don't want him to see me cry half the night.

It's Friday now, the end of this dreaded school week. But I can't go. I have zero energy to go to school today. If I have to hear one more whisper, see one more dirty look, hear one more snicker as I walk past, I will burst.

I finally fessed up, not entirely, to my parents. Letting them know that I have been getting bullied at school and I needed a day off. My Dad stayed back with me and cooked me an amazing breakfast and my Mom took Josh and Lindsey to school.

Sitting around at home was just the thing I needed, I decided to just sit back and marathon Ancient Aliens. It made me miss Cassidy and Nick, all three of us watch this show constantly. Dmitri found it to be too far-fetched and didn't care for it that much. But if he got drunk enough, he would enjoy it.

It's lunchtime at school so I decided that it should be lunchtime here. My Dad made some mac and cheese last night that makes for the best comfort food. As soon as I settle down, it is as if it was magic, I get a facetime call from Cassidy. I look like trash but who cares, I answer it.

"Oh my god, Jezzi, we may have done something bad," Cassidy says before I get the chance to say hi.

Seconds later Nick appears on the screen too, "Jez, I swear we were just trying to help. Also, we thought Craig knew."

I become even more confused as to what they are talking about. I can tell they know I am but are too busy looking at something behind them.

"Okay, so Craig came up to us and asked if we know what's going on with you. And we told him about how people have been talking about you a lot, making fun of you, putting you down. And so, we guessed that you probably needed a break from all that so that's why you are at home. But then Nick," Cassidy cuts her eyes at him. "Nick told-"

"I told him that I found out that the main source of the rumors and trash talk that people were spreading came from Travis. Cas and I were plotting his slow demise but Craig is now... I think he is about to kick his ass."

It was Travis? Why would he do that to me? I know that we didn't end things on a good term but why would he go out of his way to cause so much hatred towards me?

"We're gonna get a better look and show you what's happening," Cassidy says as the camera shuffles as both she and Nick scamper off to get close to Craig. The lunchroom is so loud I can barely hear him but then they decide to stand directly next to him. I guess they have no reason to hide.

She turns the camera around and I can see Travis sitting looking smug with these other dudes, who I refer to as the herd because all they do is follow around Craig and Jude. And I guess Travis now. Craig is standing in front of him and he does indeed look as if he is going to kick his ass.

"You feel good? Do you feel good making Jezebel feel like shit? For what reason do you need to tear her down like that?"

"Because she is a cheating whore, which you know all about," Travis grins getting the hype from the guys around him. My heart drops to my stomach. Hearing him say that makes me feel so sick.

"And you're a spineless, pathetic, weak, piece of shit that isn't even worth being on the bottom of her shoe!"

Travis makes an overexaggerated Oo and laughs with the others. I don't even recognize him. "Dude, she cheated on me with you! Do you honestly think that I care about anything you say? Why don't you go to the band room and cry while you play some moody song about your sweet new whore."

Craig huffs out some air and paces a bit, trying to hold back his anger, and most likely the beast. He snaps back around and towers over him. Travis tries not to show it, but I know he is scared. Craig is both taller and has more muscles than him. Also, Travis doesn't know how to fight.

"Why don't you stand up, be a man, and take this fight up with me, instead of attacking a girl? Oh wait, you would never do that, because you are the biggest pussy I have ever met! You attack Jezebel with words because you know it would get to her, you didn't try to step up to me because you knew that you wouldn't win. Notice how no one is saying anything negative about me? Because I run this bitch, Travis." He leans down and gets closer to Travis' face. "The only reason why you are getting any recognition right now is because you are dating Candice, who by the way has slept with all of these dudes who are around you, it is no secret so if you feel so inclined to call a girl a whore maybe you should look at who you're dating. You chose to use manipulation to try to get ahead and feel superior but guess what Jezebel doesn't need to do that, she won me over with just being herself, and I guarantee you that she will do that for the rest of my friends. My ex cheated on me too, but you know what I didn't do, spread nasty things about her throughout the whole school because I am a man and not an insecure little boy. I wish Jezebel was here so she could kick your ass in front of everyone just to show them how much of a little bitch you really are. I'm not going to put my hands on you, I'm not trying to get detention or get suspended. But what I will tell you is that you can get your insignificant, sorry, manipulative, virgin, bitch ass away from my table and my sight. You can call your mum and maybe she can use her therapy skills to give you a false sense of not being a worthless fuck."

I smile, I smile big. Grand gestures like that always seemed so cheesy but having this happen to me right now, I love it. I hear Cassidy, and Nick cheering and going crazy much like the rest of the people around them. I have never been more attracted to him in my life. I should have told him sooner. I wish I could give him the biggest hug and kiss him. Travis gets up and pushes past him. That was harsh and humiliating but he deserved it.

The camera turns back to Cassidy and Nick, they are beaming just like me. They speak over each other in excitement while I can't stop smiling.

"That was awesome!" Nick starts.

"Our plot was to slowly drive him insane with anonymous notes that were slightly threatening. Also, I was going to try to get him fired from Starbucks. But this was waaay better!" Cassidy giggles.

Their plot was more sinister and could have possibly gotten them in trouble if anyone found out, but I still appreciate it. I do wish that Dmitri was there and had my back, but he is still mad at me. He hasn't even texted me.

After saying their goodbye Cassidy hung up. I look down at my full bowl of mac, I nearly forgot about that. As I continue to eat, I can't shake the stupid grin off my face. Just thinking of Craig is giving me goosebumps.

My parents were happy to see that I was in a better mood. I told them at dinner that Cassidy and Nick help squash the issue. Which isn't a lie, if they hadn't told

Craig there would have still been an issue. Lindsey and Josh said some words trickled to the junior high as well. Lindsey would just tell them that they were wrong, but Josh said he started a counter rumor to deflect, and somehow it worked.

Around 10 at night I get a phone call from Dmitri. I was excited to hear from him but also scared of what it might be. Nevertheless, I answered quickly.

"Belle, I'm sorry... I heard and saw what Edwards did for you today. I thought he was just trying to play with you. I thought maybe he had gotten in your head. It's not my place to intervene like that. And I don't think you're a dumb bitch," his voice low and apologetic.

"I am a dumb bitch; he isn't the safest boy I could have talked to. But I believe that he does have my best interest. At least I hope,"

"I had a long, looong conversation with him after school... He is genuine, he sounds very genuine in his intentions and feelings for you. And well if he isn't, you know I will rip his head off."

"I thought that you used that as a big threat like it was all talk, but after Monday I do believe you would actually do it."

We both laugh and the air feels less tense. He makes sure that I am feeling okay and also apologizes for not doing anything about the people talking about me. He said he didn't hear much of it, most of the time snickering people went quiet when he came around. I'm guessing it was from fear. When dudes used to bully Nick, they got very quiet when Dmitri came around.

After we hang up I settle into bed to sleep, playing on my phone until I eventually knock out.

"Jezebel". a set of light brown eyes appear before me along with a sharp tooth grin. "Jezebel you're in trouble," the voice sings like mist and the face vanishes.

I pop my eyes open; my body feels paralyzed for a moment. I turn on my light on my nightstand. My heart going double time. The room is clear, but it doesn't feel clear. I grab the remote for my TV and turn it on to substitute for the light. I'd rather have sound than light. As I ease back down to go back to sleep, I feel a cold brush sweep over me. *"We're coming."* I turn around and face the TV, for the fear of what will happen the next time I close my eyes.

The Council

I finally let Craig come over, after what he did on Friday. I used to hate the white knight trope but I know he only did it because he knew how hurt I was and acted out of pure instinct. I still haven't told my family about us. We haven't necessarily called it, but I think it is a given that we're together. The feeling of impending doom makes me hesitate. Who knows what will happen with us being together?

He brought over his homework so that we could work together. The only classes we share are English and gym, so there is only one assignment we have that we could do together. But we are doing math because neither of us feel like reading Gatsby right now. He is taking pre-calc and I'm taking trig. English, French, and history are my only AP classes. He takes all AP and his AP history class is AP Euro. Being an overachiever, he took US over the Summer. Since he has already taken trig, he's helping me out. I can't offer him any assistance.

"Your popularity and looks make me forget that you are at the top of the class. Normally people like you aren't at that status."

"How dare you stereotype me, I'm more than a body Jezebel, I have a mind too," he teases.

I gently push him. "Oh shut up. Also, isn't your mind kind of a cheating factor? You literally have a super-brain,"

"It's not my fault that my kind are mentally superior. It's a hard pill for humans to swallow, I know."

I roll my eyes at him and act as if I am fully indulged in my homework. He laughs and snuggles close to me.

"I'm kidding... mostly," he chuckles. "It is a very common thing for us, ambobestia," he says in his most snooty tone, "to have extreme intelligence but some of us don't inherit that. I mean look at Candice."

Candice? She is an ambo too? Are the rest of them one too? A small feeling of concern for Travis' safety hits me, but quickly fades away as soon as I think about how he talked about me.

"They all are, if you're wondering. Bridget, Jude, and Jeanette. Candice is a half breed. She is half human, so that probably explains how she isn't the smartest."

I shouldn't be surprised. I have so many more questions that follow but I don't want to learn anything new right now. In some weird, nothing makes sense, life I am living, the fact that his best friends are also ambos makes perfect sense. Our school isn't very diverse so when Cassidy finds another black person, she tries to befriend them, Nick does the same if he finds another Jewish person. Maci is Lithuanian and a lot of her friends are eastern European. It's nice to have people around you who get it.

"What's up?" Craig inquires. A part of me wishes that he would read my mind so that I wouldn't have to say things out loud. I have spent years keeping the weird things that happen to me to myself because no one would ever believe me. This is the first time I could tell the truth, the full truth. I spent a summer in a psych ward because I thought that I was possibly schizophrenic. So many times, things just didn't feel right, that nothing was in place. My thoughts, feelings, and sometimes my speech was scattered. Something felt like it was invading my mind but at the time, it seemed impossible.

"Someone or something has been watching me or getting in my head. I keep hearing these voices and seeing things that aren't there. And occasionally these things alter my reality," I confess. I keep my head buried in the textbook, afraid to see what his reaction might be to this.

His hand slides behind my back around my waist pulling me into him. I still keep my eyes locked on the book,

"Jezebel." I don't respond. He takes his other hand to close the book and sets it aside. For a moment, his hand goes from my knee to my thigh, sending electric shocks through me. Swiftly he takes that hand to my chin and gently guides my face to lock with his. I expected his eyes to be lustful but instead their black. Pitch black.

A whirlwind of flashbacks is the best way I can describe what is happening. A wormhole is sucking me in, tumbling me through my head at high speed. Snippets of sound come through each second. Sounds from my memories. Until I stopped. I hit the ground, everything is black except for a white light, this light is comforting, loving.

Jezebel. Do I have your permission to enter your memories? Craig's voice surround sounds. He appears before me like mist. I don't see any part of my body; I feel as if I am physically here but I'm not. *Do you consent?* Chills get sent down my spine.

"Yes," I peep.

His figure disappears and I feel a rush of emotions sadness and emptiness. It's the night I came back from Dmitri's on Black Friday. But in a second, it's gone. Nerves settle in me. Everything is jittery but there is a small feeling of hope that follows. Quickly it is crushed and turned into heartbreak. I just talked to Travis for the first time after everything to try and get him back. I can't describe the emotions that I am feeling, I just feel garbled. Every .5 second that passes it's a new emotion, while short it is strong. My mind feels like it is being ripped, torn apart. Ten thousand voices, feelings, images turn and hit me. Leaving me feeling small, trapped.

It finally stops and I'm left softly whimpering. I open my eyes and I am back at my house. My shirt is stained with tears and my body is trembling. I don't know what I just went through but every part of me feels violated. Craig holds me close. As he does it's like a blanket dropped over a fire. My tears stop, the shaking stops. A feeling of a restful calm I have never felt before fills me. The serenity, comparable to meditating in a tropical paradise with the gentle song of birds and rush of a waterfall tranquil to your soul. The type of tranquility that people can only imagine having. There isn't a single conflicting thought, no worries, no distractions that could break me from this feeling.

I look up at Craig, who moves his head from resting on mines. "You feeling okay?" Craig murmurs, his voice like honey.

I nod and nestle back into him.

"I'm casting a soothing aura onto you," he continues, "I know how hard it is to have someone enter your memories. The rush of emotions that follow is... painful to say the least."

I didn't know he could do this; I didn't know any powers of an ambo could be used in such a good manner. I never want him to stop this. It's the first time I have felt this at ease in years.

While I feel relaxed in his embrace, I can feel how tense his body is. Stiff like a rock. But for some reason, I can't bring myself to care. I feel like I'm in nirvana. Then suddenly it stops. Craig isn't next to me anymore, he is at the window, looking out to my backyard. I didn't feel him get up, I could feel him next to me, his arms embracing me, my head against his chest.

I get up to walk towards him, he is unmoving.

"Jezebel, I don't want to sugar coat anything. I saw-"

BONG! A loud grandfather clock ring echoes, interrupting Craig midsentence. I look around trying to find the source, I don't recall having a grandfather clock, but perhaps my parents just got one.

The ring gets Craig to turn around. He looks anxious and filled with dread. BONG! Another ring sets off. This time louder. The soundwaves shake the floor. This isn't coming from some earthly object.

Craig is at my side; he takes my hand causing me to share his anxiety with him. "We are being summoned."

"By who?"

"The Council."

"Wha-"

BONG!

In a millisecond I am being warped through time and space. As fast as light my body travels, I see nothing, hear nothing. Before I know it, I am standing in a hall of a magnificent building. Glimmering in fantastic high beams and decorated walls of art. Tall Roman columns that made me feel smaller than I am. Marbled statues of fantastic magical creatures lined the walls. The ceiling, dome-like with windows letting the sunlight in; allowing for the gold in the room to shine in a way I have never seen. The tiles on the ground look hand-painted with the most careful detail, with a high glossy finish. With each step someone takes you can hear a clean clack from the heels. It as if I stepped into the Vatican or Versailles. It's a cross between both. Everything is so elegant, rich, with an old type of class that isn't seen in modern buildings. It exudes wealth, power, and royalty.

I finally turn to look at Craig who doesn't look impressed in the slightest bit. As his eyes cut to me and lock with my doe-eyed wonder, they look cold as ice. He looks mad about my excitement that I have, which quickly makes me diminish it into a sorry frown.

"The 3rd high Council has summoned us and you're looking around like you're at a museum?"

I try to apologize but I can't find the words. I was so struck by the beauty of this place, it feels as if I just stepped into history, that I forgot why we were even here.

Normally when I look apologetic, he lightens up, but he is still hardened, giving me a scolding look. He takes my hand and pulls me to the side where there is a golden bench, that is surprisingly comfortable.

"I was too light with you about all of this. I thought that everything was going to be fine."

"No, you didn't," I counter, prompting a confused look on his face. "You said being with you would come with consequences."

He sighs and drops my hands, somehow managing to look even more exhausted with me than before. "I thought that they would be keeping a watchful eye on us. That I would get some light reprimanding. I never imagined that we would be summoned!" He growls at me.

I scooch away a little. Afraid of what might happen next with him. I have never seen him this upset with me.

He puffs out some air and fixes his hair a bit. "The severity of being summoned by the three courts is very, very severe. Ninety nine percent of the time is a crime so bad that it is either near treason or is treason."

I blink trying to process everything, to get on his level of worry. I can't figure out why I am not that worried but seeing how Craig is acting I can tell that this whole thing is a huge deal. I normally don't follow into anything blindly without any semblance of fear, but for some reason I feel tremendously at ease. I decide that it is better to give him reassurance of my understanding; I fear if I brush it off nonchalantly it would only result in him imploding. Most of the time Craig is as cool as a cucumber, stress doesn't appear to be his friend.

Craig sits hunched over, relaxing his arms on his legs. His body in a gentle cadence as he jiggles his leg up and down. His eyes dart everywhere but at me. I want to offer him some comfort but there isn't a chance that there is anything that I could say that would ease his stress. I have never felt so far away from him but so close. A stranger is sitting next to me. For once it is like I am fully seeing Craig in a human light, he has always been larger than life, better than the rest. But seeing him look so small, scared, and worried, forces me to recognize him as the barely 17-year-old that he is.

"Jezebel," he murmurs.

His voice catches my attention, I snap my head in his direction. His eyes are pleading, and I can't help but to want to hug him and make him feel better like he has done to me. But I can't create soothing auras. I don't possess the magnetism that he has. Nevertheless, us sitting at the Council, waiting for what I presume is a court hearing, is making me feel more connected to him. That I am truly a part of his life.

I smile at him with comfort and push his hair out of his eyes. Another first, normally his hair is perfect all the time. But because he has been messing with it from stress it has fallen all out of place.

"What's gonna happen at this hearing?" I stumble on my words. I try to mimic his way of speaking that always relaxes me.

"I don't know. I thought I would have more time before anything would happen. I haven't gotten to explain nearly enough to you." He pauses and looks around.

All of the presumably ordinary and fantastic creatures move about the halls as if we were invisible. No one looked our way. I wish that they would dress more brilliantly like you see in different fantasies. The creatures who aren't painfully obvious about their species; I can't tell if one creature is a vampire or if it is a witch. I am in awe of what I am seeing. I believed in this stuff as a kid, my great-grandma Claribel would tell me fairy tales and read me different fantasy books. I believed that I could have been a secret witch when I was a kid. Perhaps she knew of this world, maybe that's why she never discouraged me and never told me it was fiction.

"Your grandmother knew of the Immortal Realm?"

The creatures in passing suddenly took notice of us. Looking at Craig with great pleasure until they noticed me. Their faces didn't look as pleasant. My calm awe was starting to diminish, and I feel more threatened and unsafe. I swallow my newfound fear and bring my attention back to Craig.

"Um, no. Probably not. She told me a lot of stories... But I highly doubt-" I trail off as I remember that I never said that out loud to him.

I spring off the bench and scowl down at him. "You read my mind?!"

"Please," he reaches for my hand and gently pulls me down back on the bench. "I didn't mean to. I don't listen to your thoughts all the time, I'm just incredibly stressed and I have been keeping us invisible, so I just lost control and I accidentally heard."

The invisibility explains the fact that no one was paying attention to us earlier, now it's like we are a star attraction at a circus. That feeling of awe and slight excitement has no trace in my body. This is the first time I have felt the crippling fear that I have been neglecting since Craig has exposed my mind to this world. I start to notice each and every creature that passes us.

A slender, strikingly ordinary looking, pale man floated pass, his eyes soulless and hollow. A deep brown color to match his slicked-back hair. His emotions are hard to read, pleased to see Craig but almost disgusted by my sight.

A spright like woman goes past, each step was like a dance. But she wasn't joyful and smiling, but every bit of her gave off that feeling. A spring green light softly illuminates off of her, but it is subtle. She doesn't shy away from staring or passing judgment. She actually stops for a moment.

Craig encourages my head to face him. "Hey," he coos, "Don't focus on them. It will only make it worse."

I peak at the earthly lady but she was walking down the hall with her head held high.

"She is a nymph. And the man before her was a vampire," Craig explains.

"Well she seemed to have a real problem with me," I grit shakily.

Craig pulls me in closer rubbing the small of my back. "Don't worry about her, all nymphs are like that. They think they are better than everyone else."

He tries to chuckle, though it quickly turns into silence. But he continues to rub my back and it sends shivers and tingles down my spine. It keeps me calm but it also makes me want to wrap myself around him.

"We have been sitting here for a while and I fear that they soon will be coming to bring us to the court. I don't have the time to tell you even a fraction of what I wanted to say. But I need to tell you one detail before going in." He pauses and looks at me as if he is asking if I am ready to hear what he has to say. I prep myself and nod. "When I was in your memories, I saw a figure and felt several energies. Someone or a group of people are after you. They have been watching you and have been getting in your head since you and your friends first went after Aiden. And I believe even before that."

My jaw drops and my blood runs cold. I knew I wasn't going crazy. I knew I saw something in my room, I knew that there were some weird things happening in the hallway. Maybe it was them this whole time. Maybe all these strange occurrences were from ambos getting into my head. I thought I was hallucinating.

I feel sick to my stomach. I search around for the nearest trash can or bathroom, but I see nothing. I try to get up, but Craig catches me and brings me back down.

"Hey, hey, hey," he gently coos in my ear as he places his hand on my stomach. "It's going to be alright. I just need you to listen to what I say in there. Do not speak unless one of the judges addresses you. Follow my lead and I promise everything will be okay,"

His words and his touch put me in a trance-like state. Compelled with the mist like nature of his words and the wave of stillness in my stomach, I nod and look at him with grateful eyes. His crystal blue eyes look different, deeper maybe. I don't make too much of it.

He removes his hand from my stomach and the nausea disappears. As he rises, he takes my hand and interlocks his fingers with mine. His thumb caresses my hand; though seconds later his grip becomes a little tighter as a large ogre looking creature approaches us. He is what I would describe as robin's egg blue, bald, with bulging brown eyes. Yet, he was well dressed in one of the most finest suits that gave an almost dashing look to him, aside from the fact that he has a very brute like appearance.

With the fakest smile I have ever seen, Craig greets the beast. "Igor! So nice to see you," he gleams.

Igor grunts and speaks to Craig in a language I do not understand. But Craig does, as he chuckles and responds. "I didn't expect myself to be here either, yet here I am."

They share in a laugh and we start walking behind Igor as he leads us to where I presume is the courtroom. I wonder if it would be like in the Mortal Realm, will we have a jury of our peers, will we get a lawyer, if we are found guilty will we be sent to jail or death?

Everything you thought will not be happening. We stand before the judges and only them and it is our jobs to defend ourselves. We don't get a lawyer in the 3rd high court. And if we are found guilty then it would most likely be death. At least for one of us. Craig's voice calls in my head. I jerk my stare to him, and he is staring straight ahead keeping face. I squint in annoyance. Well since he is listening; I thought you said that you don't listen to my thoughts.

I don't. I try hard not to, but, in this instance, I need to communicate with you without Igor hearing anything. Also, keep your thoughts undamning. My Dad will be one of our judges and he is legally obligated to listen to your thoughts randomly throughout the hearing.

I understand Craig's stress, why he was so worried before. At least when you are at court in the Mortal Realm you are able to have the privacy of your thoughts, but here you can't even have that last bit of security.

We reach a large double door, while beautiful in its décor it is intimidating knowing what is waiting on the other side. Igor looks back at us. "I will let them know of your arrival," he thunders.

As Igor disappears into the room, Craig quickly turns me into him, hugging me. His body melts into mine. "Everything will be fine. I promise. Just remember what I told you," he says breathlessly. His nerves are kicking in hard while I feel as if I can no longer feel anymore.

The doors open and we are prompted to enter by Igor. As we walk in, I am taken away by the beauty of the room. The room has windows lining the left side allowing for the sun to bask the room in a heavenly glow. A circle indention in the middle of the room was decorated by a strange symbol or perhaps a crest. It consists of 4 images, a full moon in the background, bat wings that span just beyond the moon, In the center is a wand and a slithering snake that is somewhat wrapped around the wand as it's body spans over the left wing of the bat. Symbols of each creature that Craig said rules in this court; the werewolf, the vampire, the wizard/witch, and the ambobestia.

A small set of steps lead to the circular indentation. And in front of it all was a large podium that spans to seat the four representatives. The podium was tall, specially designed for the people on trial to feel small and looked down on. On the sides were chairs which were seated by what I am guessing are nymphs, faeries, and goblins. They pass judging eyes as they take notes. The room feels so full yet so empty. The architecture gives the illusion of spaciousness but the room itself is on the smaller side.

The door slams behind us, making me flinch. I want to turn around and see what's behind us but I don't dare. Still, with his hand in mine, Craig walks into the circle, I quicken in pace to match him. A faery flutters in front of us. She is tall, for what you expect of a fairy. She is about 4'11 maybe 5 feet. She hovers right before the podium looking to make sure she has our attention. She clears her throat, and her voice booms throughout the room as if she is on an intercom.

"The honorable Judge Greysmoke."

A slender, tanned skinned woman comes walking up to the podium. She has long, straight, dark brown hair that is neatly tucked behind her ears. Her features lead me to believe that she is Native American or perhaps Hispanic.

She is Native, Kwakiutl to be specific. Her first name is Tera.

Good to know that Craig is constantly listening to my thoughts during this time. Now I get to have him and his father in my head. I pass a quick glare at him, knowing fully that he can hear me.

As Greysmoke sits, a full moon lights up at the head of the podium in the section that she is at. The Werewolf.

"The honorable Judge Cosmos."

A bigger lady, who is also quite tall enters. She has greying blonde hair that is messily pulled back into a bun. Her skin a deep olive tone. She has similarities to some facial structure that Cassidy's dad's side of the family has, which leads me to believe that she is Greek.

From ancient Greece. First name Airlea.

If he is going to do this every time, I don't get why he gives me the chance to speculate.

A wand lights up when Cosmos sits, she's a witch. A witch from ancient Greece, very cool.

"The honorable Judge Russo."

Another woman walks in, but she looks familiar to me in a way. She has a blunt black bob that contrasts well with her extremely pale skin. Her eyes are the things that strike me, they are green, an unforgettable emerald green. Coupled with the process of elimination and how pale she is, I know that she is a vampire.

I wait to hear from Craig, but he is silent. Maybe he stopped listening in on my thoughts. I know I wished for it when I was at home but having him actually do it, it feels violating.

As Russo sits down the bat lights up. No surprise there. And so that leaves,

"The honorable Judge Edwards"

This will be my first time ever seeing Craig's dad. This is definitely not the way I wanted to meet him. He walks in, and much like his son, light and all attention is commanded by him. He is nothing short of stunning. He has semi wavy hair like Craig, though his is a lighter shade than Craig's chocolate brown. Every strand is fallen perfectly in place. He has honey brown eyes that sunlight dances off of, giving it beautiful twinkles. He shows a slight stubble from where a beard would be. I should have expected nothing less from Mr. Edwards but I wasn't prepared for the man-

You did not spend this much time dwelling on anyone else. Can you please stop thirsting and drooling over my Dad? I have no choice but to hear your thoughts I can't bar my powers in here.

I quickly shut up, mentally. It is hard not to think about anything. To ignore all that is in front of me and around me. But having to hear my constant thoughts is something I don't want from him and I figure that he doesn't want to hear.

As Mr. Edwards takes a seat the snake lights up, and that causes all the lights from the different sections of the podium to come together and shoot the lights into strips through the floor lighting up the symbol beneath our feet. Oh wow.

"Court is now in session."

The Case

Everything that happened from that point forward was straight dialogue. I was so caught up in what was being said I didn't have time to think nor did I want to. I didn't want to risk any chance of me thinking something that could get me killed. So, for the whole hearing I just listened with minimal thoughts.

Cosmos: Mr. Edwards, I am shocked to see you here.

Russo: If anything, I would suspect your brother.

Greysmoke: Michael showed great promise, but alas.

Edwards: William, do you know why you're here?

Hearing Craig's first name will never not throw me off. It doesn't sound natural, nor does it suit him.

Craig: I have a small inkling as to what it might be.

Greysmoke: Well, let me enrich your mind. You have exposed Jezebel Bedeau to our world, all who dwell within it, the form of our government, and how it all works and ties together.

Russo: We have worked centuries to keep our world separate from the humans. This realm was created as a safe haven for our kind.

Cosmos: You're all too young to remember the prosecutions, slaughters, and hunting of the supernatural during the old years. 2,000 years I have lived, and the horrors I have lay witness, makes me wonder and be in awe that I am alive today. We cannot go back to the dark ages, Mr. Edwards.

Greysmoke: We can't, and we won't! It took far too long for us to rise out of it in the first place. My near 200 years do not compare to your 2,000 Cosmos, or to your 400 Russo. I have not experienced the Court of the Damned, but I do know all that it caused. And I know that Edwards knows this too. Yet, he raises his family in the Mortal Realm so who is to know the knowledge his family has.

Edwards: If you are implying, Greysmoke, that I did not educate my son or the rest of my children you would be wise to watch the next words you speak.

Russo: William is a fine boy. Exceptional and beyond in all his fields. Even while studying in the Mortal Realm he has maintained a perfect G.P.A, excelled in extracurriculars; all the while showing skills in his ambo training that goes beyond 90% of the students in our schools.

Greysmoke: Russo, your whole family has been in cahoots with the Edwards family since the dawn of time. I'm surprised that your cousin isn't here with them.

Cosmos: Greysmoke, don't let your bitter heart steer you to an evil bias. Russo is correct, Mr. Edwards is a wonderful boy and you know that to be true. I know we thought the same about Michael, but we cannot pass judgment for the mistake of the brother.

Greysmoke: You are right, I apologize for my outburst and for my sharp tongue towards you Edwards.

Edwards: It is alright Greysmoke, I do not hold it against you. This is quite out of terms for William. William, you know the massive threat exposing miss Bedeau to the Immortal Realm is. You do understand that giving her this knowledge is an act one step away from treason? I am positive you know what the final step would be.

    His words are grave. It makes the whole court go silent. I look at Craig to see what his reaction is. He looks intense and stern. Yet at the same time he looks shameful. The judges are all basically saying that he has brought dishonor on his family. I can't help but feel guilty. This is all because of me.

Craig: Your honors, I am well aware of the misstep I took introducing miss Bedeau to our world. I understood that there would be some ramifications. However, I assure you, I did not do this out of blind teenage stupidity.

Greysmoke: Then what was the reason?

Craig: I... I have fallen for Jezebel. And I couldn't lie to her if I wanted to be with her.

Craig pulls me closer to his side, I can feel how warm he is from the nerves and how stiff his body is. All of the judges look exhausted and annoyed by his answer. Greysmoke looks amused, Cosmos disappointed, Russo annoyed beyond a humanly point, and Mr. Edwards has his face buried deep into his hands and he groans in agony to his son's answer.

Edwards: Son, you jeopardize the security of our nation over a high school infatuation?!

Craig: It is not an infatuation; I have true feelings for her! I have never felt so happy and understood. I have been in the darken shadow of Michael my whole life. I have been expected to be perfect in everything that I do. I have been looked at as if I am two steps away from being a leader in this council. But I am just a boy. And Jezebel has been the only person to truly see me. To care for me. To ignite a light that burned out of me years ago. To fuel a passion that I never had. When she smiles at me, my heart nearly starts palpitating. I couldn't risk not having her in my life. I had to tell her the truth of what I am, your honors.

Russo: That does not matter Mr. Edwards! You are what you said, a boy! You are immortal, you have eons to find love. She will grow old and die while you remain youthful and powerful. You are an Edwards; you are Charles' son. You have a high standard to hold up to. You took an oath!

Craig: I know I took an oath! I know what I did your honor!

Greysmoke: Then why do you spit on it?! You have no respect for our land and the morals we stand on!

Craig: That is not fair to say.

Greysmoke: It is plenty fair to say Mr. Edwards. Look at who you have brought into our world. Look at how you live separately from the rest of your peers. And the three other traitorous families you have befriended are hardly model citizens of the Immortal Realm.

Cosmos: We cannot allow her to keep the knowledge she has. It is a threat to our society.

Craig: She poses no threat.

Russo: We cannot trust him to stay away from her even after wiping her memory. She must be executed.

What?! Craig pushes me behind him in a defensive pose causing an uproar in the court. The Faeries, nymphs, and goblins stand up on the side shouting jeers and excitement. Mr. Edwards slams a gabble to bring the court back down.

Greysmoke: It is what is wise, don't you agree Edwards?

Craig: No! Your honors listen to me, please. You cannot kill her.

Cosmos: We may do whatever we please Mr. Edwards.

Edwards: William you will stay inline. The next outburst from you will not end in a polite warning. You are of no authority in this court. You may be my son, but I tolerate no disrespect. Do I make myself clear?

Craig softens his stance but keeps me behind him. He takes hold of my hand, easing my worry and tension.

Craig: Yes sir. I apologize for my outburst, but you must understand... Jezebel does not know of what we fear. I will never tell her of that. She is in the dark and I plan on keeping her there.

Craig then breaks off into speaking a mixture of Gaelic and Latin. While I can figure out the language, they speak I don't understand a word of it. All I know is that he is speaking about me. They all keep looking at me with skeptical, hatred filled eyes. As he continues to speak the look of hatred lessens but is still visible.

Russo: If what he says is true then there should be no problem with Charles taking a look into your girlfriend's head.

That was the first time I have ever been called that. I'm Craig Edwards's girlfriend. It sends butterflies through my stomach and makes me smile a bit. Though soon it goes away as Mr. Edwards appears before me through the medium of teleportation.

Craig looks worried as he steps aside so that his father can fully get to me. He stands a few inches taller than Craig and holds even more beauty as he stands inches away from me. I need to stop thinking these things, he is probably listening. Mr. Edwards places his thumbs on my temples and rests the rest of his fingers on the back of my head. Like Craig did before, his eyes go black.

Every single millisecond a new image flashes by. The piercing sound of what a VHS sounds like when rewinding screams in my ears. My head starts to pound, pulsate in a pain I have never felt. The pain is comparable to having a bullet ant sting you in the face. I feel like my head is going to explode and I can't help but let out a loud yell in agony. It stops, everything is back to normal. My sanity isn't though.

Edwards: Something is blocking me. There is something that is blacked out in her memories.

He jerks his head over to Craig whose eyes are a different color; they are deep indigo. In a blink, Mr. Edwards slaps Craig across the face. I wince at the action. Craig holds his face and looks away. Oh my god. Mr. Edwards returns his attention back to me and continues what he was doing. This time it is a little less painful. And I see clear images and sounds of my Great Grandma Claribel. It sends tears down my cheek. Having to go through the emotions of seeing her and hearing her as if she is right in front of me. In seconds it is gone.

Mr. Edwards backs away from me. His eyes look a little apologetic. He glances at Craig who quickly rushes to my side. His cheek is red from the slap, and the moment he wraps his arm around my waist I can feel his inner pain. He was trying to hide any memory I had of my grandma. He didn't react well when he read my mind earlier. There is something I do not know about her. Mr. Edwards teleports back to his seat. His colleagues look to him for his response.

Edwards: She doesn't know. She is free of that knowledge as Cr- William said.

The court relaxes, yet Greysmoke looks a bit disappointed. I think she really wants me dead.

Edwards: But as my son tried to bar from me, she was told of our realm when she was a child. Her dreams and fantasies were fed as truth by her great grandmother... Claribel.

As he says this an almost uniform gasp shakes the room. Murmurs begin and dirty looks return. But this time I share them with Craig. I have kept quiet this whole time, but I cannot allow for any misunderstandings.

Me: Your honors?

They turn their heads to me making me instantly regret speaking up.

Me: I, I don't know what this thing is about me that makes you all distrust me so much. But My great-grandma did nothing but tell me fairy tales. And let me have an active imagination. I highly doubt that she knew anything about this world. She never explicitly told me that any of it was real. She just said that imagination can make anything real if you believe hard enough.

Greysmoke: You naïve girl, your great grandmother knew all too well of this world. She is dead now because of it!

My heart dropped. I stand in shock from the words that were just spoken to me. They killed her? They killed my grandmother?!

Craig: Some rebels killed her did they not? Because of her knowledge?

Cosmos: Yes, that is true. While we did not have a hand in her death, I must say we were awfully close to it.

Edwards: She knew of every bit of our world, our people, our history, and she knew how to get here. She even entered it once. To her demise, unfortunately.

Russo: It was not unfortunate. It is what she deserved for crossing over. And now we have her great grand here who will meet the fate that was failed to be given Claribel.

Craig: I promised I would not speak out of terms again, but if you will not keep Jezebel alive for the sake of my heart, there was another reason I told her about the Immortal Realm.

He has their full attention. He clears his throat and takes one hopeful look at me.

Craig: I have heard my father talking about the fear of a revolution for years. There has been an ongoing chatter amongst these halls that there are traitors trying to cause an uprising. You guys have been sending hounds on hunts that only lead to cold dead ends.

He goes on to tell them about the Beast incidents we were having in Malibu, about how he had his suspicions about the attacks. How we came together to hunt it down.

Craig: Jezebel then started to tell me of her past and of how ambos have been after her before and how she feels as if she is targeted. And as it turns out, she was. The ambo that was terrorizing Malibu was not trying to kill a bunch of people, but mistaken other girls as Jezebel.

They just ended up being collateral damage. Earlier today I went into her head and I have seen figures and multiple energies within her memories since October. I thought it was the Council at first. But I realized that you would have faced it head-on. This is the work of the traitors that you all fear. I believe that they are trying to capture Jezebel and use her against us. I told her about this world because it is better for us and her to be on our side, rather than the rebels taking her and giving her the exact knowledge that I gave, plus more.

The courtroom is silent. Stunned by the accusation that Craig made. I too feel shocked. I thought these things that have been in my head, dreams, and everyday life was trying to kill me. But they want to use me to fight against the government here? Am I that much of a threat to them?

The Council looks worried as they nervously look at each other. They look as if they are deliberating telepathically but as far as I know, Mr. Edwards is the only telepath up there.

Cosmos: If what you say is true Mr. Edwards, why would it be safe for us in either situation to keep miss Bedeau alive?

Craig: Because even if she is killed, the rebels will find another way to come after us. It is better that we have the leverage of having her with us. With me. 3rd High Council, I beg of you, please spare my girlfriend's life and trust me on what I say. Despite the feelings that I do not respect our lands and morals, I want nothing but the best for us. And if that means I have to fight for it, I will.

Greysmoke: You are merely a 17-year-old student. You are not a master in any ranks, nor do you have enough training to take down an entire set of revolutionaries. You may have all this passion right now, but what happens when you break up. Then what? You wipe her memory and then the rebels get her, and we go down? No, it is in our best interest to kill her.

Craig steps forward with his hand in mine. He stands strong and proud. His eyes are filled with determination. I bite my lip in anticipation of what he is going to say.

Craig: Greysmoke, Cosmos, Russo, and father. I would do anything to protect Jezebel. I am sorry if I am speaking out of terms, but I cannot live in a world without her. I wouldn't be able to go on without seeing her face every day. I know that certain people would kill the person who they cherish most in the name of this land, but I cannot comply. My life begins and ends with her now. Every single nerve within me sends electricity throughout my body whenever she is around. Ambos don't have much of a capacity for love, she is the exception. I love her. I am not infatuated with her; I do not worry about what happens when we break up because I know that will never happen. I am in love with Jezebel Felicity Bedeau.

Woah. He is in love with me? I look at him wide-eyed and confused, also in a bit of awe. This is the first time of me hearing this. We just started dating and he is in love with me. Perhaps ambos feel stronger than humans. I feel a twinge of guilt in my heart, I don't love him. I like him a lot, but I don't love him. He is willing to lay down his life and integrity for me. This doesn't feel right.

Craig pulls something from behind his back. It looks like a glass red, anatomically correct, heart. The glass beats with the same cadence as Craig's pulse. The Council looks in shock and his dad scowls at the sight of it. He takes my left arm and turns it around to expose my inner forearm. He places the beating glass heart on my forearm and looks me in the eyes as if he is saying trust me.

Edwards: William, think of what you are doing.

Craig: I have. I take this Heart String and pull on it to match the cadence of within. I swear to abide by the rules that it holds dear. I take this Heart String and bound it to Jezebel Felicity Bedeau. I take this Heart String to curse me if I do not follow.

A powerful wind kicks in blowing our hair around. A bright white light begins to shine from the heart, and I start to feel a burning on my arm. Craig takes his other hand and exposes a set of claws. He opens his shirt exposing his chest and begins to dig his claw into his left peck.

Craig: I cross my heart bloody and transfer the blood to her. Cross the Heart String for an eternal connection.

He then chants in Latin as the heart dissolves into my arm. Causing the burning to intensify, leading me to scream once more in agonizing pain. As the heart fully dissolves the carving of cursive WCE appears where the heart used to be. It looks as if someone took a knife to write it, though not bloody, but as if it is healing from it.

I look up at Craig shaking in horror and confusion. What did he just do? He takes his hand and runs it through my hair. Pushing the back of my head into his soft kiss on my forehead. "I'm sorry," he muttered for only us to hear.

Gentle weeping is coming from the podium. We look up to see that it is Cosmos. Greysmoke looks annoyed, Russo looks shocked, and Mr. Edwards looks pissed.

Cosmos: I am moved. Such dedication you have for her. At such a young age too! I remember when I had loved so young. It has been so long I nearly forgot.

Greysmoke: A heartstring is nothing to toy with. You seriously love her?

Russo: Of course, he does Greysmoke! Your bitterness knows no bounds does it?! I vote that we do not kill her. If Mr. Edwards is willing to make that grand of a sacrifice do you not think that he is serious?

Edwards: I agree. My son is a highly intelligent boy, he knows the severity of using the heartstring. I was skeptical at first. But his heart is true.

Cosmos: Let is deliberate then.

They all turn to one another and begin speaking in a language that I cannot decipher. That's a first. I take this time to turn to Craig and try to communicate with him.

I hope that worked. I really hoped that worked. If it did, I will explain everything when we get back. And if it didn't work? What does that mean for me; will I get the Ax of Justice? *Jezebel, please don't think of that. I can't bear it.*

They all turn back around. My heart is going a mile a minute as the silence becomes killer. In moments, my life could be over.

Edwards: In the case of Bedeau and Edwards, we find you not guilty. But, are expected to find and bring the resistance to the council. You will be held to report every new finding that you come across and the method that was used to acquire it. The court is adjourned.

As Mr. Edwards bangs his gable, we are sent back through the wormhole from which we came and seconds later we are back at my house.

I look at the clock and 2 minutes have passed. Craig looks relieved and is leaning over a chair catching his breath. He races over to me engulfing me in a warm embrace. I stand on my tippy toes to reach around his neck.

"I have so much to tell you," Craig says breathily in my ear, still hugging me.

In the blink of an eye, we are no longer in my house. But a large grand office. That is filled with books and fabulous artwork. Casting all the attention is a grand wooden desk that holds an Apple desktop computer, a mug that says "pish posh" on it, a pile of books on one side, and a photo that I cannot see the image of. But to my left, I notice a large family photo on the wall and I immediately know who this office belongs to. Mr. Edwards. The Edwards family is absolutely stunning. I recognize Mr. Edwards, Craig, Erin, and James. But there is another, an older boy, who I assume must be the infamous Michael. He looks like a carbon copy of his dad. The only difference is the eyes and hair, he has the same eyes as Craig, a soft icy blue. And his hair is a dirty blond color, borders more on the brown. Mrs. Edwards looks like a dream. She has a glowing softness to her that makes you feel warm and comforted. Her hair is blonde like Erin and I can see where Craig and Michael got their eyes from. It is kind of upsetting seeing them all together like that. Too perfect for words. It shouldn't be humanly possible; well, I guess it's not.

The door behind us opens and we turn around to see Mr. Edwards standing in the doorway. He looks drained. The door shuts behind him as he charges towards us. I prepare for the reprimanding and yelling.

"Oh, Craig!" Mr. Edwards exhales as he pulls Craig into a loving bear hug. That is not what I was expecting. He was so stern in the court. He looked so mad, so disappointed. He even slapped him!

He pulls back from the hug, his eyes nearly tearful.

"I thought I was about to lose you in there! How's your face? Is it okay? I didn't break anything did I? I'm so sorry, I didn't want to do that." He takes Craig's chin and examines.

Craig shakes him off, "I am fine dad, I swear. And I know you have to play a part. I shouldn't have interfered."

I stand looking confused by the whole situation. This is a whole new man from whom I just met in the courtroom.

He seems compassionate, loving, and he isn't calling him William.

Mr. Edwards backs away from Craig smiling. He then turns to face me, retaining his smile. He outstretches his hand and greets me warmly. "Sorry for everything that happened. I didn't want to have to meet my son's girlfriend in this manner. Let me properly introduce myself, I am Charles Edwards, you can call me Mr. Edwards."

I take his hand and accept the shake. I expected it to be one of the firm jerking ones. But he cups my hand and gently squeezes it. In a swift spin, he walks over to his desk and picks up the mug and takes a sip. He lets out all of his exhaustion as he sits down behind his desk. He motions his hand to the chairs around him.

"Please, sit," he says as he swallows his drink.

Craig takes the first steps towards a comfy looking love seat off to the side of Mr. Edwards's desk. I quickly follow after him clumsily taking a seat, I nearly sit on his lap but scoot over in the last minute. I feel incredibly nervous. I want to say something, ask some questions but everything is happening so fast. So, I sit silent, wide-eyed, just like in the courtroom.

Craig must feel how nervous I am, he wraps his arm around my waist giving me a gentle squeeze. Normally it would make me feel better, but something about this situation makes me feel so uneasy. I scoot away from him and his arm releases me. He looks at me, but I pretend that I don't notice, giving an innocent smile to Mr. Edwards. Focusing his attention back to his dad, Craig straightens up and plays it off.

"Dad," Mr. Edwards looks over his mug to show that he has his attention. "I am sorry that you had to find out about Jezebel this way."

Mr. Edwards nods and lets out a little hum. "I do not care that you are dating Jezebel, Craig. What I am mad about is that one, you got caught, and two you lied in court."

I sharply turn my head to him. He *lied*? But about what? Everything he said sounded so factual, so sure. He didn't stutter not once. It scares me how easily and with such an unarguable tone, he can lie. He can feel the heat of my glare, I know it. He refuses to look at me, but I won't have it.

"You lied, Craig? What was it, what was this lie?" I probe.

Mr. Edwards's raises his eyebrows, knowing that he accidentally caused something. Maintaining his smooth demeanor, Craig lazily runs his fingers through his hair and says with full confidence, "I did what I had to do to keep my girlfriend alive. I tried to stay honest, but those old dragons were heartless. She is not a threat."

I still sit glaring, refused to be move by his charming tone. He has yet to say what the lie is. We agreed on honesty, on transparency. He turns to face me. Meeting my glare with a semi seductive one. He naturally looks like that, most of the time. But I feel he is laying it on thick to get in my good graces. "Jezebel, everything I said about how you make me feel and how much I care about you is true. I have never felt to comfortable and happy with a person." He pauses, and breaks his gaze focusing back to his dad. I wait for the but that is coming.

"I do not love her. I had to add the flowery words for added theatrics. I wanted it to be believable."

Hearing that made my heart drop a little. I know when he said that he did in court I was overwhelmed and wasn't ready for that. But having to hear him say that it was a lie, it stings. I don't love him either, but I didn't proclaim it as a truth. Regardless on if you love the person having someone point blank say I don't love you isn't a good feeling.

"I don't regret using the Heart String. I am not in love right now, but something in me cannot bear the thought of anything bad happening to her."

"So, you put your life on the line for her? I know your heart is true, son. I can feel it and read it. But this is a serious," Mr. Edwards warns.

The longer he goes on the more concerned I get about the whole situation. What did Craig just do for me? They sit in silence. Mr. Edwards continues to drink whatever is in his mug. Craig leans into me, making the leather of the loveseat squeak. "The Heart String is a creation made by either an extremely powerful ambo or a witch or wizard. It is used to bind a witch, wizard, or ambo to whomever they chose. This makes it so that if the bound is in danger the protector knows and can find them easily."

That actually sounds good to me. It is nice to know that if I am ever in peril, I don't have to worry about calling the cops or anyone really, in the hopes that they get there in time. I didn't expect it to be comforting but it does make me feel a lot better. Craig is surprised by my reaction too. I don't fully understand the extent of his powers, but he seems to be able to read my emotions, whether they are on the surface or within.

He smiles, looking very pleased. It is the first time today that someone hasn't questioned him or criticize his decisions. I look down at my arm to examine the WCE craved into my skin. I lightly rub my thumb over it, expecting it to feel like a scab but it's smooth. There is no pain or irritation.

"Think of it like a tattoo. No one can see the mark but those who know you are bound. As of now that is you, the Council, and me," Craig states, his confidence in his actions booming. He felt unsure at first, no doubt, lying in court is never good. Also, this Heart String seems to be a big deal. But to see that I feel at ease is giving him all the confidence in the world.

Mr. Edwards clears his throat, as if to remind us that he is still present in the room. Craig and I break from our interaction. I didn't notice how close we had gotten; I'm sitting so close I could be in his lap. I blush a little and scooch over a tad bit, just enough for a little leg room.

"Craig, son, if you are going to be bringing her into this world, you need to work on telling her the whole truth and not a half or unfinished one. I know it is in our nature to leave things out but-" Mr. Edwards breaks off making a face while looking at Craig and only him.

This seems to have triggered Craig; I can feel the twinge of tension coming from him. "The Heart String has a drawback. One is that I only get the one, there are no replacements or extras," he says maintaining the eye contact with his dad; although, he was speaking to me.

Mr. Edwards glowers at him. He is leaving something else out. He is trying to hide this fact from me, but his dad is not letting it happen. I try to lean into him to push him to say more but he remains solid. Mr. Edwards lets out an exasperated chuckle and falls back into his chair. In a snap Mr. Edwards is back to sitting up but leaning in on his desk. His hands cupped together giving a dominating stare.

"What my son here, fails to mention is the fact that if the bounded is killed that causes for the protector to have its powers striped to nearly nothing for 40 years. Thus, would leave him practically mortal and he himself could be easily killed. So, if by some account you, Jezebel, find yourself being killed by these others who are after you; Craig would be rendered pretty much defenseless and he would be dead next." The severity in his tone was deafening.

Craig is breathing hard and stiff, keeping in some anger. I can see his tongue glide along the inside of his cheek in frustration. I sit gaping at what I was just told. When I thought he put his life on the line just vowing to protect me, I didn't know it meant instant death sentence for him. I didn't realize that he was quite literally laying his life out there. And for what, me? We have only been dating for a week. I can't let him do this. I guess it is too late for him to go back. We are bound together. The Council wanted me, these people who are after me wants me and only me. Now Craig has inserted himself into it. Anxiety wells in me and an insane amount of guilt. I cannot be the reason for Craig's death. I cannot be the reason for Craig's death.

"Will you both please!" Craig shouts, startling both me and Mr. Edwards. Craig blows out a puff of air and situates himself. "You guys' thoughts are like a million pine needles sticking me in my head. I cannot keep all of your thoughts out of my mind when we are in the Council Quarters. I had no other choice but to do what I did. I have no regrets in it." He rises from the loveseat and stand before us. "I do not care if I am not in love with her right now. I did what I needed to do to keep my girlfriend alive. I tried to stay honest and keep things a normal, non-theatrical state but those old bats have negative compassion sometimes! I care about Jezebel like I have never cared for a human. I don't know what I would have done if I had to watch them behead her right in front of my face. Just because they are paranoid doesn't mean they get the right to act out of fear. Does this 16-year-old girl look like she is going to destroy us all?!"

"I'm sure that's what the human's thought about Hitler at one point too," Mr. Edwards mumbles.

Craig shoots a glare at him that was so crass it felt like poison. Mr. Edwards shrugs a little as if he is saying 'I'm just saying'. Craig remains unamused, I thought the comment was kind of funny.

"Craig, I do not think Jezebel is a threat. I do not share in these old fears that the rest of my colleagues have. I am happy to see that you have someone who makes you happy. As the saying goes, if you're happy I am ecstatic. But, nevertheless, the law is the law."

"Fuck the law!"

Mr. Edwards looks shocked; it quickly turns into anger. "William you will *not* speak like that in my office! I have this thing blocked from all others to hear or to pry but I will not have any slander spoken in here. Do you understand?!" Mr. Edwards hisses.

I look between them both as they stare each other down. Both steaming in rage, neither of them cools off. I know that this is about me, but it doesn't feel right for me to be here. I sink myself deeper into the loveseat, causing it to speak again. With it being the only sound in this office right now I drew unwanted attention my way.

Craig softens up a little, Mr. Edwards follows. They both take a seat. I attempt to smile but the room doesn't feel right to do so. "I know what I did was profoundly serious, that it has enormous consequences. I'm sorry for speaking out of terms. I needed to ensure Jezebel's safety and I did the only thing that I could think of that would stop them. My main concern is not the Council, but these other supernaturals that are after Jezebel. I don't know how many, how much power they have," he trails off. Craig's voice is small, and for the first time during the start of the case have a heard true fear in his voice.

Mr. Edwards hears it too and he gets up and sits next to Craig. He lovingly puts his arm around his shoulders and gives him a comforting grin. "I know. I know the pressure that you are put under every single day of your life. You are expected to be nothing less than perfect, and to do that practically alone. But that doesn't mean for you have to be alone now for this." I didn't notice until now how smooth and easy on the ears Mr. Edwards voice is. It's like fine wine.

Craig looks up hopeful. "You'll help me?"

Mr. Edwards shakes his head, "No, unfortunately I cannot. I was a part of this case and it is illegal for me to interfere. That, consequently, goes for your mum and your siblings."

Craig looks down with disappointment. He looks as if he is contemplating something. I wish I could chime in with something helpful. But I am practically furniture right now.

"I can't ask my friends in Malibu; they would never lend a hand. Maybe Jude but still I don't know if he would be able to handle it. He has been training but we don't know what we are up against."

"I'm not talking about your friends." Craig looks puzzled as to who he could mean then. "While I cannot help you, your godfather can."

With that statement Craig sits up straight as a pin, his eyes wide as his he shakes his head. "No, no, no. Dad, you don't understand I cannot ask him. That has complications all on its own."

Mr. Edwards puts up his hand to cut him off. He gets up and returns back to his office chair and relaxes behind his desk. "I don't care about the complications at this point. This is life or death, for the both of you," he motions to us. "And it is also a case of keeping the state of our nation safe from any uprising trying to drag us back to the dark ages. If what you said is true, which I know you believe it to be, you need his help. Now go."

With a clap and a wave of Mr. Edwards hands we are teleported back to my house. I check the clock again, only a few minutes of lost time. I plop down on the couch and reach my hand out for Craig to take. He lazily accepts and slumps down next to me. He rests his head on my shoulder. His fresh scent fills me with comfort once again. After that whirlwind of events it feels nice to just sit with him. But I can't help but to wonder.

"Hey, Craig?"

He pokes his head up, his eyes exhausted but still sexy. I can barely control myself when he is close to me. I always just want to kiss him. But It's not the time.

"Who is your godfather? Why are there complications with him? Did you make him angry or something? Is he in jail?" I tease trying to keep things a little light. But as always, it doesn't work

He sighs and wiggles himself up and faces me. He doesn't want to tell me. But he has no other choice.

"My godfather... My godfather is Dmitri."

What the hell?

All We Know

Dmitri is Craig's godfather. I can't believe it. At this point anything is possible. For an unwarranted reason I became irrationally angry at Craig. It wasn't his business to share but I was still extremely angry about the news. I paced around my den shouting, cursing, occasionally resorting to French. A hundred million questions circulated in my head. But the main thing that was bugging me lead me to my first question. Which was, "How on earth can Dmitri be your godfather?! You're *older* than him! There was a four-month period between you and him not even being birthed yet!"

He stares at me with guilt but also the look someone gives when someone is ranting, and they think that they're crazy. I don't care if I sound crazy at this point. I have every right to rant and to be upset. I bug my eyes out a little more motioning for him to speak. He rolls his eyes and bites back some attitude. "Dmitri is 493 years my senior, that's how he is my godfather," he says dryly.

"Oh my freaking god!" I exclaim. Pacing the room at an even faster pace than before. A new level of anger and frustration enters me. I can barely think of the words to describe how I am feeling. I groan and growl several unfinished words. Sharply I turn, facing Craig with fiery eyes. He looks me up and down, still keeping his confused disturbed face.

"He is pale, his back healed pretty quickly after the Beast attack. His dad already looks like he is not alive! Let me guess, is he a vampire?!"

Craig doesn't respond but just raises his eyebrows for a brief second, indicating that I am correct. A loud groan builds inside me, I grab the nearest pillow and shout in it. I am in complete and utter amazement at how ridiculous my life has become. All of this, all of it should be fiction this should not be the life I am living.

Craig stands up, and takes my hand guiding me towards him. I glare up at him but I don't resist his pull. A sneaky little smile grows across his face. I can't read what he might be thinking but it makes me even more skeptical. He walks backwards and plops down on my couch taking me down with him. I clumsily straddle him. He chuckles at me while lightly rubbing my back.

"Jezebel, one of our first interactions with each other was at my party in October. You were so high strung and hell bent on checking your surroundings and worrying. I told you then that you need to relax and that you couldn't spend your time doing all that worrying."

I open my mouth to protest but he puts his finger on my lips and shushes me. Excuse me? I bite at his finger, though he pulls it away laughing at me. I break just a little and smile some.

"Jezebel, I am the one with the fangs," he says as he shows off his razor-sharp teeth. I jump back in retaliation but he holds me steady in his lap. I hate seeing him in any beast form. It is almost disturbing how quickly and seamlessly he can switch.

As if I weigh nothing, he stands up with me in the same position but now he is holding on to my thighs to keep me steady. He smiles again, his teeth normal.

"I know you have countless questions. I feel more at ease with everything. I know you aren't."

"Well, it's a lot Craig. It's a lot to take in. I feel like I am reacting the normal amount to all of this considering the news and the rate to which I received it."

"You have been shouting and cursing in both English and French. Making loud grunts of anger, pacing like crazy, and yelling into a pillow."

I squint at him and wiggle out of his hold, bringing my legs to the ground. "I just found out that my best friend that I have known since I was 7 is a *500-year-old vampire*. My boyfriend seems to basically be the next heir to the Immortal Realm ambo thrown. Hell, I just learned that there is an Immortal Realm, and that there is this hidden creature that no one knows about called ambobestia. And to top it all off, I almost got beheaded!"

He nods his head, giving me validation. It doesn't make me feel any less crazy but I thank him for not dismissing me. He goes over to the coffee table where his keys and backpack are sitting and gathers his things. Is he just going to leave me here after all of that? He pivots on his heels and as he walks past me, he takes my hand, taking me with him. "Let's go to the beach."

I look at him puzzled, after all of that he wants to go to the beach? Also did he forget that it is January, it's like 50 degrees outside. He grabs his dark green bomber jacket and disappears. Teleportation, I don't think I will ever get used to it. In a second, he is back with my pink windbreaker that was in my room's closet. I accept it reluctantly, feeling that my privacy was slightly violated. Though, he doesn't see anything wrong in his action.

"I want to go to the beach so you have all the liberties to yell whenever I tell you something new and I don't have to sound lock the room the whole time so your siblings don't hear." Seconds later there is a slow crescendo of all the sound that I didn't even know was missing. I can hear Lindsey talking on the phone with someone and Josh playing his video games yelling at whoever his teammates are. Stunned I look back to Craig, whose eyes are shifting from that deep indigo blue I saw earlier to his natural blue. Why can I never feel when he uses his powers?

"Jez!" Josh calls from the couch, still not taking his eyes off the screen. I respond with a simple yes, trying to keep my voice steady and non-suspicious.

"Will you be back by like 5? I wanted to go to the Grove and just chill a bit," Josh's voice is calm for a moment as he speaks to me but quickly turns to pointed jabs at his game again. Before I even get the chance to answer Lindsey pops from around the corner. Her eyes wild and excited.

"The Grove? I wanna go too. Also, mom and dad won't be back until like 8 so we can get dinner down there. I'm feeling pizza."

I smile and look at Craig for a second. He looks at his phone and nods, indicating that we will have the time. I switch my attention back and forth between Josh and Lindsey so I can address them both. "Yeah, I'll be back by then. Probably before. We can hang, I think mom left her credit card here so we can eat good," I joke.

This excites cheers from Josh and Lindsey. We don't normally get to eat out because dad is always cooking and mom is always baking so any chance we get to go to a restaurant is a small victory for the Bedeau kids. Occasionally we will sneak some McDonalds on the way home from school.

Craig and I say bye to them as we head out the door to his car. I try to keep myself with an open mind during the car ride so I can try to be a bit calmer at the beach. There will be no one there for sure but Craig pointing out my reactions made me feel a bit insecure of how I am looking right now.

Craig has the windows down just a crack. He looks calm, cool, and collected. A stark difference from how he was when we were at court. How can he be so calm after everything we just went through? I wonder if he is reading my mind right now. He said, when were in his dad's office that he had a hard time tuning us out. So, I guess he has to actively work to not listen in. But if he were, he would have butt in right now. I look at him. He glances at me with an easy smile.

"How are you so chilled right now? You weren't a few moments ago. You were freaked out and stressed. What do you know that I don't know?" I sound paranoid now.

This caused him to flicker between me and the road, he looks amused. "Jezebel why are you so paranoid by me?" he laughs. He is making me feel ridiculous. I sink down into the seat. "Aw come on," he pesters, patting my arm. "I am more relaxed because the way you were acting at your house, well, I found it funny. You were like this at my party and when we started investigating and I found it cute then and I still find it funny and cute now."

I feel my cheeks starting to blush. I try to hold back a smile but he can see right through my forced pout. He takes my hand and gently kisses it. "Your kisses have no effect on me. I know you're up to some bull," I say in a fake hainty tone. He brushes me off and continues to hold my hand. I guess after years of dealing with Bridget's real bitchiness my false attitude wouldn't have much of an affect.

He told me he wants to go to Pirate's Cove; it already has limited access on its own, so on a 50-degree January day no one will be there. We had to park at Point Dune and walk from there. Walking over made me feel extra relaxed. It felt warmer than what I thought it would be. The waves were a gentle splashing. The ocean air mixed well with my senses more than usual, it was as if I was in a spa with aromatherapy candles. The wind didn't cause our hair to blow in crazy directions but instead tossed it in a flattering way, like there was a modeling fan placed right before us. As we walked hand in hand along the edge of the beach, we quickly made it to the rocks that we had to cross over to get to the cove. You would think being able to balance on a beam while flipping it would mean walking on some rocks would be a walk in the park. But the difference is, the beam is smooth these rocks are not. I found myself stumbling but Craig would quickly help me catch my balance. He walks with ease; he does everything with ease.

I forgot a lot of the questions that I had in mind. I try to retrace some of them as we get closer. I want to be able to have full clarity, to know all that I need to know before 5 o'clock hits. Just as Craig stops and rolls out the blanket it comes to me.

"How did Dmitri become your godfather? What is the story behind that?" Craig sits down on the blanket, taking my hands so I go down with him. We sit face to face and he begins.

Craig explains that the Vaduva family are the Edwards to the vampires. That Russo is Dmitri's cousin but she did not choose to keep her maiden name when working for the council and uses her husband's last name. Dmitri's grandfather is the most powerful vampire and is the 1st court, Mr. Vaduva and his twin brother share power in the 2nd court, while Dmitri is the 3rd court.

"But what about Russo? Was she just a place holder for Dmitri that day? Also how is it that I have seen Dmitri age, and eat?" I ask confused. I don't get how these courts work. I don't understand how Dmitri can be the vampire representative of the 3rd court and still go to high school, swimming, and orchestra. It doesn't make sense.

Craig goes on to explain that when his dad came into power of the 3rd courts that he quickly befriended Dmitri because he appeared young. The women were very mean and condescending to him at first because he was only 24 when he started working. He told me that his dad showed such great power that he was inducted in right out of college. That being, Dmitri and Mr. Edwards became extremely close, with the added bonus of the Vaduva and Edwards families being close for centuries. When Craig was born a year later, Dmitri and Mr. Edwards were best friends and Dmitri was there for his birth. On the same day Dmitri was made Craig's godfather. He helped raise Craig and would babysit often at night and Craig saw Dmitri as a mixture of a big brother and a father figure.

When the Edwards decided to venture out and move to the Mortal Realm America when Craig was 5, Craig was very upset to be away from Dmitri and he wanted someone to be with him in America. So, Dmitri made the sacrifice to take this potion, made by a witch that was friends with Mrs. Edwards, that would reverse Dmitri's aging so he could be with and grow up with Craig in the Mortal Realm. While he is away his cousin, who was next in line, will take over his seat until he is of age at 25 again.

"Wait a minute... Does that mean he had to go through puberty twice?" Craig sits stunned by my question. I know of all the things that I could have asked as a follow up after that load of a story, that was my first question. But it is just where my mind landed.

"Yes, he did."

"Wow he must really love you for having to deal with puberty a second time, especially after all that time... If he loves and cares for you so much why did he seem like he hated you for years? He cut you off so quickly after black Friday."

"The hating thing for years was an act, much like most things we do. But him being mad at me after Black Friday was real. You guys are Dmitri's only non-family friends, other than my dad. You guys mean as much to him as his family and he asked for me to never mess with you guys. And when I got you and Nick to help me and then... you know. It genuinely angered him. If I wasn't his godson, he would have mangled me on the spot."

We sit in silence for a moment. He gives me time to digest all he told me. It explains why Dmitri is always willing to help Craig, and that he hangs around him often. It also explains why he would be a little pissed at him when he does dumb stuff. I would like to dive deeper into that, but I am willing to yield time for other pressing questions, such as the eating situation. "Why can he eat. Vampires drink blood only, correct?"

"Yes, but he isn't perfect. He is an imperfect vampire. Something that happens when one of your parents aren't vampire. Anabelle, his mom, she is a werewolf. Dmitri still needs blood to live and keep his high power but he is also able to eat meat and stuff. But he only does that to maintain his charade"

I am speechless and don't have much that I can think of. Finding all of this out about Dmitri was not something that I was expecting at the start of this day. I thought Craig and his family was the most I would have to be concerned about when it comes to the supernatural area.

"Do you feel comfortable?" Craig asks, cutting away from my thought. I nod, everything feels nice and balanced. It helps keep me calm and levelheaded about everything. "I'm glad. To be honest with you, I am using my powers to keep everything like this. It is actually pretty cold, the waves are loud, and the wind is nearly unbearable. But I wanted you to feel nice. I also immersed myself in it too."

I look around trying to find any signs that he is using his powers. Any kind of crack in the immersion. But nothing. Everything is seamless, until I look at him again. His eyes. They are that blue color again. I squint to make sure I wasn't losing it or seeing things. But that was his eye color, a deep indigo. "What the hell is going on with your eyes?" I ask in a low threatening tone.

He looks set back by my tone but I couldn't help it from coming out. I have a lot to worry about with unnatural things in my life. But I would prefer to not live in an on again off again illusion. I do believe that it has something to do with his eyes changing to that color.

"I'm a mentalist. It is an archetype that ambos can be. There are 4 types: Pyros, which my cousin is, your eyes are bright orange when you come of age or when you use your power. Brutes, which Erin is, her eyes are red, Creatives, which are the most rare type and the most powerful type. There have only been 5 in existence and Jimmy is the 5th, his eyes turn lilac. And then there are Mentalist, me, and my eyes turn indigo."

"Are these all rare things for ambos to have?" I push in an accusing tone.

He teeters his head scrunching his face up a bit. "Sort of. Ambos have been known to have these archetypes but it isn't extremely rare, but not common. The thing that makes my siblings, my cousin and I special is the fact is that we are of the late 20th century and we have these abilities. These normally have only occurred in the olden days or later in life by older ambos. That is why the council was holding me at such a high standard because they know of the great power I will have and hold in the Council one day."

The idea of this high-power Craig has is troubling to me. At first, I thought the power idea was kind of hot. Knowing and seeing the effects that he has at the school alone was a bit of an awe. But knowing what he can do, and not knowing all that he can do frightens me. I'm sure his powers, the mentalists powers are not used for good all the time. I'm afraid of what he might tell me. What if the fear is too great that I wouldn't want to be with him anymore? But I can't keep in ignorance. "What is it that you can do with the extra power."

I can tell he wants to answer me as much as I want to know. Yet, he does, and as I suspected the answer wasn't something I wanted to hear. He told me that a mentalist can drive someone to complete insanity so much so that it can often lead to death. They can take such control over ones mind they become like early iterations of zombies. They can emit a mental frequency that if powerful enough can literally cause someone's brain to explode. They have the ability to cast illusions that no one else can see and are so undisruptive to the surroundings that one could never know that they are in one. Such as the situation we are in now, and the one in his mom's car. But the illusions that are normally cast aren't as serene, but more so as putting your greatest fears in your daily life. They can easily slip into someone's mind and manipulate things without leaving a trace. The person wouldn't even be able to tell that something was wrong. Going into someone's memories is less painful when done by a mentalist, which explains why the pain from when Mr. Edwards did it, it was like torture and Craig's was some discomfort. The last thing he told me is that they can cast different auras on a person that will cause any emotion with ease.

"I only use my powers on you for good things. You must realize that. I would never dream of causing you any pain." His voice pleading as he lifts my chin so he can gaze into my eyes and I his. They are beautiful, his unnatural color. It's like two gems. Even more hypnotic than his natural color.

In an instant, I jump on top of him kissing him. Clearly it wasn't him who made me do this because as soon as I toppled him the illusion broke. He didn't seem to mind. I break away from him, tucking my blowing hair behind my ear. I bite my lip smiling down at him. "I'm sorry, I shouldn't have done that," he apologizes, as if he has something to apologize about.

"For what?" I giggle.

"I shouldn't have looked you in the eyes. When doing that it takes what ever action type feeling you are experiencing strongest and makes you act on it. I just wanted to be able to look at you. I'm sorry."

My smile drops and I rise up. I know he can't help it at times. That he wants us to be in a normal nice relationship but that isn't what we are going to be. It makes me kind of sad to think about. I get up and turn away from him trying to collect myself. I don't want to start to get emotional. Craig comes from behind me and wraps his arms in an embrace, resting his chin on my head and swaying us. "I will use my mentalists powers as little as possible on you. But you have to know, for me to protect you, I need to use my powers sometimes. It won't cause you any harm, I promise."

I turn around so I can look at him face to face; he looks genuine. No matter how much within me says to not fully trust him, for me to get through this, I have to. It is a scary thought to have, to put my full trust into the same type of creature that has been terrorizing me for so much of my life. That's not Craig though, I have to keep telling myself that he would never do me any harm.

Craig drove me back to my house after we discussed how and when we are going to approach Dmitri about all of this. He will undoubtedly be mad, so things would have to be handled delicately. I suggested that we wait until we have the whole team figured out. I am guessing once that is done we would have a whole plan so Dmitri wouldn't call us dumb or kill us on the spot. But the question on who would help us was still up in the air.

I didn't have the time to think on that today because I made the promise of going to the Grove with Josh and Lindsey. I enjoyed our time that we got to spend together. We spent way more than we should have and once our mom finds out she will be pissed at us. But if we slap on the idea of sibling bonding, she might go easy on us. Who knows?

I shouldn't have been surprised by the questions that came up about Craig. Josh's room is next door and can hear me on the phone sometimes. There were already suspicions after he came and picked us all up on Monday. I knew I couldn't hide it forever; I just didn't expect for them to be so observant of my life. Craig's initials are engraved into my arm; we are now forever connected. I suppose telling them that we're dating wouldn't be much of a crime.

It is more harmless telling them rather than my parents. Telling my parents will be followed by a bunch of questions that I don't want to answer. One of them will be about how concerned they are about me moving on so quickly. But with Lindsey and Josh it's just, "Does that mean he is gonna drive us to school? Or can he just drive me back? His Maserati is so sick," from Josh. And, "literally, that is so perfect. Maybe his brother will stop stalking me," from Lindsey.

I couldn't promise either. My guess is that Craig and I will be driving separately considering we both take our siblings to school. Except on Tuesdays and Thursdays when Craig has Jazz band after school. I told them that we could possibly ride with him then. The subject changed to what my friends think of him. It was no secret to anyone who was around us that Dmitri loathed Travis and Nick more so tolerated him. Cassidy got along with him but I could feel her being weary at times.

Josh practically idolizes Dmitri, he thinks he is the coolest person he has ever met so when he asked, I knew that Dmitri's opinion was the only one he cared about. Pandering to him I say, "Dmitri and Craig are actually super close. Their dads work together and were raised together. Nick and Cassidy like him too. They like him better than Travis." They go silent giving each other looks. I squint at them; I know what they are doing. They are talking crap about me via the *look*.

"Hey! You guys can speak up. Your facial expressions are very loud," I jab.

"Travis was a dickweed. I was so happy to hear you guys broke up. He was the dullest human being I have ever met," Josh says immediately.

Lindsey slaps his hand and scowls at him like our mom does to us. She is just turning into her little by little.

"He wasn't... *That*. But he was severely uninteresting and his parents were so rude to you. But he was good to you so I didn't want to say anything."

"I have been texting Lindsey separately for like a year so I could just talk about him," Josh reveals.

I sit stunned. I thought this whole time that the only person who had any beef with Travis was Dmitri. Turns out no one really cared for him. Why did they let me date him for so long without saying anything? Josh felt that this was his chance to get everything off his chest. He felt that Travis took a lot away from me, that I wasn't myself around him. The same thing Nick said. He took notice how these past few months I was getting back to who I am, and that I wasn't spending as much time with Travis.

Lindsey chimed in to stop Josh's endless ranting. Even though she is only in the 6th grade I swear she is years older than us sometimes. She switches the subject to my friends and Josh's friends. Both of us have had our core group of friends for years. Lindsey has had some issues. A lot of her *friends* have used her and taken advantage of her niceness. It is hard to see her go through that. "I'm glad you have Cassidy, Nick, and Dmitri. They have been rock solid with you for years and you guys would do anything for each other." Her voice somber.

Josh and I cheer her up very quickly, getting her mind off the topic. A part of me wants to go to the middle school part of the school and mess them up a bit, Josh wants to do the same but refuses to hit or belittle a girl. Josh tells her that the 6th graders are idiots and that she just has to hang with him and his friends and everything will fall into place.

We ended up getting back home at 9, we got some ice cream for dessert and lingered outside for a bit. Since I killed Aiden, things have been pretty quiet in Malibu. It's not going to stay that way for me, I don't doubt that one bit. Sitting out on our lawn got me thinking about the conversation we had over dinner about our friends. Lindsey is right, my friends and I are a strong hold when we are together. I already am going to have one of them on my side. Why not have the other two?

The Team

It's February 2nd, we spent the rest of January trying to plan. Seeing Dmitri at school was strange knowing what I know now. Thinking about how frustrating it must be to have to develop all the things you know, having to deal with having the mindset of a teenager; but knowing you have the capability to be so much more mature. That could explain why he is an asshole sometimes.

Every time I see him I just want to tell him what I know. But Craig says we have to handle things delicately. Craig comes over almost every day, usually later at night because of my gymnastics schedule. It ended up working out because Craig started to take saxophone lessons on Thursdays. So, whatever time isn't spent with me, at school, or with ambo training, he likes to practice. Within that time, he has been hanging out with Jude a lot. I was pleasantly surprised to find out that Jude was happy to help us. He said, "Dude, you're my best friend. Helps that I am bored, so a little trouble would be nice to get into. Also, Red is a boss, it'll be fun."

I didn't want to bring up to Craig my idea about having Nick and Cassidy help us. While he hid his stress pretty well, I can still tell this whole thing is getting to him. He would get silent and stare off into the distance. Such as now. For some reason I am awake and Craig teleported in my room to check if it was safe. He has been doing this for weeks to make sure that there is no one here. He has been actively practicing fortification so that he doesn't have to be near me to make sure that I am safe.

Chopped is on and we are snuggled up in my bed. I wish he could stay the whole night. I like warming up in his chest, feeling the gentle thumping of his heart. No matter if he is using his powers or not, I always feel relaxed like I have never been when we are like this.

"I feel like I could make it on here," Craig interrupts the silence between us.

"You cook?" I question, keeping my eyes on the T.V.

"Sort of. My Mom likes to show me a bunch of her recipes. I am trying to learn how, I have a pretty good grasp on Mortal Realm food, but preparing dishes that are eaten in the Immortal Realm is more complicated. You see, humans are simple creatures with simple recipes that their brains can comprehend," he jokes in a forced snooty tone.

I grab one of my pillows and smack him across the face with it. He tackles me and we start to play wrestle.

"I am stronger than you, I can take you down Edwards!" I grunt in-between giggles. I wiggle myself from his hold and pin him down. I know he let me do it, but I still feel triumphant. I get really close to his face, our noses touch. "Take that you ambo bitch," I taunt.

Craig gets a wicked glint in his eyes and in seconds I am sitting up on the bed pinned to the headboard. He is eye to eye with me, in a crawling stance. One hand is down on the bed in a fist for balance, while the other is around my waist. His eyes look intense, threatening.

"What are you gonna do, eat me?" I joke in a small voice. The moment feels right, but a large looming thought shreds through my mind. Trapped, scared, broken. I can hear the man's laughter and taunting words.

"I'm sorry," Craig apologizes in a whisper.

It snaps me out of my feeling. He looks soft and apologetic. He begins to back away a little. I cup his face and shake my head, "No, no don't. It's not your fault. I was having fun and then-"

"I scared you," he slumps down and rests his head in my lap. He doesn't know, he didn't look that far into my memories to know. Part of me wishes he had. I never talk about my rape. I try to push it as far back as possible. I hid from it, never owned up to the reality of it. Even after it happened, I just felt lost and dirty. I sat in my bath for 3 hours hugging my knees as my Mom comforted me and my Dad dealt with the legality of it. Turns out taking a bath wasn't the best decision to do. Made it difficult to prove my case. My parents didn't leave my side that night. I laid between them; my Mom held me all night and my Dad was right beside me not daring to close his eyes. I told my friends about it some months later and confessed immediately when Travis and I started dating. He always made me feel safe but would grow tired of me getting freaked out if we ever got too close to doing anything sexual.

But with Craig, it is different. He is an ambo, he is what attacked me, stole everything from me. But it wasn't Craig. It was some disgusting man who had a look so sinister that just from one look your skin would crawl. Craig isn't that. Craig would-

"I would never hurt you. I know I sound like a broken record, but you *know* that right?" Craig breaks me from my thoughts and paralysis.

"Hm?" I respond while I start to play with his hair.

"You look at me, sometimes, with all the fear in your heart. A lot of ambos aren't inherently evil creatures. We don't randomly kill or torture for fun. Well, not anymore. I am not like the one who kidnapped you or like Aiden."

Swiftly I slide down so I am lying next to him, eye to eye. I kiss him softly and quick.

"I know. I'm sorry it just takes some getting used to."

He presents a weak smile. I know he craves just for a small bit of normalcy. I do to, but that seems impossible. But this weird, having to watch over our backs isn't too bad when it is with him.

Things go silent again. I look at the clock and it's nearly 11:30. Craig has the same thing in mind and is already out of my bed.

"I'll see you in 1ˢᵗ period. Hopefully no sooner," his voice goes low at his last words. Paranoia has been surrounding us since we were summoned. Things were all too quiet. We give each other a parting look and then he is gone.

I am running through the secret passageway; it has been raining heavily causing these backways to have a mildew smell to it. The dark bricks only illuminated by the sparce candles; they drip with the slow trickle of rainwater. My dress drags behind me picking up slight trails of moisture. With each clack of my heels along the ground the closer I am to freedom. I can feel the brisk summer night air refreshing my lungs. The Palace has been suffocating. Everywhere I go he is there. He is my oldest, and pretty much my only friend; but life with him has become laborious. I could kill him, open Pandora's box. But would I grow to regret it?

"So, you want to kill me?" Rory.

I stop cold. Slowly I turn around to face him. Tired, beaten bloody, but something tells me that most of that blood is not his.

"Rory, you forget yourself," my voice trembles. A tremendous atmosphere of fear looms above. "I am your princess, you are simply-"

He breaks out in a booming cackle. Holding his side, he begins to morph. I stand and watch, unable to move or tear my eyes away. My head begins to pound as a growing ringing shatters through my ears.

"If you want to kill me Jezebel, kill me!" He cackles even louder. "You have done it once before. Ambo killer!" His voice

echoes in a continuous loop. Ambo killer, ambo killer. "Simple bullet through the head. Then dump me in the ocean!" A bullet wound appears on his head, the exact spot where Aiden's was.

The bricks crack, dust falling off them. I crouch down covering my head bracing for the collapse of the tunnel. Rory still laughing as his body starts to decay. He squats down and crawls after me until he is right in front of my face. There is a rancid smell of death mixed with the ocean. "What is a princess to do without her bodyguard? What are you going to do without your pistol?" He takes his cold, slimy finger and glides it down my neck to my chest. His nail sticking straight into my cleavage. "You're so pure, Jezebel." I quiver as I wait for what is going to happen to me. This isn't right, this all seems wrong. The ringing has become deafening.

The corridor opens back up, the bricks go back into place. The candles burn brighter making everything lighter and warm. I fiery pit grows in me and I rise up taking Rory by the neck. He gags as he struggles to claw me off of him but it doesn't help. He goes back to his normal self as confusion and fear strikes in his eye. "Vous ne valez rien," I spit at him, pinning him against the wall. With a sinister smirk I watch as he struggles to breathe.

"Jezebel!"

I jerk awake, a pair of pale blue eyes and a silhouette hovers inches over me. "Shh," he says quickly before I get the chance to scream. It causes me to go silent as if on command. It's just Craig.

Using his telekinetic powers, he turns on my nightstand light. The soft glow my light casts on his body is distracting. It's the first time I have seen him shirtless. I feel tempted to graze my hands along his chest and his abs. I almost didn't notice the fact that he is wearing sweatpants. Of course, he would be. His hair is disheveled but it looks cute. I try to find some words to say but I just lay there looking dumbfounded as I gawk at the boy in front of me.

"Jezebel," he snaps his fingers at me. I blink and smile at him, averting my gaze back to his face. "They came after you, that was not a normal dream."

What? I knew something was off. I rub my eyes and inch my way up into an almost sitting position. "Was that you? Were you the light, the warmth?" I ask my voice groggy from my first words. He nods, looking exhausted and a bit defeated. He pulls at his hair a bit before plopping back on my bed.

"We need a team. We need to start investigating. We have been waiting for them to do something and it finally happened," he groans in his hands. I feel like there is no better time than now to hit him with my plan.

"So, I have been thinking," I say hesitantly. Craig peaks his eye at me, intrigued. I hope he react semi well. "I was thinking that since we have Dmitri, and Jude, why not just enlist the help of Nick and Cassidy to complete the team," I fumble out their names quickly. Craig doesn't say anything, he remains dormant as if I never spoke a word. I so badly want to break the silence; he isn't even looking at me anymore.

Nervously I reach to pat him on the shoulder, he shoots up in an upright position before I get the chance. It startles me and I instantly recoil. He looks at me with cynical eyes. He isn't going for this.

"Jezebel, Jude is an ambo, Dmitri is a vampire, why on earth would we enlist the help of two humans to help us seek out a potentially dangerous supernatural group? What can they do that could possibly be of any good help? We don't need more human lives to worry about, one is enough." His voice condescending. How dare he? He has a lot on the line, I get it, but he is acting like I am some naive child who doesn't understand the severity of everything. My life is more on the line than his. He has the protection of being and Edwards, while I have to trust two teenagers who are still in training. Dmitri is the only safe bet and we don't even have him on board yet.

"You don't have to be so condescending about it. You don't have a better plan. I know your reputation is on the line and your life, but I am as good as dead if things don't work in our favor, so I am not just spitting out some hairbrained suggestion," I hiss at him.

His face softens. He fixes himself on my bed so he is sitting cross legged facing me. His eyes tired, he holds his lips in his mouth. My cue to speak. "Nick and Cassidy aren't as useless as you think."

"Oh?"

I ignore his patronizing behavior, "We need to do an investigation, not some type of battle royale. If we do need to fight, we have you, Jude, and Dmitri... And me, I killed one already,"

Craig sighs and rolls his eyes, preparing himself to say something that will be undoubtably demeaning. I put my finger up to stop him before he even gets the chance to speak. "Nick is my partner in crime when it comes to things like this. You saw how good we are together when we were trying to figure out Aiden. You know Nick is useful."

He agrees with me, he doesn't look pleased about it but at least he recognizes that I am right. I got one down.

"And Cassidy, isn't she against all this sleuthing stuff?" Craig counters.

He isn't wrong, she is. But she would have our backs if we needed her. "Cassidy, is a hacker."

Shock and disbelief set in Craig's face. It is a reaction that most people get when they find out Cassidy is like a computer whiz. She is great with coding and will most likely major in computer science in college or go into mechanical engineering. They always see her as a pretty face and a cheerleader. But she left cheerleading to focus more on coding and started looking into college prep physics classes.

"Cassidy Papakonstatinos is a hacker?"

I nod with a cocky grin, "A great one. We will most likely need to get into some phones, laptops, maybe security cameras..." I trail off getting distracted as Craig moves closer to me.

I hold my breath; he still smells incredible even after sleeping and sweating. "You smell so good," I exhale. I didn't mean to say that out loud, yet, every time I do. He nods and backs up.

"It's an ambo thing. Like a siren's voice," he mutters quickly. Clearly, he wants to move past it. Are sirens real too? I don't have time to dive into that.

Craig's eyes flicker to the clock on my dresser, I look with him. It's 3:50am. Definitely too early to be having this conversation. "Alright," Craig says breathily.

"Yeah? You'll let them join us?" I get excited. I can barely contain my smile. It feels like a huge weight has been lifted off of me knowing that I wouldn't have to lie to them. It's bad enough I have to keep this secret from my family.

He nods and gets off my bed to stand before me. "We can work out the details at school in," he looks at the clock again, "3 hours." He squeezes my hand to say goodbye. That's not gonna work for me, he looks too good right now. I pull him down to me wrapping my arms around his neck and kiss him. He pulls me deeper into him for a split second before pulling away. I wish he didn't.

"It's 4am Jezebel, we have school in 3 hours. Control yourself," he winks at me teasingly. Then he is gone.

I have never been more excited to get to school. As I was getting ready, I was thinking of the logistics on how we would tell them about the Immortal Realm, about Craig, Dmitri, and Jude, the whole trial, then finally ask for their help. Lunch couldn't have come sooner.

Walking to the lunchroom Craig holds my hand as he smiles and has quick quips with the people who pass. Everyone is always so engulfed in the allure of Craig. He says it is an internal magnetism that ambos have. The more powerful you are the stronger it is. It is annoying to deal with right now because I am trying to speak to him about the plan but every few seconds another person speaks to him. We are on a mission we don't have time for this. I feel like Nick, I get his frustrations now.

Fully annoyed and all out of patience I pull Craig along the hall faster so he doesn't have time to speak to anyone. He chuckles at me, "In a rush?"

I glare back at him, "Yes, god Craig, we are about to ask my friends to be a part of the most daring thing we have ever done! We need to talk logistics before they get to the table but we can't do that with you chit chatting and dazzling." I keep my fast pace as I charge into the lunchroom, I feel like a battery ram going through everybody.

I rush over to our table finally letting go of Craig's hand. He is still laughing at me, he takes things so lighthearted unless the danger is presented right before him.

"Is there something funny?"

"Yeah," he takes a seat next to me, "you acting like Nick right now. I see why you two work so well together," he teases. I know he read my mind, at least a little.

I squint at him. I will not respond to that right now. "How are we gonna present everything to them? Shall we just lay it all out right now?"

His eyes grow large in disbelief. "I know I have asked this before, but seriously, are you mad? No, we aren't going to tell your friends about everything right now in the middle of school!"

It is a bit risky I admit, but I think the method of ripping the band aid off is the best one to go for. It doesn't give them the chance to give little sounds of judgment in between or to clock out before the explanation is over.

"How did you tell Cassidy about our investigation and Aiden?" He questions, as if he has me in a corner. But he is wrong.

"I went to her house, we ate baklava and sweet potato pie, and then I blurted everything out to her at once," I say with pride. Taking some enjoyment with the displeasure in Craig's face.

He disregards my less than delicate approaches to breaking news and suggests that we instead invite them to hang out and let it naturally come about in conversation. A less straight forward method but it could work.

"We can invite them over for some tea and sandwiches," Craig proposes.

"Tea and sandwiches?" I question. Craig nods. "Oh, I'm terribly sorry, I didn't realize that we were going to be dining with the queen and discussing politics," I mock in a faux British accent.

"Bugger off! My parents have people over for tea and sandwiches when they need to make a deal or discuss things of a serious matter."

I fake pout at him and tease him a little more to get him to smile, it works. He playfully swats me away and takes a bite of his sandwich. "What do you suggest we invite them to then?" He makes sure to cover his mouth when he talks to be polite.

I take a moment to think on it. I know it can't be a movie night, even though it is Friday and it is what we normally do on a Friday night. Perhaps just a normal hang at one of our houses. I suggest it and Craig quickly agrees, to my surprise Jude is joining us for lunch. He plops down across from us with a huge grin. I can't be too rude to him now, considering the help he is giving us.

Nick arrives soon and communicates with me via looks about his confusion of Jude's presence. Since we started dating, we have been getting unwelcomed guest at our table whenever Craig joins us. So, for the most part Craig sits at his normal table so the crowd won't suffocate us. They are absent today; I think Craig used some ambo trick to keep them at bay.

Nick takes a seat next to Jude and puts on a big cheesy grin. Jude eats it up and tries to make conversation with Nick. Quickly saved by the conversation, Dmitri and Cassidy arrive with the same look of confusion on their faces.

"Why the hell are you here?" Dmitri doesn't hold back. Without even saying his name Jude knew he was talking to him. Looking a bit fearful but still with a dumb boyish grin he responds, "I was missin my boy!" he reaches over to slap Craig's arm.

"Then why don't you and *your boy* go sit at your table," Dmitri threatens taking a sip from his water bottle. I have never seen someone look so intimidating while drinking from a water bottle. I can't help but to think that there isn't water in there, but instead blood. But his teeth would be stained red, wouldn't it?

Jude laughs but there is a nervous energy behind it.

"Dmitri stop being so rude, Jude isn't hurting anyone," Cassidy interjects as she is opening a package of fruit snacks. Like clockwork she hands me one, knowing they are my favorites.

"He is hurting my energy. His frat boy vibes unaligned my chakras, spiritually, I will never be right," Dmitri responds. Nick jeers at Dmitri tossing a napkin at him. We laugh, even Dmitri, making Jude feel more relaxed.

Lunch carries on with normal conversations, somehow it shifted from countdown to Spring break, even though we just got back to school, to hardships in discrimination. I believe the connection started when they were talking about college and what colleges look at in terms of race and religion. Cassidy mentioned how she feels like she has to work twice as hard to seem equal to a white person who has done the same things she has so that she stands a chance; which is why she quit cheerleading so she can focus on an academic leg up. Nick chimed in saying that just dealing with the ignorance of everyday people gets too much for him at times. Because he has "prominent Jewish features" people are quick to describe him as the Jew or say willfully ignorant things to him. Cassidy experiences the same thing, being called the mixed chick or stereotypical "black names" and ignorant comments. Unfortunately, it would happen in cheer sometimes.

"I get ignorant comments all the time when people find out I am Apalachee," Dmitri chimes in. We nod in agreement, we have heard it throughout the years, it is very frustrating to him because they try to challenge him on his heritage.

"What is Apalachee?" Jude asks, lost.

"It's a Native American tribe and people," Craig responds. I can tell he is hoping Jude will hold his tongue on any ignorant responses.

"You're Native American? You don't look it at all. I guess you have the cheek bones for it," Jude says exactly what Craig was hoping he wouldn't.

We hold our breath hoping that Dmitri won't rip his jugular out. It would be entertaining to watch Jude be put in his place but we already caused a scene in January with Travis.

"Get your friend," Dmitri growls at Craig.

On cue Jude says, "You know I think I will go back to our table, gotta appease the crowd," he gathers his lunch and chuckles nervously.

The air clears and Dmitri starts to go on a rant about what happened, with some added dramatics and animations by Nick. Dmitri raised his hand in the air and flicked Jude off from afar. Cassidy tried to warn him against making a scene, but of course Dmitri challenges her and gets louder. It makes the boys laugh. It was funny I have to admit, Cassidy is starting to break but just groans and puts on her sunglasses like a celebrity incognito.

"I am not with you guys," she says trying her best to hide her smile. She fails and breaks out in laughter.

Craig slips his hand on my thigh and squeezes it lightly. I get goose bumps. As always Craig is not giving any indication that he is doing anything. He reaches into his bag of chips then leans into me.

"We should ask them now," he whispers. He puts two chips in his mouth and raises his eyebrows.

It is perfect timing; everyone is in a good mood. It would seem natural to ask about weekend plans. I take a swig of water and plan my next words carefully. "So, guys, what do you have planned for this weekend?"

"I am glad you asked," Cassidy chirps immediately "because I have been dying to hang out. We hadn't really hung out much since... Black Friday." The word almost sounded like a curse. Craig's party, the extra credit project, and Black Friday are things we don't bring up. If we do, it is as if the air goes cold as soon as the words escape our lips. The Black Friday incident has an extra eerie feeling, because Cassidy and Nick are in the dark of why it went south. I know they felt confused when Craig and I got together without having any clarity as to what happened between us in the first place.

Despite one of the unholy trinities being mentioned Dmitri and Nick were in agreement about wanting to hang out. Nick said that we need to properly induct Craig into our group. Both Craig and I are pleased with how smooth things were going. Not even an interjection from Dmitri. He was all on board with the whole idea. He even suggested that we hang out tonight.

"My house is free, no one is coming over and at least two of my brothers will be out the house," Cassidy offers. "Oo, I can make some mac and cheese for us!"

"I can bring a rotisserie chicken," Nick chimes in.

Dmitri looks at them confused, so does Craig. "Why are you guys 40? Why not a pizza maybe some wings and chips?" Dmitri criticizes. I personally am not opposed to the chicken and mac; I could ask my Dad to make some roasted red potatoes.

"Now, now... don't down the idea of the chicken and mac. I can bring some potatoes to the mix."

Cassidy and Nick exclaim in excitement. Craig and Dmitri laugh at us but agree to it. It could be like a nice dinner party. It could have that professional feel that Craig was thinking of earlier. I guess now, I have no room to judge his tea and sandwiches since we are making a full dinner to just hang out.

We agreed to meet at Cassidy's at 5. It didn't give me much time or warning for my Dad to make the potatoes. He also found the request odd but went along with it. He was just happy to see that I was going to hang out with them again.

Craig came and picked me up, I still haven't gotten around to telling my parents. It feels wrong but I feel after we get the team together, I will feel more at ease to tell them about our relationship. On the way to Cassidy's we discussed how we would bring it up to them. I suggested that once we start eating, we go with the classic line of, "I know you are all wondering why we have gathered here today." Craig thought it was a good theatrical approach but still wanted things to be more delicate. His word of the week. He believes that we should send Nick and Cassidy to go and do something in another room while we talk to Dmitri first because he will be the toughest to deal with. We arrive at Cassidy's house purposefully a little late. We wanted to give them time to loosen up before we arrived to drop the gauntlet. Craig said he will be in their heads the whole time to see where their minds are going in the event that it starts to go south, he would be able to recover the situation.

"You have a lot of big brain power when you want to use it you know? I don't know why you don't apply it all the time. Such as the night at the club. Taking a drink from a stranger at a bar, tsk tsk tsk. Sometimes it is just beauty and no brains," I say while checking my nails, sliding a sly look at him.

"Well thank god I had my big, strong, gun totin', American by my side to protect me," he says raising his voice to sound like a girl. He pulls me in by the back of my neck. "suga, I don't know what I would do without you," he changes to a southern belle accent as he flutters his eye lashes and kisses me. I push him off and giggle. Craig cuts the engine and we head inside. I am so excited, I hope it goes well.

The night couldn't have been more perfect. We immediately started eating, having a stomach full of good food puts everyone in a good mood. We moved the operation to Cassidy's room where we started to play some card games. Normally uno would end in some slight hatred amongst friends but that even felt lighthearted. I am currently looking like the winner but I have a strong feeling I am about to be betrayed. I know Nick has been cooking something up, him and Dmitri are in cahoots and I refuse to believe anything else. I tried to get Cassidy to start an alliance with me but I had her draw four and she is still kind of salty about it. I do believe that Craig has been going easy on me.

"I know you have some heat in that hand Edwards. You have been playing chump cards all game," Dmitri gestures at him.

"You can't let her win just because you guys be smoochin!" Nick jeers. Cassidy eggs them on. They are just jealous of my superior uno skills. I usually win.

I cut a glare at Craig; he matches me. He gives me a mischievous, sexy smirk. He puts down a draw 4 then changes the color to blue, which I so happen to not have and only pick up one in my 4. Cassidy plays a blue 5 but Dmitri throws down a draw 2. To everyone's luck we are stacking.

"Nope! You are not getting me," Nick says slamming down another draw 2 bringing the number up to four.

Craig glances at his cards with his fingers dancing over them. "So sorry darling," he says with fake sympathy.

I shake my head at him as he puts down a red draw 2 causing me to draw 6.

The rounds continue with more betrayals some not pointed towards me. But I am still no longer the one who is winning. Cassidy managed to slip in, she has one card left but I have few tricks up my sleeve. Nick and Dmitri put down normal cards. I have my handset for me to put down my skip. But as I look at the deck again, I see a skip already put down. I shoot a look of utter betrayal at Craig.

Cassidy exclaims in excitement putting down her last card. Everyone is happy for her, she normally wins the least. I flick Craig off but he grabs me and pulls me into a hug and tells me to not be a sore loser.

"We should do it now," Craig whispers in my ear still holding me. I look up at him and nod.

"Well once you are done gloating," I say with fake saltiness. Cassidy sticks her tongue out at me. "can we get some ice cream?"

She agrees enthusiastically. Being the super host that she is, I knew that she wouldn't ask for us to get the ice cream ourselves even if we offer. And Nick, wanting to do as much as he can to impress her, offers to help without me having to push him.

As Cassidy scampers out her room with Nick following close behind it is our time to strike. Craig and Dmitri are talking and laughing but I can't wait anymore. I have been keeping this in for weeks.

"Alright, cut the crap Dmitri I know you are a vampire," I blurt out. Both of them look at me in utter shock. "I know your family is the most powerful vampires and I know about your de-aging and the fact that you are Craig's godfather."

"What. The. Fuck," Dmitri says dryly. If looks could cut Craig would be completely eviscerated right now. "Why would you tell her that? Sharing what you are and your family business was your idiotic decision. Who in the hell gave you the right to out me?!"

"Dmitri, I had no choice but to tell her. We were summoned and we needed help. My Dad told me to enlist your help and demanded that I tell her about you. I fought against it."

Dmitri looks slightly softer but still red with intense fury. This could go either way; I wouldn't count out a bloody mess happening within seconds.

"I believe you, that sounds like some bull Charles would pull. I don't blame you." Craig and I both exchange shocked looks. I was not expecting that from him at all. I thought he would deny until the sun came up, threaten Craig's life, or storm out the house.

"So, are you going to help us?" Craig asks cautiously.

"Of course. Whatever it is I will help you. You're my godson and Belle is my best friend. No matter the stupid thing you guys got yourself into, I got your backs. Also, the Council is always on some bullshit when it comes to human affairs."

Craig tries to interject. Probably to tell him that the Council isn't the threat but feeling giddy I bounce on my toes and clap. "I am so happy, thank you, thank you, thank you." I launch myself at him and hug him tightly. His body is so solid, I nearly broke some bones in my face slamming into him. I can hear Cassidy and Nick returning and I quickly break away and act as if nothing happened.

They come walking in with two trays of ice cream. The group favorite, Neapolitan. You get a solid 3 for 1. We all take a bowl and thank Cassidy. As we eat, I wonder about Dmitri. I know Craig can enjoy sweets but I wonder if ice cream is even appetizing to Dmitri. I have seen him eat it with us multiple times but it could have been like Craig said that when he eats food it is more of a formality.

I know I can't handle things how I did with Dmitri; it needs to be a slow introduction. But none of the conversations we have been having would lead to it. Naturally, Craig takes over the conversation to sway it over to our favor. "Hanging out with you guys is a stark difference from when I am hanging with my friends. I actually enjoyed myself 100% of the time without having to get blazed."

Cassidy flips her hair behind her shoulder, clearly taking pride in his words. "And you are a wonderful addition to our group."

"No lie, it gives us an extra wall of immunity since we have thee Craig Edwards hanging around with us," Nick says with his mouth full of ice cream. Cassidy punches his thigh. "What, it's the truth!" Nick exclaims.

He isn't wrong, there has been more people paying attention to us and being super friendly this past month because of our connection with Craig. I know the rest of the Elites hate it, minus Jude. Cassidy has been enjoying it but plays it cool in front of Craig, she is still somewhat starstruck and wants to impress him.

Craig laughs it off, "I do have to admit, there was an agenda about wanting to hang out today." He takes my hand for support. "Jezebel and I have something we need to tell you." He hides his nerves behind his confident smile and smooth voice but from the grip he has on my hand I know he is not ready to speak his next words. Cassidy and Nick also look not ready, going off by the way he phrased everything and is holding my hand, they are probably thinking pregnancy or something as such.

After taking a deep breath, Craig slowly and carefully explains everything to them. They hang on every word and with every new detail Cassidy looks even more confused and a little disgusted while Nick looks completely astounded. Dmitri didn't know what he agreed to help us with and was equally shocked as Cassidy and Nick when Craig explained. As Craig reaches the detail about Dmitri, they both turn and look at him in utter shock, probably going through an inner monologue that mirrors my words and thoughts when I found out.

"We need a team; we have Jude and Dmitri on board and Jez-"

"I want you guys to help us, I want you guys to be a part of this portion of my life. I couldn't just go around lying to you, I have to do that with my family and I couldn't handle doing that to you guys too. It kills me not being able to let my family in on any of this, I need you guys. It is like an investigation like Craig said, it won't be like when we did the extra credit project. The moment it gets to that point you guys are out, we wouldn't put you in danger like that."

I bit my bottom lip darting my eyes back and forth between the two waiting for their reaction, some kind of indicator of what they thought of all of this, about helping us. But it is silent, their faces hold in the same look of I can't believe what I just heard.

"Holy shit!" Cassidy yells.

"Cassidy Pandora! What did you just say?" Mrs. Papakonstatinos calls from the next room in a threatening voice instantly after Cassidy's exclamation.

"Mama that wasn't me, that was Jezzi!" I mouth "what" at her with a sharp stare.

"She will beat my ass, take this one for me," she grits in a whisper.

I shake my head and call out, "Sorry Mrs. P, I'll watch my mouth!" Dmitri snickers at the scene but quickly stops as Cassidy shoots daggers at him.

"So, you're the same creature the Malibu Beast is? Yet you sent us on a wild goose hunt just to figure out his name. Even though you have these all-powerful telepathic powers?" Nick finally speaks up.

Craig hangs his head in shame then looks back up at him. "I needed a source; I didn't even know where to look. But you and Jezebel seemed to have a good start.

Nick is pleased with his answer and doesn't say anything else.

Cassidy didn't hold her tongue but started to grill Dmitri on him lying to us for years and trying to figure out logically how he can be a vampire. Dmitri counters her by saying he didn't lie, that we never asked in the first place. And he explained his aging down in more detail than what Craig told them and explained how now in the

Immortal Realm there is vampiric sunscreen that he douses himself in so he can survive out here. That bit I did not know.

Cassidy then grilled Craig to which Nick joined in on. Craig replied to their liking with each new question. They looked more at ease with every answer because it revealed how harmless Craig is to them and is more of a powerful ally.

"This is insane. But I am down to help. Hell, I was already somewhat a part of it in the beginning," Nick says.

We look to Cassidy, but she looks less than happy to comply. She looks scared almost. I don't blame her. "I didn't want to do the extra credit project. I had nightmares and was afraid for my life after that." This is a big ask and I can't expect her to be cool with doing this, even if we tell her that we will keep her safe, anything can happen. And she has every right to not want to be a part of this. But that means Craig will wipe her memory and I don't want that.

"I know, having been the one that it attacked and everything else following that day, and that you have probably been living a nightmare Jezzi," she says as she scoots closer to me and then hugs me deep. I drop my hand from Craig and embrace her, it almost makes me start to instantly cry. "If being a part of this team can help your life be just a touch less nightmarish, for you to have some freaking peace. I'm in."

I knew that I could count on them. While Cassidy and I are still cuddled up I look around at everyone. This is our team, minus one. I should feel all of the confidence in the world like I was this morning, but something settles in me that feels... off.

The Seer

Telling everyone about the plan went way better than I expected. Dmitri and Cassidy's responses really shocked me. They do seem the most apprehensive about it. Craig suggested that I give them, Nick and Cassidy, time to fully digest everything. But I didn't listen. Over the next week Nick, Cassidy and I have been meeting at Nick's house so that I could fill them in on all the details that I knew.

"None of this makes sense. None of it. How are you okay with any of this stuff?" Cassidy questions. She awaits my answer, Nick isn't paying attention to us; he is too busy going over all his notes. The truth is, that I'm not. I'm not okay with any of this. But I know saying that isn't the most reassuring. But what am I supposed to say?

"I'm not necessarily okay with it, I've more so accepted it for what it is." She gives me a skeptical nod, unimpressed with my answer. "It is what it is, Cas. I can't change it." She groans and looks back at the books that I convinced Craig to let me borrow. Nick is still buried in his notes. He is the only one of us who was excited about the whole thing. He has always wanted this world to be real, and now he has his wish.

"Jez, this is all so amazing," he mumbles still not taking his eyes away from his focus.

"You shouldn't have to accept this reality," Cassidy grumbles under her breath. I roll my eyes. If she knew that she was going to be like this, frankly, I don't know why she agreed to join.

"I know this Cassi, but even if Craig wasn't in my life I would still have to put up with it. I invited you to join the team because I thought you would have been supportive about it."

"It is a hard pill to swallow, Jez," she responds coldly.

She is right on that, I didn't really have the right to be frustrated with her, it's pretty much how I reacted after the court case. She is new to all of this, she isn't Nick. I apologize to her for my short tones. Reluctantly she accepts and keeps reading.

Seconds later Nick's door opens and in walks Dmitri. His hair is damp and in a bun. There is still a faint smell of chlorine. What is he doing here? I try to gather the books that I have around me. He wasn't supposed to be here. What if he tells Craig? Nick slams his notebook down and grins wide.

"Well if it isn't our resident vampire!"

Dmitri mocks him and takes a seat next to him. Cassidy and I share in a confused glance. Nick seems to be the only one aware that he was coming. Nick can never keep his mouth shut, can he?

Dmitri catches the confused looks of me and Cassidy. "Nick texted me and asked for me to come over. Said you guys needed help." Nick smiles at us as if he just did us a huge favor. Quite the opposite. Cassidy slides the book she was reading over to me. I try to slyly slip it into my pile of books that I am keeping hidden. Yet, Dmitri still catches it.

"Is that Folklorika? Edwards let you borrow their copy?" He asks leaning over to examine the book. "Much better shape than mine."

Cassidy stays quiet and looks at me nervously. I don't know what to say. Why did Nick do this?

"So, what's up with the cold shoulder? This is why I didn't want you guys knowing about the supernatural world and me. I'm still the same Dmitri. You guys just now know that I drink blood and am technically dead," he says so nonchalant. It makes Nick laugh. I have to say something.

"Can you not tell Craig about this?" I ask in an almost whisper.

Dmitri sucks his teeth. "Bitch, I'm not a snitch! Besides do you think I am so concerned over what Craig thinks? I am his superior, he listens to me."

Well damn. Cassidy and I relax our tension. It is as if I can breathe again. I might have been holding my breath since he walked in the room. It's good to know that Dmitri is the "adult" in this situation. Craig means a lot to me, I like him a lot and he is definitely the brains in our relationship, but when it comes to high pressure related thinking, Dmitri would be the guy for that. Even when we got attacked and none of us could think straight Dmitri was quick with a cover up.

"Why don't you want Craig to know anyway?"

"He didn't want us deep diving into the details of the Immortal Realm because he is afraid of the Council," I answer honestly.

Dmitri laughs, we look at him baffled. Is he not worried? He didn't want me with Craig for my safety, but now he is laughing about Craig fearing the Council?

"I swear, the Edwards, no matter how big and bad, will remain paranoid," he says catching his breath. I'm not following.

"What are you talking about?" Cassidy pipes up.

Dmitri remains unbothered and shrugs at us, "You guys already know about the Immortal Realm, things that are kept secret are most definitely not in a book. That takes some digging in the Immortal Realm, which you guys aren't doing."

But we *will be* digging in the Immortal Realm, aren't we? Dmitri's lack of concern about the Council troubles me. I mean he worked for them for years, he would know better but Mr. Edwards seemed so worried about our safety. However, Craig called me and told me his dad was significantly less stressed about the situation, knowing that Dmitri was on board. Still, I wonder.

I pull out my phone and text Craig

Hey, Dmitri said that we don't need to worry that much about the Council. Since we already know about the realm. And that we aren't digging for secrets. As far as me, Cassidy, and Nick learning about the IR

I put my phone down beside me and tune into the conversation that is going on. I feel like I have missed a significant point because Dmitri is talking about killing people. It shouldn't come as a shock; I mean he is a vampire but hearing him talk about him draining someone or doing little feedings. Apparently, it is true about vampires being able to compel people. He speaks so candidly about how he has done it to people so that he is able to get a meal and have them forget about it.

Cassidy asks him if he does it often, if he is blood thirsty. This makes him chuckle, "In my younger days, yes. By the time the 19th century rolled around I wasn't as blood thirsty as before. I obviously still hunt but I'm not as wild as I had been," he reminisces with a smile. That is so disturbing. There isn't an ounce of regret in his voice. He is basically saying that his blood thirsty ways calmed down with age but he looks back fondly at his times as a murderer. Good to know.

"Can we see your fangs?" Nick asks, which I know he has been dying to let out since everything was revealed to him. Cassidy shakes her head. I'm guessing hearing what he just said, seeing his murder weapons of choice is the last thing on her list. But as soon as Nick asks Dmitri opens his mouth and shows them, two sharp pearly white fangs. They don't appear that threatening, somehow it adds to his attractiveness. I see why it is a stereotype of vampires posing that feeling of a daunting threat but you can't help but be drawn to them. And when they show their fangs it is scary but electrifying.

Nick leans closer to him with his finger going towards one of them. "Can I touch it?" he asks inches away. Dmitri swats his hands and retracts his fangs. "Get the hell away from me, creep." Dmitri and Nick share in a laugh while Cassidy still looks a bit uneasy. Dmitri notices and comes next to her and toys with her until he can get her to smile.

My ringer goes off full volume, startling all of us. Crap, I must have accidently turned it up. And like a fool I left my phone facing upward, so everyone saw that Craig was calling. I didn't think he was gonna call he said he was in training and then was gonna practice.

"Jesus Belle, mute the damn thing or pick it up!" Dmitri exclaims.

God, I don't want to answer this phone right now. I reluctantly slide to answer and put it to my ear.

"Hello"

"Hey, what are you talking about with Dmitri? I don't see anything in the group chat about that. Are you with him?" We formed a group chat with the whole team so we can easily communicate.

"I, uh"

"Hey Craig!" Nick calls. I shoot him a glare as I put my finger to my lips to hush him.

"Is that Nick, are you guys all together discussing things?"

I stumble to find words and keep making short sounds to try to piece a sentence together.

"He is not supposed to know, Nick!" Cassidy hisses. And of course, Craig picks up on that too. I should have just ignored the call but then that would have been even more suspicious. I can hear Craig going off on his end about me going behind his back as Nick and Cassidy go back and forth with each other. Nick is going on about the good of the team while Cassidy is talking about loyalty to me. I stare blankly ahead not knowing what to do. I feel like I just messed something up. It feels like a bad omen almost. I'll be the death of us all.

My phone slips out of my loose grip, I look to my left to see it is Dmitri slipping it away from me, I don't tighten up my grip to resist.

"May I?" he asks, his tone as sweet as artificial sweetener. He seems to have just asked as a formality because no matter my answer I do believe he would have taken the phone anyway. He puts the phone on speaker.

"Well hello, hello," he says loud enough to cut the mini argument between Nick and Cassidy.

"What are you guys doing!?" Craig sounds furious, it puts a pit in my stomach.

Dmitri plays with him for a bit, in a way an older brother would pester their younger sibling. I can tell with each growing second Craig was becoming more frustrated with the lack of answers, while Dmitri was having fun.

I snatch the phone from him to put an end to this. Dmitri is still laughing at his own amusement. Upon hearing my voice Craig loses some of the spice he had with Dmitri.

"Jezebel, what is going on? My first question has still not been answered. What were you talking about with Dmitri? What he say== to you guys?"

"You snitch!" Nick spits

"You're the one to talk! Look who is here with us!" I spit back gesturing at Dmitri.

"Where are you guys?"

"My house"

"Where at your house?"

Nick looks confused, "My room?"

Craig hangs up and in a millisecond, he is standing in front of us. Cassidy lets out a quick startled yelp and covers her mouth. Nick jumps back, "woah!" =*

Craig looks pissed as he notices the room, with all the notes and the books, he knows exactly what was happening. I can feel a bit of his trust being tested with me. I feel bad but it felt like the right thing to do. I suppose if I explained things to Craig, he would have been okay with me doing this. He hasn't been controlling or demanding.

Dmitri smiles at him but Craig does not match one back. He walks over to me; with each step he takes I feel his shadow casting down and I feel smaller. But he sits on the ground next to me so we are leveled. "Why are you going behind my back?" His voice almost sounds hurt. I shake my head and shrug. "just read me," I say weakly. Soft enough for only him to hear.

"Jezebel, I see what you were trying to do. I get it but you need to tell me when you're diving into the supernatural." I nod at him, and he pulls me close. He reads my fear. He knows I want to over prepare as much as we legally can, not based on strategy but on the fear of losing my friends, Craig, and my own life. One slip up or one misunderstanding and it's gone. We have been reading up on things for a week without taking action. It is driving me nuts.

"So, you can teleport wherever you want, just like that? No wind, no sound, just poof. You're here?" Cassidy asks. Her tone is genuinely curious. For a second, I forgot that Nick, Cassidy, and Dmitri were even in here. I think Craig did too. But he responded to her, letting her know the answer is yes. I expected her to give a sarcastic great but she just nods. She fears this whole supernatural world but for some reason she feels no threat with Craig. Maybe because of who he is, because she has never seen him in beast form. We all know what he is capable of but it doesn't seem possible.

She has been looking at Dmitri weirdly whenever she sees him eat, much like I did. Since we all know that it is all for show. But he just has to speak and she snaps out of her funk, it makes her realize that he is still the same guy we have been friends with for years.

Nick on the other hand looks a bit disturbed by the fact that Craig is so seamless in his supernatural ways. I think he is used to the idea of supernatural creatures having some sort of tell, that if you look hard enough you can see. But ambos, they are designed for this very thing, of hiding in plain sight. And I get him being unsure about it, because I am on his side with that.

"So, why are you and your dad being babies about the Council? You are just doing what they said for you to do. Nick and Cas gotta know book level information about the realm if they are gonna be of any help," Dmitri asks.

Craig didn't tell him the full truth; he is so good at doing that. We didn't tell any of them, not even Jude the full truth. Craig found that for us to be able to truly hunt this group down we will need to dive into some underground secrets of the Realm. These guys aren't operating on surface level. So, this already dangerous mission has become a double edge sword. Not only do we have to worry about this rebel group but also the Council.

Dmitri isn't liking the silence. Neither is Cassidy. Nick just seems like Nick. He has a smirk on his face. He knows that we are hiding something and is just dying to hear the bomb drop.

"This mission is going to be more complicated than we thought," Craig finally speaks up.

"In what way?" Dmitri asks, giving him the same looks Mr. Edwards was giving him in his office.

"Craig says that we have to look into some underground stuff to really get a hold of this group. So, we have to go beyond what we were permitted to do by the Council. That's why I was keeping things hush hush when having these little educational meetings with Nick and Cassidy," I blurt out before Craig has a way to beat around the bush.

I don't want to talk us out of getting a harsher sentence from my friends, I would just rather lay everything out on the table."

"Oh my god, Jez, no way!"

"Jezzi! You didn't mention that we would be going rogue! Now we are true outlaws. Outlaws of a realm I haven't even been in!"

"I want to murder you both, you guys are idiots! Are you kidding me?! If the Council catches a whiff of what we are doing... Craig that is treason."

Hearing those words made the pit in my stomach grow even larger. I knew this was bad but I didn't think it was treason. This brings a cold air to the whole room. Nick no longer looks excited and Cassidy looks so worried that she might cry. They know from the readings I gave them what the punishment for treason is for humans. Certain death. The stakes were already high but now I feel like we are digging our own graves and have one foot inside it.

"I didn't think it would go that deep but the fact that they have evaded the Council for so long makes me believe that they are operating under something so secret that we have no choice. Look, I'm scared too. I don't even know where to properly begin to start the search," Craig confesses.

We go silent, the room, the whole house is dead. No house settling noises, no sound from the wind, no footsteps of Nick's family even though they are all home. It's like an isolation ward. A quiet padded room left for us to only have our thoughts to go mad thinking of possibilities. What may come, what is already happening without our knowledge, what we know, what we don't. Soon nothing starts to make sense.

"What about a seer?" Cassidy peeps, her voice unsure.

Nick snaps and agrees, "Yes, a seer! It said in one of those books that they can see beyond what the person even knows. They can see the past, present, and future."

"A seer just needs a subject. They can probably tell us what we need to know about the rebels. Just the smallest hint. Jezebel, since the both of us touched Aiden either one of us could be used. This is brilliant! I don't know why I didn't think of one," Craig says looking grateful at them for the suggestion. They both look proud in themselves for being able to give that small bit of help.

"So, do we know a seer?" Nick asks.

Craig has a sly smile on his face as he turns to Dmitri.

"Dmitri?" I ask. I hope he isn't a seer, why would he need to be an apex predator who happens to be the 3rd most powerful in the world and a seer. That's too much.

Dmitri shakes his head, "No, no we are not using her. We aren't dragging my family into this. They don't want to be bothered by matters of the Council." Well at least it isn't him, but still not a great thing that it is another powerful vampire who is a seer.

"We need her, Dmitri," Craig pleads.

Dmitri groans and sighs, he stands up with his hands outstretched for someone to take. Craig smiles and takes hold of his right hand. The rest of us look at each other puzzled but follows along. I take Craig's, Nick takes mine, and Cassidy takes Dmitri's and Nick, we form a little circle in the center of the room.

"Sick, so are we gonna go to Romania?" Nick asks.

"Nope... Florida," Craig says excited.

It clicks, we aren't going to the vampires. We are going to the werewolves.

"Motalis ut Immortalis," Craig says clear and quick.

Just like getting to the Council we are warped through time and space for a few seconds before we hit the ground. We are standing in a grassy field; it is warm with a bit of humidity. Nick stands off to the side to catch his bearings.

"What the hell was that?!" Cassidy asks looking around mortified.

"We are in Immortal Realm Florida," Craig explains, his hands on his hips as he looks around.

Dmitri looks like he is going to be sick, you can tell that this is the last place that he wants to be. Everything seems normal around us, to what I assume. I have never actually been to Florida. I've seen things in movies or on the internet. It is warmer here than it is in Malibu, I can tell you that much. I like it now in February, but if this was Summer, I know I would absolutely hate it.

I look behind me and see a house in the not so far distance. It is a good size, not too large and gawdy like you would see with a lot of LA homes, I'm sure they have some like that here as well. There are palm trees that are carefully placed surrounded by beautifully matched shrubbery and flowers. The house is a soft sandy beige with enough wide windows that it would allow for the best rays of natural light. But the windows are covered by thick drapes that block any means of entrance. Even by the patio door, shut and blocked. They don't want to be bothered or to be seen.

"What was that?" Cassidy asks looking around frantic. I didn't hear anything. I open my ears to try to search for the sound she heard.

I think I can hear some rustling opposite of the house. It is very faint though.

We start to look around, see what we can see. But the land, it looks void of anyone or anything. Just then I hear giggling. I have heard this before But I cannot pinpoint from where I have heard it.

"We need to go. Now!" Craig calls. He begins to take off running and grabs hold of my hand. My friends follow, things feeling a little too familiar.

The rustling is no longer a faint thing in the distance but footsteps, multiple footsteps, charging in our direction. I manage to keep up with Craig, but he is pulling me a fraction.

"Don't you have super speed?!" Nick yells to Dmitri, extremely out of breath.

"Yeah, but that wouldn't be too fair."

"Dude let me piggyback, I'm dying!" Dmitri and Nick stop for a second as Nick hops on his back. Dmitri moves so quickly over to Cassidy I didn't even see him take the steps. In one swift motion he picks her up and holds her in his arms and in a blink, he is gone. But so are me and Craig.

We are suddenly standing at the front of the house. Vampire super speed and ambo teleportation, I wish we had this back in October, perhaps I wouldn't have almost died. Dmitri already has Cassidy back on her feet and Nick is jumping down. Cassidy looks at me and we share the same look.

"Are you thinking what I'm thinking?" I ask.

"October?"

I nod, we share in a relieved smile from making it out of there, I feel kind of exhilarated as well. That rush of adrenaline is coming back to me. It is a good and bad thing. I think it is the first time Cassidy is feeling it. I think Nick has been feeling it since last Friday.

Dmitri franticly rings the doorbell and knocks so hard I think he is going to go through the door.

"Whose house is this anyway?" I ask Craig, he is looking around to see if anything else is coming.

"Chepi," he says breathlessly.

My stomach drops. I never thought I was going to have to see that woman again. I thought she was going to eat me the last time I saw her. And now that I know she is a werewolf my odds of being her dessert seem even greater.

"Who is Chepi to you?" Cassidy asks.

"My aunt who I know is in there and better open this goddamn door!" Dmitri pounds louder.

The doorknob twists and I instinctively grab hold of Craig's hand, he squeezes back.

"Will you relax! This is why I got my house fortified with material so strong that not even a vampire can break it down," Chepi says scowling at Dmitri.

She is wearing a long emerald green silk kimono robe that has accent Japanese blossoms on it. Her hair is in a ponytail. It gives the illusion that she just woke up but she looks so put together in the face.

Dmitri pushes past her and barges into the house.

"Welcome," she snaps letting the rest of us in the house.

I take back what I said about the lack of flaunting of wealth. This home's interior says otherwise. It isn't like the homes in Malibu but instead it is like you just stepped into a luxury villa that is giving you a "Native American experience". The difference is that her stuff is 100% real and not tacky, it looks tasteful and elegant, full of culture, and pride.

"A hunt is happening by the way. If you didn't open this door they most definitely would have smelled my friends' blood," Dmitri calls from the kitchen as he raids her refrigerator.

"My favorite nephew what do I owe this pleasure? Did you bring me some snacks?" She drapes herself across her couch and looks back at us with a wicked glint. Please not this again. I hug myself as close to Craig as possible.

She tilts her head and examines all of us one by one. It's like a snake sizing up their pray. She clicks her tongue, "Craigie, you two are together? Tsk tsk tsk, you have been letting my nephew's bad influence run off on you. I never pegged you as a boy who would dabble in such taboo."

"First of all, I advised against them dating so don't put me in that. Second that is a lie, I am not your favorite nephew, Lee is," Dmitri says coming back downing a red drink, blood.

"Now what makes you say that?" She pouts in fake curiosity.

"He is practically your son."

"He is an orphan Demetrius, what was I supposed to do, I would have been a terrible aunt if I did nothing."

Chepi rises from the couch and offers us some water. Nick readily accepts, for all of us. As she saunters into the kitchen our attention is directed to Dmitri who's licking his blood-stained teeth clean.

"Traveling to the Immortal Realm makes me very thirsty. Craig probably needs to eat too."

The three of us snap our head in Craigs direction, I let go of his hand and move back a little as well.

"I am hungry but-"

"Here," Chepi appears out of the blue with some meat on a plate. I really hope it is not human. "Eat this, it will hold you."

Craig thanks her and sits down next to Dmitri and to my horror upon smelling the meat he morphed into half beast. Cassidy gasps and clutches Nick's hand. While Nick looks fascinated.

"Your waters," she says presenting a tray of ice-cold water. We all take one, but Cassidy's petrified look doesn't waiver. So, this is what happens when he becomes hungry. It's frightening, as he tears into the meat, the "human side" is barely visible.

"So, what brings you guys here anyway? Do your parents know you're here?"

Craig and Dmitri simultaneously respond no, short, and sharp. This makes Chepi's sly and easy look switch away.

"For legal reasons, my Dad cannot know I am here," Craig says.

Chepi takes a seat across from them and demands an explanation. Craig and Dmitri share in telling her of everything that happened and what we are doing now. With each new detail her eyes grew more and more fearful. She is scared and jittery at the mention of the Council most of.

"Why are you guys here? You can't have Lee. I have kept him safe and hidden from the Council for years, if he helps you, they will recruit him," Chepi says in a rush frantic tone.

Dmitri shakes his head, "I wouldn't do that to Lee, I already have two cousins who met that fate, I don't want a third. We need you to see for us."

Her eyes dart to me then to Craig, who is back to his human form.

"We are stuck, we need a lead to know who this group is. We need you to look into Jezebel and see what you can find."

She squints her eyes and stands up. "And whose suggestion was this?"

"Theirs', kind of." Dmitri points at Cassidy and Nick. They instantly freeze up

"We didn't say your name, we suggested a seer. Craig was hinting towards you and Dmitri eventually agreed," Nick says to clear their names.

Cassidy nods viciously. "Please don't kill us," she peeps.

After giving us humans a once over with a look that makes me believe she will turn into a wolf at any moment, she bursts out laughing. "You humans, so fragile, so easily spooked. Follow me."

With that she saunters off in the direction of the stairs and we follow after her. Cassidy and I let out a breath of relief but we hold each other's hand as we walk. Dimitri leads us with Nick by his side, his forever bodyguard. Craig is behind me his hand lightly rests on the small of my back making me feel a little calmer.

Chepi stops at a room that has a decorated skull of an animal on it. She opens the door and welcomes us in. It looks like a very sacred room. She asks that we remove our shoes upon entering. The candles dance as they light up the room in an almost haunting glow. She stands in the middle of a flower petal and pebbled circle. She does some ritualistic movements that look almost like a dance as she chants something under her breath. She looks at me, her eyes golden and glowing, she summons me to join. Carefully I step into the circle with her. She takes my hands and instantly the petals and the pebbles rise off the ground. I look to my friends hoping they wouldn't look worried or scared, out of luck on that one. Nick is biting his nails, which he only exclusively does when he is nervous, Cassidy is wide eyed and biting her lip as she plays with her fingers. Dmitri is still as stone but he has never looked more concerned in my life. But then I look at Craig, he looks at me, caring and sweet and mouths, *it will be okay.*

Chepi starts to chant in Muskogean. After every phrase the candle flames grow larger and larger, the room heats up. A wind whirls around whipping our hair in a turbine. A surge of power grows in the room, there is a feeling of extra spirits present. Then suddenly it is dark, the candles whoosh out, the pebbles and petals drop down like dust. Chepi has her eyes closed and is looking down, her hands still gripping mine. *Thump thump.* My heartbeat so loud I think it can be heard by everyone. I wait, I wait for her to enter my mind like an ambo would. But it doesn't come, the pain doesn't reel through me. The sudden flash backs don't happen.

She looks up, startling me, her eyes still glowing a bright gold. It is like a personal candlelight for her face. It gives it a haunting glow and she smirks at me and whispers, "I knew you were always going to be trouble." In a second the candles come back on. The room goes back to how we walked in. She drops my hand and lets out a huge breath. We all stand around waiting for her to speak, to tell us what she saw, but instead she wipes the sweat off her brow and leaves the circle and opens the door. She exits. We look at each other in confusion. Dmitri starts off by leaving and catching up to her. We proceed behind him. He calls her name but she keeps walking as if she doesn't hear.

"How was it?" Nick asks in a whisper, though Cassidy and Craig heard and also wanted to know my answer. The thing is, I don't know what to tell them. There wasn't pain, there wasn't any emotion, just other things that tingled my sense of touch mainly. I felt a spiritual presence but that was the most weird sensation I had. I shrug, "I don't know, it was weird but it mainly felt oddly neutral. Like I was just the pawn." They nod, accepting the answer. I know our main goal is to hear from Chepi. But for some reason she doesn't want to speak. I wonder what she saw that made her say that she always knew that I was going to be trouble. I don't think anyone else heard that part of it though.

We catch up to her in the kitchen as she stands by the island looking a little frazzled.

"Aunty, come on, what did you see?"

"Chepi, please, even if it is hard to hear, we have to know," Craig pleads.

She takes a sip of water and looks at us, her hand is shaking a little. I don't know if this is normal behavior after performing a seeing but it really makes me wonder what type of danger she saw.

"You guys are in for way more than you bargained for. This is huge. It's not gonna be pretty. Lives are gonna be lost from this."

"Whose?!" Cassidy blurts out.

Chepi looks at her and smiles, "I won't tell you that, things can change depending on how you play things out. Others will join you though, it won't just be you guys. I couldn't see who the leader was, but I did see a connection with that boy who was in Malibu. He was made, by the way. Four kids. Look into the sources of Hayden Norris, Donna Leighton, Sarah Nichols, and Mitchell Green. Those people are going to help you get your answers."

Nick is typing the names into his phone while Cassidy double checks him. I'm sure Craig has already engraved it into his mind. Dmitri thanks his aunt and makes sure she is okay. Apparently performing a seeing job takes a lot of energy out of you. Cassidy and Nick question Craig if he has ever heard of those names. Craig tells them that he hasn't. It seems to frustrate him a bit. "We have something though. Thank you Chepi, we will get out of your hair. And I promise you that the Council will not know of this," he says. She nods taking his word. Chepi and Dmitri share in a hug. We join hands together like we did to get here.

"Wait!" Chepi calls running up to us, she takes hold of my arm and looks at me very seriously. "You hold great power Jezebel," she looks to everyone with the same look, "all of you need to remain on your guard, you aren't just stepping into a small investigation. This is the start of a war."

I gulp and turn my head to face my friends again.

"Immortalis ut Mortalis," Dmitri chants.

Back in Nick's room we sit around looking at each other with grave looks. A war. We are going into a start of a war? I didn't want to get Nick and Cassidy involved in a war.

"So, on a scale of one to ten how freaked out are you guys?" Nick breaks the silence.

"There is no number I can think of to explain," Cassidy says monotoned.

"I won't let them track you guys. Jude and I can make it so you guys leave no trace. You have my word that I will keep you safe," Craig promises.

It seems small but I can see their faces lift a bit from it. But within seconds the room is quiet and we are all left to our thoughts.

"Let's go get smoothies or some shit, that was way too heavy," Dmitri says.

Slowly we smile and get up, gathering our stuff. We go downstairs and pile into Nick's Prius as we go to get some smoothies... or some shit.

Take My Hand

Living like we didn't know what we know was the hardest part after visiting Chepi. The idea of this investigation turning into a war is one of the worst possible outcomes that we could have heard. Along with the thought of lives being lost without the knowledge of who it is. I guess it is a good thing, we wouldn't be living in constant fear, looking over our backs for when the death comes. The uplifting bit was that she said things can change.

Craig filled Jude in on the visit to Florida. Jude was pretty bummed out that he missed it. But like Craig told him, it was a spur of the moment decision to go. It wasn't an intentional exclusion. After him wasting about 30 minutes by whining and moaning about it, Craig moved on to explain how when we went to go get some smoothies we hung out in Craig's yard. In addition Craig and Dmitri got high as a kite, Nick was curious but chickened out.

Cassidy and I abstained. We slowly came to the idea of me, Craig, Nick, and Cassidy being investigation while Jude and Dmitri are basically the muscle. It would be best for them to not do any of the digging because it would technically be aiding in an open case. It was set for me and Craig to handle this. But since they have zero power over Cassidy and Nick, they can do whatever they please as long as they don't get themselves into something so deep and get caught.

So, we each took a name after Cassidy does her thing to hunt them down. For safety reason we each handle a person of the corresponding gender so Cassidy and I have Donna and Sarah while Nick and Craig will take care of Mitchell and Hayden. As we speak, Cassidy has already been making her way into the Beverly Hills High School's student database to see what she can find on the student body. After all, that's where Aiden was located, so it only makes sense for his connections to be there too. At least we hope.

While Jude and Craig are off doing some ambo training stuff, Craig let me hide out in his room so I can do some homework. I manage to get it done a whole lot quicker than I expected. But now I am just sitting in his room bored. I look around and notice some pictures on his dresser. There is one of him, Erin, and Jimmy making "ugly" faces but they still look incredibly beautiful. Then there is one with his parents at a band concert, he is wearing the tux with his sax around his neck. The others are him and his friends. A few of them have pictures of people I have never seen; they must be from the Immortal Realm.

One picture catches my eye, it has him and the rest of the Elites in it, they are at some ski lodge and he is all cuddled up with Bridget. It strikes a nerve in me. But they are friends, it was all fake, it wasn't like me and Travis. Deleting all our pictures together was hard. I wasn't going to delete them off Facebook and Insta but when I saw he did it I figured that it would look sad if I didn't do the same. I haven't been on social media in a while, I think I am afraid to see that Travis posted something that would mess with me.

"We need to take a picture together, I need to post us looking all cute," Craig says in my ear as he hugs me from behind. I stiffen up for a moment then place the picture I was examining back down. I wish he would announce himself when he teleports.

"What's wrong?" He asks, still holding me.

"How's Bridget?" God, I wish I didn't ask that. It makes me sound jealous and like I don't trust him. He drops his embrace and backs up. I turn to face him and he is sitting on his bed. "I'm just wondering because she hasn't said anything snarky or rude to me since we got together. And you never fully explained how you ended things.

He raises his eyebrows for a second. "Well, Jude is keeping her entertained still. But she's doing fine. Candice is the nightmare." I can hear the hurt in his tone when he mentions Jude. I know he was never truly okay with them constantly hooking up, even if the relationship was fake it is still a blow to know your best friend would do that. But I try not to pry into that. It bugs me to my core though. I don't even want to know what Candice is up to. She seemed so sweet, compared to the rest of them.

Turns out she's a snake. At least Bridget and Jeanette keep things on the surface. I shake the thoughts from my head and bop over to him.

"Is Jude still here?"

"Yup, he's outside the door."

My smile drops as I see him walking through like a sitcom entrance. Well it gives us time to talk, I guess. I ask them if they want me to get my friends on skype so we can talk. Jude shakes his head; he looks tired and rubs his muscles like he is sore.

"Nah, I'm gonna get going. Erin kicked my ass. I need to rest and regain my pride."

"Aww, don't feel bad, she's a brute. But also, a 12-year-old girl," Craig says with a fake pout teasing him.

They wrestle around a little bit before Jude says his final goodbyes. "Don't leave me out of any good stuff next time!" Craig pushes him out the room and locks his door. He looks back at me and jumps on the bed so he is lying next to me.

"So, why did you want to know if Jude was here?" His voice is suggestive. I act like I don't notice so I can play with him a little bit.

"I wanted to talk about the investigation. Don't you think it is weird how little they are interacting with me?" My playful redirecting turned into a real question. Why are they being so slow, so aloof? Aiden was taking direct action. It seems so odd. It's like they are playing with me.

Craig is looking out his window at a bird that is posted in his sill. He is acting like a distracted dog. "Hello?" I wave my hand, but he rises up, his eyes still locked on the bird. He takes a hold of my hands and slowly looks at me. His eyes indigo. He begins whispering so low that I can't hear what he is saying. His eyes make a hard cut to the bird again. His pupils shrink and shake back and forth in small but rapid movements. A loud shriek yelps out of the bird. I jump back cowering into Craig's body. What is happening, what is he doing. In Seconds the bird is nothing but a pile of feathers. Did he just explode a bird?

"They aren't all ambos. There is a witch, maybe a wizard with them," he whispers, this time he is looking at me. His eyes are back to normal. I don't leave from him.

"What? How do you know that?"

"That bird wasn't a real bird. It was a familiar. They are keeping tabs on us, they are calculated," he gets up closing his curtains, but before doing so he looks around.

"Jezebel, this is bad, who knows who else, what else they have working with them. What if they have a demon?"

I'm sorry a what? I gawk at his mention of a demon. I cannot believe that is even a possibility. Demons? We have demons that are just lurking around, we don't even have to open a possessed thing or open a portal. What if they did? Oh my god!

"How do you know about the demon?"

"I didn't say that they have one for sure, but usually when there is a witch or wizard that is into the dark arts, they have a little demon friend." I can't believe, I can't believe that I keep thinking that I can't believe anything new that is presented. I should know at this point that anything is possible. What if one of us gets possessed?

"We need to warn the rest of the team!" I grab Craig's shoulders and jerk him.

"Jezebel."

I drop my hands and lie back on his bed. "I'm sorry, I just didn't think we would have to worry about demons as well. It is a jarring discovery. I haven't read about them yet."

He takes his phone out of his pocket and starts texting. His thumbs working in over time.

Craig: *I have some information about the rebels. They have at least one witch or wizard. There was a familiar at my window. There could be a demon so heads up.*

Cassidy: *I'm sorry did you say a demon?*

Nick: *Sick, does that mean we can get possessed? Should we get some holy water?*

Dmitri: *We would need a whole exorcist team for that.*

Me: *So, we can get possessed?! If I get possessed just let me die.*

Craig jerks his head at me. "Don't be so dramatic."

"I'm just saying possessions seem like a lot of energy"

Cassidy: *I kind of agree with Jezzi on that.*

Dmitri: *Being possessed and living to tell the tale is something fantastic, quite the story to tell. Don't be little bitches.*

Me: *You speak as if you have been possessed before.*

Nick: *would explain somethings.*

Dmitri: *I don't have a soul to be possessed. I'm dead remember??*

Craig: *guys, the witch/wizard. That is an issue that we need to get back to, we don't even know if there is a demon.*

Cassidy: *Why is witch/wizard a huge issue?*

Craig: *outside of the IR I cannot tell a witch/wizard apart from a human. I can't smell the difference unless I am in beast form and I can't exactly go about like that.*

Nick: *Dmitri can smell the difference, right?*

Dmitri: *I'm not supposed to be investigating shit, I'm here to beat people up, possibly kill if necessary.*

Me: *He's right, but... can't you just sniff around when we are closing in on a potential target??*

Jude: *I'm late lemme catch up.*

Nick: *Come on now Jude... The muscle of this group is something else*

Dmitri: *Keep talking smack Aronthal and I will be in your room.*

Craig: *Guys... This familiar that they are using is a black bird with electric blue wings. If any of you see that let us know. Jude and Dmitri just kill it.*

Me: *How many familiars can it have?*

Craig: *As many as it can conjure.*

Jude: I am back. There has been one of those in my lawn for a few weeks. I don't know why or how I didn't clock it as a familiar.

Cassidy: How was Craig able to clock it as a familiar after one look and it took you up until now? You guys are the same creatures.

Jude: Hey! Craig is a mentalist he is specially designed to detect things better than me!

Craig: Have the rest of you guys seen any other animals that have been sticking around your houses or anything that is out of the ordinary?

Nick: Negative.

Me: nope

Cassidy: no

Dmitri: nah

Craig: Great, so this wizard seems to only be interested in the ambos. Since Cassidy is working on hacking. Nick and Jezebel, can you look into wizards and witches. Specifically, dark magic and why they would be looking into me and Jude.

Dmitri: We should hunt, go to the woods and see what we can find. Jude, I guess you can come to.

Jude: Aye, I've never hunted with a vamp!

Dmitri: Don't bother me or it will be your last hunt. Ever.

Jude: aye aye captain.

I have to look into dark magic. I hope I don't accidently hex myself or something. There could actually be things online about that as well. Wizards and witches are more well known. Everyday people practice witchcraft. I wish I knew someone who was into voodoo. I bet they would be useful. There could be a coven nearby, maybe a bookstore. A hunt for a witch or wizard seems way easier than trying to hunt down a band of ambos. At least they have a variety. I wonder if this will take us out of the state. Who's to say that they are operating in California? They have the ability to teleport and such, they don't have to be bound to Malibu. God, I hope they aren't in the south. I can't be around that energy. Any place that still has "sundown" towns in the 21st century cannot be trusted.

"You're so cute," Craig chuckles. He is lying next to me propped up on his arm. He is looking at me with admiration, it makes me blush. "When you're in deep thought like that you look very cute."

I try to hide my ever-growing redness with a pillow. But he takes it away from me and hovers inches above my face. I can feel the heat of his body on mine. "Does the thought of being spied on by some dangerous witch/wizard get you in the mood?" I tease.

"I don't know, maybe," he steals a kiss from me. "Maybe the thought of being a wanted man gets me going. Danger can be hot." He pins me down, taking my breath away. "Don't you agree?" woah.

He doesn't wait for me to respond. He kisses me deeply; I return matching his passion. Every time I kiss him like this it's like currents whipping through my body. My hands begin to explore his chest like I wanted to when he came in my room after I had that nightmare. Just as I thought his skin is so soft and beautiful to touch. I grace my hands around each curve and line of his muscles, with each passing second, I want him more and more; a soft moan escapes my mouth. He rises up and removes his shirt, mine is ruffled allowing for my own abs to be exposed. For a moment I look at him, even in artificial light he looks so perfect, no matter how light hits him he will look luminous. He comes back down trailing kisses from my lips to my cheeks to my neck. He starts to move down; he lifts my shirt a little to expose my stomach a little more. He trails little kisses on my stomach, giving me butterflies. My mind drifts into darkness.

"You need to relax babygirl. I'm gonna take care of you. I don't know why you're so scared. Now come here." He drags me over to him. His large hands explore over my chest. *"Your little heart is beating so fast. I knew you liked this."* He lifts up my shirt and slithers his hands up it until he reaches my chest.

"Get off of me!" I screech. I squirm and kick until he is off of me. My heart is pounding. I cower back into the back of his bed. He isn't here. He isn't here. Just focus on your breathing, it's not happening. It's over, he is not here. I feel my cheeks become wet with tears. I start to dig my nails into my legs and rocking. I need the rhythm. Back and forth, back and forth.

Craig slowly moves towards me and outstretches his hand. "Don't touch me!" I spit at him. He instantly recoils and looking frightened and confused. Back and forth, back and forth. How many blue items does he have in his room? 1,2,3..4...5.

"Jezebel, are you okay?"

I shake my head, curling myself further into myself.

He cautiously steps towards me again, like you would approach a feral animal. "What is going on. I didn't turn into half beast, did I? I should have asked you if that was okay. I went too far."

I can't respond. I feel like I am frozen in time. I have never reacted this strongly, I would recoil from touch but never like this. I want to tell him; I need to tell him.

"You don't have to talk; can I sit next to you?"

I weakly nod. I bury my face in my knees letting my tears fall freely. I want to be able to tell him everything I am feeling and why but I can't bring myself to talk about the details. I have never brought up the grit of it since it happened and I had to go to the police. My friends nor Travis know anything other than when I was thirteen, I was raped.

"Please... help me," I weakly simper.

I feel Craig's body shift over and get closer to me, I still cannot feel his touch. "What- how do you want me to help you? Is it okay if I go into your mind? Do I have your consent?"

I lift my head to look into his eyes, he meets my pain, he badly wants to comfort me but he respects my space.

"P-please don't make me feel any of the pain. Can you go through it without me feeling anything?"

He nods and straightens up. He shuts his eyes and takes in a deep breath.

Ellington Baddox

Jezebel's mind

It is a warm August night; the air is fresh and comfortable. Jezebel walks down the street holding a pink stuffed bear that she got from the carnival. Her ponytail is bouncing with each step. She isn't far from her house, that's why she chose to walk back. It is a quiet neighborhood, nothing exciting happens on the streets. Suddenly there is a man across the street in a dark green sedan. He calls out Jezebel's name. She looks over to him in confusion. She has never seen this man in her life. But something about him seems trusting.

She stops and responds, "Hello?" she calls back. A smile spreads across his face, he beckons for her to come to the car. Like under hypnosis Jezebel approaches the car.

"What are you doing walking alone at this late hour? That isn't safe young lady," he says giving her a once over.

Jezebel giggles, "I'm like a block away from my house. Nothing happens here."

The man looks around then focuses his attention back to Jezebel. "I guess you're right. Still it isn't very safe. You should get in so I can take you home.

Apprehensive Jezebel doesn't move. She squints at the man, who she does not know but he seems so familiar. He seems to know her though. But Jezebel agrees and hops in the back seat.

Once she is buckled in the man takes off. What should have been a quick ride around the block they travel a little farther. His amber eyes look at Jezebel through his rear-view mirror. He is in his 30s and extremely handsome. He has stubble where his beard would be. He keeps giving a sinister, crinkly smile in her direction, making small talk conversations until everything goes black.

When Jezebel wakes, she is in the living room of a house. A glass of wine is sitting on the coffee table in front of her. She looks around bewildered and scared. She lost time; she is in a strange place. And she is alone.

"Hello?!" she calls in a panic. She looks for her purse, it is on the chair next to the door. She looks around one last time to see if someone was there with her, but nothing. She quickly gets up and grabs her purse. She makes a break for the door, then suddenly, the man from before, appears. He stands in front of the door blocking it. Jezebel backs up slowly, wanting to get as far away from him as she could. She can feel the danger that she didn't feel earlier. The man follows her holding his own glass of wine.

"Jezebel, I got you something to drink, it's late. You can stay here. Just sit here with me. Relax babygirl." His voice slick, but still Jezebel sits down on the couch. She doesn't touch the wine that is presented in front of her. He takes a seat next to her, getting so close that she has no where to move, there is not a sliver of space between them. He drinks down his glass of wine and places it on the coffee table.

He slips her purse out of her hand and takes hold of her face, his breath filthy of alcohol. "Now, now you just need to get comfy. It's gonna be a long night if you don't relax."

Jezebel closes her eyes, thinking that if she closes her eyes this nightmare that she's living will be over. But to her horror, it's not a nightmare. His hand slips up her thigh and she can feel his stubble scrape her neck. "Jezebel, you're so pure."

Tears start to well in her eyes until some escape, starting a gentle weeping. She is trapped in a home she does not know; with a man she does not know. She wonders how she got here, why she is here. But each question leads to another painful one. She needs to escape but cannot find a way to get out. The man takes in a big inhale of her hair and notices her fear. It seems to fuel him. He becomes more exhilarated. He kisses her neck. Jezebel tenses up, balling her hands into fists. She recoils as far back as she can but she can't seem to escape him. He catches her neck and forces her to look at him.

"You need to relax babygirl. I'm gonna take care of you. I don't know why you're so scared. Now come here." He drags her over to him. His large hands explore over her chest. "Your little heart is beating so fast. I knew you liked this." He lifts up her shirt and slithers his hands up it until he reaches her chest. Jezebel cries for him to stop, but he doesn't, he keeps going and becomes hungrier.

She wants him to stop, she tries to push him off but he is heavier than her. He has her pinned down, puts all his weight and strength on top of her. "I like a fighter," he growls in her ear, "Makes it all the more rewarding." He begins undressing and doing the same to her. She fights to get him to stop but he grows claws and rips her shirt off. His face morphs into a demonic beast with a black venomous tongue. He laughs at her tears, at her tremendous dread. "You can make this much easier on yourself."

Jezebel finds enough strength to bite hard into his arm, hard enough to break skin. He lets out a thunderous roar and she slips from his hold. Grabbing her purse, she runs to the door again but he appears in front of it again. He looks down at her with menacing eyes and a cocky, disgusting grin. He throws her onto the floor and gets on top of her. Before Jezebel gets the chance to fight back, he has already stolen what was hers to give away. Excruciating pain ripped through her with each movement he *made. She screams and begs for him to stop but she knows it won't help, that it won't make it end.*

She goes silent but then sees the wine bottle and a thought comes to her. She reaches for the neck and smashes it over his head. He hollers out in pain but that just makes him be even rougher with her. She shrieks and cries before she thinks to stab the broken bottle into his neck. He roars and topples off of her trying to stop the blood. "You little bitch!" he spits at her.

Without thinking Jezebel gets up and runs out the door. She knows that this is her last shot to escape. She runs down the street calling for help through her tears but no one comes out, no lights come on. In fear of the man coming back she dials 911.

Craig looks at me shaking, tears roll down his cheeks. I feel nothing but peaceful. He reaches out to me, I accept and collapse into his arms. I have never felt so relieved of that. I read about this when studying up on ambos. He took my memory and shared it and absorbed the energy behind it so he could feel the pain, so for a temporary time I was free of it as my mind relived it.

"Jezebel, I'm so sorry," he stammers stroking my hair holding me as tight as he possibly could. I snuggle up closer not wanting him to let go. The memory is still mine. I have the weight of it. But now I am not alone. I have someone who feels my pain.

"Jezebel, why didn't you tell me earlier. I wouldn't have even-"

"Because... I know that normal couples of the school ya know... do things. It frustrated Travis at times. And I know that you are used to certain things. And-"

"No, no that is insane," he breaks from our embrace so he can look me in my eyes. "You been through something so... Jezebel you were raped. I don't care what everyone else is doing. Which they aren't by the way, they all have big talk but most of our classmates have barely had any kind of action. I don't expect anything from you. Things with me and Bridget was a whole different story we are both ambos. I never think that I am entitled to anything from you. It, was... We were both into it so I assumed at the time. I'm so sorry, Jez-"

"Shh, can we just lie here? I don't want to talk. I just want you to hold me," I say. He wraps me around him so that I am cuddled on top on him. I nestle myself into him as he gives me a soft kiss on my forehead as if he is saying one last time that he is sorry.

We ended up lying there in silence for much longer than I thought. Two hours went past. To be fair in the last 30 minutes we were asleep. I was late to dinner at this point. Craig helped me pack up all my things and drove me home. When he arrived at my house, he wanted to come in. I told him that he shouldn't that it would be too suspicious.

"Why would it be suspicious?"

I haven't told him yet that I still have neglected to tell my parents about us. I just never got around to it. I guess in my head they already knew but when Craig wants to come by when it is later it hits me that I never told them. I had been so swept up in the investigation and everything.

"I haven't told my parents about us yet."

He looks at me in utter shock. "Are you serious? We have been dating for over a month, got sentence to near death and you haven't even told your parents that I'm your boyfriend?"

I look away trying to play coy and innocent but he just rolls his eyes at me. I know I have to tell them. What's a better time than the present? I tap his leg twice, "Alright then come in, I'll tell them tonight!"

'Really', he says to me with his eyes. He shrugs and unbuckles his seatbelt enthusiastically. This is my second boyfriend, things can't be as bad as it was when I introduced them to Travis, that was followed by a painful dinner. My Dad seems to think that dinners are the best way to get to know any new people. A week after me and Travis were dating, we were forced to have a joint family dinner, the memory still haunts me.

Nevertheless, we walk up to my door and walk in. Thankfully everyone is still in the dining room. Gives me a bit of time to think. Craig closes the door.

"Jez is that you?" My Mom calls.

Never mind. "Yeah it's me. I uh, I have a guest."

Tip Toe

I was thinking that we were in the clear. My parents took to Craig pretty well. They recognized him as the boy I brought back from when I went out to a party. I nearly forgot that he had to stay at my place after Aiden drugged him. I'm glad my parents didn't hold it against him. My Mom was a bit reserved about the idea of us dating at first because of me and Travis breaking up so recently. Also, she didn't care too much for him being a guest after the Aiden thing. He explained himself and apologized profusely to get on her good side.

All the while my Dad had his arms crossed and just stared at him for an uncomfortably long time. Craig pretended to not notice and just kept his attention on my Mom who was giving him question after question. I didn't know what my Dad was thinking. Normally he is the one who is the talker. I bet he can sense something isn't normal about Craig. Well, he has never been suspicious of Dmitri, then again, he adores Dmitri like no other. Even if he did notice something off about him, he would ignore it.

The more I think about it, I can't believe that I didn't clock something was up with the Vaduva family the moment we met his parents. His dad screams vampire, to be honest I don't even think I saw him breathing. I guess when you aren't aware of the fact that such creatures can exists, why on earth would someone be suspicious that someone isn't human. I jokingly think people are aliens. Aliens, I wonder if they are roaming the earth too.

"Charles Edwards!" My Dad exclaims breaking me from my nonsensical train of thought and stopping Craig and my Mom's conversation.

"Excuse me?" Craig asks politely. I can see the panic in his eyes. He is probably thinking how he knows his dad's name. I know I am.

"You're Charles Edwards' boy, aren't you?" Oh my god he knows his dad. Was everyone in my family in cahoots with the Edwards family except for me?

Craig gives a weary smile and nods. Not sure where this is going.

My Dad slaps his hands together and smiles. Making a small exclaim of excitement he pats Craig on the shoulder. Thank god my Mom looks equally as confused as I was. I have never heard Dad mention Mr. Edwards once. And he is always rambling about his friends.

"Rae, Craig is Chuck's son!"

Chuck is Mr. Edwards? Chuck is short for Charles... He has never said that man's last name. I guess this is a good thing. My Mom's eyes light up and smiles also now recognizing what he was talking about.

Chuck, Mr. Edwards, is one of my Dad's good friends who he golf's with. He says that Chuck makes it tolerable down at the club. According to my Dad a lot of the men at the country club are far too conservative for him. My Dad prides himself as being as far left as he possibly can be. He always talks about how Chuck shares so many ideas that he has and that he is a breath of fresh air. He did mention that he is British, but to be fair, Craig wasn't on my radar when we were first told this.

"You know my Dad?"

"We're good friends, and golf buddies. Every Sunday afternoon, it's me and Chuck!"

Craig has a stroke of realization. He nods and points his finger, "You are Chris," he states already knowing the answer. The amount of people knowing each other you would think we live in a small town in the middle of nowhere. What are the odds? It seems that me and my Mom are the only ones who has no ties to the Edwards family prior to Craig.

In theory this is a good thing. Everyone knows each other, almost. But no, this actually just accelerates the thing that I dread the absolute most.

"We should get the families together and have dinner,"

Craig looks at me, I warned him about this before. My Mom is shaking her head at my Dad, ferociously trying to talk him out of it. I told Craig about how much of a disaster our last dinner was with the Hart family. I don't think it would go up in smoke but the fact that Craig's family isn't human gives me a new set of anxiety. Craig said that they never go out to restaurants as a family. He says when ambos eat, like really eat, they transform. Like what I saw when we were at Chepi's. That would be a sight to see.

"Um, it's late, I have an early morning practice. Craig, can you come up stairs with me for a sec, I want to give you something," I tug at his arm looking at him expectantly.

Craig looks relieved about being able to escape this dinner conversation. He shakes my Dad's and hand gives my Mom's a polite hand squeeze. "It was a pleasure meeting you," he schmoozes. Oh brother, I roll my eyes when my back is turned. I tug on Craig's arm subtly to get him moving. The longer we stay here the higher the possibility of being roped into this family dinner.

Finally getting him to break free we make our way around the corner, but my Dad calls after us. "Wait, love birds, remember this, L'amour fait les plus grandes douceurs-"

"et les plus sensibles infortunes de la vie," Craig finishes.

Both me and my Dad look at him impressed. I forgot that he could speak French, but I didn't think he would know de Scudéry. I thought I would have stopped finding little things about him that amazed me.

We continued to make our way to my room. I can hear my parents' loud whispers about their approval of

Craig. He is bred to please; it shouldn't come as a shock. I quicken my pace up the final bit of stairs and rush us into my room. I make sure to not slam the door and to not make a sound. I don't want to cause any attention.

As I turn around, I bump into Craig, I didn't know he was standing this close to me. He chuckles at me and helps me regain some balance. I shake him off of me and rush to my bedside. I feel incredibly uneasy tonight. I don't feel a presence but my mind, it's like there is an ever-growing tick that refuses to leave. I started to feel it when we dosed off at his house. I'm not sure if it's paranoia thinking about the witch or wizard possibility, or the uncertainty of what could be out there. Either way I don't think I will be getting much sleep tonight.

"Can you stay?" I plea. He meets my sorrowful gaze with apologetic eyes. I already know the answer before he says it.

"We are going to hunt tonight, see what we can find, otherwise I would." I didn't know that they would be hunting so soon. Maybe that's why I felt so uneasy. Maybe something isn't going to happen to me, but to one of them. I want to beg him to not go, to do it a different night. But I can't allow for my suspicion to get in the way of furthering the investigation.

I would feel better if I could be with them, though I'm sure they wouldn't let me go. Well, Jude probably wouldn't have a problem. "Can I-"

"No, no you can't come. It is far too dangerous and... I wouldn't want you near any of us when we are hunting. We are even less human than we already are... I don't want to risk you being hurt."

"You guys would never-"

"Dmitri is a blood hungry killer Jezebel. He overindulges before he comes around you guys so he feels little to no thirst." I pause, Dmitri told us that he is no longer *that* blood thirsty. Did he lie? "He has incredible control, don't get me wrong, but anything can happen on a hunt and he can turn on you in a second. Same goes for Jude... and I'm afraid me."

My heart drops thinking about it. He has never admitted to being a danger to me. He has said things around us getting together would pose a threat but never himself. That bit kept my fear that I have for that beast side of him shadowed. To know that he has more humanity than monster. He is a carnivorous beast under the guise of a human.

I try to hide my apprehension towards him. Yet, I feel that he can tell how I am truly feeling. He has the same hurt look in his eyes that comes whenever I recoil from him. I've never heard him call himself dangerous or a monster. He doesn't seem too tortured about what he is. Though, the shame that comes across his face when I look as I do now speaks volumes.

"I gotta get going. You'll be fine tonight. I'll talk to you tomorrow," his voice hurt.

I smile at him dimly and take his hand, but he slips it out.

"I'll show myself out, give one last good first impression with your parents. Good night."

Before I can stop him, he has already disappeared down the hall. I let out a long sigh and change into pajamas. I would love to stay up and look into some witchcraft but I have to be in Beverly Hills at 7am which means I gotta be up at 5:30am to get ready. I remember the last time I had an early morning practice like this. Travis came and got me, he brought me some breakfast on the way and just hung around the area till I got out. He wanted to spend as much time as he could with me because I was swamped with homework for 2 weeks straight. He surprised me with a picnic when we got back to Malibu, it was the most simplest and sweetest thing he did for me. I almost cried when I saw it. The stress was getting to me and he did the smallest gesture, because he knows I am not fond of grand ones, that he could think of to relax me.

My heart pumps out a sorrowful beat in my chest. I miss so much of that. Of the simple romantic things that I was able to do. The simple life I had when I was with Travis. Things went wrong in my life, sure, but when he came around it was like being carried by the current, there was no work involved. Dmitri swore up and down that he was just instilling a false sense of security and normalcy in me. He always believed that Travis was grooming me into a "perfect obedient patient". I shake my head of the thoughts. All that is over, it's never coming back. I chose to be a part of this, and besides, even if I didn't, I just would have been swept up into it without any authority and probably would have ended up drowning. I made the right choice.

Be safe, please don't leave me and die. I text Craig.

I promise you the sweetest pleasures, not the misfortunes... at least not now anyways lol. Get some sleep

I lay back in my bed shutting off the light. As I stare at the ceiling starting to doze off, I think of the saying, in English, "Love makes life's sweetest pleasures and worst misfortunes."

I couldn't stop myself from going over every little detail of what was presented in front of me.

1. *I would never be able to tell the difference between reality and an illusion*
2. *No matter how much he claims, Craig will never be able to keep me and my friends safe.*
3. *Every second I am with Craig the more I put myself in danger.*

"You regret it don't you?" No, I don't. I don't. It was inevitable. I just now know who and what I am up against. "But it wouldn't have happened in the first place if you didn't leave me."

I turn my head sharply to face him. Travis sits looking at me smugly, the way he would look whenever he had an 'I told you so' moment. It always made me seethe. His self-assurance. I shake my head and ignore him and continue to read. "You avoid me to hide how you are truly feeling." You don't know what you are talking about, you're just trying to manipulate me.

He laughs and appears on my left and coos in my ear. "Jez, babe. You miss me. Things were so simple and nice; don't you miss that. Why let one little thing mess everything up?"

"No!" I rise up out my sleep panting. I look around my dark room searching for a set of eyes, a shadow, anything. I'm alone. I don't want to believe that I dreamt that on my own. I don't miss him; I don't wish I were still with him.

"You okay?" Craig asks.

I jerk my head around to see a shadow figure standing near my bed. Is this still an illusion? Why can't I see him, or why isn't he letting me see him.

"Craig?" He doesn't answer or move. That's not him. But why isn't he here with me now, can't he sense that I am in danger? I look down at my left arm, WCE is still there.

"Craig, why aren't you moving why aren't you talking to me?" The figure stays still and silent. I look at the door and measure how fast I would need to move to get out safely to get to my brother's room.

When I look back the figure is walking towards me in a slow haunting pace. No, no, no, no. I gather up my comforter and throw it off of me and race for the door. I go to open it but it is locked, glued shut. I desperately wiggle the handle and bang on my door screaming for help. Where is he? Where is Craig?

The door finally gives out and I burst it open ready to run but in seconds it is shut.

"It's okay, whatever that was, it's gone," Dmitri says in my ear pulling me towards him. How did he get in my room? Too afraid to turn around in fear that this will be some other illusion, 'Dmitri' does it himself.

"Belle it's me, Craig used an energy transfer to teleport me to come and get you." I take a good look at him, he is wearing a black tank top and black pants, his long hair is slightly wild but still tamed. What strikes me are his eyes, their blood red and his fangs are exposed. This isn't Dmitri. I shake my head and back up trying to leave again. But I am careful with my sounds. I don't want to endanger the rest of my family.

"Belle, no, no. My eyes are like this because I was hunting. We were in the middle of a hunt and Craig felt you were in danger. He is in full beast right now and didn't want to freak you out so he sent me." I don't know if I should believe him. What if he was that shadow figure and changed forms?

"Prove it,"

"What?"

"Prove to me that you are Dmitri."

"Any type of shapeshifter cannot replicate abilities of a supernatural creature, only the look. Want me to prove it?"

Before I get the chance to respond he bites into his arm leaving two fang marks and deep burgundy blood dripping down. "Drink it?"

"What?"

"Drink my blood; blood of a vampire is so sweet and enticing that it should be considered a drug."

I look at the blood, it is like it's almost calling me, whispering my name. No. "I believe you... I don't want to drink your blood. That's not sanitary." Dmitri laughs at me and pulls me in for a hug. I resist at first but give in and just let my body flop into his. Ever since I was told he was a vampire I expect for him to be cold like all the readings, myths, and legends say. But I forget that he has Werewolf blood in him as well, making him warmer. His body is still very solid, like stone.

He walks towards my bed and beckons for me to follow him. Is he inviting me to join him in my bed? This is weird. I cautiously walk towards him getting comfortable on my bed. "Hey, do you have a ponytail holder I can borrow?" He asks gathering his hair. Still confused by what is happening I go into my nightstand and pull out one and toss it towards him. He skillfully catches it and ties his hair into a high bun.

"Are, are you sleeping over?" I ask him standing at the side of my bed. He has slept over before but never in my bed, especially with me in it. I don't think anything would happen but- I get distracted by him licking the blood from when he bit his arm. He takes it slow, it's almost seductive. The two bite marks are gone, completely healed. Not a scar left to tell the tale. He notices me staring and winks at me playfully.

"Really should have tasted it. Would have changed your whole life. But you most likely would have became obsessed with me," he jokes.

I take a seat at the edge of my bed; his eyes still haven't changed back to green. Is he thirsty? I keep thinking about what Craig said about him being blood thirsty. I wonder if he was laying it on thick just to steer me away from wanting to go on the hunt.

"Your eyes, they are still red. Are you still... thirsty?" He looks at me inquisitively. "Are you afraid of me, Belle?" His voice is darker than usual. I don't respond but he starts to move towards me. Before I get the chance to react, he grabs me and pins me on the bed in a speed so fast it causes a slight wind. He towers over me his fangs bared. He lunges down to my neck. I brace myself for the bite and shut my eyes as tight as I can.

Dmitri loosens his grip and begins laughing and rolls over to his back. "Oh my god, too funny," he bellows.

I lie paralyze trying to process what just happened. This was Dmitri alright. Typical asshole behavior.

"I'm thirsty, yeah, but not so thirsty that I would feed on you or kill you. Worry not. I'm here to act like a guard. Think of *A Nightmare on Elms Street*. You're Nancy and I'll be Glen... except I'll do my job and stay up."

I angrily situate myself and turn my back on him. It's 2 am. Hopefully I can get back to sleep. Does he not need to sleep? No, I don't have time to get into vampire questions right now. I need rest, I gotta get up early.

My alarm goes off, deafening me. I fumble to get to my phone to quickly get it off. 5:30 is far too early for me to be up. I peak over my shoulder, expecting to see Dmitri, but he wasn't there, instead there is a note.

Left at 5. I needed to leave before the sun came up, ya know, don't wanna burn – Dmitri

Right, probably a good call that he left. At least he stayed for a while. His handwriting is really nice, especially for a guy. Knowing that he was born in 1502 helps, they had better penmanship back then. I wonder what happened with that.

I didn't have another dream but the one I did have still left me feeling extremely unsettled. And guilty. I don't think that I made a mistake, I want to be with Craig, I don't want Travis back. I wish I never kissed Craig in his car while I was still with Travis. I wish I would have fessed up sooner to him. But us ending things was the right thing to do. At least that's what I believe.

Bzz Bzz. I look back down at my phone, it's a text from Craig. *Are you naked?* I squint at my phone. Am I naked? Why is he asking that? *No,* I respond back. I toss my phone back on my bed and turn on the lights in my room. Unexpectedly, I am being hugged, the scent is unmistakable. I hug Craig back without hesitation.

"Jezebel, I'm so sorry I couldn't be here. I was in beast form and couldn't change out right away, I didn't want you to freak out." Craig continues to ramble on and on about everything that was happening and how he panicked and sent Dmitri because he didn't know what else to do. He said that he was blocked from getting in the dream. He said that it is a definite sign of a witch. Just having woken up I can hardly process what is happening and try to digest everything that was being said. I ultimately fail. I get on my tippy toes and kiss him on the cheek.

"I don't really get what you are saying but I am not mad or anything. Thank you for sending Dmitri. I gotta get ready though. We can meet up after my practice. Can you meet me here?"

He nods and wishes me luck at 'rehearsal', this isn't band but I get what he means. In a second, he is gone. *You regret everything.* Travis' voice whispers in my ear. I jerk my head around. Not now, please not now. I don't need whispers when I am trying to focus on gymnastics. I could seriously hurt myself if I don't focus. I think about what Dmitri said about A nightmare on Elms Street. What if whatever is whispering to me is like Freddy Kruger, if I ignore it, it'll lose its power?

I wanted to talk to Cassidy and Nick and fill them in on my dream but I want to ignore it as much as I can now. I just texted them and told them to meet me at my house at 11 am. Craig, Dmitri, and Jude will be there too. I asked my parents if it was okay before I left, granted they were half asleep, though they still agreed. My Dad groggily said he would make finger sandwiches. My Mom said that they could have the left-over dessert she had from a catering gig. I don't believe they fully understood what I was asking, but I will take the free food.

When I get to the gymnasium Maci could tell something was bothering me. I told her I had a nightmare and it kind of got to me. It wasn't a lie, just a simplification. She accepted my answer and offered me her second breakfast sandwich to try to help with my fatigue look.

During warmups she kept me good and distracted as she told me about how things were going in Beverly Hills, it was good to know that the hunt for Aiden's killer has strictly stuck to their area. She said that it is kind of sad because most of the people at her school, she went to the private school close by his, kind of stopped talking about it. That no one cares about it anymore at her school. I suppose it is more of an uproar at his school. But at hers, they have a Spring formal coming up that has been distracting everyone. She says she has her eyes on this boy named Thomas who she has been casually flirting with the whole year.

Talking to her about her school life made me feel old, it felt like those times for me were years in the past. My life has been so consumed in this supernatural world and being Freddy'd every night that I can't even enjoy what is supposed to be the best years of my life.

As I wanted, practice was a perfect distraction. As I often do, I tune out any extra thoughts and just focus on my moves, my coach, and the music. I am focusing on my floor routine and the uneven bars. I love my floor routine; I convinced my coach to let me do it to Eurythmics Sweet Dreams. I have nearly perfected it, every step I get more and more fluid. There is a difficult tumbling section that has been kicking my butt for weeks but I am determined to get it down. Maci says this is the best I have ever done with any routine. She says she can tell my heart is in it. Coach agrees.

My uneven bars have been a bit rough; I focus so much energy with the floor I hardly put my all into the bars. My focus has to be razor sharp on these. When I pass between the two, I feel a sense of freedom, for the brief second, I am flying. I always catch myself on the bar but it is shaky. Sometimes it is a close call. I powder my hands up and shake out any nerves and loosen up my muscles. I take a deep breath and go.

I was focused, this was my best run yet on the bars. When I was about to pass over to the lower bar, I hear *You betrayed me! It was always us!* I lose my focus and miss the bar and fall straight down landing on my back. Rory? Is he real? Is he here? The force of the fall knocks the wind out of me. Coach is crouched beside me the rest of the girls come around looking shocked and worried. I cough as coach helps me up. I look around to see if I could find Rory. Or maybe a shadow figure, but nothing.

I didn't think he was a real person. He has been in my dreams but I thought that was it. Has he been the one controlling my dreams all this time? As I sit on the side watching my teammates practice; since the fall was pretty bad and there was only about 15 minutes left of practice I was told to sit out, I fidget on my phone typing then deleting a text to Craig. He has never thought I was crazy or that I was making anything up but this seems so impossible. I'm also afraid on what he will say. What if he knows who Rory is? And it's not good... No, I want to tell him in person. I want to see any change in his face when I say his name. If I text him, he might try to withhold things from me.

Dmitri is an old man, and has actually worked at the Council, he probably knows more. Wait, I forgot, he can't tell me about things like this. It brings him into the case. I don't to get him involved like that. But still, saying a name wouldn't hurt, would it? I start a text to Dmitri but then Maci comes bopping over to me. She has a new ice pack for me. I lay on my stomach and let her ice my back.

"What happened out there? You were doing great. It was the best run you did," she asks. I can hear all the concern in her voice.

It sucks that I can't explain to her an ounce of the truth. All I can say is, "I just lost focus. I don't know... it was weird. My mind went blank."

I peek back at her; she doesn't look like she is buying it but doesn't press anymore. My favorite thing about her. She never pries into people's business, never pushes an answer out of someone.

I race home, eager to get back, I need to shower before anyone gets there. I am being paranoid, I know, but I asked Craig to sit watch in my bedroom as I shower just in case something happens. He was happy to oblige, he still feels guilty for not being able to help me last night. He wasn't able to see the dream either, he just knew that I was in peril. I'm glad, it gives me the chance to explain things to him, I wouldn't want him taking things the wrong way. If I learned anything from last year, I can't keep things from someone just because it might hurt them, or it might be an awkward conversation.

I can't change what I did, and I keep thinking about it, but I truly do wish I would have just talked to Travis about Craig, and how I felt that he was dismissing me. I just spent the better half of my life keeping things secret. But being with Craig, I have been able to have full disclosure with everything in my life. Granted he has to keep certain things secret with me, so I can keep my head; it feels so nice knowing that I don't have to worry about secrets for the first time in my life.

When I get to my house, I see Craig's car already parked outside. I pull into my spot in the driveway but Craig hasn't gotten out yet. I grab my gym bag and walk over to his car. As I approached, I expected for him to come out or roll down the window at least, but he stays looking ahead. I see him put a joint up to his lips. Got it.

I knock on his window, he rolls it down letting the smoke escape his car. I crunch up my face and wave the smoke away from me. I don't know how he is able to stand that. He looks at me and his eyes are weary. He is upset about something, I wonder if he did see my dream.

"What's up? Why are you sadly smoking in your car?"

He takes another hit before putting it out. He rakes his fingers through his hair; he tugs at it, he's stressed. "Your dad called my dad to set up a dinner. We are having one tonight at my house. My mum thought it would be best for the whole family to be here. Michael is coming in; in two hours he will be here."

His older brother Michael, right. Craig never speaks of him. I only have the brief explanation that he gave Nick back when we started our little investigation. I know that he hates him and clearly his presence upsets Craig greatly.

I didn't want to ask him too many questions before because we hardly knew each other, but now, it seems justified. I lean on the passenger side window. "Can you tell me about the whole Michael situation when we get to my room. Also, the dinner. I definitely need to know about the dinner."

He tries to smile but I can tell it is forced. He rolls up his windows and cuts the engine. I reach my hand out for him to take. I hope my Dad is in the living room. I would just love to have a chat with him about this dinner. I guess my Mom couldn't get him to tone down that enthusiasm of his. After 15 years of marriage I think my Mom has nearly completely given up with trying to get my Dad to not act on instinct as much.

I am sad to see that he isn't in the living room. I can hear our patio furniture moving, I'm gonna guess my parents are outside. This house carries sound like a library or an empty museum. I have no clue where Lindsey and Josh could be, they normally live in the living room on the weekends. I don't give it too much thought, makes it easier to get Craig upstairs.

Before I miss my window, I hurry him along, taking no time to look back or to stop. I hear the patio door opening and I quicken my steps to a jog. This makes Craig chuckle at me.

"My parents would never allow for me to have you in my room with the door closed, especially when I am showering." I whisper as I shut my bedroom door behind us. He raises his eyebrows at me and plops down on my bed. As I disappear into the bathroom Craig begins explaining the story behind Michael.

Michael is 4 years older than him, when they still lived in Surrey, permanently, Michael lived with them. Craig always tried to get his attention and wanted to play with his older brother. Michael didn't have too much of an interest but was still nice to him. It wasn't until Michael turned eight did he really start to ignore Craig, even though he was a toddler he took notice, but loved him, nonetheless. When it came time for them to move to Mortal Realm America; which Craig told me they moved for a secret reason that not even he knows the full story, he can tell me that he knows that his dad was ordered by the 1st high court, Michael refused to move with them. He didn't want to leave behind all of his friends and his life in England. The idea of living around humans disgusted him. His parents tried to get him to want to come along with a different angle. They told Michael they wanted him to be there for Craig so that he wasn't so alone. But Michael didn't care about his brother's feelings, only his own and chose to stay with their grandparents. That's when Dmitri came into play. When Dmitri came over a few weeks before they were supposed to leave, he saw how upset Craig was and it broke his heart to see him like that, so he took the sacrifice to be with him.

When they moved to America their family would go back and forth to visit often, Craig would always be super excited to see Michael but the feeling was never reciprocated. Craig didn't hold Michael's decision to stay in England against him because he was only 9 and Craig was 5 and didn't understand too much. Yet, each year Craig became more and more tired of the way his brother would blow him off. The last straw happened in the summer of 2007 when Craig was 12 and was visiting

Michael once again. Michael was 16 and got into drinking. He would often drink every night. Craig hated seeing him destroy himself, no matter what he tried, even tapping into his newly formed mentalists powers, he couldn't stop Michael. He ended up having to take him to the hospital because he had severe alcohol poisoning. It was traumatic to see his brother like this.

Ever since then I kind of gave up on him. He never stopped drinking and became an alcoholic, which is why I don't drink. Erin still adores him and Jimmy doesn't think he is that bad. He keeps going on recovery tracks but fails every time. It is tiring. All the weight of the family name fell on me. So any small lapse I make, it is like it's Armageddon. As you saw in our hearing. My family praises him for every little minor thing he does. And he tries to make up for being an arsehole to me for 7 years but I-I just can't fully accept him.

Craig speaks to me through my head, I couldn't hear him with the shower going. I see where he is coming from but I think he should try to give his brother a chance. I wait for him to respond, but he doesn't. I have never had a relationship like that with my siblings. We have been pretty close. We have jabs at each other and fight but nothing out of the ordinary of a typical sibling relationship. We still get along pretty great and love each other.

I quickly dry off and change into some lounging clothes. When I step out the bathroom Craig is already sitting up on my bed waiting for me. He beckons me over eagerly. He holds on to me by my thighs, making sure not to wander too north to my butt as he gently massages my legs.

"They are so firm, I wanna see you out there. On the mat, being a badarse gymnast," he pulls me in close, his head at my stomach. I giggle running my fingers through his hair. I normally am very insecure about my body; I don't have that slender feminine frame like Bridget and Jeanette. But Craig seems to like it.

"I have a meet on March 3rd. I'm really excited about it. But," I tilt his head up so our eyes can meet. "We first gotta get through this dinner tonight."

He stands up and slides his hands up to my waist.

"I grilled my Dad about that, by the way. He is such a sneaky git." I look at him confused. I thought my Dad was the one who called about this dinner. "I should have known something was up when after the trial he was happy to accept us dating. The whole time he was friends with your dad. For years he has been fraternizing with the Bedeau's, he just kept it under the radar. That's why he was saying that he was upset that we got caught." He lets go of me and walks towards the door smiling at the revelation. If anything, I feel more confused. I thought the beef was with me. Not my whole family. Is my whole family on the most wanted list there?

"But, Craig-

"Jez, we're here! Get on down!" Nick calls from downstairs.

Craig opens the door and motions as to say, 'after you'. I wish I had more time.

Craig, Jude, and Dmitri briefed us on what they found on their hunt. Dmitri caught onto a scent early on, both Craig and Jude went full beast to help track. What they ended up finding did not disappoint. They found a ritual ground that had fresh blood in the center. There were signs of extreme burn damage around the pentagram.

"They have a demon, don't they? The fiery pits of hell... I summon thee..." Nick trails off not daring to finish.

"The familiar, the one you guys have been seeing is a common form of a tracking demon," Cassidy chimed in.

"They can help a witch or wizard get into the minds of the ones they are tracking... But you can counter that right?" I ask looking to Craig, then I look at Jude, "You too, the both of you can help counter that?"

They look to each other apprehensively. They know another bit that we don't know. If it were that simple, they would have just answered.

"Well, Red, they haven't been coming to you so they aren't trying to get into you guy's heads. Trackers do a little something different to supes."

Dmitri looks down, he too knows what they are referring to. "It's completely illegal though. But if they cared about legality we wouldn't be here right now," his voice is low. I try to search my head on the very little I was able to gather, it was a very brief reading. I was going to deep dive this evening but I have a dinner to attend.

"Mimik! It is Mimik! They aren't trying to get into your heads or ours. They are trying to see who is close to us, who we interact with to... fuck with us!" Nick exclaims passionately.

Oh wow, okay then. Cassidy looks equally as shocked as me. Dmitri is trying to hold back some laughter and just looks away.

"Um... okay, who is Mimik?" Cassidy asks.

"It's a common trickster demon. The more it sees of the person it embodies the more natural it can become with its impersonations," I explain.

"Sometimes it evens kills or engulfs the target of imitation," Nick replies, less heated but still annoyed. "Is this what your Aunt meant about lives would be lost. Will this demon kill a love one of ours?"

Stillness fills the room. We figured that one of the lives would be one of us. Not someone who was simply in our lives. I didn't think that the stakes could get any higher. The targeting has been only on us so far, me mainly but now we have to worry about our family and other friends.

"We can't act out of fear or anger. Whatever we do we need to keep things logical. Mimik cannot do a perfect impression, especially for a long time. Prolong any interaction you have with someone that seems off," Dmitri warns.

"There was something else," Craig adds in. "We know who all is involved, other than Aiden. There are 4 individuals. A witch, two ambos, and a werewolf."

"Thank god, they don't have a vampire with them. We don't need two fast creatures. I can take another ambo down and a little wolf, easy," Jude says confidently.

"Don't be so sure of that, a matured werewolf can rip your head off with little fight. You're sixteen years old, kid," Dmitri humbles him. He gives us all a look, extending the warning to all. We are all just teenagers. We don't know the ages of everyone else. Just because Aiden was our age, that does not mean the rest are.

"Aiden was turned. We know that from Chepi. Also, we know from that, that there has to be an adult or a matured ambo in the mix; a teenager cannot turn a person into an ambo. I can't even do that. That's something you learn and develop when you go to college," Craig chuckles nervously. The weight of what we are up against is settling in. Every time we get a new detail it brings up another even more daunting fact. It almost makes me want to hide under the covers and use the rule of if you don't see it, it won't be real, it's not there.

"I found one of the names in the Beverly Hills High School student directory. It was Donna Leighton. I got into Aiden's Facebook and Instagram and he was friends with Donna, they have several pictures together. From his Instagram I was able to see her profile. I think she may be hiding in plain sight. She has a very witchy vibe to her. She can be dressing goth and seem like she is into wicca because she is actually a witch," Cassidy informs us.

That would be the easiest to hide under without actually covering up what you are. They probably believe that she is some weird goth kid. It is comforting to know that at least one of them is a teenager. But how will we get the other three? They aren't in the high school. Wait, The place in the woods. We can scope it out, in the daytime of course. We could see if they left any small tell as to who they are. One of them wasn't subtle at all, the other is hiding in plain sight, who's to say that the other three aren't the exact same?

"Red, that is way too dangerous, we can't take you guys there, besides, they probably cleaned up the area by now. You can't just have that stuff out in the daytime. They can't be that dumb. We should just go alone again," Jude responds to my thoughts.

"Stay out of my head, Jude," I warn him in a low threatening tone. Craig shoots him a glowering look to match.

"These guys don't seem too careful. We should go to the sight we found but during the day. No supernatural creature would ever have the gall to operate in broad daylight. Inexperienced or not, they would at least know that," Dmitri defends me.

Nick looks excited by this prospect. He loves onsite sleuthing. Craig looks a little apprehensive but doesn't say anything, as if he is biting his tongue. To no one's surprise Cassidy looks the least enthused. "In the least offensive way possible. This is exactly why most horror movies are of groups of white people. Why on earth would you guys want to go to the belly of the beast? We have such little knowledge on these people. Don't you think we should wait it out just a little bit and see exactly where their powers lie?"

There is a pregnant pause then laughter, we know she is right. She is 100% right about that. Even the smartest person in horror movies almost get killed from doing stupid things like what we are doing now. The only one of us who I don't have much to any fear for is Dmitri, I have strong confidence that he has more power than any of those guys. Craig's mentalists powers come in clutch as well as an extra layer of protection, but still.

"It was one thing to happen upon it, but to go back when we don't know how powerful they are is dangerous: incredibly irresponsible. I'm glad you spoke up Cas," Craig extends the gratitude.

We agree to hold off until we get some more information on them. At least one more. It is better to have half rather than a quarter. Cassidy and Nick are going to pursue Donna, Dmitri will be joining them for some muscle. Since those three are the only ones who have not had any interferences with these guys, they are the safest to send out now. But they naturally come to me, so I just gotta keep living and stay sane so Craig can catch them. Jude is going to try to get as much information as he can about any parties in the hills without over crossing any boundaries. Since he is being followed by Mimik he has to watch his back.

Once we get some research and a few more answers we are going to meet at Dmitri's house. Apparently, he and his parents put up a big act so that we wouldn't want to come over much. His dad isn't great at concealing that he is a vampire. Dmitri was appalled by the fact that we thought that he would speak to his mom that way. According to him she is a rose and he would never disrespect her. I applaud the dedication to seem scary and dysfunctional to ward away any guest, it seems very theatrical and on brand to Dmitri, apparently it is in the blood. Nevertheless, it feels good being able to make some progress on this. I hate that I have to offer up my sanity to do my part. I have come to the realization that my main purpose is to act as the bait. It's not a good feeling.

The Dinner

I wanted to get into more research about witches and look into werewolves as well. But seeing that Dmitri's mom, and I was told that almost a third of his family on the Vaduva side and all of his mom's side, are werewolves he said that he could just fill us in on any details that we may have. He never mentions his mom's maiden name. It seems like a security reason. But another thing that I forgot about was the fact that Cassidy was supposed to sleep over tonight. All her brothers are at the house and she needed a break. I told her that she can still spend the night, I'll just text her when it's over.

After they left at three, I went to go confront my Dad about the whole situation. Whenever he is faced with any kind of confrontation he usually smiles and takes the polite approach to deal with it. I have rarely seen that man upset. I go into his office and knock on the door; I'm upset but I don't want to be rude.

"Come, come," he says enthusiastically.

I barge in and place my hands on my hips, trying to look as hard as possible. His smile doesn't waiver, "Care to explain this dinner, dad?" I press, tapping my foot.

"Ah yes! So, Craig told you? Great, we are going over at 6! Dress nicely, Chuck tells me that Maggie is cooking up quite the meal," he enthuses.

"Father why?" I groan throwing my head back.

He laughs at me and says that I am being dramatic. It'll be fun, a magnificent bonding experience he says. Just as I suspected he would find no wrong in his action. He is like an innocent child. Losing all hope, I go to my only ally in this house on this.

"Mom!" I whine as I thump up the small set of stairs going into our four seasons room. As soon as I come in she sees how defeated I look and opens her arms to me. I get on my knees and collapse in them.

"I know," she says. "I tried to stop him, I kept telling him how horrible of an idea it is. But you know how he is when it comes to any event or outing with food."

"Like a kid in a freaking candy store," I mumble.

My Mom chuckles, "Well, the Edwards actually seem nice. They're English they have to be polite."

I pull away from her and give her a funny look.

She laughs at me, "Perhaps it won't be a dumpster fire like the last one. Your father," she glares off in the direction of his office cursing him, "he commissioned me to bake some kind of dessert. This was supposed to be my night off. Un pied en avant et le cœur plein d'espoir, best foot forward Rae, he says. Stay positive and hopeful for tonight" she mocks him and tosses her iPad to the side. "Do you want to help me bake it?" I nod and get up. I might as well. I need to do something to clear my mind for tonight. I wish I could be at the Edwards' house; I wonder how they are preparing for this. I love my Dad dearly he is a walking ball of happiness but his enthusiasm is gonna be the death of us one day.

It is 5:58, my Dad is huge on punctuality, and we are all in the family car driving up the hill to get to the Edward's gate. I put on a simple periwinkle dress, I noticed blues and purples looked best on me. I tried to do a nice makeup look but I kept messing it up. I wish Cassi was there to help me, she is so much better at it than me. I can barely do my makeup for gymnastics; Maci always has to touch me up. I'm not sure if my family is fully prepared to see the beauty that is the Edward's family and their home. I was a bit overwhelmed seeing both Craig and his dad together but seeing the family as a whole, in the flesh. My god, it will look like we are in the presence of the divine.

Craig texted me right before we left to warn me and my family about his mom. It isn't anything severe, it's just that his mom has a thick Scottish accent. He says it is so thick and she speaks so fast that new people have a hard time understanding her. I was confused by that because I thought his whole family was English but he explained that his mom is English by blood, but she was born and raised in Scotland so ethnicity wise, she is Scottish.

My parents are discussing the proper etiquette to deal with the situation if his mom says anything that we don't understand. I think we fully know how to properly handle someone who has a strong accent, we aren't ignorant idiots. We would never be offensive. But my parents slowly became on edge the closer the time came. It isn't like with the Harts. These are the Edwards, socialites, near royalty out here. They want to make sure as a family we give off the proper energy. I didn't get it at first, considering my Dad is close friends with Mr. Edwards and Josh is best friends with Erin. Not to mention Jimmy being obsessed with Lindsey. But much like us never seeing all of the Edwards together, they have never seen all the Bedeau's together and that is a whole new impression.

As we arrived at those golden gates the awe set in. Expecting are arrival, the gates opened as soon as we drove up. Only Josh and I have seen their home, but for my parents and Lindsey it was a shock to their system. As we pulled around into the circle drive the gawks and awes became ever present. I get it, it's like pulling up to a palace.

We didn't even have to ring the doorbell; the moment we approached the door Craig is standing in the doorway. He looks breathtaking. He has Italian leather shoes on with a black fitted suit, the jacket open exposing the perfectly fitted white button down he has on. A modern-day prince. His flawless smile gleaming instantly making me melt. But his eyes, they are indigo. He sneaks a look at me, a cry for help.

"Welcome Bedeau family," he says smoothly. He greets all of my family members as they enter. I walk in last; he guides me in, his hand on the small of my back.

"You look lovely," he coos in my ear. "I am in hell right now," he continues.

I quickly look at him and then I finally see what is going on. Dishes, furniture, food, decorations, are flying around the house. I look to him and then to my family, they don't notice, they are just looking around in utter amazement of his house.

"We went hunting before this so we wouldn't have any... accidents. But it went longer than expected and now my mum and dad are speed preparing the house. I have to cast an illusion on your family."

My stomach sinks thinking about what kind of accident that could have happened.

We join my family and Craig turns his charm up to a 10, he is like he was at his party back in October. He gives them a little tour of the house, carefully avoiding all of the flying objects or redirecting the objects. I knew that Craig was powerful but being able to cast an illusion on 4 people at the same time, talk to me, and telepathically move objects at the same time. Well, it really makes me wonder how much his powers extend.

As we reach the dining room, which a den sits across from, Craig quickly herds my family into the den. There must be something going on in the kitchen that he doesn't want them to see. Within seconds his mom appears. She is even more gorgeous than the picture I saw. That picture couldn't even compare to the beauty that was in front of us. Her golden hair is neatly in a French twist, I normally find that hairstyle ugly and extremely unflattering but she is working it. She is wearing a black dress that hugs her curves showing her perfect hourglass figure. Her eyes sparkle like Craig's and her smile, much like her son's and her husband's, warm and inviting.

"Aye, hello! It is so nice to meet cha all! I'm Margret, but you can call me Maggie," she chirps. Her voice is not in the slightest bit of what I was expecting. I thought it would be more melodic and proper. But it's warm, homey, and a bit harsh like you are in the countryside. As Craig warned her accent is extremely thick. As she went on about her enthusiasm, it became harder and harder to understand her.

"Mum," Craig warns, noticing our confused faces.

Mrs. Edwards turns red as a tomato, "Oh, I'm very sorry. When I go, I go. I'm not with me family, am I?" she laughs a very infectious laugh. "Well, dinner is in the oven. I would love to talk to ya before then. Christophe, Raven care to join me? My husband should be somewhere around these parts."

"Josh! Thank god you're here! Come with me! Lindsey, you can come too," Erin appears out of the woodwork. But before she pulls Josh away, she looks to my parents and greets them politely. She then turns to me and says in my head, *take care of that one, he is losing it*. She winks and scampers off with my brother. Lindsey follows along so that she isn't alone. Once my parents leave, I see Craig's eyes go back to the normal pale blue.

He takes a breath in relief and sinks into a chair. He looks incredibly tired and stressed. He doesn't let go of my hand, his fingers dance along my hand as he sits looking at the wall. I know my silence is what he needs. I sit on the arm of the chair and use my other hand to smooth his hair. "You look really handsome."

"You have no idea the amount of stress I have been under today. I am dreading you guys meeting Michael. That man has no humanity. He wasn't raised fully by my parents. My grandparents see humans as one thing and one thing only. I don't know why they invited him," he grumbles. He wants me closer to him, but with our families walking about the home I don't want to sit in his lap and cuddle up.

I gently turn his face towards me and smile, "Well Erin is extraordinarily strong, if he gets out of line, she can physically hold him back, right?"

"Erin could crush every bone in his body, but that tosser has an unworldly rejuvenation rate. Which is why he isn't dead yet," Craig laughs.

"You say that as if you've tried to get rid of him before," I tease.

Craig looks at me and then back at the wall playfully. I lightly smack his arm and we share in a laugh.

A man appears before us.

"Willy, how are we supposed to dress tonight?"

Oh hello. To my guess this is Michael. He stands damp with a towel around his waist. His hair wet and slicked back. His perfectly chiseled body has little droplets of water clinging to his muscles.

Craig jumps out of his chair and balls his hand into a fist and points it outward towards the entrance of the den.

"What the *hell* are you doing?" Craig hisses at him getting into his face.

"I didn't know the attire for tonight, sorry. Oi, who is this then?" He redirects his attention over to me and pushes past Craig. "You must be Jezebel, pleasure. I'm William's older brother, Michael," he says taking my hand and kisses. Craig knocks him away. His accent is so different from Craig's and Mr. Edwards.

"We are dressing formal as you can see, can you get back upstairs and put some clothes on?!"

"Willy, always the feisty one," Michael chuckles. He gives me a parting wave and disappears. That was quite an introduction. Despite Craig's fuming I am happy to see how warmly his family have accepted us. But I wonder what he means about his brother not having any humanity. I don't want to deep dive into that now.

"Do you need a smoke?" I ask him. He laughs at me taking my hands again.

"I wish, I can't be inebriated in any state tonight. Let's go find our parents."

I nod and we walk around his house in a calming silence trying to locate our parents. He could have just teleported us near them but I think he wanted this time to just be alone with me. It's good to know that it's not just me who is extremely worried about this dinner.

As we walk around his wealth maze of a house, I ask him about the hunt. He tells me how they first went up to the redwoods of Northern California. But that wasn't enough. They were still extremely hungry, so they went up to the Yukon territory next. And since they were close by, they went to Alaska afterwards. They finally felt full enough after visiting the three places. He explained they normally don't do that much hunting just for one day, they normally take their hunting to the Immortal Realm. Those creatures fill them up more than mortal creatures. I wonder why they didn't hunt for humans, but when I asked, Craig just shook his head. I'm not comfortable by the idea of his family eating humans but I try to put it into perspective. There are some things about the beast side of himself that he isn't quite ready to disclose. It's not from distrust but out of fear of how I would react. So, I don't push.

We end up giving up trying to find them so we just settle in his kitchen. Things are still flying around and being prepared via telekinesis. I didn't know that ambos could do this stuff remote. I look around at all the food, and it's a lot of food. How much do they expect us to eat? It all looks so delicious but my family and I could never finish all of this, even with the help of his family this seems impossible.

Craig comes close to me and locks me up to a counter. My heart starts racing as blush rushes over my face. He looks down at me, his eyes hungry. He presses his forehead against mine. "Do you want to be my chef's assistant?" He asks me. I struggle to find my voice and just nod. He slowly slides his hands to my waist and helps me up on the counter.

He slides over to the pot on the stove next to me and seamlessly takes over the spoon. He begins chopping up some extra ingredients while humming a tune. I sit staring at him in awe, it's like he has extra hands the way he is working. Once he moves from another station, he floats the vegetables my way to add to the pot. He moves over to the oven and takes out some chicken that has been cooking. His hand glows red just like it did at lunch the first day we went public at school. He picks up the chicken as if it isn't fresh out of the oven. He skillfully chops it up and flies the tray over to me so fast that it nearly hits me. He laughs and apologizes.

I giggle and use a knife to slide the chicken into the pot. He comes over to me stirring the pot again making sure everything is mixed in together. He adds a few more seasonings and takes a spoonful of the soup. He gently blows on it and puts the spoon up to my mouth. He raises his eyebrows anticipating my reaction.

I carefully swallow the hot soup. Oh wow, oh wow this is good. This is incredible. He chuckles at my silent reaction. My face isn't hiding my feelings. "It's good?" he asks.

I nod, my eyes big still allowing the flavors to dance on my tongue.

"Mind if I taste?"

I look puzzled but then he starts to get closer to me, his lips inches away from mine.

"We eat here, Craig," Jimmy says interrupting us.

Craig stops right before reaching me and chuckles. "You're right." He helps me back down and puts a lid over the soup. He turns the heat down to a barely simmer.

Jimmy's eyes are lilac. That is more jarring than I expected it to be. Craig's indigo eyes are unnatural but it's still somewhat in the spectrum of being realistic. But seeing those bright purple eyes is jarring.

"Plants?" Craig gestures at Jimmy. Jimmy nods and takes out a can of sprite from the fridge.

"Mum wanted some more greenery in the dining room," Jimmy responds. Mum? I guess if everyone else in your family has an accent you will pick up on a few things. That brings my head to an earlier curiosity.

"Hey, why does Michael have a British accent but it sounds different from you and your dads?"

The mention of his name made Craig go stiff but he responds anyway, "We live in Surrey as you know but my brother spent most of his time with my grandparents up north. They live in Manchester. His accent slowly changed overtime. See, hardly part of this family," Craig mumbles the last sentence under his breath.

"Erin and I don't talk like we are from Surrey; we have American accents. Are we barely a part of the family?"

"You guys are slowly getting one. Certain words you say with an accent. Just wait until next year when we are there permanently."

"You should be lighter on Mike."

"Well maybe he should have been a better brother. And you aren't the one who is getting the blunt end of all his mistakes. You just go about your days hardly even being an ambo ignoring your responsibilities to draw. So shut it Jim," Craig barks storming off into the dining room.

Jimmy looks hurt. I give him a caring smile and put my hand on his shoulder. "He doesn't mean it," I reassure. I don't even know if it is a true statement. But Jimmy is so sweet.

He smiles back at me, "He sort of means it. He gets really mad when we sympathize with Mike. He isn't that bad, now. From the stories I heard he wasn't the greatest and Craig has every reason to be mad. But we're family ya know. Mum always taught us to be strong and hold on to family. In her words, blood is thicker than water, hold on until you can't anymore... even if they're shite."

That's quite a saying. We laugh and he downs his Sprite and goes into the dining room as well. When I enter the room, Mr. Edwards appeared next to Craig. He has his hand on Craig's shoulder in a concerning way. He is muttering something to him, only for their ears. I do catch him asking how he is doing and if he is tired. Their eyes glance in my direction then back at the table.

"Why is Wil half beast?" Erin's voice sounds next to me suddenly.

I look back at Craig and see nothing different. He looks the same.

"I sympathized with Mike and he did not take it too well." Jimmy explains nursing a plant.

"He is hiding it from you girl," Erin says.

I jerk my head back around to him; I don't see a change in his eyes. I guess when you are in an illusion you can't see it. Makes sense.

"Everyone take your place, it is dinner time," Mr. Edwards calls his voice like a megaphone. Michael appears at the table, this time dressed. Mrs. Edwards comes floating into the room with my family. She joins her husband to the right of the head of the table. They stand behind the seats in age order so unfortunately Craig has to sit next to Michael. My Mom looks at my Dad then at me. We follow what they do and scramble about to get in the same order. They all look so perfect, it's hard to not feel inferior when you are standing right across from them. I know I shouldn't be shocked by his family's beauty but they all clean up spectacularly.

As if a shock hit Mr. and Mrs. Edwards they spark up and scurry out of the room bringing multiple rounds of food in on silver trays. The children all stay standing looking picturesque. I squint at Craig to try to find a tear in the illusion but nothing. I wonder if he stopped. *Looking for something?* He says in my head. I break my stare and focus my attention to my siblings. Erin and Josh are making faces at each other while Jimmy is staring hopelessly at Lindsey. She is avoiding eye contact as much as possible. My parents are whispering to each other about how impressed by the spread they are. And debate on whether they should help. They decided that they should at least offer. They go off to the kitchen. *I'm not casting an illusion anymore. I know you are curious.* He winks at me. You'll make it through this. *Next to this bollocks? Who knows?* I roll my eyes and he smiles.

The parents return, my parents did help, they brought in the drinks. Looking at this spread is making my mouth water. If the soup is tasting that amazing, I can only imagine how the rest tastes. Returning to their spots Mr. and Mrs. Edwards grin big. "Dinner is served," Mrs. Edwards gleams.

Just as I suspected the food was unworldly. My parents asked for recipes so that they can try to make them themselves. After eating the soup and salad we did a round table introduction. But by the time dinner rolled around everyone had met everyone. All except Michael, who Lindsey could not keep her eyes off of. I still could not see what was all bad about him. He blends in well with his family, you would never be able to tell he has never been around humans. As far as I could tell my family liked the Edwards. My Mom and Mrs. Edwards became quick friends. She is a lovely woman, Mrs. Edwards, she is so kind and spends all of her extra time volunteering, fundraising, and she even opened her own animal sanctuary. She is like a modern-day saint. But she didn't have a god complex, she still feels like she isn't doing enough. My Mom already invited her to come to the bakery after hours and to come out for a girls' night.

Our dads were gabbing like the best of friends. They were making fun of the men down at the country club. Talking about the stuffy nature of the people they encounter on the daily. They joke about work; you would think they were coworkers the way they knew about each other's work life. My Dad even knew the other judges by name. It was interesting to see them interact so well. The elites more so keep to themselves. When they interact with humans they still stand out and seem so inhuman. But at this dinner you couldn't even tell the difference between human and ambo. Between the conversations and the jokes, it was as if we have been together for ages. It was interesting enough to see and be privy to Craig's magnetism but to see the whole family at work, amazing. You'd swear it was a scene out of a movie. The functionality, the way everything moved so smoothly from one convo to the other.

"So, Craig, have you thought about college yet?" My Dad asks before taking a bite of his food.

Craig looks a little sullen. We've had this conversation before. "I am going into law, like my Dad... and my brother. So, I will probably major in criminal justice and political science."

His dad looks pleased with his answer, a well-rehearsed one. His mom looks down at her food and gives a look of pity. She looks as if she is debating to speak up.

"That's very impressive, Jez is looking to major in history. But still will keep her gymnastics. The goal is UCLA," my Mom gushes. This sparks a discussion about my sport, and future major. It's nice, oh so nice that the Edwards genuinely care. The Harts kind of brushed me off and told me how it wasn't the most lucrative path. But the more we talked about me pursuing my passion the more in despair Craig looked. He tried to hide it with smiles, but I could see right through it. He hates so much how his future is laid out in front of him. He knows the moment he goes back to the Immortal Realm his freedoms will lessen greatly.

"Craig here is a patron of the arts. A bright musician. He plays the saxophone. If it wasn't so set in stone with the family, he has been telling me recently that he is very interested in musical therapy," Mrs. Edwards beams about Craig. It puts a smile on his face.

This sparks my parents interests even more. Both of them love the arts. They were so happy when Lindsey joined orchestra and also showed interest in percussion. My parents love the arts but I don't have a musical bone in my body and Josh is more interested in goofing off. Another reason why my Dad loved Dmitri so much, the moment he learned that Dmitri played cello, he was sold. I'm glad he knows that Craig plays saxophone now, perhaps that will hinder his minor obsession of him wanting me and Dmitri to be together. He did see Craig play before, at the holiday concert, but that was before he knew who he was.

Mr. Edwards looks proud of Craig but has a look of sorrow deep in his eyes. I believe he is saddened by all the pressure that is put on Craig. His younger siblings get a bit more freedom. For now, at least. But he carries on talking about how Erin is in kick boxing and how she is stronger than most guys despite her size. That makes her sit up straighter and bask in the praise. I wonder if it is considered cheating the fact that she is a brute and is naturally much stronger than even the average ambo.

He also mentions how artistic Jimmy is. And how he gardens. "All of the plants you see in this room was grown by him actually." It was the one time I saw Lindsey actually look impressed by something about Jimmy. This makes him blush.

I couldn't help but notice how quiet Mike was being. He didn't have much to say but he sure was nursing his drink. I can tell he was trying to be extra careful. He does look a bit nervous and on edge. He pours himself another glass of wine. He excuses himself and returns with a shorter glass with a brown liquid, this causes Craig to side eye him a bit.

He offers some to the adults at the table, it's brandy. Josh and Erin lift their empty glasses. Michael gets up and takes their glasses. "Mike, I-" Mr. Edwards starts but Michael gives him a secret wicked grin. My parents look nervous about the situation. My Mom begins to get up but then Michael returns as quick as he left. He has two identical glasses to the one he had with a few perfect pieces of ice. He sets the cups down in the middle of the table to make a display of it. He pulls from behind his back some apple juice and pours it in the glasses. Everyone cracks a smile and laughs. He slides the glasses to the two then pick up his drink, "Cheers," he toasts tilting his glass to them. Craig laughs and smiles with the rest of us but I can see the annoyance in his eyes.

"Mike, you're a junior in college, right?" My Mom asks. Lindsey eagerly turns to give him her full attention. She is fully smitten.

"In my third and final year, I go to Oxford," he boasts after taking a sip of his drink.

"Oxford? Following in your father's footsteps? A legacy thing huh," my Dad teases. "What do you study, you know, your steppingstone into law for grad school?"

"PPE, Philosophy, Politics, and Economics. But I dropped the Economics bit after my first year,"

"How is it? Oxford?" I ask. I have been avoiding conversation with him all night but I am so curious about this. Like my Mom said the plan is UCLA but school overseas sounds interesting.

"Well I am in my last year, like I said. It is a 3-year thing. But the course work is mad."

He doesn't actually go to Oxford. It is an act.

"I would recommend not going if you like fun. Willy here is just buzzin' thinking about when he will be there in two years." He puts his arm around Craig's shoulder and shakes him a bit.

Craig takes a breath. There seems to have been some kind of salt in Michael's tone. "Well someone has to restore the legacy. Besides, you managed to find a way to have nothing but fun the whole time you were there. Or can you not remember past this morning?"

"Don't be snide, Willy."

"Okay!" Mr. Edwards says breaking the tension as he claps.

My family becomes frozen in time. The Edwards are all looking at the two brothers. Both of them teeth bared.

"Aye, yer two stop this! We have dinner guest," Mrs. Edwards hisses at them.

"I have been on my best behavior all night. I make one joke and this one gets personal!" Michael defends.

"Your best behavior, your thoughts are very loud and 90% of them have been about how good they would taste," Craig snaps back.

He has been thinking about eating my family? I don't feel very comfortable being around him anymore. What if he acts on it?

"Don't worry, they would never let me," Michael rolls his eyes as the bottle of brandy floats in and pours into his glass. Did he just read my mind?

"Stay out of her thoughts," Craig threatens through clenched teeth.

"Since when do we stay out of human's heads? We are ambos, it's what we do, yeah?"

Craig squints and his eyes flash indigo. Michael holds his head and cries out in agony and his glass breaks. I jump startled by the glass breaking. What just happen?

"William!" His parents scold.

"Wil what is your problem?"

Michael collects his bearings as Mrs. Edwards tries to help soothe him.

"He isn't used to being around humans, come on Craig you know that," Jimmy adds.

"He isn't a wild animal! But I guess he can't control his thoughts considering he has been drinking all night. But he is sick right? That's not his fault either?" Craig snaps at everyone.

Mr. Edwards disappears for a second and returns cleaning up the brandy and the glass shards. "You need to get some air, Craig. When I bring the time back you excuse yourself." Mr. Edwards turns and gives me an apologetic look. Another glass appears and is filled to where it was before time was stopped. I see what he means, about the family dynamic being off with Michael in the mix. I can't help but feel bad for Craig, I don't know what was being said in Michael's head but I can't imagine it was pleasant. Craig wouldn't have reacted the way he did if it was minor.

Mr. Edwards returns to his seat and everyone goes back to the original pose that they were at before the time stop. I feel like I shouldn't have been a part of that. That seemed like a private family matter. *Clap!*

Craig stands up and smiles apologetically. "I'm sorry for my outburst. Sorry Michael. I just need some air. I'll be right back." Before any of us got the chance to react he was walking out of the room. Without letting the moment seep in, the Edwards engaged my family in conversation. "That croquembouche looks real good Mrs. Bedeau, can we dig in?" Erin asks.

This engages everyone in the dessert excitement. I wonder where Craig went. I should go and find him. I stand up and tapped my Mom on the shoulder and told her I was going to find Craig. She nods and says that is probably best.

I speed walk out the room and start to search. Where would he go. He said he would get some air, but did he actually go outside? Maybe he is in their backyard. I race over to the back of the house. I open the patio door and he was sitting on a step, his back to the door. I see some smoke blow out in front of him. Thank god. "I thought you couldn't get inebriated?" I poke, teetering towards him.

He turns to look at me and playfully blows smoke in my direction. I cough and swat it away. He puts out his joint and guides me down to sit in his lap. "Yeah, well they already think I am the villain for attacking the family drunk."

"What did you do to him?"

"I emitted a sound frequency that was so loud and violent that it caused him a pain even greater than a common migraine and has the ability to crack his skull if I did it for longer," he responds coolly.

I push away from him, "Craig! I know you don't like him, but to crack your brother's skull?"

"I could have... I didn't. Just awfully close to doing it. No one but me heard all those vile things he was thinking and imagining. I honestly could not tell if he would act on any of it. He isn't worried about the safety of the family or anything. He just doesn't care about humans in general. I don't think less of any ambo who doesn't have humanity. To each their own. But him? Such a mistake bringing him here." He shakes his head and holds me close.

God, what was he planning on doing to me and my family? I try to rationalize it in my head. Like if I were to be in the presence of a cow. Would I imagine all the ways I would kill it and how much I would love to eat it, if it was standing there living and breathing? Can't say I would. But I think some people think like that. Like people who hunt and eat what they kill or when people do that with fishing. Still it is weird to think about. Not to mention he was reading our thoughts the whole night as well. I have no proof of that, but just going of him reading my mind and then saying 'since when do we stay out of humans' heads.

That's probably how he was able to be so natural and quick witted with any questions that came his way. Ambos don't play fair, I knew that. But I was so used to how Craig and his family were, I didn't think too much on how unfair things could be with them. Why would one play fair when attacking a lesser being. Humans certainly don't play fair with other creatures. This makes me think of the investigation. We need training. We need to work on how to be able to fight and properly rival against these creatures. I don't want to bring this up to Craig right now. I want him to be relaxed and happy.

"My Mom made a croquembouche, it is physically impossible to be stressed and mad while eating a puff pastry."

He smiles up at me and gets up. "You're right."

We finally leave at 9. As soon as we got in the car, I texted Cassidy. She was elated to hear from me. She was tired of all the male energy around her. There are three girls in the house right now but there are five boys and I can 100% see why she needs to get away from that.

Craig wanted to hang out with me and Cassidy but he has to fully make amends with his family. Despite the small outburst my family loves the Edwards. Even Lindsey warmed up to Jimmy by the end of the night. We were all amazed the most by how much they can put away. All of them are fit as a whistle but they ate most of the food. Whatever we couldn't finish they gladly took care of it.

Cassidy met us at my house and was super eager to see we still had some dessert. Before we settled in my room, she took some of the pastries with her upstairs. But she wants the full details of everything that went on. While I washed my face and got ready for bed, I filled her in on all the details.

"Craig almost killed his brother?!"

"Well, almost cracked his skull. I'm not sure if that would have killed him."

"Jesus, Dre makes me wanna pull every hair out of my head but I have never wanted to crack his skull. I guess supernaturals have more violent thoughts."

I return to my bedroom and shrug. "I guess. But look at this," I pull out my phone. We all took a picture together, she needs to see how ridiculously out of this world they look.

As soon as she sees the picture her jaw drops. "Damn! The whole family is hot!"

I agree and I demand for her to rant out all of her frustrations. Her Greek grandparents made a surprise appearance, or as she calls them yayá and papús, and Cassidy nearly lost it. She loves them greatly, but she does have a slight preference to her black side coming over, while her whole family is abrasive the black side is slightly more subdued. Both sides are very fun and loving.

Volume can be an issue for sure. She was happy to see her grandparents but she wanted a chilled night. She got swamped with questions, mainly on why she quit cheerleading and why she doesn't have a boyfriend. Her brothers chipped in on some relentless teasing while throwing in some humble brags about themselves. But Cassidy is always quick with a comeback. Her wit goes unmatched when she is challenged. She taught me the art of playing the dozens. Something she can thank her brothers for. She thanked me for the sanctuary that I offered her tonight. She says that she gets the best sleep when she is here. We always do stuff as the four of us but me and Cassidy need our girl time and time just to rant to one another without the boys interfering. As Cassidy says, a quick vent between girls gives you clear skin. Cassidy is always ready to help me. Granted I am usually more in peril than she is, but whenever she asks for girl time, I am ready to drop everything.

We end up talking until 11:30 but we aren't even remotely tired. So, we decided to scour through Donna's Instagram. Cassidy managed to hack her way into her account as well. From what we saw she is definitely hiding in plain sight.

"Her style is cool, you gotta admit. I would never be able to pull something off like that. Well for one, my granny would think I turned into a Satanist," Cassidy jokes. "We should make Dmitri seduce her. He has the look. He has a lip ring for Christ sakes. Get him to put those good looks into use."

"Why not, girls are usually made to be the sexy bait in these situations. Dmitri can show off that swimmer's body a bit and help us out."

"Yes, let's sexualize our men." We burst out laughing. A little too loud because my Mom calls for us to get to bed.

Obviously, we aren't going to actually go with that plan. The last time we tried to seduce one of these people, Craig ended up drugged. Investigations in the shadows is the way to go. But the other way would have been fun too.

Divine Intervention

Craig managed to smooth things over with his family. They didn't know that he gained the ability to shield them from his thoughts while creating false ones. He told them how sorry he was and it was just all the stress he was under. In return he was forced to have tea with Michael. He swears it was the most painful 2 hours of his life. Drama queen.

I became burned out on all the investigating and studying the Immortal Realm that I'd actually wanted to do homework. I never thought I would say those words. Trying to do physics is somehow more soothing than looking up the magical insight of witches and wizards.

Lindsey is practicing in her room, every once in a while, when she gets the melody right it is kind of nice to hear. I wish she would practice her drumming instead; it may be loud but at least it won't be a screeching high pitch wrong note. Violin, couldn't do cello, or bass? She still would have been out of tune at times but at least the notes would be lower. Josh is trying to counter her practicing with loud music to drown her out. Her room is far enough from him that it wouldn't be much of a bother to her. But for me, the clashing of sound is making it impossible to concentrate.

My Mom is with Mrs. Edwards, she invited her out to come to brunch with her, Mrs. Papakonstatinos, and Mrs. Babicz, Nick's mom. I was shocked to hear that she invited her out to meet the girls so soon. It has only been a week since they first met. I have been telling my Mom that her and the others are like a cult. Mrs. Vaduva was welcomed in after the holiday party. And now she is fully engulfed with their shenanigans as well. I guess they are going to suck Mrs. Edwards in too. It's nice having your best friends' parents being friends, you have more free range when hanging out with them. But they also share too much information about us too.

My Dad ended up getting swamped with some work dealings, he has been on call with France all morning. He sounds super stressed but let's me chill in his office with him to work. This doesn't turn out to be an any better situation. Has my house always been this loud? Maybe if I go work in the attic, or maybe the basement. I think I have become too spoiled to Craig's sound proofing. I'm not going to get any work done here. I have no clue how Cassidy does it with her full house. I was thinking about texting Nick to see if he would let me come over so I can get some work done, but I know he is knee deep with a group project. He loathes working with anyone who isn't us. 'Incompetence, all of these people are incompetent and a waste of my time!' he has been yelling this whole week. We all roll our eyes at him but we know how much of a pain doing group projects are for Nick. In his defense, he does do 90% of the work.

I stare blankly at my textbook, I got completely sidetracked by my thoughts. It is chilly, but I'm going to take my work outside. I wave at my Dad and whisper good luck to him. He signs the cross across his chest and twinkles his fingers at me. Midafternoon on a Saturday and I am pacing about my house to try to find somewhere to do homework.

I settle in the backyard with one of Craig's hoodies. He hardly wore it so he gave it to me. He said he heard that's what humans do. I looked at him funny when he said that because I'm pretty sure that's what a lot of couples do, human or not. To be fair, I am his first real relationship. His scent never left the hoodie, I think that is my favorite part of it.

As I cozy up, burrowing my body into a warm ball, my mind feels clear enough for me to actually work. While I'm not flying through my homework, I am getting way more done than I was when I was inside. I know I will never use any of this information past this year, but I still need to get at least a B in this class. I wish I could be like Dmitri in the sense that he doesn't care what he gets in any class. He always rode heavy on the C's get degrees motto. Which, in some cases he is right. But knowing that once he graduates, he is going on vacation mode until he is 25, makes his so lax attitude towards school all the worlds difference.

Getting all caught up with the excitement of these rebels that we need to hunt down, I nearly forgot about the SATs. My friends and I originally were going to take it in March, but none of us figured we would be ready next month to take it, so we bumped it to May. Craig and Dmitri are supposed to help us study for it. Hopefully, we can make some waves on this stupid investigation so our lives can continue.

Something woken in me this past week and made me want to go back and re-read all of my old dream journal entries. See if I can find a connection. Something about the Rory character seems so real. He is an ambo. It got me thinking that perhaps he is one of the people who is a part of this rebel group. Though he was not one of the names Chepi mentioned. The more I look into everything, the more I feel like I am losing my mind. I can draw a connection from what I ate for lunch two weeks ago to this investigation.

Bzzz bzzz. I snap out of my thought and pick up my phone. Craig is calling. My heart beats a little faster.

"Hey, you wouldn't happen to know anything about electromagnetic radiation, would you?" I say as I answer.

"I do, but I'll help you with physics later if you don't mind. Can you spare a few hours for me?"

"Depends... what do you need me for a few hours for?" I respond feeling playful.

"You humans criticize ambos for being too sexual. You guys are the deviants," he teases making me laugh. "I just wanted you to come to lunch with me... and my friends."

His friends? He wants me to go to lunch with 5 ambos, where 3 out of the 5 hate me? And ambo or not, I definitely don't want to spend time with Candice. I can't believe I thought of her as the nice one of the group. Well, to be fair, she might actually be, but she was awfully quick to jump to Travis.

Craig notices my hesitation and jumps in to cut the silence. "We won't be eating human... if that's what you're worried about," he blurts out.

That wasn't my first concern that was running through my head, but now it is definitely the number one spot. "It's not that... that didn't even cross my mind to be honest, Craig. The issue is that your friends hate me."

Craig starts laughing as if I said something amusing instead of stating a fact. It's like he has amnesia. Did last year fully escape his memory? He admitted that his friends didn't like me when we first started talking.

"They don't hate you Jezebel."

"Oh, you are 100% full of crap, Edwards. You said last year that the girls were dreadful and now you want me to hang out with them? They don't even call me by my name! Not to mention one of them is dating my ex!"

"To be fair, you are dating me, and I'm Bridget's ex so, you know."

I let out a low growl and roll my eyes. He knows it's not the same, unless, he was lying to me about how serious him and Bridget were.

I do suppose it is only fair for me to hang out with his friends, he hangs out with mine. But mine are nice and love him.

"Listen, I may have overstated the girls' dreadfulness. Bridget is like me, humane wise, she wouldn't hurt you, in an ambo type of way. Jeanette doesn't have much of an opinion on you, she was mainly mean to you because of Bridget. And I don't think Candice will even be there. Please, can you come. I told them that I wanted you there and that I was inviting you."

His pleading voice is starting to break me down a little. While I still don't think this is remotely a good idea, to be a fair and just girlfriend, I should go. I sigh and give in, making Craig very happy. I have t-minus 20 minutes to get ready for this lunch. It's at the Farquhar's. Which I didn't know upon agreeing to this lunch.

Craig is super excited for me to spend time with him and his friends. He keeps trying to reassure me that he said what he said last year to get in my good graces. 'People like it when you hate the people they hate, makes them trust you more.' I wanted to slap him; it is much different when they are your friends. The subtle things that he does that are just normal ways that ambos act is simply wrong in human interaction. The amount of times I have to tell him that some of his ways of growing closer to someone can be borderline manipulative. Such as reading someone's thoughts to know how to react or what to say so the person will have a positive reaction. He is genuinely confused about that one.

"I get that, but in the same manner I don't think it is that bad. I don't want to offend you, I want you to trust me and like me. It's not like these aren't truthful words from me, they are just perfectly manufactured for the most positive conversation. I don't do it all the time, just when I first meet people. I'm not being fake, if they think something I don't like, I don't switch to their side. People fumble on the right things to say when they first meet a person, is it so wrong that I ensure that things go a little smoother?"

"Craig, dear, it is still wrong. I'm human, I cannot read your mind to do the same to you. Nor am I used to people reading my thoughts. Not everything has to be calculated and planned. Some of the best first impression interactions are made from spontaneity."

He squints but nods reluctantly. I'm not mad at him. Very seldom does he use his power in that manner. I get it though, if I had the ability to read minds, I would do wellness like checks to see if the person is perceiving me correctly. It took some time, but seeing how Craig interacts with our classmates compared to me and my friends, I know that he is 100% genuine with us. I trusted him back in January that he didn't manipulate me to have feelings for him. But I couldn't stop thinking if he was putting on an act sometimes with my friends. Turns out he really is that easy going and charming. Almost sickening to think about how perfect he is.

"Do you wanna know the moment I knew that I liked you?" He asks me, gleaming. The soft glow of the sun casts a perfect angelic light around him.

"Yes, I want exact details. An exact transcript of your thoughts." I wanted to know this with Travis but he wouldn't share. He said it sullies the moment or some profound nonsense that I can't quite remember.

He rolls his eyes at me says okay in a mocking tone, as he pretends to backtrack his thoughts to get the exact wording. "When we were doing the whole get to know you thing when we spent time alone for the first time, ya know, after I sat too close to you," he slips me a little playfully sinister look.

I scoff and encourage him to continue. He *was* sitting too close to me then. I had every reason to be a little nervous.

"Well when I started talking about my travels with my friends and how they were basically being teenagers, but I wanted to experience culture more rather than party, this impressed you because you were on the same wavelength as me. However, your thoughts didn't go how I expected it, you thought this about my friends, and I quote, People like them don't deserve to be well traveled, they don't know what to do."

I look at him skeptically. That. That was the moment that made him realize that he had a crush on me? He reads my skeptical face and chuckles.

"I'm serious. I have told girls about me traveling before and how I prefer to take in the culture rather than party, and they just normally go all goo goo eyed on me, which is fine. But you, immediately going into anger over my friends not doing the same. I don't know," he trails off smiling thinking about the memory. I don't get it but seeing him smile so fondly and warmly about me gives me butterflies.

He starts to lightly chuckle about something. I ask him what it's about and he shakes his head. "It's corny. You're going to make fun of me."

"I might, but I would still like to hear."

He shakes his head again. "No, no, I'll tell you some other time. We are here."

Jude and Jeanette's house is big and spectacular just like the Edwards. But their house is more modern looking. Incredibly open with windows and boxy features. I take my time opening the door to get out. Craig opens it the rest of the way and takes my hand leading me out.

Somehow, it is so much brighter over here. All the light is bouncing off the extraordinarily white house and outdoor décor. Craig's house is a palace, beautiful and astonishing but only the lucky can be allowed in. But the twins' house, is extravagant in a minimalist, simplistic manner. The house in a way is more exposed. All the corners of the house are clean cut, crafted perfectly to a fine detail so that no piece is out of place. Even the cars outside match with the clean, expensive look. Three cars sit in the driveway, shiny and black. They are so pristine it looks as if they have never seen the road. As we approach the house, I notice that it still gives off the same vibe as Craig's home, welcoming, while still being exclusive. While the Edwards' home feels warm the Farquhar's feels cool.

"Are you sure they want me here?" I ask Craig squeezing his hand tighter.

"Yeah, Jude is excited to see you and Jeanette didn't seem too moved either way."

That's good, I guess. "And what about Bridget and Candice?"

He keeps smiling but won't look at me. "Candice won't be here. She is with Travis."

The way he refuses to give any explanation on how Bridget is feeling gives me all the answers I need on her. I sigh, a little too loudly. It catches his attention and he strokes the back of my hand with his thumb.

"Don't worry about her."

I huff and shake my head. Easier said than done.

He stops walking and moves in front of me. He takes both of my hands and lifts them up to his lips, as he gives them a soft kiss. "Darling," I will never admit it out loud but I love it when he calls me that. With his accent it sounds so alluring and makes me melt every time. "I would never put you in a situation where you would be ostracized. Bridget isn't the happiest, no, but she likes that I am happy and will grow to like you more and more. We were friends first and fake lovers second. Please don't fret over her," he strokes my hair and his fingers linger on my wavy ends. "Everything will be okay, I promise." He leans in and kisses my forehead softly.

Just as the outside, the inside is just as incredible and modern. I almost don't want to sit on anything or touch anything, every piece of furniture and decoration is so carefully place to balance the room. Black, white, and light wood with touches of green are the colors of the house. Sterile? Maybe sterile isn't the right word but is the only fitting adjective I can use to describe this home. In perfect silence, you can hear the clicking of heels in the next room. Much like at Craig's dishes are floating around. Not in the hectic manner but in an organize fashion, like it was in his kitchen.

"Red!" Jude calls, spotting us first. He has a large sharp knife in hand as he comes jogging up to us. He grips me in a bear hug; Craig slips the knife out of his hand and places it on the table. "So, do you like my house?" He asks parting from his hold.

I smile and nod. It's not that I don't like the house, it just makes me feel uneasy. I shouldn't have thought that, they could all be reading my mind.

"Well, come on and make yourself comfortable. Chat with the girls about girl stuff," he says leading Craig away from me. Oh no, no, no I will not be left alone with Bridget and Jeanette. Craig resists him and insists on staying with me. He locks his body to mine with his arm around my waist.

Jude still manages to break us apart and claims that I need to be alone with the girls so they can truly get to know me. "They won't bite, as long as Craig is here. Nothing to worry about Red," Jude pats my shoulder.

He makes his way deeper into his kitchen as I scowl at him. "Must you always steal my boyfriends?"

"Stop dating such sexy men," he counters as he starts to play with Craig's hair. Craig swats him away as Jude lets out a roar of a laugh.

I want to remain annoyed but that was a great comeback. I quickly turn so he cannot see the spreading smile.

I go over to the next room that somehow commands the most light, in there is a dark marbled table where Bridget and Jeanette sit. Their hair perfect, as always, glowing under the sun as their skin shines in radiant beauty. They are giggling about something and don't seem to notice that I'm even here.

Jeanette is the first to turn around. While Bridget has the looks of a beauty queen, that classic kind of beauty; Jeanette is like a femme fatale. Looks so stunning and striking it reminds me of Megan Fox. Both Bridget and Jeanette together, it's like seeing Eris and Aphrodite at the same table. Jeanette smiles at me, "Ginger bitch, glad you can make it." And just like that, the magic is gone.

I walk over and take a seat across from them. They have the fakest smiles I have ever seen plastered across their faces. I make sure to study their eyes, to see if anything wonky is going on. Bridget's hazel eyes are looking dazzling and sparkle like light does on water and Jeanettes chocolate brown eyes are so sultry I even feel mildly seduced looking at her.

"So, let's get rid of the elephant in the room," Jeanette breaks the silence. She gestures to me and Bridget. Both of us look at one another in a challenging glare. Up until this point I have no clue why Bridget has hated me so much, years of being rude to me and now I am supposed to kiss and make up?

"Oh please, so the ginger stole your man who wasn't really your man," Jeanette says nonchalant.

"She kissed him, three times, while we were still together."

"You were never really together," I defend myself.

"But you were on such a high horse calling me a stuck-up bitch and Jen a catty whore! You never even gave us a chance but you wanna play the victim."

My eyes grow large and I back down. Of course, she heard my thoughts. I didn't think those things until somewhat recently. Well since the 2nd half of freshman year.

Jeanette laughs, taking a lot of amusement out of the situation. "Hey, to be fair Bridge, it's true," she continues to laugh. Bridget scowls at her but Jeanette does not stop.

"Oh come on, Bridge, you know it is true! Besides, she doesn't know any better, cut her some slack." I'm surprise by how lenient Jeanette is being towards me. I thought she hated me as equally as Bridget. Though Bridget's hatred does seem to be softening but only when she looks at Jeanette, the moment her eyes lock with mine I feel as if she will turn into a beast and murder me on the spot.

"Do you want to know why I am the way I am? Do you want to know why I am such a stuck-up bitch as you say?" Bridget asks me, her voice is calm but the tone is threatening. Before I get the chance to answer she is already starting her sentence. In middle school everyone started to treat Bridget, Jeanette, and Candice differently because of the fact that all of us were awkward middle schoolers and they looked like tween models. They got the attention of all the boys and us girls turned on them or flocked to them. It was the situation of you hated them or wanted to be them. They could hear all our thoughts and it slowly got to Bridget to the point that she just decided to become what everyone thought she was. Since everyone thought she was a bitch she started acting like one to gain that fear and respect.

"I have to admit, once I got Craig on my arms the power really went to my head. It was amazing to see what a power couple could do," Bridget reminisces fondly. But her face turns to rage quickly. "And then there was you, you turned Dmitri against me. You told him how horrible I was, and how fake you thought I was."

I try to resist my urge to cower back in my chair and stay tall. "What does that matter? Dmitri probably doesn't like you because of who you are, not what I said."

Bridget holds her rage in silence leaving me feeling awkward. You can hear the boys in the kitchen laughing. God, I wish I were in there instead of here.

"You're not gonna continue? Bridge, come on girl," Jeanette nudges, but Bridget doesn't budge. "Bridget had a crush on Dmitri before she got with Craig, but because you had been bad mouthing her, along with the rest of the student body, Dmitri held those things to be true and rejected her harshly. Thus, turning her to the strong bad bitch you see now," Jeanette finishes with a smile.

A boy? All these years, her hatred towards me all came from a boy? Are you kidding me? Craig told me this was the reason why they started fake dating but I had no clue this was the reason why she hated me! This is ridiculous. I shake my head and get up.

"Stay!" Bridget barks, halting me. "Please, sit back down."

I follow, on my own free will. I cross my arms, keeping the attitude. "Look Bridget, I'm sorry for saying what I said when I was 12," I apologize with salt in my tone. She catches it.

"I know it sounds childish and stupid but it did hurt, okay?"

The table goes silent and for the first time I see hurt in Bridget's eyes. And concern in Jeanette's.

"You need to think of things from our perspective Gin-Jezebel," Jeanette quickly fixes. "Imagine growing up knowing exactly what everyone thinks of you. Every good and bad thought. You never have to worry about the whispers because you already know them. Having people judge you for being something you didn't ask to be. To hear and see the boys get praised but we get torn down. Or have to hear disgusting thoughts from boys. I know we aren't humans but, we still have feelings."

"You humans never watch your thoughts like you do your words when you speak. You think no one can hear you," Bridget says.

"After hearing all of those thoughts it just made it all the easier to not care for some of the humans around us. I personally became neutral or hate you guys."

"What happens when you hate us?" I ask not really wanting to hear Jeanette's answer. I have a strong inkling on what it might be.

She snickers, "Well, I don't like to keep hated company around. But don't worry. My pray is strictly men." Jeanette reassures me. Didn't make me feel any better though.

"She prefers to just love her ladies," Bridget teases. It makes Jeanette blush. Is Jeanette, gay?

"I'm a lesbian, yes. I know you're wondering."

I smile and look down embarrassed. "So, is that why you never gave Nick any attention?" I try to joke.

It works and they both laugh. "Nick is a cutie, he is one of the few boys who respects me for my intelligence as well as looks. If I was feeling adventurous one night, I might have made his whole world."

Apparently after years of hearing men and boys think the most disgusting things imaginable it really turned her off from men. Her eyes always wondered to girls but she denied it for years; but all of those thoughts really solidified it. Also, she thinks girls are superior in all ways. They smell better, they are softer, and they know how to express their feelings. For the most part. I can't blame her, if I could hear people's thoughts and I looked like her, it would turn me off too.

The conversation goes on to how they feel about humans in general. Bridget is like Craig, as he said, and she sees them in a more humane light but still grows tired of them at times. She feels more human range of emotions towards us rather than Jeanette who is neutral or just hatred. A good thing to note is that my friends and I are on the neutral side for her. And that she was only mean to me and Cassidy because Bridget doesn't like us. "Girl code, you can't break it. If my best friend doesn't like you,

I don't like you either." She also claims the lovely name of ginger bitch is a term of endearment. Somehow, I doubt that.

Jeanette excuses herself leaving me and Bridget alone. I try to peak into the kitchen to see if the boys were almost done so I don't have to be alone with her too long; but she scootches over and blocks my vision. She looks at me with deep sincere eyes. I look back at her skeptically. I wonder where this is going.

"I don't like you, I'm not going to lie to you. It is going to take some time. But I care about Craig a lot. He is still my friend and you make him extremely happy. I have never seen him light up as much as he has since you've been around. It's kind of gross," she chuckles. "Since you mean a lot to him, I won't be mean to you. But note, we are not friends, we are tolerable acquaintances." I give her a weird look and smile and agree. In her own way, what she said was sweet. Still not the nicest, but with good intentions. It's like getting a blessing from a god. It may not be what you want but you are grateful for the presence.

Jeanette returns with mimosas, I decline the offer and stick to water for now. She boos at me and cheers with Bridget. I feel incredibly lame for not taking one now. I feel a strong need to impress them. They command respect and fear. Even though we are sitting on the same chairs on the same ground, they feel higher than me. Like they are looking down on this lesser being.

"So, is it true?" Jeanette inquires.

I stop drinking my water and look confused. Is what true? What has Craig told them? Or maybe she is reading my mind and heard me thinking of myself as a lesser being. That would be so embarrassing. I need to compose myself and look cool and natural. "Is what true? You're gonna need to be a little more specific," I return with a cool edge to my voice as I pick up the other mimosa and take a sip. Oh sweet Jesus this is stronger than I thought. I nearly gag on the drink as I swallow. What is this? 85% alcohol and 15% orange juice. I keep my face as relaxed as possible.

"The council. Did they actually summon you?" Bridget responds rolling her eyes. She can tell I am trying too hard. Maybe I should dial it back a little.

"Yeah, and did Craig really break out the Heart String?" Jeanette adds. Her eyes filled with excitement. Bridget looks like she couldn't care less.

I nod making Jeanette even more giddy. She asks me if she can see the mark. A little apprehensive I put my arm on the table. Jeanette gently glides her soft warm hand up my sweaters sleave and pushes it upward until slowly the WCE is revealed. A tiny gasp from the both of them escape their lips.

"Woah," Jeanette utters in a barely whisper. She glides her fingers along the letters. It gives me goose bumps. Her touch feels so nice. It reminds me of Craig's in a way that it pulls me in. Feeling too awkward to meet her gaze I look at Bridget who has a small pout on her face. Is that jealousy? She pretends to act uninterested but I catch her eye looking.

"Such an idiot sometimes," she grumbles, finishing off her drink.

"He had no choice, he needed to make a statement so that I wouldn't get the ax," I defend.

Jeanette and Bridget look at each other and laugh. Once again, I fail to see what is funny.

"The Ax of Justice isn't real. Well it is but it is never used," Bridget says in-between giggles. Wait what? No, that can't be. Craig seemed so worried, they said that they were going to kill me.

My confused look makes them laugh even more. I have never wished to be one of them more than right now. I want to be let in on this little secret.

"The Ax of Justice is like a folklore, a fairy tale of sorts. They use the tale of the Council using the Ax of Justice as a cautionary tale for us as kids to behave," Jeanette explains.

"I know we have some dark fairy tales but I have never heard 'oh you better behave otherwise the government is going to decapitate you'!" I exclaim, a little too loud. This makes them laugh louder.

I open my mouth to speak but then the boys come back with a tray full of gourmet looking sandwiches and drinks. "The sammies are here!" Jude announces cutting us off. I instantly cut my eye to Craig. He smiles but he has worry behind those eyes, as he should. Did he lie to me?

"What's going on? Were you two nice?" Craig asks sitting next to me resting his hand on mines. I want to jerk it away but why cause a scene. The girls quiet their giggles and nod taking a sandwich each.

"See, told you that they wouldn't bite," Jude says muffled, his mouth full of food.

"Dude, you told her the ax was real?" Jeanette amuses. Craig looks like he is taken off guard. He puts a sandwich on my plate and his before he speaks.

"Well yeah, because it is. I know they haven't used it in years but-"

"You said it like they use it all the time, Craig," I point, looking him directly in the eye.

He turns to face me, his eyes dreamy and soft. "Jezebel, what I said in my Dad's office still stands and everything before. I would do anything to keep you safe and I would not lie to you. If I didn't think that the ax was an issue to bring up, I wouldn't have mentioned it. You're a special case and I was genuinely worried that they would use it on you," he coos, soft enough that I think only we could hear. I nod back at him and turn towards my plate.

Upon turning back around I can see Jeanette giving the aw look and Bridget looks disgusted. I guess they could hear. It wasn't what he said, but how he said it. Jude doesn't seem too worried about our conversation; he is just stuffing his face.

"I am starting to like her Craig," Jeanette says smoothly sliding my hand away from Craig's. She plays with my fingers and she looks at me with a naughty smirk. "She has some fire in her," her velvet voice sings. I feel myself starting to blush before Craig pulls us apart. He leans in close to Jeanette,

"I'm tired of you Farquhar's trying to steal my girls. If you don't stop trying to seduce my girlfriend, I will make those gorgeous brown eyes red," he threatens with a heavy sexual undertone.

Jeanette leans in making their faces so close they could probably feel each other's breath. "Oo, Craig you really know how to ravish me," she says breathily. They part and laugh. Jude and Bridget don't seem affected. "I'm just messing with you both. She is cool though."

Okay, that was weird, I guess I was right about my assumption of them being hyper sexualized. I shake off the moment and compose myself. I go to pick up the sandwich to take a bite but then I stop and look at it. I scooch closer to Craig, "This isn't human is it?" Craig stops chewing and looks at me, he is giving me the WTF face. "What? I have never seen cooked human. I don't know if we are red meat or not." I look back at the white meat sandwich.

"It is turkey, darling. I wouldn't try to make you into a cannibal... We have to be dating for a year to slip that in," he jokes. I scoff nudging him and taking a bite.

Even the way they spoke to each other flowed in a seamless matter. The conversations barely over lapped and when they did it was as if it were planned. Their laughter sounded melodic and pleasing to the ears. I've notice that Jeanette and Craig muse together the best, they are both witty and play off each other well. They dominate the conversations, commanding most of the attention. Jude reminds me of Dionysus in his laid-back manner, just drinking and eating. Bringing pleasure and party wherever he may be. To my surprise Bridget is the most reserved. She stands out with her soft commanding beauty but she is quiet and aloof.

Somehow the conversation goes to me being a wild card and talking about the night I shot Craig. I can't believe he told his friends about that. But it seems to have been a good thing because they thought it was hilarious. The twins had the same reaction of being won over the moment Craig told them. "You didn't even hesitate Red, I knew you gingers were freakin' crazy!"

"You said take one more step then, BOOM!" They crack up. I join in on the laughter. I felt really bad after doing that to him but seeing how lightly everyone was taking it, it makes me feel better about the whole situation.

"I must admit. After I woke up and saw you, I was scared for a moment but then I knew; this girl right here, she will never be too afraid to be with me," Craig pulls me closer to him looking at me in admiration. Who knew killing Craig, temporarily, would have brought us together? It's weird to think. Ambos are so weird. "You do always call me mad," I poke with a sneaky grin.

"From what he tells us, he has every reason to think so," Bridget smirked. Her tone sounds a little sour but she looks like she meant it in a good way. I let out a forced chuckle not quite sure how to take it.

The conversation continues with me being a badass and they talk about Aiden. That is a harder topic to talk about. But Craig keeps his arm around me lightly rubbing my shoulder, keeping me calm. Jeanette is disappointed that he was gay, she says drugging people is, in her exact words, some straight people shit that we don't want in the gay narrative. "Straight guys already think gay men are predators after them. At least it was Craig, he is an ally and knows the truth. Also, he is a little bi-curious," Jeanette slips.

I jerk my head to Craig and raise my eyebrows. I knew that kiss looked too convincing. Craig looks unsurprised as he sips his water. "I thought he would sense that I was an ambo and that I wasn't in real danger. Also, I'm not bi."

"You frenched him!" Jeanette came back.

"And you've had sex with men."

Jeanette purses her lips out as if to say fair enough.

I wouldn't have guessed that I would have gotten along with his friends so well. It's not like how it is when Craig is with my friends, no, it is more enigmatic. I can see why people flock to them. To impress them. To never want to leave out of their light. Their energy is contagious yet you can never fully match it. But the very fact that they let you be a part of it, is enough.

It's a little after three now and Craig is driving me back to my place. The car ride is silent, but a contempt kind of silence. He is playing Jason Mraz, some nice easy listening after we just stuffed our faces. As we get closer to my house I turn to him and smile.

"What?" He says as he peaks a glance at me. He takes his right hand off the wheel and rests it on my thigh. Another impossibly attractive thing that he does that he doesn't seem to notice that drives me wild. Or maybe he does and just likes to see the sudden change in my mood.

I shake the feeling and say, "I judged your friends too harshly." He raises his eyebrows at me looking shocked. "I think as a student body we judge you guys too much. Even Bridget isn't that bad. Candice is still in the air though."

He chuckles and grips my thigh a little tighter. I let in a sharp breath. He has to know what he is doing. "Despite Candice mugging you off and taking your man, she is a sweet bimbo." I squint at Craig a little puzzled. Mugged off? Craig mainly speaks like an American with a British accent, but sometimes he slips into that British slang. Sometimes I know it, mainly from TV and Harry Potter, but he lost me on this one.

As we pull into my driveway, I can see that my Mom is back. I also had the sudden remembrance that I have homework to finish. We are going to church tomorrow and having dinner with my aunt. We haven't been to church in a while. In light of the attacks a lot of the sermons have been about them and my parents hated that.

I turn to give Craig a quick kiss goodbye but he stops me, caressing my cheek looking me deep in my eyes, as if he is reading me or wanting me to read him. His pupils are dilated then he pulls me in. His kiss is soft but makes me go weak in the knees. He lingers on my lips before barely pulling apart. "Thank you for coming," he whispers.

I bite on my lip slightly and pull away. "It was nice to be in the gracious presence of the Elite," I tease.

He makes a cross and mutters patris et filii et spiritus sancti. "You've been blessed."

I laugh and mock him as I get out. He playfully sticks his tongue out at me.

Beverly Hills

I nearly forgot that it was a leap year. An apocalypse and leap day all in the same year. Amazing. Craig is over, hanging out with me and my siblings. He brought Heathers, saying it is a must-watch, 'If you like Mean Girls you will like Heathers.' Things have been so quiet, no weird dreams, no illusions, no voices. It makes me think that they are planning something, something terrible. I tried to suggest to Craig that we get some kind of training for combat. Yet, he is convinced that Cassidy, Nick, and I will not need to fight. With two ambos and a vampire, I'm inclined to think the same. But I worry.

He set up a buddy system. He watches out for me, obviously, Jude watches out for Cassidy, and Dmitri does the same for Nick. It was supposed to be reversed for Nick and Cassidy but Nick called dibs on Dmitri quicker than

Craig's speech. I still worry though. Anything could happen, and if one of them can't get to us in time... I just want to be able to stand a chance.

"Look at how he is dressed, Veronica wasn't able to tell he was trouble the moment she saw him?" Josh asks with a mouth full of popcorn.

"It was the 80's about to be the 90's," Craig starts but then stops as if he is deep in thought. "Well I guess even for back then, it was still a bit suspicious."

"Lindsey would fall for him," Josh pokes.

Lindsey whacks him in the back of his head with a pillow. It nearly knocks his bowl of popcorn out of his hand.

"Hey, you're just mad because it's true! Jez, back me up."

I duck my head and act like I'm not here. I'm not getting involved. Josh is not wrong but I can see her little cheeks redden at the conversation.

"Ah, it's okay Lin," Craig pulls down the pillow she is hiding her face with. "Everyone is in love with JD. Looking past the murder he is just an art or English student," Craig jokes around, making Lindsey laugh and feel better. I love it when Craig comes over and spends time with all of us. I don't know if it is his built-in enhanced magnetism or if it is just his personality, but my siblings and I can't get enough of him. Josh even threatened me, it was only to ignore me for two months if I ever broke up with him. Lindsey told him that he needed to get over himself but I know she would also be devastated if Craig was gone too.

Bzz bzz. I look down at my phone and it is a text from Jude in our group chat.

We still on for this party tonight?

Party? I didn't know anything about any party. I thought we were going to discuss the stuff we found on the witch while we had a stakeout. Also, Jude found some information on the other ambo, Hayden Norris. Cassidy was able to find him in the police database. Petty crimes like shoplifting and vandalism were his crimes. But he is 19 years old.

Cassidy: I thought we were getting hot chocolate and doing a stakeout. What is this party? I need to prepare.

Good, I'm not the only one who is confused. Craig still hasn't looked at his phone, he is too preoccupied watching the movie and passing around the bowl of popcorn.

Jude: Hayden will be there. I told Craig about it. I thought he told you guys.

I nudge the back of Craig's head with my knee. He looks back at me. *Look at your phone!* I mouth. Why didn't he mention this party to me? He has been over here for 3 hours, and he didn't think to inform me of this not once?

He sneaks a peek at his phone, careful to not let Josh see, who is sitting next to him on the floor. I can see the exact moment he realizes his mistake. "Sorry," I hear him utter under his breath. He is franticly typing now.

Craig: Sorry, sorry. It slipped my mind. But yeah, we are going to Beverly Hills. Sorry Cas, no hot cocoa.

Nick: What is the point of your superior mind if you still forget things. Shouldn't you have evolved past that or something?

Craig and Jude simultaneously send a middle finger emoji directed towards Nick. I let out a giggle. This draws the attention of Lindsey.

Nick: I'm just sayin

"Did you see a funny meme? Lemme see," she reaches towards me. I lock my screen and flip my phone away from her.

"No, it was a text. But um, we are going to have to cut movie night short."

"Aw, I wanted to watch Crazy, Stupid, Love next!" Lindsey whined.

Josh twisted himself around and scowled at me. "Yeah, come on! What's going on?"

Craig and I exchange looks at each other. *I'll take the lead.* Craig states in my head. "Jezebel and I have a party to go to tonight. I'm very sorry. I almost forgot about it, but my friend just texted to remind us."

Lindsey groans louder and dramatically flops back on the couch. Josh's eyes light up. I know the idea he has in his head before he even speaks. He wants to come to the party. He believes that partying is the cornerstone of making your teen years the best you can. He just turned 13, he is barely a teen.

"So, where is this?" Josh inquires with a real slick tone to his voice.

"Beverly Hills," Craig answers looking at his phone.

"The hills?" Lindsey shoots up. She dreams of living there. She doesn't mind Malibu, but beaches aren't really her thing.

"Oo, a hills party. Sick, what time are we leaving?"

This catches Craig's attention. He looks up and gives Josh a funny look with a smile.

"You aren't going, you nub," I say getting off the couch. "This is a high school party, an upperclassmen high school party. I'm not taking my 13-year-old brother with me."

He scoffs and crosses his arms as if I said something to offend him.

Craig laughs at him, "you're not missing anything," he says.

"What will be there? Drugs? Weed? Alcohol? Hot babes?" Josh lists off, enjoying the thought of 'hot babes' a little too much.

"Well, I suppose yes to all of those. Perhaps you are missing something." Craig sees the disapproving look I'm giving. I don't want him encouraging those things to him.

"I'm kidding. Those are not things to be glorified," he says with an unconvincing stern voice. He nods but then winks at him.

I slap him in the arm. He chuckles at me as he stands. He pulls me into his side by my waist. "Jezebel is right. You can't come, we probably won't really enjoy it much either. We can all go to the hills on the 4th, the day after Jezebel's meet." Lindsey looks excited about this proposition. Josh looks a little less impressed but accepts anyway. I guide Craig upstairs so we can freely talk about this.

A party on a Wednesday? We have school tomorrow. They couldn't think of another way to confront Hayden? It's a leap day party, he said. I know it only happens once every four years, but still, it is no reason to party on a Wednesday.

"Could we not go?" I whine as I collapse into Craig, burying my face into his chest. I would much rather stay here and watch movies all night. I just want one normal night. One night to not talk about the investigation, to pretend that none of this supernatural world exists. I wish my only issue was worrying about tests, college, and the SATs.

"I'm sorry," Craig mumbles, resting his cheek on my head. "I can erase all that you and your friends know... Let you go back to a normal life." Was he listening to me? I part away looking up at him.

"Where are you getting these thoughts?"

"Your dream. The night I had to send Dmitri. I didn't want to bring it up but I noticed small differences in your mood since."

"You saw," I groan as I flop on my bed. I should have told him. I should have just explained my feelings.

He nods a defeated nod. I stretch my arms out to him, he takes my hands. I guide him to sit next to me. In one swift motion, I sit on top of him. I rest on my knees so I am taller than him. I cup his face smoothing my thumb along his jawline. I smile warmly looking into his eyes. They sparkle even when he is sad.

"I don't know how much you saw. But this makes me happy, actually." He furrows his brows at me in reaction. "It makes me happy because it proves that you don't listen to my thoughts all the time. If you did, you would know that every time we are together, I feel like I am in a dream. I have never felt so happy yet in total peril being with someone," I stumble on my last words giggling. It makes him smile too. "Yes, I want normalcy. But I don't want them with Travis, I want them with you. I can spend hours, days, weeks, listening to you talk, to see you smile, making witty jokes. I love when we sit in total silence watching something and you go into hyper-focus mode. I didn't notice, and don't let this get to your head, but my friends and family like you, us, better than Travis. They notice how much you make me light up without even trying. Not to mention I love to see you fumble on your words. Seeing you be an unsmooth teenager is a masterpiece."

He gawks and places his hand on his chest. "This is slander. When have I ever fumbled on my words with you?"

I bite my lip; I have been waiting to break this out. "Does the 'you are a rose... but not like a real delicate flower, but like a fake plastic rose. Like a mixture with the magical rose from beauty and the beast,' Ring a bell?"

He shakes his head looking wounded trying to get me to shut up. "I was flustered, stop it, stop it, I get it."

"Aw come on, it was cute. It was filled with so much corn I thought I was back in the Midwest, but so cute," I joke.

He rolls his eyes and blushes. This is the first time I have seen him blush. I tease him with an over-exaggerated awe, toppling over him. We are now lying down with me on top, my hair sweeping over his face like a privacy curtain. We can't stop laughing and I am starting to lose my strength from it. He finally stops, sort of, as he lays smiling. He tenderly smooths my hair behind my ear and cups my cheek.

"I suppose it could have been a nightmare. Having some weird ghost ex talking in my ear would be a nightmare for me. Especially Travis, he might as well be the serpent of Eden."

I look at him quizzically. What does he mean by that? He chuckles and shakes his head. "Don't worry about it." He pulls me in and kisses me. My last bit of remaining strength leaves me and I fall into him. My heart starts pumping faster, and I feel my stomach flutter. In a quick, hasty motion Craig moves from beneath me. I look at him, catching my breath, tucking my hair behind my ear. He smooths his shirt and smiles at me. Why does he leave? He keeps leaving.

"I can call Jude and tell him we can do this another day. Let's stay in and watch movies with Lindsey and Josh," Craig says, switching the subject. I wish I could get into his head sometimes.

"No, no, it is fine. We can be normal some other time."

He watches me as I bounce over to my closet. "What should I wear. I don't know how to really dress at these parties."

He smirks and walks over going through my clothes. "What, you've never been to a Leap Day party? You're wasting your youth," he says with a sneaky grin.

My parents are gone for the week, they won't be back until Friday, i.e. just in time for my birthday. It's a good thing too because I know for a fact that if they were here there was no way they would have let me go to this thing. Before we left, I made sure that Lindsey and Josh were squared away for food. Gave them the whole rundown of not answering the door, keeping everything locked yadda, yadda.

We are meeting up at Dmitri's, as it was originally planned. So we can all arrive together we are taking the Vaduva family SUV. As we get there, I see Cassidy's jeep but no Prius, I don't know what Jude drives but I imagine he didn't arrive with Cassidy.

We didn't even have to knock, the moment we reached the door Cassidy swung it open. She is smiling big at us, showing her infectious smile. "You guys look killer! Come, come," she beckons us in, guiding us over to the den as if she owns the place. She looks gorgeous, but is that a surprise? Without even trying Cassidy always looks so pretty. She isn't even wearing foundation. If she were her freckles would have been invisible. While uncommon with her skin tone, she has the cutest speckles of freckles along her nose. But, in the winter they are barely there, so if she wears the tiniest amount of foundation, it covers it up.

"Is this you just quickly putting something together?" Craig jests giving her a quick once over. He looks impressed and not lustful. Cassidy flips her hair and fluffs her pony as she saunters off to the mirror to take a look at herself.

"Yeah, it is what I could do on short notice. You know, I gotta look good enough to scope out any potential... mates," she looks over her shoulder like a burlesque dancer making me laugh.

"We are here for the investigation, there will be no time for scoping," Craig says.

"There is always time for scoping," Cassidy and I say in unison.

Craig squints at us while smiling. He gets up and shakes his head. "Where are the people who actually live here?"

"I have no clue, I think upstairs. Dmitri put me on door duty while he went to talk to his parents."

Craig clicks a quick thanks and separates from us looking for the Vaduvas.

Apparently, we are also on the hunt for Donna, I did not know this. Cassidy just explained to me that she is also supposed to be at the party, it was on her Instagram. For some reason, this made me even more worried about tonight. They are both teenagers though, so that does give me a bit of peace of mind.

Just then, the sound of footsteps approaching the house. Well, now I see how Cassidy was able to detect us so quickly. We both go to the door to greet either Jude or Nick. But as we open it, it's a bloody Mr. Vaduva. He looks just as shocked as we are. He looks down at us and smiles, his fangs are exposed and equally as bloody. Cassidy and I both shudder and jump back.

"Excuse me," he says politely as he walks into his house. "Ana!" he calls, his voice almost sings. In seconds Mrs. Vaduva, Dmitri, and Craig are at the top of the stairs looking down. Craig fits right into their family, strangely. It's like an extension. Well, I suppose they are.

Upon seeing her husband, Mrs. Vaduva flies down the stairs, racing up to him. She starts franticly saying things in Romanian to him while he just smiles at her. She doesn't look as pleased. Dmitri and Craig join us. Dmitri has his lip ring in, he hardly ever wears it. Odd.

"Vlad there are *humans* here right now! What were you thinking?!"

"I thought they would be over later. I was thirsty." I shudder once again at his words; I wonder if he did what the Edwards did and hunted an animal.

Mrs. Vaduva swats his arm and pushes him deeper into the house. She says a quick hi to me with a sweet smile, but then just as quick scowls at her husband reprimanding him once again in Romanian as he softly chuckles.

"How long have they been married?" Cassidy asks.

Dmitri looks up and counts carefully in his head. "Well come July it will be 611 years."

Cassidy and my mouths drop. 611 years? I cannot imagine being married to someone and still being so in love for a little more than half a millennium!

"What would have been 611 years?" Nick asks.

We jerk our heads towards the door to see Jude and Nick walking in. Nick looks... Different. His hair, normally a bit unkept, sits in perfect soft curls. He is wearing a navy blue and white striped t-shirt with a dark khaki pant. He looks like a member of One Direction, and somehow it is working for him.

"My parents, they have been together for 526 years. Dude you look-"

"Not like myself, I know. I feel like I am in a boy band but I figured I needed to blend in tonight."

"You look really handsome," Cassidy stumbles on her words. She looks flustered, if she were able to blush, I think she would be.

Nick also picks up on this and smiles a triumphant grin.

Somehow Nick manages to upstage Jude for a moment until he finally speaks. "Everyone looks hot, ladies," he gives us a thumbs-up as if we accomplished something. "fellas," he gives them finger guns. "But we are running late, we gotta go." Jude rallies us to go outside but Craig stops him.

"We need to talk strategy."

"Strategy is for the weak," Jude replies.

"Strategy is for the people who want to stay alive big brain. What do you got, Brit?" Nick intervenes.

"We are running late, we can talk about it in the car," Dmitri says. He grabs his coat and Cassidy's off the coat rack by the door. He calls goodbye to his parents; they wish us luck and tells Dmitri to call if anything goes south.

The strategy is simple, or seemingly simple. We all had a hand in to think of the best way to execute everything. Craig suggested that we form groups. We cannot all be together and neither Craig nor I can be seen by the targets. The moment they see us they will know it is a setup. Nick and Jude offered to team up together, I didn't see that coming considering that Nick thinks of Jude as more of a loveable idiot. But Jude says that he can talk to Hayden and distract him and Nick said that he can steal his wallet. We all paused at his suggestion. Nick says that it is to get more information on him, get his driver's license, see if he is a member anywhere, etc. He says that since he has been practicing magic for years he has gotten to near "expert level" at the art of the sleight of hand. He says he can also get any keys off of him as well. Jude vouched for him saying that Nick showed him out in front of Dmitri's home.

While skeptical on their end of the plan we moved on. Craig and Cassidy will be with each other; they will be on the hunt for Hayden's bedroom. Another new fact, this party is actually at Hayden's house, hence why he will be there. They want to find a laptop or anything laying about. Craig wants to scope the energy and see if he can tell what kind of ambo he may be. He has a feeling, much like Aiden was, Hayden was created.

That left me and Dmitri together. And to me and Cassidy's surprise, everyone agreed to have Dmitri seduce Donna. Dmitri was shocked by this. He didn't like the idea of being used as a seductress. But he fits the bill. He is near irresistible to a lot of girls, with his height, deepness of his voice, his aloof way of being. But the fact that he looks like the type of guy Donna would be into, it is perfect. To add to his allure Jude suggested that he let his natural accent fly. Dmitri rolls his eyes at this but agrees. Cassidy and I try to contain our smiles. We were joking about using him in this manner, but it is quite funny to see it actually play out.

I am set to hang in the background by Dmitri, to check for anything that is off. Craig says that I have a particularly keen eye. That even when he is doing his best illusions, I still find the tiniest cracks. I am to call attention even if I feel something is the slightest bit off. It is nice to not be the bait for once.

We pull up to the Beverly Hills mansion, one I just know Lindsey would have loved. We unfasten our seatbelts and get ready.

"We need to remember to not get distracted. We are here to get information, and if we are lucky, maybe some interrogation," Nick lectures us. Not surprised in the least.

"Nick is right, we also need to stay connected. And I found a way of doing so. I can temporarily connect us for about 3 hours tops before I get burned out. Think of it as an internal walkie talkie. All you have to do is think it while thinking of all of us and we will hear it," Craig nods, looking at us for a sign of consent.

"Will this hurt?" Cassidy asks.

Craig weighs his options before saying yes. Well, at least he is honest. He says only the initial connection and when he disconnects us.

Despite the pain, we agree knowing it is what we have to do. Craig's eyes turn indigo, it freaks Nick and Cassidy out. I forgot they have never seen that. But this time it is as if they are glowing. And before we even got a chance to react, we all wince in pain, holding our heads. It's like chimes are banging in my ears and I'm going through electroshock therapy. But in seconds, it's gone.

Did it work? I hear Nick say in my head. Judging by us all facing him, I think we all heard it.

Brilliant! Let's go. Craig cheers. We file out of the Vaduva SUV and ready ourselves for our first big step into this investigation.

The feel of the party is very similar to how it is at the Elites' parties, yet it is much darker. The music is softer, the homes aren't as spread apart, they are pretty close together. The house isn't as filled with people either, but still enough that we can get lost in the crowd. Before we parted, we did a quick scan of the scene. We had to make sure Hayden nor Donna was nearby, lucky for us, they weren't. Quickly we parted into our three groups. Nick and Jude off to hunt Hayden, Cassidy and Craig went upstairs to try to find Hayden's bedroom. And Dmitri and I started to look for Donna.

The home is large but not as large as Craig's. I feel like I can't get lost in here, which I appreciate. I know some homes can be just as large and obnoxious as the Edwards'. Everything is very open though, I thought the Farquhar's home had an open feel, this place is as if there are no walls. I feel so exposed. I make sure to stick close by to Dmitri; I'm latched on to his arm. I look like a scared child.

We are walking outside to the patio when I see her. Her ebony hair slicked back into a messy ponytail. Black ripped booty shorts with distressed-looking red fishnets underneath. Black platform boots that really make a statement, and a black tank top under a sheer mesh off the shoulder shirt. She will be like putty with Dmitri.

"That's your girl," I say soft enough for only us to hear. I feel the muscles in his arm tighten as he notices her.

"She is a poser and I know it," Dmitri scoffs looking at her up and down.

"I don't care what you think she is, go over there and flirt girl!" I push Dmitri over in her direction. I need to find a place for me to post up. I wonder if Maci is here. I look around to find a nice semi-discrete spot to hide, this open floor plan is really not working in my favor. I should have worn a wig and some sunglasses.

We just hit the motherload. Craig says. I look in Dmitri's direction and he is finessing Donna. A googly-eyed mess she is right now. Playing with her hair, laughing way too much. I think he has this handled. I'm going to wander and see if I find anything.

About an hour goes by without a single disruption. But then, a woman walks in, she looks as if she could maybe be in college. She takes off her coat and looks at me and smiles. She gives me a wink and continues up the stairs. Something doesn't seem right by her. Suddenly a weird feeling overcomes me. Something doesn't seem right with this party either. Oh no, Cassidy and Craig.

Cassi, Craig, you need to get downstairs now. Some woman just went up there and something is not right about her.

Just for a second, I see blood trickling down the stairs and then it is gone. Oh shit.

Cassidy and Craig appear next to me scaring me, making me yelp. "Didn't mean to startle you," Craig says taking my hand.

I look down at Cassidy's hand and she is holding a laptop. She definitely did not come in here with one. What is up with my friends and theft when we are doing investigations? "Cas, why do you have a laptop?"

She waves me off as to say, 'don't worry about it.' "Who is this woman you saw?"

"I thin-"

The opening of "Get Low" starts blasting through the speakers catching all of our attention. This is such a banger and it is our mission to dance whenever it comes on. Craig looks down at his watch. "We have time." As if that was our cue, we run over into the living room where the music is coming from. Dmitri also came running in with Donna, and Jude with Hayden. The only person missing is Nick. I'm pretty sure everyone at the party is in this living room popping off. Cassidy and I started a grind train ending with Craig behind me. We all screamed 'to the window to the wall' and hollered the rest of the chorus.

Where the hell are you guys? I have his keys, his phone, and his wallet. While everyone is distracted, we need to do some sleuthing! Nick lectures us. I don't think anyone of us is listening because we all continue to dance as if nothing was said. *You guys are with them, aren't you? You know there is an option to not dance when Get Low comes on.*

That is the biggest lie. Jude says, making us laugh.

About halfway through the song I hear a growling roar above us. I look back at Craig who has stopped dancing and is looking at me in concern. I look over to Jude who is still dancing but looks more timid. Dmitri and Cassidy seem unaware. This is an illusion to distract the party-goers. That woman was weird, I did see blood. What if she is the 2nd ambo or she could have been the werewolf. She's Sarah. I gasp at my realization and grab Cassidy's arm to get her attention.

"Someone has either been killed or is being killed upstairs," I warn. Cassidy stops smiling and looks from me to Craig.

Everyone meet in the basement. Jude bring Hayden, Dmitri bring Donna. It's time to tell them what we know. Craig commands.

Dmitri and Jude look at us and gives a small nod of understanding.

Oh, what the hell? The brit gives orders and y'all listen? Nick exclaims, appalled.

Many apologies for not listening earlier, meet us in the basement. Craig apologizes just to appease him.

Jude, I slipped some fake coke in your pocket, use that to entice Hayden. Nick suggests.

Cassidy, Craig, and I were already on our way to the basement when Nick suggests this, but that made us stop dead in our tracks.

You put what in my pocket?!

Just do it, the dude is a junkie.

"Nick is hardcore... glad he is a part of our team," Craig says entering the basement. Cassidy and I look at each other cynically.

The plan is to interrogate. Jude is going to stop time so that we have no interruptions, but first Dmitri is going to bring Donna down here. We don't know what Cassidy and Craig found but they both agreed that exposing that Dmitri is a vampire is the best option for Donna to start talking. The basement door flies open and panicked footsteps barrel down the stairs.

"Nick, could you be a bit quieter?" Craig hisses. I can't even see him but Nick whispers an apology and joins us in our hideout nook.

"Where did you get this fake coke?" Cassidy asks him in a reprimanding tone.

"I made it, watched some videos. Don't worry about it."

To cut their bickering short I told everyone about the woman I saw and the blood. Also, the growl that happened during Get Low. Which no one but me, and the ambos heard. I thought that Craig was just saying that I am good at detecting breaks in illusions to make me feel less useless but I guess he was being honest. Craig admitted that he sensed the illusion a little before I called to him and during our dancing break. But he said that

that isn't an uncommon thing for ambos to do. Even at gatherings with other ambos and supernatural creatures, they often do that for an escape for all the guests.

"But I suppose they used it for a cover-up," Craig says.

"See, told you guys you shouldn't have gone grinding on one another, hope it was worth it."

"It was," I jab. It's dark but I can feel Nick rolling his eyes at me.

I continue to tell them that I think that woman who went upstairs is Sarah. Craig and Cassidy think the same after I tell them what she looks like. Apparently, when they said they hit the motherload they found all the people in their little group on his laptop. Nick thinks that we should go into Hayden's car and see what we can find in there. The time is getting late but it is worth the look. The plan is to interrogate and if we have time go into the car

Craig directed Dmitri to come down with Donna first and then once we have her incapacitated, Jude brings down Hayden. It is very obvious to us now that none of them are from the Immortal Realm, Donna would have instantly known who Dmitri was had she been. This makes things easier for us in the long run. Since they are not of the Immortal Realm that means they are not under the protection of the Council and we can do what we please.

The basement door opens again and I can tell from the giggling that it is Donna and Dmitri. A light comes on in the corner of the room and Craig puts up a fist, I think he just made us invisible. The two of them come into our line of vision. Donna is up on her tippy toes as they kiss. Dmitri opens his eyes and looks in our direction. Can he see us? He leads Donna over to a chair and pushes her down in it. She bites her lip and pulls at him hungrily.

"Where did you say you were from again?" She asks, playing with his hair."

"Transylvania," Dmitri responds with his natural heavy Romanian accent.

"Like Dracula," she teases as she steals a kiss.

Show yourself. Craig commands Dmitri. Obeying orders Dmitri tilts Donna's head up with his finger to her chin. He smiles and outcome his fangs. It is unsettling seeing Dmitri like this.

Her mouth drops and she stands up. "Exactly like Dracula," he whispers in her ear, "And I know you're a witch." She trembles at his words. He slowly drags his nose around her neck as his lips gently glide alongside. I get goosebumps just watching it. She lets out a soft moaning sigh and says, "kiss me," he obeys. His kisses trail to her neck and that's when Craig says *bite her.* Cassidy, Nick, and I gasp at the sight of Dmitri sinking his fangs into her neck. At first, she moans with pleasure but it quickly turns into pain. He isn't drinking her blood; he is poisoning her. She struggles to get him off before he pushes her away, his mouth stained with her blood. He wipes it away with the back of his hand and is gagging in disgust. She doubles back into the chair crying in agony holding her neck.

Craig lowers his fist; she jerks her head over and tries to stand but she can't. He *was* keeping us invisible.

"I hate witches' blood!" Dmitri exclaims spitting, "It's like poison!" His voice is back to an American accent. After using an American accent for 12 years it is probably more natural when he is speaking English.

"Craig, Jezebel?!" Donna questions looking frightened. It almost makes me feel bad. She is only a teenager, who knows how she got herself into this? She could have been forced.

She reaches into her boot and takes out a wand, "percutiet!" She contorts her body and screams out in pain. Her wand stops glowing and she drops it to the ground. I look at Craig, his eyes indigo. Maybe she isn't an innocent soul.

Nick rushes to the ground and picks up her wand. "Oh wow," he says examining it.

"Get your hands off my wand you- ahh!"

"Watch your mouth and stay still. We have some questions for you," Craig says calmly. He looks to Dmitri and nods his head towards Donna. Dmitri drags her in the chair over out of the light and stands behind her.

Bring Hayden. Craig orders. Donna looks like she is trying to get out of the chair but physically can't. Dmitri isn't holding her down. My mind goes back to when I was attacked by Aiden and I couldn't move despite him not touching me. Craig is not like them. He is good... he is good. It still doesn't make it any easier to see.

We scurry off into our hiding place as we wait for Jude and Hayden to come down. In the darkness, I can hear Donna wince in pain. I know I shouldn't feel bad, considering what she was probably thinking of doing to us, but I cannot help but think that what we are doing is no better. "Is she gonna be alright?" I ask in a whisper.

"She'll be fine, she is a witch remember? The venom will not have as damning of an effect as it would on a human," Craig reassures me.

"Also, not to mention the fact that that spell she was about to use was going to obliterate us," Nick adds.

Cassidy and I sharply turn our heads at him. She was about to do what?

"He's right," Craig confirms. Oh my god. Well, I hope the little witch suffers.

The basement door opens again and we hear Jude raving about the coke he has. Pure and uncut, a specialty made in the undergrounds of the Immortal Realm. It is kind of sad how hooked this guy seems to be. I need to stop feeling pity for these people. They are evil and trying to kill us, there is no need to try to seek out the humanity in them.

The lights come on and light up the entire basement. One of them gasps in horror. "Donna!" Hayden shrieks running down the stairs. "Who the fuck are you?" he says to Dmitri. Dmitri pushes Donna in her chair towards Hayden like she is nothing with a sinister smile on his face showing his fangs. This makes Hayden back up. Craig steps out from the darkness and we all follow behind him. Upon seeing us Hayden backs up but has a wide pleased grin.

"Ah, a setup? Craig Edwards," he peers around to look at me. "and you brought the bait." Something boils within me and I lunge at him. Craig catches me as if he is holding back a guard dog. "Oo, she bites," Hayden continues to taunt. As if on instinct I pull Wendy out of my bag and aim it at his foot.

"I shoot too. But you should know that. How's Aiden?"

He growls at me and his eyes start to change into the beast style but then he is on his knees groaning in pain. Craig towers over him, his eyes bright indigo. "Be nice to the Lady before I let her use you for target practice."

With both of them subdued the interrogation begins.

Interrogation

J ude is by the stairs, keeping the room soundproof and the time frozen on the other side. Dmitri stands guard behind them in the event either of them tries anything risky. Cassidy and Nick stay a little further back looking into Hayden's phone and laptop. What Cassidy and Craig found that was the 'motherload' were profiles of all the people in their group. Cassidy and Craig switched off going down the list.

Craig started with Donna, a witch who was orphaned after her parents were killed and was adopted by a coven of vampires, hence her fascination with Dmitri being one. She has no true family of her own and has learned all of her magic from a dark warlock who is of unknown origin. Being a rogue witch with no true coven she was picked up by Hayden, who seems to be the leader of all of them. She has never been to the Immortal Realm and knows very little about it.

Cassidy goes on to share about Hayden. He is, as Craig suspected, a created ambo. Stolen from his home at the age of 16 and turned by an unknown ambo and left to fend for himself. He is unaware of his life before he was turned and has no loyalty to anyone. He is aware of the Immortal Realm but doesn't know much of it. Because he has come to his powers on his own, he lacks discipline and is a wild card. Making him a ticking time bomb of destruction.

Before they go on to the others Hayden starts to laugh wildly. Donna follows soon after. "So, you know us. You know our names and what we are but that's it," Hayden laughs crazily.

"You can torture us all you want. It doesn't matter, there's more," Donna hisses.

"Yeah we know, you psycho, there are two others," Nick responds. This makes Donna laugh even more.

"Other groups you degenerates! We are just one group in this whole grand scheme of things. As you said, we basically have nothing to lose. Torture us. I can take the pain." They both laugh uncontrollably.

These guys are unhinged. Have they been sniffing bath salts or are they always this insane?

"Who are the others?" Dmitri asks.

They proceed to lists the names: the Bandits, the Ghosts, the Rogue Agents, and the Royal Court. And they are, in a very fitting name, the Unhinged. It's almost like I guessed it. None of us like the fact that there are others a part of this. And who knows how many are in the other groups. And on top of it all, who are they working for? They can't all just be separate groups with no leader.

"Who do you work for? Who is in charge of you? "Craig asks.

Hayden reminds Craig that even though he is a created ambo he can still block Craig from entering his head. He says that he can block him from getting into Donna's too. Craig takes the challenge. "Wanna bet?" He does something that causes them to have milky eyes and have a blue fog form around their heads. What the hell?

"Who do you work for?"

"The Ripper... like Jack the Ripper," Hayden answers smartly.

Craig rolls his eyes and snaps his fingers making Hayden groan in pain. "He isn't lying," Nick shows us his phone, emails from someone named the Ripper.

Craig scoffs at this, "What an arrogant arse!"

It's a pretty good name to me, a bit jackass like but I love how theatrical it is. I can tell that Nick appreciates it as well.

"The Ripper just wants the bait. He doesn't care about you or the others," Donna chimes in coldly.

"And to what use am I to this 'Ripper', why does he or she want me dead so bad?"

"You misunderstand. The Ripper doesn't want you dead, no, we need you alive. Like I said, you are the bait sweetie," Hayden sneers.

I shoot my gun at his foot. He cries out in pain and it causes Craig to lose his concentration. "Jezebel! What in the world?!"

"Call me bait one more time and it will be your head!" I threaten Hayden as he is working to heal his foot.

Dmitri is laughing and I can hear Jude laughing at the stairs as well. "We need them alive for right now to get answers. Stop being so trigger happy," Craig scolds me.

"He was asking for it," I say. Cassidy and Nick agree without even looking up from the laptop. Cassidy is transferring files over to a flash drive. I smile at the victory.

"Okay, maybe he was but can you give me a bit of a warning the next time. I still have a bit of PTSD from when you shot me," Craig mutters low enough for just us to hear. I nod and we get back to the two.

"If all you want is Jezebel, why follow me and Jude around with Mimik?"

Donna remains silent but twitches in pain from the venom slowly making its way through her body.

Craig groans in frustration and his eyes go back to indigo. "Donna, answer me!"

"The Ripper likes the hunt, makes it more fun for him. She isn't quite ready yet."

Chills go down my spine. The hunt? They are playing games with me just for the sport of it? And what does she mean that I am not ready? I feel even worse after doing this interrogation. If anything, I will be watching my back even more.

Dmitri is like a blur and within milliseconds is holding down Hayden who is in half-beast form. "I have been trained to kill more powerful than you, kid. Make one wrong move and it's lights out."

I instantly grab hold of Craig who is already putting me behind him in defense. He looks down at his phone.

"We have school tomorrow, we need to go."

"Go, what are we gonna do with those two?" Jude comes jogging up to us.

"And Sarah, she is upstairs," I remind Craig.

He takes a moment to think before saying, "We gotta keep them here."

"I can take them. I do have a dungeon," Dmitri offers.

"I knew it was a dungeon!" Nick exclaims standing up, "Do you use it for sex too?"

"Come on now, only on the weekends," Dmitri jokes with a wink, biting at his tongue.

Cassidy and I react in disgust while Jude and Nick laugh. Craig is still in thought as to what to do with the two. "Dmitri, break his arms, and suck the venom out of her, they can't move until I release them. Jude, I'll help you do a permanent soundproof and we'll lock the door from the outside."

"Dmitri? I thought your name was Caesar," Donna winces.

"Well, it's one of my names," Dmitri is quick with a reply.

"What about his stuff?" Nick asks, holding up the phone, keys, and wallet.

"Destroy the phone, keep the keys, leave the wallet," Jude suggests. Nick shrugs. He drops the wallet and kicks it into a corner, pockets the keys, and tosses the phone to Jude to break.

"I got it!" Cassidy exclaims hopping up with the flash drive in hand. She looks at us very happy and accomplished. I feel like she missed all that happened. When she is in hacker mode, she tends to block out the world. Craig smiles and nods.

"Let's wrap this up then," he nods to Dmitri, who grabs hold of Hayden's arms, despite Hayden's begging not to, he snaps his arms with an unforgiving swiftness. That makes me and Cassidy cringe in horror. Seconds later he is over to Donna who is screeching until Dmitri covers her mouth before taking his fangs into her again, sucking up the venom. He spits a black substance on the ground and shakes his head in disgust. He mumbles that he needs some fresh blood to get this taste out of his mouth. I feel compelled to offer but thinking about him sinking his fangs into me makes me shudder.

Nick is examining her wand. "Hey, can I keep this?"

"No!" Donna wails racing towards Nick.

Before she can make it Craig is in front of her and says, "You will be in rigor mortis for 5 days you will not utter a word until then, If you try to break this you will feel a pain so intense that it will put you right back in shock." And she collapses on the ground in front of us.

"Holy shit I almost pissed myself," Nick whispers clutching the wand.

Hayden is wailing in pain cursing at us.

"Why don't you just kill them?" Jude asks.

"We may need them for more answers. We should hold off with getting their blood on our hands until we are 100% done with them," Craig replies.

We make it up the stairs, Dmitri suggests that we don't look back and keep moving. As we enter the main floor of the house again, we see the scene of the frozen party. Craig and Jude finish up their soundproofing and lock the basement.

"Let's do it," Craig says. On cue, Jude continues time and All Star starts in the middle of the song. People run past screaming the lyrics and jumping around. We walk out of the party feeling triumphant but also a little shaken. We got our answers but we got even more of a reason to be afraid. But I have to admit, it makes life a little interesting, to say the least. As we leave the house the last lyrics of the song that we hear is "My world's on fire, how 'bout yours? That's the way I like it and I'll never get bored". It makes me laugh a little. No one else gets what I am laughing about. On the way back to Dmitri's we ended up looking up the Shrek soundtrack, hearing All Star got us in the mood and jamming to it as a bit of a victory.

A Happy Birthday to Me

Today is my birthday and I went through some meticulous planning with Dmitri, Cassidy, and Lindsey for the perfect outfit. I needed something cute but also practical for the weather. I am wearing a heather grey puffy shoulder sweater, red skinny jeans, and black wedged converse. Cassidy got me a curling wand as an early birthday present. It really helps me more than I thought. I bought a new body mist and even did some light makeup, that surprisingly looks good.

As I come racing downstairs, Lindsey and Josh surprised me with a birthday banner and an attempt to make Mom's crepes. The effort is there but it isn't very edible. My parents will be back at one so we, including Craig and my friends, will be having a dinner and game night in celebration.

Josh, who apparently has Craig's number, texted him and asked if he could pick us all up and bring a backup birthday to-go breakfast. Lindsey knew they were doomed after they messed up their first crepe and so asked for Josh to get reinforcements.

Sure enough, the Edwards came to the rescue with street style strawberry crepes. Mrs. Edwards made them for us. We got to school a little early and Cassidy, Dmitri, and Nick were waiting for us there. I feel like everything was done in such a calculated way, with perfect timing every step.

I was greeted with a loud happy birthday and the covenant birthday tiara and balloon. Only worn by me and Cassidy; Nick said he would die of embarrassment if he wore that and Dmitri is always conveniently "sick" on his birthday. The balloon is a simple red helium balloon that I have to wear on my wrist all day as if the gold birthday girl tiara wasn't enough. Cassidy takes a series of pictures of me in the get up before letting me be free.

Craig walks me to my locker before we go to class, he has to stop at his too. But before he leaves, he hands me a perfectly wrapped metallic green present. He said that he went a little above and beyond what he was planning but didn't regret it. I was a bit confused by what he meant until I opened the gift.

He got me an exact replica of Anne Boleyn's iconic B pearl necklace. Complete with natural pearls and a 24K gold B. The necklace lays perfectly on deep burgundy velvet inside of a glass case with a gold bottom.

I look up at him in amazement, my mouth wide open. I am completely dumbfounded. I don't even know what to say.

"Do you like it? I remember you talking about how much you want a collection of royal jewelry to have your own mini museum someday. And since Anne Boleyn is one of your favorites, and you wouldn't let me celebrate valentine's day-"

I cut him off with a kiss. I love this so much I cannot believe he got this for me. And with natural pearls, it must have cost a fortune. "How, where did you get this?" I say finally parting from the kiss.

"Our family's jeweler. I had it custom made. I found some online but I wanted it to be extra special.

I shake my head and kiss him again, "You are incredible," I say in-between kisses.

"I'm glad you like it; I'll see you in class soon." He parts from me and heads off to his locker.

I can't stop staring at the necklace, I am still in awe. I tuck it safely on my top shelf before grabbing my history textbook. When I close my locker, to my surprise, Travis is standing there. He smiles at me, weakly.

"Um, hi," I say trying not to show how shaken up I am.

"Happy birthday."

Suddenly I remember my get up. I laugh quietly and nod. "Ah, yes, the tiara and the balloon. It's-"

"Tradition, I know. Also, I didn't need the get up to let me know. I remember. We dated for two years and only recently broke up."

I agree and nod keeping my head low. I feel so incredibly awkward and I don't quite know what to do. I didn't even know we were speaking again. We have a moment of silence before Travis breaks it. He starts to apologize to me. He says that he was completely in the wrong for saying the stuff he did to everyone. He was just hurt and didn't know how to deal with his emotions properly. He also apologized for not telling me about Candice before making it public. He claims that it wasn't planned, that it just sort of happened. When I tried to apologize, he stopped me and said he knows how I feel, because I apologized a thousand times already.

The next thing really made my heart sink. "Just because we broke up, doesn't mean I don't care about you. Yeah, we hurt each other, but I loved you. I know I never said it, but I did. The love is still there but we clearly aren't meant for one another and that is fine. I just want us to be okay."

He loved me; he still has love for me. This information hits me like a ton of bricks. I don't know what to do but to stand and smile.

He starts to ask me about the present Craig got me. Apparently, he saw it. To him, he thinks it is a bit much for a relationship that just started. "A great gift still, at least he listens. Just a tad bit flashy if you ask me."

"Well good thing I'm not asking you," I jab in a light tone. He laughs at me and we share in our first normal moment in months.

"Here, this is for you. I must admit, this was your Christmas present. But no time like the present. Happy birthday." He hands me a little red gift bag. Before he leaves, he softly kisses me on my cheek then walks away.

I couldn't get what happened between me and Travis out of my head all day. Why would he tell me that he loved me after we broke up? A little too late it seems to me. Why on my birthday, why give me this gift, why even hold on to it, why did he have to kiss me on my cheek?

I try to cover up how shaken I am about the situation at my mini party. Cassidy, Nick, Dmitri, Craig, and Maci are all here with my parents and siblings to celebrate. My parents did not disappoint with the food, as per usual. Maci brought over a bunch of board games for us to play, but we ended up spending way too much time getting into Scattergories, Uno, and Mario Kart to play much of anything else.

The night ended with an amazing chocolate and strawberry layered cake that my mom made and presents. I never want anything too grand whenever my friends ask, I say I want little things. But on my 16th last year, Nick got smart and got me a very expensive miniature of the Palace of Versailles.

They did keep in the guidelines this year. Cassidy got me a total care skin package with all essentials of keeping my face and body as smooth and radiant as a dolphin. Nick got me a collectible Grace Kelly Barbie that I told him about in confidence. While slightly embarrassed, I loved it. Maci got me sapphire mini star earrings and a pack of scrunchies that match every leotard I wear for competitions. And Dmitri fed into my constant hinting of items I wanted from Bath and Body Works. I have an unhealthy addiction to that place, and him getting me 10 items from there isn't helping it, yet it is welcomed. My family got me an exclusive private historical tour of Paris for when we go to France over the Summer. They are tickets for two, while they didn't say who would be going with me, they implied heavily that Craig would be the one accompanying me on the tour.

I wanted to bring up as we were eating cake about the Travis situation, but It didn't seem fitting. Everything was so nice and happy. I didn't want to throw that stone in the water. I haven't even opened the gift. I want my mind completely clear and ready for my meet tomorrow.

Somehow after everyone left and my family went to bed, I convinced Craig to spend the night with me. He warned me how ambos often go into half-beast form when sleeping. I told him that I didn't mind, that I just wouldn't look at him. I was very happy to find out that he sleeps in just pajama pants. Deep royal blue ones, to be specific. I wanted to match his attire but all of my pajamas are mainly my dad's old shirts or ratty shorts and tank tops. But thank god for both Maci and Cassidy, I found in the bag Cassidy's gift came in, at the bottom, a pink satin nighty with a card that says, "when the time comes, Cas & Maci" They are ridiculous, but might as well.

When I came back to my bed Craig smiles at me giving me a once over. "You look adorable."

I crawl into bed and snuggle up next to him. "Well enjoy this while you can, I don't look like this when I wake up"

He traces his finger along my lips down to my chin lifting to his mouth. "I enjoy the imperfections of humans, it's less frightening than going to sleep next to a beauty and waking up to the beast." I scrunch my nose at him giggling. He gives me soft lingering kisses then whispers a last happy birthday like a sweet melody in my ear. He holds me to him like a silk ribbon fastened around a delicate gift.

The Meet

Craig made a swift exit before anyone in my family got up. Also, he woke up before me so I didn't even see him in half-beast form. I hadn't slept so soundly in years. Who knew just sleeping with Craig beside me would give me such a relaxing slumber?

The meet is in 3 hours but I need to get to the gym like now. Craig is coming with my family and is going to meet one of my aunts, my uncle, and my grandparents at tonight's dinner. I asked him if that was too much, but then he reminded me that he has bound himself for life to protect me so meeting some more of my family isn't that daunting.

We got there in enough time for me to shake some nerves out and to hydrate and go over some of my steps. Right before the meet was about to be begin, I went off to the side and asked Craig to help stretch me out. I wanted this time to talk to him. I finally opened Travis' gift. It was a snow globe; one we saw at a very cute antique store that I could not keep my eyes off of. I remember that whole day so clearly, I thought he was going to tell me he loved me that day, and I was so ready to say it back. I need to tell Craig about it. Something like this doesn't feel right keeping from him. The gift, his confession, the timing of it; it has left an occupation in my mind. Like an earworm, it won't leave. Eating away at me every passing second.

He helps me stretch out as he bops to the loud music we have playing. He needed some slight guidance on how to stretch me out. I teased him about it because he is always saying that marching band is a sport so he should know how. It made him go on to a rant about how it is a sport but they don't really stretch each other out that much. He has never seen me do any of my gymnastics things, besides the small bit from when we broke into Dmitri's house. He is impressed by my flexibility. I wanted to make a joke but I need to keep serious so I can tell him about Travis. My body temperature rises and the loudness of the music seems to dissipate, making me more nervous. As if all the focus is now on us.

"Hey, so, Travis and I spoke... on my birthday," I say cautiously waiting for his reaction. Yet, he doesn't show one, he just continues to focus on massaging my leg.

"What did you guys talk about?" he finally asks.

"He actually apologized for his behavior and... he got me a present. It is a snow globe. One I saw at an antique shop. He said it was supposed to be my Christmas present."

Craig nods but doesn't say anything. I can't tell if he is holding something back or if he genuinely doesn't care.

Either way, I would like some kind of feedback. My palms become sweatier.

"He also told me that he loves me," I blurt out. This makes Craig strike his head up. "Well, that he loved me, and that he still has love for me. But but that we aren't meant to be. And then he kissed me on the cheek and walked away. But not before saying that your gift to me was too flashy and grand." Word vomit, that is the only way I can describe what I just did.

I can't tell if Craig is in shock or if he is enraged. He just has his hands frozen on my leg and is looking at me with such sharp eyes. "I can give him the snow globe back."

"Do you love him?"

"NO! No, I do not love him. I did, or I thought I did. But I don't love him. Sure, I care about him but like-"

"Jezebel, it is okay if you have love for him. You guys have dated for 2 years. You only broke up in November. I trust you. Completely."

My heart melts and my heart rate goes down to normal. He isn't mad, at least at me. "Well, I don't love him. I do care about him in a way that I don't want harm to come to him."

Craig laughs and stands up giving me his hands so I can stand up with him. "I'm not going to harm Travis if that's what you're thinking. I feel bad for the git actually. The move he pulled was very manipulative and it still didn't work." He winks at me and wishes me luck on my 'performance', it's not wrong but not quite right either.

"Your leotard and scrunchie look great." I give him little poses making him laugh as he joins my family in the stands. I am wearing one of the metallic green scrunchies Maci got me to match our team's metallic green and gold leo.

I was a nervous wreck when it came for my time to compete. Maci is all around amazing, getting near-perfect scores in vault, bars, and floor. She came out with a perfect score on beam. I do vault and beam as well, but I am not nearly as good as I am on bars and floor. I got a 9.4 on my bars. Surprisingly, though this shouldn't be a shock at this point, whenever I looked to Craig all nerves I had washed away as if I just rose from a cleansing. Seeing him so amazed and smiling at me, brought me to serenity. I don't know if he is doing it with his powers or if he naturally has that effect on me. My family's loud cheering also aided in my confidence. It is unworldly how much their voices carry.

Now it is my time to do my floor routine. Maci gives me a tight good luck hug, while coach hypes me up. She says there is no reason there shouldn't be a 10 after this. I step onto the edge of the mat and my name is announced. I smile. I peer into the crowd to find my family and boyfriend. All smiling faces, excited to see me perform. *You're going to kill it.* Craig says in my head. It startles me at first, then edges me out. I shake out my final nerves and go.

The song starts and I am on the floor. I think in my head over and over, 1,2,3,4,5,6,7,8. Keeping the beat is the most important part of my concentration. It helps me time each tumble, each movement, each step just right. The beat takes over and I no longer feel like I am at a competition but putting on a show of a lifetime. I hit every tumble with such precision that I even surprise myself. I feed off the crowds' energy and become sassier in my movements.

I get to the breakdown section when everything goes dark. Flashes of images go through my head. Violent, bloody. "hold your head up" another sharp disturbing image, this time met with a pain in my stomach. "Keep your head up, movin' on". I try to shake the feeling. I keep going, though I cannot focus. In-between each lyric another flash. A scream, my scream. Cassidy, Nick, bloody on the ground next to me. Dmitri, burning. "Movin' on." Every second that passes a new flash distorting my reality. Tears roll down my cheeks as a warm bright light disrupts the images. Craig's light. Until it is gone.

I hit my final tumble combo ending with my final pose into a split, looking over my shoulders to the crowd with a satisfied impish look. The crowd goes wild. My family stands up cheering. I get up waving with a huge grin. I go to wipe my tears but they are gone, my face, only a little damp with sweat. I look to Craig; he is smiling at me clapping and standing with my family. He looks proud, happy. But worn and traumatized. I run off to my team, as I am met with excited hugs and praises. Something happened. Something lingering, that I cannot fully comprehend. Though in the back of my mind, a terrifying feeling lingers.

Maci won 1st in everything, no surprise there. I got 2nd in bars, and to my surprise, a perfect 10 on my floor giving me that 1st place spot. I can't even remember the ending half, except the final tumbling pass. I just know my body was fluid like I was on autopilot.

Once the meet is over my family comes down to congratulate me. Josh gives me a bear hug but instantly regrets it upon noticing how sweaty I am. We couldn't go without taking some horrendous looking pictures of me and my medals, and then with me and Maci. They make me take a few with Craig, which I hate. He looks amazing and I look sweaty, a little red, and my hair is not as neat as it was when I came here. I wish they had taken these when we first arrived.

Before leaving for dinner we took a few more photos as a family, a few selfies with Josh, Lindsey, Maci, and Craig, and had to hear a mini speech from my dad about how proud he was.

I go to change and ask Craig if he could walk with me. When we were a good enough distance away, I ask the question. "What happened?"

"You did an amazing job and I have never been more impressed, wowed, and a little turned on in my life."

I slap at his arm and hold back a giggle. "You know what I mean. What was going on in my head?" I ask in a more grave tone.

Craig's smile fades, he looks straight ahead. "I'll tell you about it after dinner."

Craig won the heart of my grandparents and my Aunt and Uncle fairly easily. But as the dinner progressed the more things slowly came back to me. All of the images were less quick flashes but clear scenes. Horrific scenes of my friends being killed right in front of me. Me being tortured. Jude being ripped apart. Dmitri being chained to burn in the sun. And Craig, decapitated next to me, while I am bound to the floor, screaming...

I hold my composure as if nothing happened and kept it up. As we got home, I called to my family that I was going to shower and head straight to bed.

"A shower is probably for the best. I didn't want to say anything. It's not like it is too bad, but you aren't super fresh right now. Craig probably noticed too, he was just polite not to say anything," Josh says in a snarky tone.

Wow. Wow, he has a lot of nerve saying that. "Oh sorry, I just competed in a competition and worked my butt off, sorry that I may have sweated."

"Just sayin, Jez, No harsh feelings. You did your thang."

My thang? Okay. "You have a lot of nerve saying that considering you are a 13-year-old boy and we all know the odors you permeate."

"That is natural man musk, sweetie. And some women find it very sexy."

I fake gag and head into my room.

"Whoever told you that is lying or hates themselves," I hear Lindsey say as I close my door.

I immediately text Craig, who already headed back home, to see if I can come over. He has a huge bathtub and I need to soak and talk to him about what happened.

Craig: And what about your parents and siblings, won't they notice you are gone?

Me: No. I said that I was turning in for the night.

In a second Craig is in my room. I give him a weak smile and gather my things for a bath and my pajamas.

Craig sits outside of his bathroom, facing away from me to give me my privacy. He tells me how Sarah and Mitchell were there. They arrived later, under the radar. Sarah is the werewolf and Mitchell is the ambo. He was implanting visions into my head. Ones that may or may not come true. It is a way to slowly torture someone. To cause them to have random visions or nightmares of these scenes and perceive them as real. It can cause harm to my psyche and to me physically.

I sit in the tub, holding my legs to my chest. The hot water keeps the submerged parts of my body warm but the exposed half is filled with goosebumps. I stare blankly ahead. When will this end? When will any of this stuff end? The words of Donna, of there being more of them, haunts me. Even if we get rid of all of these Unhinged, there will be more. And who knows that even if we beat them, this Ripper person won't have more in its arsenal. My mind goes back to when we were in Dmitri's basement with all of that weaponry. I still don't see how his family legally has all of those things, they need to be regulated. But they probably aren't legal. Nevertheless, I can sort of see why they have all of those things when dealing with the creatures and beings of the Immortal Realm. They stop at nothing and will go way beyond what is normally expected.

How much is all that he put in my head true? Is that's what to come? Chepi said lives would be lost, but I didn't imagine, more so I didn't want it to be like that. My heart starts to beat at an alarming rate and I can feel my body shutting down.

"Craig!" I cry out to him.

"What, What's wrong?" Craig still is facing away from me.

"Come in here. Please! I don't care if you see me naked just please come here!" My voice shaken with tears as I tremble.

Craig comes racing in and kneels at my side. He runs his fingers through my wet hair as he coos in my ear. I tip over and rest my head into his neck as tears continue to gush. I thought that things would go a little slower, that we would have time to breathe.

"I killed Mitchell," Craig whispers in horror. I pull my head up and look at him in utter shock. He did what? He is going to get summoned again or thrown in jail! How, when? I didn't see anything to support this. When did he even have the time?! People would have noticed.

"I-I exploded his head," Craig's voice breaks a little. "When your mind was clear, when you finally were able to be broken from his visions... That's why, I caused his brain to explode using a concentrated mental wave. It is draining, for me to do. A-and difficult to know that I have killed one of my own. I have never done that. I didn't even mean to..." Things go silent between us. He is now sitting on the ground hiding his face in his hands while he does hard staggered breathing. "Jezebel, there is another reason why there aren't a lot of young ambos with special abilities like me, my siblings, and my cousin. Kids like us normally get killed because we are incredibly unstable. But because our dad is who he is, we got to live. He trained us well. I thought I had great control. I was just trying to deter him, but then I got so heated and, and-" He trails off. "I won't get in trouble with the Council, he was not part of our world. But that still doesn't change the fact that I lost control like that."

I pull my arms out from the water and run my fingers through his hair, now making him wet. He looks up at me, eyes full of sorrow and disgust in himself.

"It was so violent. The power ripped through me and there was nothing I could do. I stopped time to get rid of him. Sarah ran."

"How did you get rid of him?" I ask afraid to hear the answer. But he doesn't give it. He just shakes his head and says that he doesn't want to say. But he, Mitchell, is gone, forever.

I sniffle and reach in the water to drain the bath. Craig gets up and hands me a very plush robe to give me some privacy again.

After I dry off I join Craig in his bed. I cuddle up next to him without saying a word. All I can think of are those visions; they are more like recent thoughts. Craig said that I won't be randomly haunted by them anymore, but I will remain aware that they were implanted in my head. The only way he can get rid of it is if he erases that part of my memory, but I am afraid to go through that process. And as it comes to be, not only me, but Nick, Cassidy, Jude, and Dmitri had the same vision. They texted us in the group chat about it. Jude and Dmitri knew what was going on, but Nick and Cassidy are feeling just like me. But since Mitchell is dead, his vision will not stick to them, just the same as me.

After 15 minutes of silence, Craig speaks. "We need a vacation. All of us. Four weeks, we have Four weeks until Spring break. Mitchell is dead and Donna and Hayden have already dealt with us firsthand. I think they will be out of commission for a little. My family always goes to the Hamptons for Spring break. The rest of my friends have homes out there too and they go as well. Since Jude and I will already be there: you, Nick, Cassidy, and Dmitri should come. We all need to get away."

I agree with him, I do believe we are due some sort of break. But I always spend Spring break with my family. "My family always goes up to Northern California to camp. I don't want to leave them."

"They can come too. We have room for your family and the others. There will have to be some room sharing but I don't think that will be an issue."

I have never been to the Hamptons. Nick has an aunt and uncle who has a home out there. My family does love the annual camping trip, but I think with the work of both me and Craig we can swing them to go.

I don't want to sleep alone tonight, and neither does Craig. He allows me to stay with him and makes a stern time of 4:30 am that I need to be in my own bed. "Yes, dad," I tease him. He rolls his eyes at me and rolls over to turn off his lamp. He kisses my forehead and whispers, "four more weeks."

The Hamptons

Craig was right, they did stop. Our guess is they had to regroup after all that happened. It gave us the chance to be teenagers again. In both good and bad ways. In the good we got to hang out more, without having to worry about doing any research. I have even hung out with Craig's friends a few times. Bridget is slowly warming up to me. Candice has been mysteriously missing every time I came around. I wonder if she knows what Travis said to me. I try to keep Travis in the far reaches of my thoughts. Craig is an easy way to make me forget. He fits right into my group of friends like a glove. I am getting used to seeing Craig and Dmitri be so civil towards one another. For years Dmitri played up the whole 'I hate him' bit. You can tell Dmitri truly loves and cares about Craig deeply. Sometimes Nick gets jealous, it is kind of funny.

The last big hang out we did was Nick's birthday party. His parents booked this gigantic upscale hotel in L.A. It was the four of us, Craig, and some of his cousins. But two days after that was the SATs. Dmitri and Craig did end up helping us study. They are both extremely proficient in the job. I have never felt more stressed in a scholastic setting than in that moment. I had some peppermint tea before going in to try to soothe me. It sort of worked. However, Cassidy, Nick, and I left feeling good about it. Stress nonetheless, but good.

When I told my family, during one of our dinners, about Craig's proposition, to my surprise, they were stoked to go. I thought there would have been a little more fight with our annual camping trip, but it was as if that trip never existed. Actually, we joined together, the Edwards and Bedeau families for breakfast two days before we leave to discuss everything.

As it turns out, we will be leaving in two separate jets. If it wasn't enough, the Edwards have two private jets. "Well, we need backup, just in case the other fails," they say. People normally say that about food, maybe cars, staple fragile décor in a home. But no, the Edwards use this for their jets. My family and his family, sans me and Craig, will go on the first jet, leaving at 7am and we are getting on the second jet leaving at 9am. Our families will get there at 3 and we at 5. The sun will be setting about 2 hours after that so Dmitri won't have to wear an abundance of protection. His parents were invited but they wanted the "alone time". Dmitri gagged at the thought and said his home will need a spiritual cleansing.

We met at my house before we went off to the airport. Jude and the rest of the Elites are already there, they got there the day before. But, seeing that Craig can teleport he visited them on their first night. The jet was beautiful and it added on to the list of perks that having Craig around provides for Nick. Thank god for Craig's sense of humor; I swear one of these days Nick's mouth is going to ruin him. He means no harm, just very disconnected at times. Cassidy was overjoyed for this vacation; she has always wanted to visit the East coast. But all her family is either west, Chicago bound, or in the south. None of them had much interest going to New York or anything.

When we arrive to Craig's Hampton home, which we took a limo to, we were a bit tipsy, minus Craig, from the champagne from both the plane and the limo. His mansion in the Hamptons is in Amagansett, technically a town within East Hampton. Amagansett is quieter, big trees surround the home, and it is very close to the beach. Though it is relatively close to the livelihood of East Hampton. His mansion and his friends are a pod almost. They are each other's neighbors, separated by the mass amount of foliage. They chose to be over in the far end for privacy reasons, much like they are in Malibu. But they do spend a lot of time in the South Hamptons, which is where Nick's family is, without a problem because of the whole teleportation thing.

It has 8 bedrooms so there will be light sharing like he said. Our siblings took on the burden for us. Lindsey and Erin will be staying together and Jimmy and Josh will be staying together. Thank god that they all like each other and that worked out nicely. To my parent's knowledge, I will be sharing a room with Cassidy, but I will be sneaking over to Craig's. Everyone else get's their own room. The place is beautiful. While their home in Malibu is gorgeous, I have mentioned many times how it is a labyrinth. This home is easy to navigate. Just like in Malibu, the décor takes your breath away. The Edwards have very exquisite taste.

Dmitri declared to us that he will sleep until 7 when the sun starts to go down, and for the rest of the vacation he will take on his natural nocturnal state. We were making plans for the day when Nick popped in. Craig is excited to see him and tells him about wanting to break in their first night with a little herbal remedy.

"Like tea? We come all the way over to the Hamptons and you want to drink tea? I want to party with these rich east coasters!"

Craig laughs at him. I roll my eyes and groan. "He is talking about smoking, Nick," Cassidy clarifies for him, sounding as if she is suffering from second-hand embarrassment.

"Oh. No one has ever asked me to smoke. What are we smoking? Weed I know, but like is it special or anything?" Nick plops down on the couch in between us.

"It is laced with a little something that gives it an extra kick."

"Is it crack?" Nick asks.

Craig laughs even harder. "No, it isn't crack, with miss goody here, do you think I can get away with that?" Craig motions at me. I shove him away. I know he is joking, well I hope. "It is an herb found only in the Black Forest of the Immortal Realm. It is really trippy. So we only use a little."

I do worry for Nick, he has never smoked before and it takes a lot for Craig to be able to get high, another ambo biological thing. I worry that this will be too much and Nick will be tripping balls in a ditch by the morning.

"Nick, don't go overboard. I don't want to have to rush you to the hospital," Cassidy pleads. I'm glad she said something first.

"Yeah, Nick. You have never had anything in your system other than some alcohol."

He pouts and puts his hand on his heart. "Ladies, love your concern for me, but I think I am in good hands." Nick puts his arm around Craig. He side eyes Nick a little and nods.

Craig continues to talk about his plan to invite his friends over, even Candice, to smoke with them to just 'vibe' as he says. Nick was excited about the idea of Jeanette being there. He may be completely in love with Cassidy, but he lusts after Jeanette like no other. Craig breaks it to him that she is gay. I expected him to be a pig and sexualize on that fact, but instead he says, "that explains why she didn't take to my advances. We are perfect for one another. A smart sexy little minx like her and me together; the world just wasn't ready." He confidently sits back with his hands laced behind his head.

Craig tries to stifle laughter. Cassidy sarcastically agrees with him. I just bite my tongue. You can't say that Nick lacks confidence. This will be happening at around

8 tonight. Cassidy and I will not be participating, we instead decided to drive into town to the East Hamptons to hang out with Craig and my siblings. We will probably end the night on the beach with a bonfire. I do wish I could see Nick high; I think that would be interesting.

"Until then, what do you guys wanna do?" Cassidy asks us.

"I actually have a little party for us to go to in an hour, Cas. I know Jez and Craig could use some stress-free alone time. So, I got us invited, thanks to my cousin, to a party in the South Hamptons."

Oh. I did not expect that from Nick. He reads our shocked expressions and soaks it in. "How's that for being a socially unaware robot?"

"Well, thank you Nick. That was very sweet of you to think of us," I thank him. He soaks up the praise.

Craig lets them use his Corvette, which I cannot believe he has, to get there. It is a 45-minute trip so they rush off to get ready. Craig pulls me closer to him and kisses me. "Alone time. No supernatural rebel group after us, no school projects, papers, or SATs to worry about. What do you wanna do?"

My first instinct was to say cuddle and nap, but attached to his family's property is this gazebo that overlooks the beach, and a pathway leading down to it. It looked so peaceful and nice I thought it would be the perfect time to spend our few hours of solitude together.

It was nice to just be able to talk, with no constant worries trailing in the back of my head. Our conversations started light with some jokes here and there. But then we slowly started to go into deeper conversations. I asked him about some things he would miss the most about the Mortal Realm/ being in America. I told him he can omit the obvious being friends and me, I wasn't searching for any validation. His answer was that he would miss the sun, warmth, and beaches of Malibu. He has a whole different wardrobe more fitting for England. The slow pace easy going nature of everything, his freedom, and marching band. Specifically, competitive marching band. It isn't my fault, we weren't together during the marching season, but I still wish, and feel guilty that I wasn't, able to see him march.

His ultimate dream would be to go to school down south, study music therapy, and minor in jazz studies. He would have liked to go to, as he calls it, not a southern school that screams 'we vote red' but a southern school with some flavor, with some diversity. He listened with so much zeal about me being excited to go to UCLA and how it has been a dream of mine since I was 13. I don't have many back up plans, I should really get one, but there is no place I would rather be. I go on and on about their gymnastics team there and how amazing they are. And how after college I want to go to France to do some pre-grad school research projects. Maybe get an internship if I am lucky. Whenever I talk about my passions his eyes light up and his smile becomes cozier. I feel the opposite, because, while I love how much he genuinely cares about me fulfilling my dreams, I know he puts in a little extra heart for the fact that he can't have his. It isn't fair, and I know I sound childish saying so, but he has so much talent and drive for music. It is a shame that he cannot pursue it.

He told me that he has been working on combining playing music with his powers and asked if he could show me. He disappeared for a second before he came back with his sax. He has been working on a way to manipulate, for the better, one's emotions and state of mind depending on the music he is playing. He played me a piece by Chopin, which he informed me is not normally, hardly ever, played on saxophone. Didn't make any difference to me because I have never heard it. But as he started to play my mood was instantly transformed. It was like he took me to another dimension. I knew I was lying by his side but my mind felt like I was brought to a new land, a romantic, carefree place. Where I felt safe, safer than I have ever been. It was dusk and as I looked into the sky it was as if the stars were dancing with me. I felt myself go deeper and deeper. Not knowing if I could ever come out but I didn't care. But then he stopped.

I snapped back into reality to find him looking at me concerned. Apparently, he almost pulled me in too deep. It was a work in progress. I know he is concerned about going too far with his powers at times, but moments like this, I wish he would never stop.

We end up going off on a tangent about the summer. We are making it our priority to make the most of it that we can. The plan is to be outside most of the day and night. He wants to soak up as much sun as he can before he is shipped off to 'grey England'. He loves his motherland, as he calls it, he just wishes it were sunnier and warmer.

We buzz off in silence, nestled together as he slowly traces his fingers about my body, never wandering to places he has never been. Naturally within the silence and the soft touches we move into kissing. But we have never kissed like this. It was sweet with some hunger, that's not out of the ordinary; but it was also passionate, hypnotizing, begging for more and more. We got so swept up in the moment We didn't notice how much time had passed until we were interrupted.

It was a series of texts from Nick saying that him and Cassidy were on their way back. And for us to finish up any nefarious acts we were doing. I groaned and rose up from Craig. He shares in an exaggerated sigh and escorts me back to the house.

As we get back to the house Erin is in the living room on her phone, alone. Craig goes to put his saxophone away and I join her.

"Why are you alone? Did Josh do something weird or stupid?"

"No, he is taking a nap," she giggles at my insinuation, still not looking up from her phone. "What were you and Wil up to?"

"Just talking about life, ya know."

"Did he whine to you about his fate with the Council again?"

"I wouldn't say whine."

She laughs and finally puts her phone down. She commends me on always listening to him about it. She then goes on to tell me how she finds the idea of everyone, just because you are part of the family, getting to be in the Council. According to Erin, the only Edwards kid in this family who should be in the Council is her. The brutes are superior in her mind.

With perfect timing Craig and Jimmy appear in the room. I switch my eyes back and forth between them to see what will transpire. Erin looks back at them with an all knowing grin. "I'm right and you know it. Jimmy, you are too spineless to be in the Council. You creative types are way too empathetic. And Wil, you mentalists have the mindset to really set a new rise in the government but you lack the gall."

"Oh, you mean we don't want to resort to violence right from the start? That we want to use some logic and reasoning?" Craig snaps back.

"If a brute was in charge you would never see any change," Jimmy chimes in.

"It is called playing the system, James," Erin says in an all knowing way.

"Playing our corrupt, stuck in the old days, government? No, there needs to be a change within the system, with someone who won't play by their rules!" Craig exclaims. "No offense to you brutes, but with your temper, you guys are better suited for bodyguard duty. Not government decisions."

Erin stands up and narrows her eyes. They turn blood red. "Wanna bet?"

Craig meets her challenge, his eyes turning indigo. I instinctively back up. I do not want to get caught in this ambo crossfire.

They begin to charge at one another when Jimmy's eyes turn violet and a force field bubble pushes them apart. Erin and Craig propel back flat on their butts.

"You two need to behave. There is a *human* in the room." Jimmy walks off into the next room, feeling good about what he just did.

"That kid is too OP," Erin grumbles getting up.

As if nothing happened Erin and Craig are sitting on the couch watching TV. Hm, peculiar. But I go with the flow. I sit down next to Craig as Erin flips through their DVR. She puts on an episode of Gossip Girl. To my surprise Craig watches the show quite often. He says that it is Erin's favorite show and she got Jimmy into it as well. And so naturally he ended up watching too.

"It is not a bad show, it is good for ridiculous drama," Craig defends.

Amused by him I continue the narrative. "So, who is your favorite?"

"Well, all the characters are flawed in their own way. But I gotta say Nate."

"He has such a crush on Nate. I swear, if we were on the upper East side Wil would swear they live almost the same life," Erin teases.

I giggle and play into it. He shoos us both away. I ask Erin her favorite, and before she even answers I know it is Blair, and I am correct.

"But who is your least favorite?" I ask Craig and Erin.

"Jenny. No doubt," Erin answers without missing a beat.

"Do you even have to ask? Dan! He is just a self-righteous, pretentious arse!" Craig exclaims. I burst out in laughter. I had a feeling he would say that. Some of Dan's savior mannerisms remind me of Travis and I feel like Craig sees it too. Speaking of which, I wonder if he is here. If he is going to be joining Craig and his friends tonight. I want to ask but he is already hyped up because of Dan Humphrey. My favorite feels very random but I enjoyed Eric the most. And my least favorite is Vanessa.

Watching the show made me question why him and the rest of the Elite were attending the public schools instead of private. Craig informed me that it is for the same reason why his family and Mancini family were told to come to the Mortal Realm. Which is a reason he cannot disclose to me. He found out the Mancinis were sent like his family a few years after he met Bridget. The Farquhar family is here for their own pleasure, and I found out that they are new money. But their parents went to public schools and wanted the same for their kids. And the Bennett family is here because her dad is a human and they chose to live this lifestyle and wanted her to be in public schools.

The night came up quick after we logged in a few episodes of Gossip girl. By the time Dmitri came down the stairs, Craig, Erin, Jimmy, Josh, Lindsey, Cassidy, Nick, and I were all sitting in the living room completely enthralled by the show.

Dmitri looks well rested and at ease. I thought it was a myth but night really does give vampires an exhilarating energy, especially if they got their proper rest during the day.

Cassidy and I round up the siblings and head out. Dmitri says that we should stay. That having some sober moms around will ensure they don't do anything too stupid. "I haven't seen you guys all day and you guys are gonna ditch because of drugs? Grow a pair and stick around," Dmitri says to the both of us. His arms around our shoulders.

"YOLO!" Nick calls from behind us.

"We will come back in an hour, okay?" We make the compromise, pleasing Dmitri. He shakes our shoulders a little to hard and woots.

When Cassidy and I return we find our friends and the Elite completely blasted in the basement. Everyone is laughing, has glassed over eyes. Candice and Bridget are dancing together, Jeanette is lying across both Craig and Jude as they touch hands and reach out to this invisible force, and Dmitri and Nick are talking to each other in Hebrew and Romanian. I think Dmitri is also switching to Muskogean. Cassidy and I look at them and just sit and observe.

"I thought they were smoking weed?" Cassidy says to me over the loud music.

"Craig said it was laced with this psychedelic herb from the Immortal Realm. Guess it is really strong."

We catch the eye of Dmitri and Nick. They excitingly invite us over to them. Reluctantly we join. They join us all together in a group hug.

"I love you guys," Nick says, his words getting out slowly.

"Love you too Nicky," Cassidy pats his arm.

"Love ya," I respond

"I didn't even know my Hebrew was still this good. Guys this is insane! The lights are dancing," Nick bobs his finger to the beat and encourages us to join.

"Your hair smells like strawberries," Dmitri says burring his face in the top of my head. He calls to Craig to come and sniff my hair. Craig saunters over and crouches in front of me. Even when he isn't even in the same layer of the atmosphere as me, he is incredibly attractive. He looks at me and says something in Greek. Cassidy turns shocked. This is news to me as well, I didn't know he could speak Greek.

"He says that you smell like strawberries and cream and you are fresh like summer rain," Cassidy translates for me.

It makes me laugh. Me and Cassidy both. While we are very confused as to what is happening, it is very entertaining to watch. Starships by Nicki Minaj came on and it got everyone excited. Dmitri, Cassidy, Nick, and I know every word and could not help putting on a performance. Candice and Bridget built off our energy and kept dancing wildly. Jeanette, Jude, and Craig cheered us on and started bouncing to the beat at the beat drop. While I am not 100% sure what they were on, the night was entertaining to say the least.

Bugged

We have been here for a couple of days and I can see why they would want to live in the quiet, less bustling parts. It is quieter, there is no noise from neighbors. You feel like you woke up on your own private island instead of a neighborhood. It makes it more of a getaway rather than a second home. One of the highlights for me is every morning we come down and the chefs have a full meal prepared for us with freshly squeezed juice. I feel so spoiled. The cutest thing is that Mr. Edwards wakes up at dawn to spend time with Dmitri until twilight turns into sunrise. Dmitri and Mr. Edwards wanted to hang out more but a 16-year-old hanging out with the 40 year olds just would have seemed very weird.

Us kids have been kicked out the house tonight. The Edwards have a benefit tonight. Mrs. Edwards has promised that they were going to raise 4 million dollars for a homeless shelter in Riverhead New York. My parents are skeptical about the amount she believes she will raise but Mr. Edwards is confident in his wife's ability. They already put down the 1st million. They seem to have an extra over abundance of money, but at least they are philanthropic.

Craig said that we can go to this bar in the South Hamptons tonight. We have been spending every night in the East Hamptons so it is nice to finally see the Hamptons that you always see on TV. Dmitri is excited, he says the bar we are going to has the best drinks. He hypes Nick up saying that he can probably find him an east coast girl. Nick has always liked the idea of a long-distance relationship. He feels like a normal one right now would smother him. Dmitri and I tease him about it, because the reality is that he compares every girl to Cassidy and they never live up to her.

After breakfast, once our parents leave for a bike ride around town, Dmitri heads back upstairs for the day. He has to make an appearance every morning so my family doesn't notice his nocturnal behavior. Craig leaves to go over to the Mancini house to hang out with his friends alone. I didn't mind, gave me some time to hang out with Nick and Cassidy.

We spent our time at the incredible infinity pool in the backyard. I could spend the rest of my days here. Nick and I rest at the edge of the pool looking out at the trees. Cassidy is lying on a pool floaty humming a tune. Lost in thought Nick plays with his Star of David around his lips.

"Hey Jez?" Nick asks still playing with his necklace.

"Yeah?"

"Have you and Craig... done anything yet?"

I blush at his question. "No. not yet. Well, he sort of tried but I freaked out. I think I am too nervous to do anything with him for the obvious reason, and because he is *Craig Edwards* and has had a lot of experience and I wouldn't know what to do."

"You are dating a slut," Nick says dropping his chain out of his mouth.

I scoff at him and playfully splash him.

"Jezzi, I love Craig but Nick is right."

I laugh at them both knowing they are correct. I mean I have said the same thing and he has admitted it himself. We joke that he is a recovering slut. Out of practice if you may.

"Anyway, like I said I wouldn't know what to do, or where to start."

"Well don't look at me, I am just as inexperienced as you," Nick says.

We both look over to Cassidy who is oblivious to our stares. Soon she notices our silence and pushes her sunglasses up on her head. "Why are you two looking at me?"

"Well, we aren't experienced in that area and you are the only one who is," Nick says gingerly.

Cassidy scoffs at us looking wildly offended. "Oh my god, I have *never* done anything in that nature!"

"Why are you offended? You are the one who said you have hit a couple of bases with Dmitri!" Nick accuses.

"Yeah, we got to second base, we have made out with some light under the shirt touching. But I was still wearing a bra and he barely touched it! Also, since you guys are so nosy, we haven't done anything since summer. We ended that for your information."

Nick and I look at each other trying not to laugh. Oh sweet Cassidy. "Cas, that is not second base. That is more like 1st maybe halfway to second," I inform her.

She looks even more confused by this. "Then what is second base then?"

I look at Nick trying to hold back laughter. He nods to me as if to say he's got it. "Well the most wildly accepted idea of 2nd base is more so full under the shirt play and ya know some," he makes some gestures with his hands that makes me laugh and Cassidy looks shocked and disgusted.

"Ew, no! Dmitri and I never did that! I've never even seen *it*." Nick and I laugh harder. Cassidy eventually breaks and smiles, putting her sunglasses back down over her eyes.

"Hey, do you still have those macarons that we got from that little shop last night?" Nick asks me, still recovering from laughing.

"Yeah, they are in my room. Do you want me to get them?" I respond, I too recovering from our laugh.

Nick gives me a puppy dog look. "If you could be so wonderful."

I scrunch my nose at him playfully and swim off. I grab my towel and wrap it around me. Slipping on my flip flops and scurry off into the house.

As I reach my, aka Craig's room, I hear Dmitri talking in his room a few doors down. And then I hear Craig. That's weird. He said he was at Bridget's. I know I shouldn't spy but the last time I found them speaking alone some very important information was being withheld from me.

I sneak over and peek in the door. Their backs are facing me and they don't notice. Dmitri looks like he is comforting Craig. He is holding him as Craig is saying something to him that is muffled. Dmitri pulls him back off of him and I can see Craig is crying. What happened? My heart breaks seeing him like that and I want to rush in but I keep myself where I am. If he wanted me to see this he would have came to me. I should leave.

"I messed up, Dmitri."

"No you didn't. It isn't your fault that the Council is the way it is."

"I wish you could have been there."

"Well I'm glad I wasn't. Now I can be here to help you."

"I feel so stupid, so weak! I said that I could handle this, that I was able to get this job done. I showed that I was mature and strong... and now look at me?! I am crying in the arms if my godfather like a little bitch."

"You're just 17 Craig, it is fine to be scared. Chuck and Maggie didn't raise you to harbor emotions until you get to this point. And no one would think you are a little bitch for crying now. If I was tasked with what you were at your age with little to no guidance, I would be spending some nights crying too from being overwhelmed. It isn't a pussy thing to do."

"I *am* scared. They have been too quiet for too long. I thought that being here would make me feel better but I keep thinking and dreaming about them striking. What if what they put in you guys' head is true. What if that happens here?"

"Kid, I got your back. I have dealt with and killed many others that were worse than them. I have no problem ripping them to shreds if that means keeping my best friends and you alive... even Jude."

"I can't tell Jezebel. It will just freak her out. She has been so calm, so worry free for the first time in a long time. I, I-" Craig trails off getting choked up.

Dmitri pulls him in again. "Don't worry about it. You are stronger than you think and even though I don't like him Jude is a pretty good ambo as well. If you lose control every once in a while, I mean you are 17 it is expected, I think it is better on scum like them."

I don't want to hear anymore. I shouldn't be hearing any of this. I run back to Craig's room and grab the macarons and head back to the pool.

I tried to act like I didn't hear what I heard. When I got back to the pool Nick and Cassidy could tell something was wrong but I just told them I started to worry a little bit about the Unhinged. That was not entirely a lie but not the full truth either.

As the sun went down so did our time in the house. We all congregated outside of Craig's house. We didn't know that the Elites would be joining us. And this time they brought Travis. To my horror. Candice, the moment she saw me, ran up to me apologizing saying that she never meant to hurt me and that Travis was telling her how horrible I was to him and she felt so bad and it made her hate me and all that stuff. I couldn't help but to advert my glare over to Travis who is mouthing he is sorry.

"You seem totally chill and I wanna start over. I just thought because Bridge hated you and after what Travis said, that you were some evil bitch." She pulls me in for a deep hug. Her overwhelming sweet marshmallow scent consumed me. I lightly patted her back so she would get off of me. As she parted, she gives me a huge grin and I smile back, but in a way of shock and wanting her to stop holding my hands.

She then goes on to give Cassidy a series of compliments. Cassidy is also very confused by Candice right now. Not to mention the presence of Travis. Nick and Dmitri did not flounder on letting him know that he was not welcomed in any sense. I ended up telling them, Nick, Cassidy, and Dmitri, about what Travis said to me on my birthday. The boys had the same, with more hostility, reaction as Craig. But Cassidy was just as shocked as I was when I first heard him say it. She feels just as uncomfortable with his presence as I am. It is just too soon.

"Ugh, can my brother and Craig hurry up! God, I need to get to this bar. I have had such a long dry spell, I will literally take anything," Jeanette complains taking a hit from a joint.

"Even a Long Island girl?" Bridget asks taking the joint from her and taking a hit for herself.

"I will take a Long Island girl, a girl who isn't even gay or bi, those types who wanna experiment. Hell, I'll even take those drunk girls who just want attention. It has been too long!" Candice, Bridget, and Jeanette laugh and we all join in.

Apparently before they got super high, Jeanette and Nick bonded. It is weird seeing them talk and joke around. Dmitri and Bridget are even being civil and having conversations. They join as a group of four and converse with one another. They are making plans of finding people to take home for the night, or in Bridget's case, someone to buy her drinks all night. Apparently, Dmitri and Bridget make excellent wing people. Candice stopped hugging up on Travis and went to talk to me and Cassidy. Well she is more so talking to Cassidy. After Travis and I broke up her and Cassidy stopped talking up until this point. So I guess she is making up for lost time. I still feel weird around her but I am not going to stop Cassidy from talking to a friend. Especially now that I got from between the lines, that Travis painted me as villain to her and that was the reason she decided to pounce after all this time. Craig told me that Candice would flirt, but she flirts with everyone and respected our relationship.

I smile and walk off getting my phone out to text Craig when Travis cuts me off.

"Hey again."

I look up like a deer in headlights. I give a weird half-hearted smile and a small hey.

"This is a little weird, huh? Seeing the two groups come together like this?" Travis continues.

I try to speak but I am tongue tied. Are we really going to continue on like he didn't say what he said to me on my birthday? That Candice didn't just tell me that he was talking shit about me for like 3 months?

"No, actually it's not. My friends know how much Jezebel means to me and they are making a great effort to be nice to her and her friends. Even with past aggressions they can set those aside," Craig says behind me. Oh thank god. I let out a breath and put my arm around him. He does the same to me and gives Travis a snarky little grin.

"Come on Craig, you don't think it is a little weird. I mean Bridget and Jeanette hated Jez's friends and her not so long ago."

"It is called growth, and maturity. Also, we went on a psychedelic trip together a few nights ago and brought us all closer together." His remark is quick and sharp, made perfectly to get a rise out of Travis. Everyday I see more and more of Dmitri's influence on him. But Travis is right. It is odd to see them interacting so well. It feels like we are in some bizzarro world.

Travis opened his mouth to say something, judging by his face it was going to be judgmental but then Jude swooped in. "Hey Trav!" Jude escorts him away and began talking to him about some nonsense. Jude looks back at us and winks.

"I know you still have reserve about Jude, but you can't say he doesn't pull through," Craig says in my ear then kisses my cheek. We join the others and they exclaim in exasperation over his tardiness.

"How are you late, meeting in front of your own house?" Jeanette jabs at him as she extends the shared joint his way. Craig takes a hit before saying, "Quit your bitching Jen and get in the car." She sticks her tongue out at him and laughs.

We pile into two different cars. Me, my friends, Craig, Jeanette, and Bridget ride in the SUV. While Jude, Candice, and Travis are riding in Candice's convertible. Jude took one for the team to spy on them for us. I told him it wasn't necessary but I think he read my mind a bit and knew that I was secretly loving it. We would have teleported over to the South Hamptons but Travis doesn't know about them. It makes me feel a little better. I guess since Candice is a human hybrid herself, her being interested in humans isn't far-fetched.

On the 45-minute ride over I can tell that something is bothering Craig. I have a feeling that something is the conversation he had with Dmitri earlier. I don't draw any attention to it. I have a feeling he just wants to get lost in everything and have a good time tonight.

When we got to the bar, they didn't even card us. The moment we walked up they saw the Elites and let us in. I don't know if they called ahead or if they used their "influence" to get in. They had a table set aside, almost like a VIP area. Even with all these rich east coast adults around us the Elites steal the spotlight. There are some teenagers here, who actually have fake IDs as I see them give them to bar tenders. They quickly notice us too, well the Elites. Some girls look intrigued by Dmitri when he was standing up, his height was a big selling point. I don't normally like the bar scene. It is always a little too much for me. All things considering the last time I was at a bar/club I ended the night killing someone. But something about now feels different. I have m friends here with me, Craig is here, but it is a different one. One who I can fully trust. One who isn't this larger romanticized version. I might actually be able to have a good time tonight.

Before we got the chance to fully settle in the talk of shots started. It was declared by no other than Jude first, then was quickly endorsed by Dmitri second.

"The question is which ones to get," Candice entices the group while playing with Travis' hair. It is still weird to see them together like this.

"I vote straight Patron to get the party started!" Jude exclaims. The girls sneer at this while Jude and Dmitri get excited. Jude mocks the girls for wanting more fruity shots to which Bridget is quick with the comeback.

"Just because we want something that taste good doesn't mean that we can't take a shot."

They bicker back and forth over what they should get. Craig looks wildly uninterested and very disconnected from everything. I know what is bothering him and it kills me that I can't say anything without outing the fact that I was eavesdropping earlier.

Travis used to be highly against Dmitri getting drunk, but I guess it's okay when his new girlfriend and her friends do it. He doesn't utter a word. Kind of funny. I bite my tongue not wanting to start any unwarranted controversy. Instead I engage back to their 'what shots to get' conversation.

"What kind of shot do you like?" Bridget asks Nick.

Nick stumbles on his word trying to think of answer quick. He has never had a shot in his life. He has seen Dmitri take many shots but he has never had one himself. He prefers wine over all things.

"I have not had a shot before. I've had a little bit of bourbon and whiskey, that's as hard as I get. I normally go for a wine."

"Nick you are precious," Jeanette purrs as she lingers her hand on his. It makes Nick blush. If she didn't tell me herself that she is a lesbian I would think that she was into Nick. But then again, she is like that with me sometimes. I think Craig is right when he said that she is just flirtatious. Nevertheless, I see Cassidy glare at her in, could that be, jealousy?

"I just never had the chance to party too much. Cas and Jez don't drink like that and Dmitri goes way too hard."

"Of course they don't," Bridget comments in a snarky tone. Jeanette snickers at her comment. Candice is lost in flirtation with Travis.

I sneer at Bridget and Jeanette as Craig puts his arm around me rubbing my shoulder.

"Just because we don't want to ruin our livers by 25 doesn't make us lame," Cassidy cuts back.

"Okay, what about a round of Parton shots, then a round of one of my favorite party shots, Woo Woo, and then finish it off with two Kamikazes," Dmitri raves.

The Elites share in excitement. Nick looks a little confused but is smiling anyway, not knowing fully what he has got himself into. Travis just looks happy to be there. Seeing him so silent on the matter is odd.

"Nick don't go too hard," Cassidy warns, her concern written all over her face.

"Yeah Nick, you can do the Patron, maybe a Woo Woo. We gotta see how you are after that, then perhaps you can have a Kamikaze," Dmitri says patting Nick on the back. This relaxes Cassidy's face a little. Even when Dmitri is in party mode, he would never let anything bad happen to Nick.

"I'll get the shots, who is all having one?" Craig asks coming back to life.

Dmitri, Jude, Jeanette, Bridget, and Nick all chime up. Candice debated back and forth on whether or not she should partake in shots because she dove them there.

"Babe it's okay, I'll drive back. Have fun tonight," Travis says.

"Thanks babe!" Candice replies with a quick kiss.

I try not to make a face, I try really hard not to make a face but it is hard not to. I think back to when that was us only 5 months ago. And how he is here cuddled up with Candice calling her babe. I may be here with Craig but we aren't like *them*. I shouldn't care. Emphases on the shouldn't.

"You have daddy's credit card?" Bridget asks Craig in an almost flirty tone. It breaks me from my thoughts.

Craig reaches into his pocket and pulls out his wallet. "Duh," Craig responds flipping out a black credit card. Craig gets up to head to the bar.

"I'll come with you," I blurt out standing up. Craig looks back at me taking my hand guiding me through the crowd. It is a relief to get from that table. Something about dealing with the Elites in a party setting is a bit exhausting. Their godly status elevates and I feel like a peon. Oh my god, Cassi, I shouldn't have left her there. I look back to the table that is getting lost in the crowd.

We reach the bar which is filled with people as well. Normally one wouldn't be able to find an empty spot at the bar but as Craig approaches it the people move out of his way. The bartenders are assisting other people but he doesn't seem to mind this. He leans on the bar and buries his face into his hands. I rub his back. God I wish I could just tell him what I know.

"You okay?" I ask in his ear, trying to get my voice over the loud music. Are we under a speaker or something?

"I'm fine. Just a bit exhausted." A lie.

"You can tell me if something is wrong Craig."

He stands up straight and looks me in my eyes. "I'm just a little worried about the Unhinged. Their silence and lack of action is worrying me just a little bit. Also, I was really looking forward to a relaxing night tonight. I completely forgot about my parents' charity benefit tonight. Also, I'm sorry about Bridget and Jeanette they get extra catty in settings like this. They are basically in hunting mode."

Them being in hunting mode makes me wanna run back to the table and steal Cassidy. I didn't mean to leave her with the wolves. I try to peek over to see if I can make anything out but once again, a failure. I sigh and turn my attention back to Craig. "I'm more annoyed with the presence of the duo of Travis and Candice. Do they have to be so kissy, huggy, all that stuff in front of all of us?"

My disgust makes Craig finally crack a smile. He isn't just a little bothered by the Unhinged, it is occupying his full mind. I hate that he feels alone in this because he isn't. I'm right here. "Hey-"

"It is crazy how much jealously Jeanette can bring out in people," Craig says looking over the crowd to the table. I try to see what he sees but I'm too short.

"What do you mean? Who's jealous?"

"Cassidy. Jeanette can read how defensive Cas starts to get when she becomes a little flirtatious with Nick. So she has really been playing it up to get under Cas' skin a little bit."

"I thought she was a lesbian."

"She is, she is just playing around."

Why does he find this amusing? That is not amusing that is mean. I squint and get myself ready to stomp over there to confront her but then Craig stops me mid charge.

"Woah there. No need to charge over there and kick any body's butt," he chuckles bringing me back to him. I huff and swing around knocking his arm off of me.

"That isn't funny, it is mean. To both Cassidy and Nick!"

"She is doing it for Nick. Cassidy has a little thing for Nick but doesn't really know it. Jeanette lightly flirting with him is bringing out some jealousy with Cas thus speeding up the process a bit."

"Cassi has a thing for Nick?"

"It is kind of obvious," Craig snuffs. How is it obvious? Dmitri and I have been trying to get Cassidy to maybe see Nick in a beyond friendly light and to us it didn't seem to be happening. Ambos, they think they know everything.

I cross my arms still not amused. "So, it's one of you guys' ambo mind games?"

Craig looks at me sweetly but I can tell he is about to be patronizing. "Sweetheart."

"Dear," I hiss between my teeth.

He rolls his eyes at me and brushes my chin. The bartender finally gets to us and Craig orders the shots. And two Sprites and a Coke for me, him, and Cassidy. He also got a water for Nick just incase he needed one. I reminded him about Travis and told him that he likes coke too. He reluctantly got him one. He still hasn't totally forgiven him, no matter how many times I say it is fine. Craig is convinced Travis is a snake. Which is funny, coming from the guy whose kind is literally marked as a snake.

Out of the crowd I see Cassidy stomping over to us, she looks pissed.

"What is Jeanette and Bridget's deal?! You said that they were nicer." Cassidy points an accusing finger at me. They were nicer. I didn't lie. I thought we were done with behavior like that from them.

"What is wrong?" Craig asks as if he is oblivious. I snarl at him but he ignores me.

"Jeanette, who I was under the impression was gay, has been messing with Nick this whole time. She keeps touching him, playing with his hair, and trying to influence him to get black out drunk and stuff! And every time I try to tell him that he needs to be careful they tease me and make fun of me, calling me his mom or his over protective girlfriend. I just..." She trails off.

"Care about him. You're a good friend and you're looking out for him," Craig finishes her sentence.

"Yes! God, they are killing me!" Cassidy exclaims.

I apologize for leaving her with the wolves. She told me that I would have to make it up to her. "The most dreadful minutes of my life" she says. The bartender comes back with the shots and the drinks. Craig leaves a very generous tip as another male steps out from behind the bar with both trays to follow us. Swerving our way through the crowd Craig takes hold of my hand, and I Cassidy's. The server is very steady with the trays, it is quite impressive. Not a drop spilled.

Right before we get to our table Craig stops and let's the server through. The table cheers and begins divvying up the shots. Craig turns to me and Cassidy and says, "Listen, give the girls a little bit of time to warm up, get a few drinks in them. They are like this in party settings all the time. Jeanette isn't interested in Nick, she is just a flirtatious person and likes to tease. Nick knows that, I think. But watch, in like 30 minutes or less she is going to find some girl and be way to preoccupied with her to even mess with you. We only have two more nights here after this. Let's have some fun." I suppose we will have to take his word on it. I hope he listens to himself and has some fun too.

I pull him to the side as Cassidy joins the table again. He looks at me a little concern from the severity I am showing on my face. "I know you are super stressed Craig, it is written all over your face. But we have been good here in the Hamptons. I think we are safe. Can you follow your own words and have fun tonight?" He doesn't reply at first but he does crack a small smile.

They knocked down those shots fast. Nick was only able to handle half of the Patron shot and a full Woo Woo. He ended up skipping the Kamikaze, which Jude gladly took off his hands. Cassidy ordered some food for Nick because he didn't take to the shot too well. I ended up splitting some Mozzarella sticks with Candice. She was actually very pleasant. Just as Craig described her, a loveable bimbo. She never really talked to me much, she always just spoke to Cassidy, and Travis of course. Travis looked pleased and nervous about us getting along. I think Craig actively chose to ignore Travis. He spoke only two sentences to him.

Sure enough, Craig was right about Jeanette. After taking their shots she quickly found a girl who caught her eye. Tall, shoulder length blonde hair, almost as stunning as Jeanette herself. But she didn't leave Bridget in the dust. Both her and model blondie helped scope out the room for a non pervy looking guy. All of them were kind of gross so Bridget went to Jude, where they spent their time as a quad.

Nick's stomach finally settled so the five of us felt safe to leave the table and hit the dance floor. Candice and Travis abandoned us some time ago to grind on the dance floor. Dmitri wanted to take Nick around the bar to find a girl for him. Cassidy did not trust him because after taking the four shots Dmitri ordered two more very strong drinks. Let's just say his accent is a hybrid of English and Romanian, so not fully drunk yet, but getting there. I told Cassidy to go with them and give me and Craig some kind of signal if she needed reinforcements.

Dancing around actually got Craig to fully lighten up. I forgot how good of a dancer he is. Dancing with Craig is like in a movie when everything goes black and there is a spotlight just on the two of us. The magical music surrounds us and the crowd slowly comes back bringing you into reality again but you are so dazzled in the moment you don't even care.

We dance through about 6 different songs before we need to go back to the table to take a break and drink some water. "Cassi hasn't signaled us yet, so I guess that means they are doing good?" I say in between sips.

"Let me see if I can find them." I expected Craig to get up but instead he remains by my side. He is searching for their thoughts. I wonder what that is like. A few seconds go by before he exclaims, "got em!" They are chatting with some people near the bar. Well Cassidy and Nick are. Dmitri is flirting with the bartender and it is actually working. Nick and Cassidy both found someone to talk to apparently. Good for them.

"Do you wanna go over there and see what they look like?" Craig asks with a sneaky grin.

"I don't wanna throw off their game."

"No, no it is fine. We will get close enough to see them but not close enough for them to see us," Craig assures me. He has a trickster glint in his eyes. I kind of love it. I giggle and agree. They better be up to the standards. Cassidy and Nick are wonderful people and only the best deserve their time. Even if it is for one night. We get up and begin to indiscreetly make our way over to them when Candice comes running up to us. She looks panicked and her eyes are wild. She is pushing us back to the table and throwing her keys at Travis telling him to get the car. What is going on?

"They are here! Those Crazies, the Insane. Whatever they are called they are *here!*" Candice franticly tells us. The Unhinged? Is that who she means? They are here? In this bar? I haven't seen them. I begin searching around and Craig tries to calm Candice down.

"Candice, please, please slowly explain what and who you saw to make you believe this," Craig calms her.

Candice takes deep breaths shaking out her hands. "Okay, okay. So like I really had to pee right? And I went to go search for my girls, because a girl cannot go to the bathroom alone in a bar. Who knows what will happen. Though you meet the nicest girls in there sometimes-"

"Candice, back to the story," Craig instructs.

"Right, sorry. So, I went to find Jen and Bridge but I didn't see them. I saw the girl Jen was with but no one else. I went to go up to the girl but then I noticed something really weird about her. I ran to the bathroom hoping maybe the girls were there and they were! They were sitting on the ground bewitched!"

"Oh shit," Craig and I mutter at the same time. I shoot up and stand on top of the seats to find Cassidy, Nick, and Dmitri. I find them and they are all doing fine. But then I see Nick and Cassidy start to move in the direction of the bathroom. Oh no. No, no, no! I hop down and try to race towards them but Craig Takes my arm, again. I try to jerk him off of me but he won't let go.

"Dmitri is getting them! I alerted him, look!" Craig exclaims to me. I jerk my head back and see Dmitri grabbing them and dragging them over to our direction. A shadow starts to loom behind him before a loud screeching noise echoes and it is gone. I look back to Craig whose eyes are fading from Indigo.

Jude comes over to us with Jeanette and Bridget in a zombie like state. "What did they do to my sister?! What did they do to them?!" He exclaims. Dmitri arrives soon after with Cassidy and Nick looking in a similar fashion. His eyes filled with panic as well. Yet, no one else around us is fazed by all of this. It is as if they can't see us.

"They're bewitched!" Candice shouts getting over worked again. "And, and they left this note," she trembles. Candice hands the note to Craig and he reads out loud, "Come and see what we have waiting for you tomorrow at 9pm. See you at Alberts Landing."

Trapped

We race back to Craig's place ignoring all the speed limits and stop signs. Jude Squeezes in the SUV with us and tries to get Bridget and Jeanette out of the trance. He fails with them and with every passing second he becomes more and more frustrated. He is able to partially get Nick and Cassidy out of the trance. Dmitri and I keep them talking and asking questions so they don't slip back under. Craig is attempting to keep his cool but he is gripping the steering wheel so tight I think it might break.

Going at least a hundred down the streets we get back to the house in record time. I can't even think. I can't form a thought to comprehend what just happened. How it happened. Why is it that no one at that bar noticed anything that happened? How did they not see Bridget and Jeanette on the bathroom floor? That large shadow figure. Was that all a set up to get to us?

"Jezebel!" Craig hisses between his teeth. A tone I have never heard him take with me. "Please quiet your thoughts... please," he says in a calmer tone. I don't respond but look back to our bewitched friends and try to think of a way out of this. I try to log back to the things I read about bewitchments. There has to be something that can snap them out of this that doesn't involve the use of another witch or wizard. I know I read something. It was a potion or maybe a chanting spell. Still we would need to use magic. But ambos are almost like magic. Closest creature we have at least.

The car jerks to a stop flopping me in the seat a little bit. We rush file out of the car and sneak the bewitched into the back of the house. As we rush in we can hear the clamoring of the people at the benefit. Snaking through the kitchen the smell of all the amazing food is almost distracting. Everything is being prepared remotely but as dishes are plated they are floated over to a server.

We make it into the sunroom that Craig and I spent our first day and many nights at. Sitting the bewitched down, Craig joins in with Jude to try to get them out of the hex, but they cannot muster enough power. Candice pops in the room with us. She startles me and I let out a small yelp. She says that she "put Travis to sleep" a term Craig taught me. Lulling someone into a sleep inducing coma for however long you need them out. I hope she knows how to get him back out.

"I'm going to get Chuck," Dmitri calls already running off as a blur in the distance before Craig had the chance to protests. Craig curses under his breath and looks defeated as he stands back up. I haven't spoken up much. I am trying to keep my panic inside. Jude is freaking out, rightfully so, at the feet of his sister. Trying with all of his power to get her back. I wish I could think of the way to reverse this. Nick would know. Nick always knows the answers to these things. Why did they have to target them and not us? Mimik. The trickster demon. It has been following around Jude and Craig. It transformed itself into a person that would entice Jeanette. It knew what Jeanette would want because of it following around Jude. And they it did the same thing for Cassidy and Nick from following Craig. Since I am around them a lot, and in turn so is Craig, it latched onto them.

My heart pounds more and more. If anything were to happen to Nick and Cassidy, I don't know what I would do. I can't live without them. What if this is permanent? No, no it can't be. I go to their sides and hold their hands. They look like their consciousness is slipping away. That they are losing more and more of themselves with each passing second. I start to mutter a chant under my breath. I don't know where I've heard this but it is worth a shot.

"It was a warning," Craig mutters. It is only loud enough that I am able to hear it. I look up at him, my eyes moist from the beginning formation of tears. One escapes my eyes and rolls down my cheek. He wipes away the tear and crouches down to meet me and Jude. Candice joins us, her eyes filled with tears as well. "This was a warning. They are sending us a message so that we know they are not ones to be messed with. They have some serious power in their arsenal." Craig's voice is grave but with such little emotion. It's futile it feels like. Nothing we do to get away helps.

Dmitri comes back with Mr. Edwards who is dressed in a tux. The four of us rise up and make room for Mr.

Edwards. "I already briefed him on the situation, anything changed?" Dmitri asks joining back up with us. We shake our heads at him. Mr. Edwards gives a reassuring shoulder squeeze to Craig and leads him back in front of the bewitched.

"No one noticed around you?" Mr. Edwards asks.

Craig shakes his head. "No one. The whole thing was a giant illusion. There is only one ambo left alive and there is no way Hayden could have done that."

So that's why no one noticed, it was all one big illusion. If Craig knew why didn't he say anything?

"The witch, do you know how powerful she is?" Mr. Edwards further questions as he continues to examine our friends.

"I have no clue. Didn't get a chance to dive deep into her powers. But she is easily subdued. At least when caught off guard."

Mr. Edwards stops and takes a longer look at Nick and Cassidy. He waves his hands in front of their faces. He looks back at Craig. "What did you do to them?"

"I tried to get them out of the trance by trying to pull them out of their own unconsciousness."

"No, you did something different, they are in limbo, they can hear but cannot get out. Bridget and Jeanette are still gone."

Hearing Mr. Edwards say that made Jude and Candice wince. What does he mean by they're gone? Are they essentially dead?

Craig looks back at me confused. "Jezebel?" Me? What did I do? Was it the chant? Did it work? Chepi said I hold more power than I thought. Is this what she meant?

"Jezebel? What did she do?" Mr. Edwards asks. He turns his attention to me as he hurries towards me. "Did you do or say anything to them?"

I stumble to get my words out, feeling very nervous. I don't want to sound ridiculous. All I did was chant, but I'm not an ambo nor am I a witch. Or am I witch? "I chanted," I blurt out. The excitement over me possibly being a witch over shadowed my hesitant thoughts. "I think I read it in one of the books about witches, wizards, and warlocks. A reversal on bewitching."

"You're not a witch so that wouldn't have worked on your own." Oh, well that kills my enthusiasm. "Perhaps... Craig were you trying to pull them out at the same time as Jezebel was chanting?" Mr. Edwards beckons for me to follow him.

"I could have been, I don't know when she was doing it."

Mr. Edwards instructs me to do exactly as I had before. But I cannot remember what I did, something came to me and it was as if I was being controlled almost. Craig is beside me as he says, "Can I work through you? It won't hurt." I don't know what he means by that, but my guess is that it has to do with going inside of my head. If that means we can get Nick and Cassidy back then fine.

I nod my head, and the moment I do everything is white. A warm yellow light is all I see. Craig is chanting in a language I don't recognize. His voice is fuzzy, static like.

"It's working Craig keep going," Mr. Edwards encourages. The light grows stronger and Craig and Mr. Edwards voices slip away. My vision slowly comes back to the current room.

"Nick, Cas!" Dmitri exclaims racing over to them. I jerk my head up to see them both awake in conscious. Jude and Candice exclaim for Bridget and Jeanette soon after. I feel slightly dizzy as I try to stand. Craig helps me up steadying me.

"Craig," Mr. Edwards calls beckoning him over. They walk off along the entrance hallway muttering something to one another. I blunt force hits me from behind. A bear hug from Cassidy. I turn around and hug her back. She pulls away and her joy quickly turns into rage. "What the *hell* happened?" she asks with a viper grip on my shoulder. I am not sure what just happened but I am glad it worked.

Jude and Candice took Jeanette and Bridget back to the Farquhar's house. Craig never returned so Dmitri filled Nick and Cassidy in on what happened and what we think we know. Which isn't much. We know that the bar was a set up, they knew we would be there and the whole experience inside was an elaborate illusion that not even the ambos could detect. Strangely enough it was only as strong as it was because of the help of the witch. There was definite use of Mimik with the people who was flirting with Jeanette, Nick, and Cassidy. And they were chosen as a method to get a message across. But that is all we know. And even that we aren't one hundred percent on. Dmitri also said Craig used me to get the chant out of my head so he was able to recite it back as I whispered the words to him. Apparently I was right about the bewitchment reversal incantation.

Nick and Cassidy do not remember anything after being approached by this guy and girl. They cannot remember what they look like or sound like. That whole part of their memory is gone.

"It felt like I was in a deep sleep, but I knew I was awake," Cassidy explains shivering. Nick backs up her statement. He finds the idea of it intriguing but is frightful about the fact that it happened to him.

"I wanna find out more," Nick says. Cassidy, Dmitri, and I look at him like he is crazy.

"You were just bewitched you dumb ass why on *earth* would you want to dig deeper into them?!" Dmitri says what we are all thinking.

"Well we are going to have to right? They had that note. Tomorrow night at 9," Nick tries to rationalize. He isn't wrong. They did call for us to meet with them. But that doesn't mean we should.

"One of us could get hurt or killed. This feels like a set up. We should not go. Do you want a repeat of what happened to Jezzi and Craig in November?" Cassidy says and I agree; this feels all too familiar. Nick tries to convince us that he is right in this but I don't see how. On one side I can see what Nick is saying. They went through all of this to just send a message. If we don't comply, they can get more and more violent. But it really does feel like if we meet them tomorrow at 9, we will be walking into a trap.

"You and Cassidy should not be anywhere near these guys. But, We do need to look into them. We can't just ignore them," Dmitri states.

"So you're backing me up?" Nick asks.

"No, not fully. I think maybe we should go to the area in the note in the day time and have a little investigation with you guys and then at 9 leave you guys here so we can go in and do what we gotta do."

"Dmitri's right," Craig says startling us in a monotoned voice from behind. When did he even get in here? "I just spoke to my dad about everything. He is concerned about... all of us. I think in the afternoon we should all go to the area and see what we can find. You can always sniff out a supes' lair."

"I'm going to go over their files tonight, thoroughly. I don't want to walk into anything without being prepared again," Cassidy says. Something that we should have been doing from the start.

Nick and Craig end up joining Cassidy in her room going through the flash drive of files that she got when we went to that leap day party. I try to sleep in Craig's room. But I cannot. My mind keeps going over everything that happened tonight and this afternoon with the conversation between Craig and Dmitri.

Giving up on my attempts to get some sleep I scurry down the hall to Dmitri's room. The light from Cassidy's is still on. So I make my footsteps as quiet as possible so no one hears me. I softly knock-on Dmitri's door. I hope it is loud enough for him to hear. But I believe vampires have like super sonic hearing.

Dmitri opens the door and before he invites me in, I push my way through. "Close the door, but quietly," I whisper. I don't think they would be able to hear me but I don't want to risk anything. Dmitri looks confused but does it anyway.

I sit on the bed and look around the room. I notice a bottle on the nightstand. "What's that?" I ask.

"Blood. Type AB positive. My favorite," he says in a sinister tone. I react in disgust making him smile. He joins me on the bed taking a swig from the bottle. "What do I owe this late night pleasure? Does Craig know you are visiting? Is he joining? That's kind of gross Belle."

I scoff and swat at him as we laugh. "I'm not trying to have a threesome with you and Craig. I wanted to talk about somethings."

"What things?"

"Things of the Unhinged nature."

His smile drops. He puts down his bottle of blood and gives me his full attention. The look in his eyes makes me feel safe.

"Since the beginning of all of this you have been pretty understanding. You rarely oppose the things we do. Do you trust Craig in all of this?"

Dmitri sighs and takes another swig from his bottle. He plays with his hair before tossing it over his shoulder. "Do *you* not trust Craig?" He asks me leaning in.

"I worry that Craig doesn't trust himself."

"What makes you think that?"

I sigh sinking my head into my chest. Dmitri isn't going to budge on this. He is loyal, it's not a bad thing except in this instance. He is going to make me confess and this will be my second offense of invading his privacy. Hind sight I shouldn't have done it at all but I am still not please that I have to confess to it.

"Listen," I pause. Should I confess to this? I definitely was not supposed to hear any word of it and I just know that Dmitri will be mad at me, probably lose all trust in me. But I am concerned. Might as well. "I heard some of the conversation you and Craig had earlier today. I know He is extremely overwhelmed from this whole thing and is unsure if he is doing anything right."

Dmitri rubs the space between his eyes in frustration. He lets out a low groan that almost resembles a growl. He looks at me with a scowl. Yup, he's mad.

"Belle."

"I'm sorry."

"What is with you and spying and sticking your nose into things of people who you care about. First you break into my house and now this?"

"Hey, Craig and Nick broke in too. And I was against the whole thing," I point. But I know that is besides the point. Judging by the look that he is giving me he is thinking the same thing.

"If you were a boy I would have slapped you by now."

I nod, "I understand."

We sit in silence. You can faintly hear the others conspiring down the hall. Everyone else has gone to bed. He still hasn't answered my question about if he has full trust in Craig. But I don't want to pester him. I think we both know the answer. Sitting in this silence is making things worse. I study the room to try to find something to talk about but my eyes settle back on Dmitri, specifically his hair. It looks different.

"Your hair looks different."

Dmitri looks back at me squinting his eyes at me. "What?"

"Your hair, it looks," I take a moment to study it a bit more to see what exactly it was, "lighter"

He runs his fingers though his hair and examines it himself. His confusion switches as he drops the lock from his hand. "The color is fading is all."

"Color?"

"I dye my hair. I have been for years. My hair is naturally dark brown like my mom's."

My eyes widen. I don't know why this is such a shocking and upsetting revelation to me. His jet-black hair is part of the whole package, him with brown hair? That just doesn't seem right.

"It's just hair Belle," he snorts at my disgusted look.

"Yeah I guess.."

He laughs harder, it makes me crack a smile.

"Moving past my hair color,"

"It was a very shocking thing to hear,"

He rolls his eyes and mocks me. "Sure, Belle. But I trust Craig's process... to an extent. He hasn't done anything incredibly stupid enough for me to break and intervene."

Well, it is an answer, not one I was looking for. It gives me a small dosage of reassurance. I still worry about Craig; I don't want him to stress himself out too much. Seeing him break down like that broke my heart.

Dmitri puts his arm around me. "Hey, it's fine. Well clearly not everything is fine. But we are going to get through this. It might be an awful journey, but still. We got the brains in the next room going over files and preparing."

"If they are brains what are we?"

"Brawn."

I let out a short laugh. Yeah sure, me as brawn. Dmitri leads me down to lie next to him. He pulls the covers up over us. "You're not the bait Belle. You're stronger than you think and you'd be shocked with what you can do once that adrenaline kicks in. Also you are an excellent gymnast making you quick and limber. Not to mention you being a great marksman."

"I've never missed a shot," I say feeling the confidence booster.

I crinkle my nose as he boops it with his finger. "See, not useless." I giggle at him. "Seriously though, tomorrow we will do some investigating and go from there. You read so much on ambos, werewolves and witches. There is nothing else you can possibly read for the general basic knowledge. Just go to sleep."

I turn my back to him as he shifts to lying on his back. He puts earbuds in as he goes on his phone. He probably won't sleep until around 5am. I'm just going to rest my eyes for a bit before going back to Craig's room.

I wake up to hear the birds chirping outside. The room is still very dark. I turn over to see if Craig is awake, but to my surprise Dmitri is beside me. He looks dead, well I suppose he is dead. I look at the clock on the nightstand. It is 7:30. I overslept for sure. I toss the covers off of me and sneak out of the room. I don't want to disturb his vampiric slumber.

I softy close the door and slowly turn around.

"Jez!" I jump and yelp. I clasp my hand over my mouth as I take a moment to catch my breath and let my heartrate slow down.

"God damnit Nick! Could you not do that?!" I whisper at him harshly. The rest of the house is still probably asleep. We don't eat breakfast until 9

"Sorry, but, come come. I have things to show and tell you."

Nick drags me down the hall to the room that Cassidy and I share. He opens the door to show me Cassidy and Craig passed out on the bed. They aren't snuggled up, just sharing the bed as if they knocked out in the middle of doing work. Nick explains how they were up all night scouring through the files on the flash drive. Nick tapped out early and headed to bed but they kept going.

"Why are you showing me this?"

"I didn't want you to think your boyfriend was two timin' ya with your best friend."

Oh Nick. "I'm not worried about that Nick, but thank you"

Nick crosses his arms, "You must trust him a lot."

"Yeah, I do. Also I know Cassi would never do that to me."

He nods and begins walking towards the stairs. "Yeah, you're right. Cas is perfect."

I can't stop myself from making a face. Nick takes notice and warns me to stop, but I keep going.

I wonder what Cassidy, Nick, and Craig found last night. I never got the chance to look into the files. I just trusted that Nick and Cassidy would do that. I do feel on edge thinking about what we may find this afternoon. Time is moving slower than usual. It is as if each second lasts 60.

At breakfast everyone was groggy. The benefit last night was a success so the celebration went way longer than what was expected. Our siblings stayed up playing video games and watching TV with one another after they came back from the store fronts. But no one was as exhausted as Cassidy and Craig. I thought that they were going to plop their faces in the waffles. My parents have been worry free about me since we've been here. Little do they know what we got ourselves into last night and what is to come.

After breakfast Craig and Cassidy retired back to their rooms to go back to sleep. I went to go and follow them but then Mom stops me. "Jez, come sit with us," she says patting the spot between her and Dad. I go over to them and take the seat. My dad cuddles me as my mom looks at me very sweetly. What is all this about?

"Comment ça va?" Dad ask with a warm tone.

"Bien," I reply.

"How're you and Craig?" Mom continues.

Ah, I see. This is a relationship wellness check. I did spring Craig on them out of nowhere after sulking around my house for a month and a half about Travis.

I smile and snuggle my back deeper into my dad. "He's good. Really good. He makes me really happy, and he lets me be me." hearing this puts a syrupy smile on my mom's face. I can feel my dad let out an exhale.

"We were just wondering," she continues.

"Were you worried?" I question.

My dad says no in an unconvincing tone the same time my mom says yes. I move out from his arms so I can look at the both of them.

My dad gives a scolding look at my mom. "Rae!"

"What? Chris, I'm not gonna lie to the girl."

Is this going to be like when Josh and Lindsay disclosed how they really felt about Travis? In that case it was fine because we were done. But Craig? I guess them getting this out early is good.

"Sweetie, it is just that you guys got together rather quickly after you and Travis. And you were really torn up about your breakup. Your light was gone," My mom says as she holds my hand.

"But, it is back. And it has been back for some months, éclat. We just wanted to make sure."

"He is a nice young man. And his mother isn't a pompous, holier than thou little-"

"Chuck and Maggie are wonderful and so are their kids,"

I giggle. It is always entertaining to see them trying to find a way to properly speak on a serious/parenting topic, because my dad likes to keep things very optimistic and sunny while my mom is more blunt with a touch of pessimism. "I have never been as happy as I am with Craig when I was with Travis. Craig treats me really well. Actually, he does the opposite of what Travis would do, he relaxes me, no matter the situation."

My dad rubs my arm and shoulder as he kisses the top of my head. My mom interlaces her fingers with mine. They release me from their hold after being satisfied with my answer. I scurry off upstairs to Craig's room. Nick decided to meet up with his cousins, so I am the only one of my friends who is awake.

I knock on the door to be polite; the door cracks open seconds later. It must be nice to be able to use telekinetic powers to open things. I go in and shut the door behind me. He is lying with his back to the door, the room dark. Is he even awake? I crawl into bed with him and he turns around to face me. He softly brushes my hair from my face. "Sorry I never came back to bed," he groggily says. It sends shivers down my spine.

I snuggle up closer to him and hum. "It's okay, I went to talk to Dmitri because I couldn't sleep and ended up sleeping there."

"Did he give you peace of mind?"

I scrunch up my nose thinking of a way to put it. "Kind of. In a Dmitri way."

He hums turning me so that he can spoon me. "So he gave some sound words but also still you felt a little uneasy."

"Spot on."

He chuckles keeping me in his embrace. I don't think I have long before he is fully knocked out. So I quickly ask him if they found anything useful last night. To which he mumbled he will tell me about it later.

It is 6pm. We slept through our afternoon investigation time. Nick got so caught up with seeing his cousins he forgot about being back by 1. He came running into the house at 4 but Cassidy, Craig, and Dmitri were all still knocked out. Nick and I worked on trying to reach Jude but even he wasn't responding. It wasn't until 5 when we were able to get people up. Jude came over after he finally saw all of Nick and my frantic messages. He was sunbathing and 'couldn't be bothered'.

We are all in the SUV rushing over to Alberts Landing. Nick, Cassidy, and Craig inform us of what they found on the Unhinged. Upon diving deeper into their lives, they found that while Donna was orphaned, she has the bloodline that can be traced to very powerful witches and wizards alike. Also, the vampires who she lived with would get her to tap into a darker power by using their blood. I remember reading about blood magic, when used it can cause for a higher dark magic but it comes at a price. That is probably how they were able to make such a large illusion at that bar. From what I remember, a witch/wizard and ambo paring can make for some extremely powerful magic.

Sarah, turns out to be the leader amongst them. She was the leader of a pack of young wolves for 5 years, until they stage somewhat of a coup because she was insanely power hungry, corrupt, and to put it quite frankly, a ravenous bitch. According to Nick and Jude, Sarah and Hayden are often coked up, making them crazier than before. They learned this from chatting with Hayden at the party. But Hayden himself isn't that powerful from what they can see. He was created and doesn't have much control over his powers and doesn't know how to use them as well as a trained ambo would. But there was one thing on his record that they could not decern.

"There was this symbol on there. I have never seen it before. I searched and searched, that's why Cassidy and I were up so late. Everywhere we looked leaded to dead ends," Craig explains with some lingering frustrations.

When the explaining stops so does any talking. We don't know what is going to happen when we get to the beach. Will they be there, will there be some kind of clue? Before we left Craig gave me Wendy, he snuck it over for me. He doesn't want to kill again, but if the time comes he said he will assist me. Rallying into the SUV felt like we were about to be deployed into battle.

The only talking that is going on is amongst Craig and Dmitri. They are going over something about Mr. Edwards. It isn't meant for us to hear considering they are speaking Romanian. I know Craig can speak quite a few languages but I wasn't aware until this trip that Romanian is his second language and his third is Muskogean; the language the Apalachee speak.

Nick and I sit in between Cassidy who is the most nervous about doing this. It is making her think of the extra credit project. We also told her that she wouldn't have to deal with anything like that, and that we just needed her to get information. Yet, here we are. Spending all that time looking into the Unhinged actually made her feel worse. Her and Craig are the biggest naysayers on going to the location after their deep dive last night. But Craig is following what his dad told him to do. Nick says that we can't keep running.

"Logically, none of this adds up to work in our favor," Nick starts. "but,"

"But what? In what way would it be wise to walk into a monsters mouth to risk destroying it from the inside when you can find another way of doing it?" Cassidy counters.

"There is no other way," Jude mumbles as he is still focused on his search.

"There is always another way. There is never just one way," Cassidy snaps back.

Craig and Dmitri don't say anything. Craig just keeps driving and Dmitri keeps looking ahead. They always tell me that I don't need to know everything, that I am not meant to know all what is said and what goes on. But their silence is deafening. They know something. Mr. Edwards told them something. Even though they told me to not pry, I will find out. I don't follow orders too well.

We know more about what we are up against but that just makes the fear all the greater. We have a dark blood magic witch, a psychotic coked out werewolf, and an equally psychotic ambo who has an extra detail about him that we cannot discern.

Jude is going through everything he can dig up from his family's personal files to see if he can find anything on this symbol. Whatever illegal thing his family does it turns out to have a lot of secret underground information not even known to the Council.

We pull up to the beach and there is nothing or no one here. Just sand and ocean. Craig and Dmitri unbuckle their seat belts. "You guys stay here for now," Craig says as they exit the car. I challenge them and maneuver my way into the 2nd row so I can get out with them.

I hop out the car and as I close the door behind me Craig and Dmitri take notice. Craig rubs between his eyes as he sighs in total frustration.

"Belle, why do you have to be such a stubborn bitch?"

"I don't know, why do you have to be such a cryptic asshole?" I quip back walking up to them.

Dmitri rolls his eyes as he tries hard not to smile. I join up with them and wait for them to explain why they are the only ones who get to be out here.

"Sweetheart."

"Dear."

Craig groans again, "We wanted to look around the area to see if anything is suspicious."

"You couldn't have done that with all of us?"

They don't respond, but they aren't blank. I can tell they are trying to think of a fake good reason to make us all wait. "Oh come on, give it up!" I exclaim, becoming exhausted with all this secretive stuff.

"Chuck saw something. When unbewitching them, he saw a little note left by the Unhinged," Dmitri fesses up.

I wait for him to continue but he doesn't, neither does Craig. I prod them to continue. "It said go underground and what you seek might be found," Craig says.

That's it, that's what they couldn't tell us? That sounds like a clue we should have definitely known. Craig notices the unimpressed look on my face. "Jezebel, that isn't it. He... he saw the vision that they put in you guys' head. But this time it was worse, and clearer. It was out here, on this Alberts Landing Road. They suffer too, not just us. They are planning a murder suicide mission."

My smugness drops. My heart sinks down to my feet. It was real. It was a premonition. We just walked into our deaths. If they knew why did they bring us here?

"Nothing is set in stone Belle. It can change, we can't let the fear over take us, then we'd be undeniably screwed."

I gape at them. I have no words. I have nothing to describe this feeling of wanting to both fight and take flight. I don't want to go so gentle, I want to fight for my life, for my happiness. But going into a trap, walking right into a trap and just hoping that we will be strong enough to get out of it? Craig takes my hand and guides me into him. He holds me tight to his chest.

"Guys! Guys!" Jude frantically calls racing up to us. I slightly break from Craig's embrace; his arm is still around my shoulder. Nick and Cassidy soon follow after him. What happened?

"He," Jude stops for a moment to catch his breath. "He, Hayden, he is a pyro!"

"Oh, fuck," Dmitri's voice low.

"He is a pyro? A PYRO?!" Craig drops his arm from around me and shouts out of disbelief.

"That's what the symbol was!" Nick yells catching up to us. "Jude here almost missed it, but I was looking over his shoulder and saw it." Jude shoots a quick glare at him but confirms it.

Dmitri is stunned and doesn't move. Craig begins to pace and mumbles something I can't hear. I am still quite confused about this.

"I thought he was made, how can he have a archetype when it is rare for a natural born ambo to have one?" I ask Jude.

"Who. Is. This. Ripper? He has something, he has some unworldly power that I can't even comprehend. How the *hell* do you give a made ambo an archetype?!" Craig snaps coming back at us.

Before Jude has the chance to say anything Craig barks at us to comb the beach for any clues. To dig under the sand. It is 6:30 and we have 2 and a half hours before they supposedly arrive. This is a fierceness I have never seen from Craig, he's practically smoking. I've seen him in a slightly more subdued state like this before and he turned into half beast.

We went in teams, our teams respective to our buddy system set in place from before. However, right now I wish I had another buddy. Craig is scaring me, he is like 2 seconds away from unveiling the beast. It is now 8:40 and we have found nothing.

Craig growls and slams himself in the sand. While I am very frightened of him right now, it is still Craig. I stand in front of him and brush his hair back with my hands. Without speaking he pulls me in by my thighs and gets to kneel so he is eye level with me. He runs his hands up my thighs to my waist pulling me in closer. "Jezebel," he whispers, "I'm scared."

The first time he has said those words to me. Something I knew since yesterday but he has finally said them out loud to me. And oddly, it feels good to hear it. I don't say anything back but I move his head to my chest as I hold him. "I don't want anything to happen to you guys," he tries to continue but I shush him. I get to be what he has been to me this whole time. He gets to finally let go and not be the perfectly put together one.

"AHHHH!" Cassidy screeches from the other side of the beach. Craig and I snap back and scramble up and run. We meet up with Dmitri and Nick doing the same. Jude is holding Cassidy, looking just as mortified as her. It wasn't until I looked down did I see it. Organs, a pile of organs. I don't know which ones what other than the large intestine. I can't look away, I cannot tear my eyes away from what I am seeing. The blood mixed with the sand, the gory mess in front of us. The smell of it... it is fresh. I feel sick.

"Oh god," Nick grumbles and he runs off to go throw up. No one says anything, what is there to say? Fresh human organs were just unearthed. But then it came to me.

"The Ripper," I whisper.

Everyone looks to me. Nick comes back, still looking green. "What?" he asks breathily.

"Jack the Ripper would disembowel his victims," I say pointing my head towards the remains.

The silence returns as we gaze upon the "clue" again. Craig squats down to get closer. Jude lets go of Cassidy and goes down with him. To our disgust they begin rummaging around. Nick turns away trying to hold back the vomit again. Cassidy can barely keep her disgust in as she turns her head looking nauseated. I feel like Nick, I want to vomit as well. Why are they in there?!

Dmitri steps away because of the smell of blood, it is getting to him. Pulling their bloody hands out Jude emerges with a kidney with a note attached to it. "From Hell"

He is baiting us, there is no doubt about that. Craig and Jude washed their hands off in the ocean before we piled back into the SUV. The note gave an address to follow. It is on the same road but Craig and Jude swear that there is no house here. But the story was different when we came up to it. It looks new, like it was just placed here.

"Are we sure, this is it?" Jude asks. Nick is looking over Cassidy's shoulder as she searches for a signal from any of their phones. She ended up finding a way to tap into them when she stole Hayden's laptop.

"This is the address at least," Craig says looking around the area.

"I hope Chuck is right about this," Dmitri mumbles pulling hair back off his face.

There are no shadows, weird glitches, no strange birds hanging around. But what does that mean? We thought we were in the clear when we were at the bar. And look that happened there.

"Guys... they're here," Cassidy peeps. She got a signal on her phone. We look around but see nothing. Everything is the same. Eerily still and quiet. We look to one another. Trying to have some kind of unspoken agreement about what we should do. A part of me wants to jump in and face them straight on, but another part thinks about what Craig and Dmitri told me. If we are going to change things, we need not act abruptly.

Jude unbuckles his seat belt. "I'll go in."

We call his name and warn him to stay put. "Guys it's fine. I'll go in first. Someone has to be the martyr." He scooches over to open the door but Dmitri clamps him down with one hand.

"No one has to be a martyr. We go in together." Dmitri's voice is serious and authoritative. Kind of hot but also kind of frightening.

He lets go of Jude and unbuckles his seatbelt too, we all do. I guess we are going in. They're here. Somewhere. I don't know what they want from us, but I suppose we are about to find out.

The door was open, they aren't trying to keep us out. This is definitely a trap and we are dumb enough to actively walk right into it. At this point I have no clue if it is considered courageous for facing them like this or if it is just plain idiotic.

The first good sign is that the door did not randomly shut behind us like in a horror film. But it doesn't take long for them to show up. A cloud of black smoke billows out of the blue. As it dissipates the three of them are shown. Hayden already in half beast form.

"We were going to wait," Sarah starts.

"But you killed one of our own. So the Ripper thought it would be best to kill one of yours," Hayden slithers out.

Without warning Donna pulls out her wand and shouts, "Rapiospiro!" As quickly as she aims her wand at Nick. Dmitri is in front of him taking the blunt of the attack and running off with Nick. From then on, it was go time. Jude and Craig transformed into half beast. Donna went chasing after Nick and Dmitri, Jude and Cassidy ran after Sarah as she shifted into a large wolf, while Craig and I are head on with Hayden.

I don't know what is happening to the others. I hear growls, screaming, crashing, heavy footsteps running. Craig is fighting Hayden off as he tries to advance at me. I feel paralyzed and I don't know what to do. Craig doesn't want me to kill, he doesn't even want me to shoot. But my heart is racing and my adrenaline is pumping. My senses are going into hyperdrive. It is as if I can hear every single little thing that is happening in this house. The whip of a spell leaving Donna's wand, the growling and snarling from Sarah and Jude. They aren't even around me. What is happening?

Throwing Hayden against an unfinished fireplace, Craig looms over him, "Who is the Ripper?!" Craig grits between his sharp teeth. He rips a sizeable gash into Hayden's leg, "Answer me!" I jerk my head to the stairs as I hear something tumbling down. It is Jude! I race over to him, he is hurt and bleeding. I try to help him up but he waves me off and weakly get's out, "Cassidy, save Cassidy." I lower his head and plow up the stairs.

"Cassi! Cassi!" I cry at the top of my lungs racing around trying to find her. And then I see Sarah, coming around the corner, her mouth bloody. Oh no. She snarls her teeth at me then starts to race towards me with great speed. I swallow all my fear and run towards her then right when she is about to reach me I launch myself into a front full twist barely missing her. I landed perfectly to my surprise and book it down the hall to the left to see if Cassidy is around. I can hear her faint whimpering. Please be okay, please be okay.

"Jezzi!" She is sitting in the corner of a dark room holding onto her arm which is riddled with blood and bite marks. I need to get her to Jude or Craig, now! I run over to her helping her up making sure to be easy on her arm. As I try to walk her out Sarah comes around the corner about to launch at us. Quickly I pull out Wendy and aim at her abdomen. *Crack!* She howls in pain and curls in her herself on the ground.

"Come on!" I grab Cassidy again and quickly lead her out of the room. As we get down he stairs I hear more things breaking and roars and growls. Then a high pitch ring echoes and waves of bright blue white light produces from the living room. It is paralyzing. I struggle to look up to see Craig floating and his eyes glowing more than I have ever seen. His hair is raising up as if wind is hitting it. Hayden is on the floor convulsing. What on earth is he doing?!

I see Jude crawling over to us, struggling to get his hand out he puts it on Cassidy as she starts to heal. He himself is all healed up. The house starts to crack around us before Craig stops. He drops down and watches Hayden as he slowly stops to shake and blood comes out of his eyes and mouth. "Give me the answers!" Craig demands lifting him up as if he weighs nothing.

"Move! Move out of the way!" Nick screams running past us into the living room with Craig. Dmitri moves soon after with a dark shadowed demon chasing after them. Donna floats past as she chants in Spanish. Dmitri rips a piece of the crumbling beam off the house and throws it at her, propelling her backwards trapping her. Even for a breaking house, that is still a large, heavy support beam. Nick collapse on his knees taking in a few pumps from his inhaler.

I don't know where to focus my attention, everything is happening so fast. I hear a girl yelp in pain at the top of the staircase. It is Sarah, she is in human form again, her clothes tattered. She is gripping her stomach where I shot her. Jude grabs Cassidy and I and pushes us out of the way. Jude takes a stance to attack but she runs past him towards the fighting Hayden and Craig.

"Hayden!" She howls. "Heal me! The bitch shot me"

"And I'll do it again!" I lunge at her. Dmitri holds me back. I struggle to get out of his hold. It was useless when he wasn't using his full strength and now it is like trying to fight a mountain.

Hayden adverts his attention over to Sarah and goes over to her, but Craig uses his Telekinesis to lunge her out of the door. Out of the door, he propelled her though the door. Wood shattered everywhere. Hayden growls at Craig and his eyes glow orange. Oh no.

"Hayden no!" Donna yells as she struggles to get out of her trap. "Help me! Erumpere!" The wood breaks slightly but she still wiggles and struggles to move.

Hayden doesn't listen and in moments fire escapes from his hands, whooshing around the room. Milliseconds, Dmitri has me and Nick in his arms on the ground. He is acting as a shield taking on the blunt of the heat and flames. He bellows in pain as the flames scorch his back. I peek my eyes over to where Jude and Cassidy are. Jude has a weak forcefield over him and Cassidy. But the force of the flames is causing tears.

The sound of the flames stop but the loud screeching from Donna intensifies. Dmitri rises off of us. He takes off his burning shirt and stomps off the flames. His back has severe burns on it. I try to scramble up to do something to help, but how am I suppose to help with burns. But his back quickly heals itself.

"That is so cool," Nick whispers as she stands up.

Jude and Dmitri run over to Craig who is struggling to hold back the blunt of Hayden's tidal waves of flames. As I go over to them. I can see Donna, she is still trapped, but is surrounded by flames. Oh my god, she is going to burn alive. Cassidy notices as well and clamps her hand over her mouth. Donna's blood curdling screams are heart breaking, something so unforgivable that it will never leave you.

"We have to help her!" Cassidy cries going towards her. Nick and I chase after her to help her. I know she is a bad person, but she doesn't deserve to die by flames.

We try to get close but the flames are too great. "Dmitri!" I call. He is by us in a second. "Help her!"

He looks at us, his harden look softens looking at our horrified faces. Was he just going to let her burn?

He starts to move towards the flames but we are distracted by the cut of Craig's roar. Snapping my head back I see Craig emit a bright deep blue light that is almost blinding. Like you are looking at a neutron star. It last a second before Hayden stumbles back with his nose, ears, and eyes are bleeding. I look to Craig, he is someone I don't recognize. He looks like a monster. This isn't my boyfriend. What did he do, how did he do this?

Hayden looks up and stumbles forward like a zombie, his eyes glow brighter and soon does the rest of him, like he is made of magma. Is he self-destructing? Jude, Dmitri, and Craig all scream no. Craig glows a soft blue, his eyes white again, he stands in front of us as a large forcefield forms around us. Dmitri is over to Hayden. He is behind him then, *SNAP!* I cringe. He snapped his neck. Oh my god, he snapped his neck. He killed him with such ease.

Hayden's lifeless body starts to convulse and glow brighter. "Oh shit!" Dmitri exclaims coming back to us. A burst of flames explode out of his body, hitting us like gamma rays of a star. Craig roars as he uses all his strength to keep the forcefield around us as strong as possible. There are no cracks, a perfect orb of protection around us. The heat seeps through but it is probably nothing compared to what is outside of us. Donna wails in agony. Louder than before. The smell of burning flesh enters my nose. Tears slowly stream down my face. Take me out of here, get me out of this reality.

"Jude! Get us the fuck out of here!" Nick yells. Jude takes hold of my and Nick's arms, the rest joins so we are touching, Dmitri holding on to Craig's leg who is still keeping us protected. Then, we are outside.

We gag, choke, and cough up the smoke that surrounded us. We are on the lawn in front of the house, but a fair distance away scattered amongst the grass. I look for Craig, he is the only one of us standing. He sways then crumples to the ground. Craig! I get up and race over to him. He is back to human form and looks lifeless. Please Craig, no, no don't leave me. My tears hit his face as I hold his head in my lap. "Jude! Dmitri! Help!" In that moment I forgot about all the fears I had about Craig a moment ago, I don't see that monster. I see my helpless, weakened boyfriend, whose life is slipping away.

Everyone comes over. The moment Dmitri sees Craig he drops to the ground and takes him from me. "No, no. Craig, come on. Wake up. Please, kid, don't leave me." I have never heard Dmitri with so much sorrow in his voice. This makes me cry harder. He can't be gone. No, no this isn't how it ends.

"Jude, do you know how to do an energy transfer?" Cassidy asks shakily. What is that? I have a vague memory of what that can be, but I can't think of anything right now. All I can think of and see is my boyfriend lying lifeless before my eyes.

"Do it, NOW!" Dmitri pulls Jude down without waiting for his response.

Without any fight of hesitation Jude moves his hand about Craig's body, hovering just low enough to see a soft glow between them. "Keep going, he lost a lot trying to keep us safe from the flames." Dmitri coaches.

Jude strains but keeps going just a little bit longer, until Dmitri directs him to stop. Jude sits back trying to collect himself. Come on Craig, wake up, please wake up. I hold his hand, rubbing his fingers. Come on, please, please.

Craig's fingers twitch then softly curls into mines. His eyes flutters open. Not even a second goes past before Dmitri crushes Craig into him. "Thank god!" Dmitri wails holding tight to Craig. "Don't ever do that again! You almost killed yourself!" Dmitri reprimands letting go of him. Craig doesn't say anything but just sits up. He keeps his hand in mine.

BOOM! We jerk our heads back towards the house. It explodes in flames. It looks like someone set off ten bombs in the house. Holy shit. One last blood curdling screech wails from the house. Donna... we left Donna in there. Cassidy jumps back with tears streaming down her face as she cups her mouth. Nick tries to comfort her but is just in much disbelief.

"We gotta get out of here," Craig says softly. He holds his hand out for Dmitri to take. Jude takes Dmitri's, I take Nick's who take Cassidy. In the next two seconds we are back at the entrance of the beach. Where the street meets the parking area.

Don't Tell

We sit on the curb. Dead silence. None of us looks at one another, none of us dares to try. Blankly we stare at the darkness a head of us. No cars drive past. No trees rustle in the wind. The oceans waves are quiet. Desolate. Craig and Jude share a joint without passing a glance, just a silent hand off. Same with Dmitri and Nick, but with Dmitri's flask. Cassidy rests her head on my shoulder and mine on her head. I didn't think it would get this far. We just went to investigate, that's all we wanted to do.

The house is still burning. They just left her there to burn alive. We didn't stop it. We should have stopped it. It has gone too far. An unspoken solace is shared amongst us. Nothing can be the same. Nothing can change what we saw. All we have is the comfort of one another.

We should go back. We should call 911 or something. We can't just leave everything like we did. I don't want a repeat of Aiden. At least they get it now. We are all feeling what I felt in November. Though I am still alone in having this being a double burden. Twice I have gone through this horror. I didn't think I could become more numb after the first experience.

The only sound between us is the sound of the whiskey in the flask and the smoke being blown. How long can we sit like this? How long until Craig's and my parents come looking for us? Someone has to have reported the smoke from the fire. The house, I have never seen a fire so big, so bright, so destructive. Everything spread so quickly. Her scream. I will never get that out of my head.

Craig crouches in front of me, I didn't even hear him get up. He looks me in my eyes, behind the emptiness he is searching. Searching for the right thing to say, searching for the solution. But there is none. At least right now. There is nothing that can be said that can fix or provide any comfort right now.

"We need to go. We have to go back to my house."

"And what will that do?" Nick responds coldly.

"Provide a clear head maybe. There is a calming energy on the house. It could possibly make it easier to think of a solution."

"We should have helped her," Cassidy peeps, her voice shaking. I hold her close to me, giving her the comfort I didn't have after Aiden.

"We should go. Craig is right." Dmitri gets up and takes the joint from Jude and puts it out. Without any further protest we stand up and begin walking towards the house like zombies. We don't teleport, we need the silence in the walk, a moment to clear our head a little more. I doubt we will feel any better.

Sirens screech from behind us. Police sirens. We stop walking and look to see two cop cars pursuing us. They halt and rush out of their SUVs. "Freeze! Don't take another step!" One officer commands.

We put our hands up and keep frozen. This is it. We are done for. "You are under arrest for the arson on Albert's Landing! Get on your knees, hands behind your back!" We obey the next officer's orders. The two of them place handcuffs on us. Frozen in fear I don't even have the strength to muster up the tears I want to release.

I don't know how they found us, how they knew we were there. We are locked up, separated by gender. We each have one phone call but Craig said that Dmitri is the only one who needs to use it. That he has to be the one to call. After arguing back and forth about this Dmitri eventually gives in and does the call. The rest of us don't question anything. What else can possibly happen that will make this situation any worse? Nick is panicking and Cassidy is crying. I try to comfort her but I start to cry too. Jude is silent, something I have never seen from him. I can hear Dmitri and Craig trying to calm Nick down but nothing is working. It is cold and harrowing. We share a cell with a distress, strung out looking woman sitting in the corner. How did things go so far that we ended up here? I look at the blue bars of the cell gate, hear the phone ringing at the desk. The staggered panic breathing of Nick in the neighboring cell. The muttering of the woman in the corner. The eventual outburst from Jude. The whimpers of Cassidy. My heart slowing down, me slipping into darkness. We have been in here for 3 hours, I count every passing second on the clock, wishing I could call my parents. But I want to trust Craig and his process. But that is what we have been doing. And look where we are now.

Somebody had to have called the cops and tipped them off. But no one knew we were there but the Unhinged. I suppose one of them could have called. There is no other way the cops would have known. We walked right into a set up and we ended with another set up. What if we end up staying here over night?

Nick is becoming more and more delirious. The officer at the desk warns him to quiet down. I try to tune him out the best that I can. I don't want any of this going on my record. How will I get into college with arson or get a job? How will my parents feel, what will I do if we end up getting sent away? Is there a possibility we get tried as adults? I cannot go to jail I would be a sitting duck. The next wave of rebels would be able to get to me with such easy access. I don't want to think about this. I look back at the clock and count the seconds going by. One, two, three, four, five, six.

The gate opens. An officer stands in front of me and Cassidy and then goes over to unlock the boys' cell.

"Aronthal, Bedeau, Edwards, Farquhar, Papakonstatinos, and Vaduva... You're free to go. Your guardian is here to pick you up."

Cassidy and I look at each other with tear filled confused eyes. Who did Dmitri call? Mr. Edwards? Nick wasted no time rushing out the cell. The officer didn't stop him. We slowly rise, holding each other's hand. As I pass the officer his eyes are glazed over, milky. Who just came and got us?

Craig and Jude follow behind us. Dmitri is with Nick; I didn't even see him leave the cell. As we are escorted to the front, I see him standing at the front desk signing our release papers. Mr. Vaduva. Nick races up to him hugging him instantly thanking him over and over again. Mr. Vaduva looks uncomfortable. Dmitri peels Nick off and tells him to get himself together. How did Mr. Vaduva get here so fast? He was in Malibu, even if he took a Jet, it would have taken him five hours.

"Sorry for the misunderstanding Mr. Vaduva," The glazed over officer says accepting the papers.

"It is no problem." He glances over at us. His dead eyes are icy. "They were in the wrong place at the wrong time."

When we pile into the Edwards SUV none of us speak. Lost for words we don't know what to say. We should have been charged for arson. There is no way we should have gotten out. Mr. Vaduva had to have compelled him. But the question as to how he got here still remains. I don't know what to make of any of this. None of us do. Craig wanted me to sit next to him so Cassidy and Nick are cuddled up in the back. Nick finally stopped his endless rambling. Jude has still not spoken a single word. He is so far removed from us. While right next to Craig, he is far away. Only Dmitri, his dad, and Craig speak.

"Dad, I'm-"

"Is Reginald here?" Mr. Vaduva cuts off Dmitri.

"No... They have their own pyro. It wasn't our fault Vlad. I swear. It happened so quickly I did my best to stop it. I just had to get everyone out, and-" Craig responds rapidly. Who is Reginald?

"Did you tell mom?" Dmitri asks.

"No."

"My dad?" Craig follows up Dmitri.

"I'm going to have to Craig."

"Vlad he will kill me! Please don't."

"They have a pyro. A made pyro. That has never been done before. I need to tell Charles. Is the pyro living?"

"I killed him just before he let out his last bit of energy," Dmitri says quietly. Mr. Vaduva groans in genuine agony. It is the first time I saw him express any kind of emotion.

"Demetrius, you killed?"

"I had no choice."

Mr. Vaduva doesn't respond. He doesn't speak another word, prompting Craig and Dmitri to do the same.

Before we knew it, we were in in front of the gates to Craig's house. Mr. Vaduva doesn't pull in. He stops just short of the gate and puts the car in park. No one speaks, the car's engine is the only sound. We sit, waiting to see who will be the first to speak.

"I won't tell Charles. I won't tell Margret or Ana either. This will be between us. I am above being watched or tracked by the Council." Mr. Vaduva turns and looks at all of us. "I can't keep covering up any mistakes that you guys make. I won't. To be frank, you are all a bunch of goddamn idiots. In what sane decision making thought made you guys to think it was a good idea to go to that house? You knew it was a set up. You *knew* that you were dealing with a psychotic rebel group that did not and does not care about their lives!"

He looks to Dmitri and slaps him in the back of his head. "You could have, once again, gotten your friends killed! I could have lost you as well! Charles trusted you to watch over Craig, I know you are stuck in the mind and body of a 17-year-old but you have the knowledge deep within to know the responsible choice!"

"You know it is hard for me to do," Dmitri mutters.

"He is your godson Demetrius and you care for him as if he were your blood! I don't give a shit if it is hard! I just ran across the country, just about tired myself out, and exerted nearly all my energy. I pushed myself to my limit in speed to get to you. But did you hear me say, sorry son, can't do that, it is too hard? It is your responsibility to keep Craig safe because Charles cannot right now and *you know* it is killing him not being able to protect his son himself! You may have the mentality of a teenager but you have all the strength and power of the 500-year-old vampire that you are! Use your head or you will get Craig, your friends or yourself killed!" Mr. Vaduva's voice breaks. "I nearly lost you once, I'm not putting up with that shit again. If you can't find it within you to fight that teenage mentality, you use all your strength to get yourself out of the situation."

"I'm sorry Craig," Dmitri barely whispers slightly turning his head towards him.

Mr. Vaduva directs his attention to Craig. "I know you have a lot of responsibility and expectations put on you but let me tell you something, I don't care what you think would be safe or not, you tell Dmitri everything."

"I can't, if I involve him-"

"Dmitri has committed four acts of treason and they haven't killed him yet. He is my father's favorite grandson and Dragomir would *never* let anything happen to him. Not to mention if anyone in the 3rd high court has anything to say he holds seniority over all of them except Cosmos, who will, and I guarantee, have no issue yielding knowing what we are up against."

"Dad, if I commit one more act of treason-"

"They created a pyro Dmitri. They hold some kind of strange power that we have never known. Up until this point, I didn't even know it was possible to create an ambo with an archetype... I am 632 years old and I am exhausted. I already had to fight in one revolution, I don't need another. Go above the law otherwise we will all meet our demise." He looks between Craig, Dmitri, and I. "Tell the Council very minimal information of what you know.

They don't need to know every detail. Tell them the bare minimum, just enough that they have an understanding of what we are up against."

Silence, once again. What is there to say? How are we supposed to react to this? I cannot imagine that Nick, Cassidy, and Jude would want anything to do with this anymore. I don't even want to be a part of this. But If I had the choice there wouldn't be a this to be a part of.

I look back at Cassidy and Nick and see fear, a fear so deep it breaks my heart that I made them go through this traumatic experience. I should have listened to Craig in the first place and not involved them. If I had to lie to them it would have been much better than them being scarred and disturbed like this. I have been targeted for years, and while I do not feel better about the situation it is getting easier to rationalize all that is happening. But for them. This is all new. These are things they never should have been exposed to.

"You need to wipe their memory," Mr. Vaduva says. Without mentioning a name, we know he is referring to Nick and Cassidy. Cassidy lets out a small gasp. "They cannot be a part of this if you want them to live. It is just going to get worse and worse."

A still air fills the car again. I wanted to avoid that. I thought maybe we could just tell them that they were done. I didn't think we would have to wipe their memory this late in the game. I wish they were never exposed to this but I don't want them to have two, almost three months erased from their memories. Craig strokes my hand with his thumb. He doesn't say anything to me, not out loud or in my head. There has to be another way.

Mr. Vaduva says something to Dmitri in Romanian and gives him a parting deep hug. He leaves the car and in a second he is gone.

Wiped

B ack in the house Craig, Dmitri, Jude, and I are in the study. Our parents were on their way to bed once we got back. They gave us a light scolding for being out so late. Cassidy and Nick are in the kitchen drinking some tea trying to calm their nerves.

"You can't be serious Craig!" I cry.

"You heard Vlad, we have no choice I have to!"

"They won't try to pursue these guys after this, there is no reason to wipe their memory. Craig, please!" I try to plea but he doesn't budge. He crosses his arms and coldly turns away from me preparing himself to erase and replace their memories with false ones. Jude gives me an apologetic look and starts to prepare himself as well. Jude is supposed to do Nick while Craig does Cassidy.

I race over to Dmitri to try to get him on my side. I know he doesn't want this either. He has been very quiet since we left the car but I know, I just know that he has to feel the same as me. They are our best friends.

"Dmitri, this is crazy. Tell him this is crazy. Even if they wipe their memory they could still come after them. Isn't that even worse?!"

He barely meets my pleading eyes. "Belle,"

"No, no, no don't Belle me! Dmitri you know this isn't right."

"My dad is right though. I need to try harder to keep you guys safe. And if that means erasing Nick and Cas' memory then," he lightly shrugs.

I cannot contain my anger any longer. It feels like Black Friday all over again. Overwhelmed with frustration I begin ranting, ranting about this whole situation. How we can't just wipe their memory and hope that will solve this huge issue that we have encountered. How we need to keep pushing forward with what we are doing. How wiping their memory won't solve what we already did. They don't want their memory erased. But they also do not want to be in this fight anymore. They can have both. "It isn't fair, and it isn't right!"

Craig comes over to me trying to calm me down. I push him off of me. "No Craig, you can't just hug me and coo in my ear and make this better."

"May I intervene," Nick interjects from around the corner. We jerk our heads in his direction. Cassidy is with him also. How much did they hear?

"If you are, which seems like it, going to wipe our memory. I have one request. Please don't wipe the fact that I know Dmitri is a vampire. I already knew that before you and Jez told me and I would like to keep that information."

What? We all look shocked. He knew what, and he never thought to mention that? How long has he known, and why did he never tell me, or Cassidy? Did Dmitri know that he knew? I look to him and he looks unfazed by Nick's request.

"You knew?" Cassidy asks.

"Yeah. Since the 3rd grade. I knew about his deaging too. And about a lot of supernatural creatures, but I never knew anything about ambos. Or that Craig and his friends weren't humans. I also wasn't aware that he was Craig's godfather either. I thought he deaged because of some deep dark government secret. So all that was a shock. I sort of knew about the Immortal Realm."

We look accusingly at Dmitri who has yet to react to this. He scoffs at us. "Okay, yes Nick knew. He caught me bloody in a supply closet with my fangs out. I made him swear to keep everything a secret and he did." He goes on to tell us that he went to school hungry one day and lost control and accidently killed someone trying to feed his hunger. Nick offered some of his blood to hold him over. Ever since, Nick knew and kept it a secret. He has hung out at the Vaduva's house plenty of times and they are extremely comfortable with Nick knowing because he kept to his word. Also, apparently Nick was in on the big act during the extra credit project that Dmitri's family put on. Which is why Mr. Vaduva picked on Nick the most.

"I can't believe you didn't say anything. Especially after we told you everything," I say still appalled by his knowledge.

"I said I would never tell, so I didn't. I only did now so your boyfriend wouldn't take that from me."

Oh my god. We look to one another, not quite knowing what to do. Craig looks as if he is contemplating. I wish he would let me into his head, share his thoughts with me. Craig, Craig listen to me.

"Let's just go to bed and revisit this in the morning. We all need rest," Craig breaks our silence. He takes my hand and leads me out of the room with him.

Without saying another word everyone goes off to their room and Jude teleports back to his house.

"Craig?" I ask.

He doesn't respond but continues to lead me into his room. Once we are in the room he shuts and locks the door. He begins getting undressed and heads to his bathroom and closes the door. I sit on his bed, not knowing what to do. I don't know what is going on in his head, I don't know if he is still thinking about wiping Nick and Cassidy's memory. I don't know if he is thinking about all that Mr. Vaduva said. I wish he would just talk to me. A word or two, anything.

"I won't wipe their memory," Craig says bursting through his bathroom door, toweling off his face. He is now wearing his pajama pants but is still shirtless. It startles me but I am incredibly happy to hear him say that. I hop up running towards him. Wrapping my arms around his neck I kiss him in gratitude. "I am going to replace their memory of what happened tonight. They don't deserve to be haunted by that. But they cannot be a part of this team anymore. And Jude doesn't want to be as involved as he is now."

My smile drops. So we lost our whole team. I figured Nick and Cassidy wouldn't be able to stay but Jude too? We are back to square one. We can't do this with just three of us. Also, Craig is going to be in England come late August and he won't be able to be here with me all the time. He will be in training for the most of it and now we are down to just three of us?

He pulls me in deep, embracing me. He strokes my hair and I let out all of my tears of frustration. "Sweetheart it will be okay. I swear it will be okay. We will find people who are more suited. The Unhinged are gone. We have some time to figure this out. Look at me," He cups my face and looks me deep in my eyes with sincerity. "I would never let anything happen to you, ever. I will screw things up along the way but I will make sure that you will always be okay."

I nod. Not just a nod to make him feel like I understand but a nod saying that I fully believe him. That I know he is telling me his full truth. I think this is the first time that I have never doubted him. That I feel like I completely trust him. I am worried about what is to come, I have no clue what is to happen in our future but I know that Craig will do everything in his power to keep me safe. That is all I need right now.

The next morning, we all come down for breakfast as usual. We try our best to act normal in front of our family. I can feel the uneasy feeling from Cassidy and Nick, they are unaware of what Craig has decided. We eat our breakfast fast and tell our parents that we are going to the beach before too many people get there.

We instead go to Jude's place. Thank god Jeanette is over at Candice's so she won't ask any questions, even though I am fairly sure Jude already told her. We stand in his den. They all await for Craig to speak or even Dmitri, but even he is waiting for Craig.

"I'm not going to wipe you guys' memory completely."

"Oh thank god," Cassidy lets out a huge breath.

"You're a saint Edwards," Nick throws finger guns Craig's way.

"But I am going to erase what happened to you last night. You guys cannot be a part of this team anymore and it isn't fair for you guys to have to keep that horrible event in your head."

"You're kicking us out?" Nick asks hurt.

"It's what's best, Nick," Dmitri backs up Craig's decision. Dmitri and Craig share in a nod, acknowledging that this is the best course of action.

Craig and Jude sit Cassidy and Nick down on the couch. Craig's eyes go indigo and Jude looks as if he is concentrating extremely hard. A light blue mist channels between Cassidy and Craig, her eyes going milky. Nick's eyes go pitch black.

After a minute or two Craig begins to speak and Jude repeats everything he says. "You will no longer pursue this group. To your knowledge, we have everything under control. There is no need to worry. When you wake up from this trance you will think that we just had an incredible breakfast and we are about to go shopping one last time in downtown East Hamptons. We had a long night and you are feeling a little fatigue from staying up so late."

Dmitri puts his arm around my shoulder and pulls me into his side. I look up at him and he winks at me. I dimly smile. "They will be okay," he reassures me.

"I know."

He pats my shoulder and drops his arm. "I feel like Nick will still be a little twitchy, not sure if I trust Jude entirely. Seriously I am going to make Craig double check his work when we get back home."

I let out a small snicker. Craig and Jude wonder what is so funny. Dmitri tells them to not worry about it.

We take our place in the room to look as natural as possible so when Cassidy and Nick come to, everything will be seamless. Slowly their eyes go back to normal. Cassidy yawns and stretches as Nick rolls and cracks his neck. "So, when are we heading out? It is our last day here. Gotta make the most of it," Nick says standing up stretching out his arms.

"I saw this really cute shop last night that was closed by the time we got there that I wanted to check out," Cassidy says scooting to the edge of the couch.

So it worked. Craig smiles at me sneakily and kisses my temple. *Told you everything was going to be okay.* Sure, everything seems like it will be okay, but this isn't the first time that things felt like they would be okay. I thought that everything would be fine on Black Friday. I thought that my meet was a safe space. We thought that coming here we would get some peace. I want to be as optimistic as Craig is right now but how could I? Nick and Cassidy are fine for now but what if they regain their memory? What if the next waves of rebels come after them still? *You worry too much.* Craig, he only listens when I don't want him to.

After going shopping we joined with the rest of the Elite and Travis for a bonfire on the beach. Dmitri and Nick seem to be comfortable with them around to hang out with. Apparently, their smoking session really did bring them together. Cassidy is slowly warming back up to Candice. She doesn't seem that bad, she did help with the Unhinged.

This is our last night and I want to just cuddle up with Craig and enjoy this night. Bridget and Jeanette haven't even said a snarky comment yet. Dmitri is good and drunk so he is way nicer than usual. Him and Jude actually mix quite well when drunk. Nick brought a blanket to wrap around him and Cassidy. I think hanging around Craig and Jude so much has given him more confidence.

None of us mention the events that happened the night before in secret passing. As I thought, Jude told Jeanette who then told Bridget and Candice. Travis is in the dark. I still wonder how Candice is able to date him without telling him about who she is. But that isn't any of my business or my concern. My concern is Nick and Cassidy. Jude and Craig seem to have done a good job at the erasing and replacing of their memory. They are both still aware of what is happening with me and Craig, they know what him and his friends are, and still knows about Dmitri. But to their knowledge the Unhinged never came back for us, and that we found out they retreated to go back to their leader, the Ripper. And for now, all is well.

Craig and I part from the group to take a walk along the moonlit beach. It is romantic, the feeling that I wanted back in November and October. There is a feeling of peace that I have been wanting on nights like this. My hand in his, we don't speak, we just enjoy each other's company in silence. I don't want to go back home; I don't want this moment to end. I don't know if he is listening, probably not, like I said, he never listens when I want him to. But that is fine, I like him not giving me a secret message in my head. I like this normal human type moment we are having right now. A moment like this would be perfect for a declaration of love, a sweet sentimental moment. I want to tell him what is in my heart, that he is my sun. Whenever I am in darkness I feel is warmth, see his light, and I know I will be okay.

I look up at him, he is smiling, a cheeky little smile is on his face. He looks down at me for a moment. He heard, without saying it, I know he had to have heard. I look away from him back to straight ahead.

"You know that thing I told you that I would tell you later? When we went over to Jude and Jeanette's for lunch for the first time?" Craig asks dreamily.

I stare quizzically. I have a vague memory of it. "Sort of."

"Well, when I was a kid I watched the Powerpuff Girls."

"You watched the Powerpuff Girls?" I gawk.

He rolls his eyes at me and brushes my comment off. "I did, it's a good show. It isn't just for girls. I digress, anyway, I had a crush on Ms. Bellum and she awoken something in me and from then on I had a thing for red heads," he gives me a sly look and winks. "But, also, my favorite Powerpuff was Buttercup because she was so fearless and tough. I liked how stubborn and a little reckless and impulsive she could be. She reminds me of you, even though you can be timid and paranoid it is because of all the things you have been through. But at your core, who you truly are, and when you let your walls down and let it shine through, you are Buttercup. And in my head, I would call you Buttercup, then when we got together, I would call you my Buttercup. I felt too embarrassed to say it out loud but whenever I call you sweetheart, Buttercup is what I wanted to say but it felt so corny and I thought you would make fun of me"

He peeks down at me biting his lips. His face is screaming in embarrassment. "That is adorable," I say smiling trying not to blush. I never thought of myself as a Buttercup, I always loved Blossom the most because she had red hair too but him calling me Buttercup, it makes me feel all fuzzy. I don't think I am in love with Craig yet, and I don't think he is in love with me, but I have never felt more secure in my life.

The Return Home

As the Edward's, the Bedeau's, and their friends get onto the jets, all seemed well. They return to the jets to which they arrived. Jezebel's and Craig's family goes on one jet while they join their friends in the other. There were no further incidents in the night and Vladimir kept to his word.

Charles was none the wiser as to what happened that night, yet he was still on edge. His eyes darted wildly the whole morning. He spoke fast and was out of his calm demeanor. His wife took notice but he told her to not worry, that it was simply some stressors from work that he has to deal with post vacation.

Once Both families were on the planes, Charles left the jet saying that he forgot some luggage. Which was not a lie, there was one forgotten carry on, but it was not an accident that he left it. For it was his plan, he needed time alone, away from his family and Jezebel's to speak to Dmitri.

To his luck, Dmitri was already semi isolated, he was about to call his parents to make sure that they were home.

"Dmitri!" Charles calls.

Catching Dmitri's attention, he walks over cautiously. Dmitri too noticed the difference in his friend's behavior. He figured that him calling him over was not of good news. Perhaps his father did go back on his word and told him of what happened two nights ago.

"What's up?" Dmitri asks.

"My son and his situation... how is that going?"

Dmitri's nerves grow with the current question. "Well, there are multiple groups after us but one of them has been taken care of."

Charles nods. "I see. Well, might I suggest something to you. For the upcoming year. As you know we are moving away to England come August and I think you all will need more reinforcements. More on the home base if you may."

Dmitri squints, unsure as to where he is going with this. His growing skepticism of the situation shows. "What are you getting at Chuck?"

"Nothing, nothing too bad, just a suggestion. You know, Craig has told me that this rebel group is quite tricky to track and I think that having someone or someones on your team trained for this type of-"

"Oh no, no, no Chuck. I'm gonna stop you right there. It will never happen." Dmitri knows exactly where Charles is going in his thoughts. It is an idea that Dmitri would never dare to use.

"Dmitri."

"The answer is no! We can find someone else. They are just kids and what you're asking for is far more intensive than what we asked of Nick and Cassidy." Dmitri shakes his head and begins to walk away.

"We are in far deeper than we thought Dmitri! I wouldn't ask this of you if it wasn't this dire," Charles calls out to him, letting down his façade. The desperation in his voice makes Dmitri stop and go back to him.

"What do you mean by that?"

Charles whispers into Dmitri's ear. As they part Dmitri looks just as worried as Charles. "How long have you known?"

"A month. I have been wanting to tell you but I didn't want to worry you. But I- you guys need them."

Dmitri shakes his head. "I cannot Chuck."

"They are hounds Dmitri; it is what they are trained to do."

"They are hounds in training, they are not ready for this!"

Charles drops his bag a little too loud and clutches onto Dmitri's shoulders. He looks into his eyes with great urgency. "It is our best bet. I know they are young but so is my son and your friend. The difference is, is they have been trained since the age of 9 to do a job just like this. They can work above the law. Hounds work for the Council or individuals in the Council, privately. And they will be working for you not Craig."

"I know how hounds work, Charles," Dmitri says with a salty tone.

Dmitri sighs and shrugs Charles off of him, giving into his words. Charles smiles knowing that he got to Dmitri. While this plan is not a guarantee of safety it is still a plan, a plan that has been better than the rest.

"I said that I would never do this to them. I hated when they were appointed to be hounds. I highly doubt their parents will go for this though."

"Dmitri, please, just talk to your Aunt and Uncle. Your cousins are our best bet right now. We need to find these people before they come for us."

Ellington Baddox

Till the fall

Bad Romance Part II